BOUND TO THE DRAKARN: DRAKARN MATES VOLUME ONE

A FATED MATES ALIEN ROMANCE BUNDLE

KATE RUDOLPH

Three dominant Drakarn warriors. Three human women who refuse to yield.

When fire meets fire, the only rule is surrender.

On Volcaryth, the Drakarn live by the blade, the flame, and the mating bond etched into their very souls. But when Earth-born women crash into their lives, desire burns hotter than tradition—and these warriors are about to break every rule.

Terra's mouthy, stubborn, and infuriatingly irresistible. Darrokar has never craved anything the way he craves her scent, her skin, her submission. She may fight their bond, but he'll seduce her into surrender—body, heart, and soul.

One sacred ritual. One forbidden witness. Now Orla is Rath's to protect—or claim. Rath will risk it all in a brutal trial by fire to keep her alive. But survival isn't enough. He wants her marked, mated, and by his side forever.

Selene is off-limits. Untouchable. The one female who tests Vyne's restraint with every heated glance. But when they're thrown into danger, resisting becomes impossible. In the wild, she'll learn just how true a Drakarn mate can love.

Fated mates. Possessive warriors. Off-the-

charts heat. If you love primal passion, growly aliens with tails, and heroines who give as good as they get, this bundle will leave you scorched.

CLAIMED BY THE DRAKARN WARRIOR LORD

PROLOGUE

DARROKAR

A soundless roar rumbled in the marrow of my bones.

I stood under the endless blood-red sky of Volcaryth, our twin suns glaring down like molten eyes. Above me, the heavens tore apart.

A vessel not of this world hurtled downward, a silvery behemoth engulfed in flames and blackened smoke. It screeched through the fiery clouds, splitting the horizon until it struck the molten surface of a distant lava lake. The impact sent shockwaves rippling across the landscape, the ground beneath my feet trembling with the screams of the dying heavens.

Lava erupted in great, fiery arcs, showering the area in droplets of liquid fire that hissed and sizzled against the scorched earth.

Then, through the smoke and chaos, *she* appeared.

She staggered from the wreckage. Her form was framed by twisting pillars of flame, long hair cascading like molten copper caught in a breeze I couldn't feel. Her eyes—striking emerald, impossibly vibrant against her soot-streaked skin—locked onto mine as though she could see me, despite the vast distance between us. It was impossible. And undeniable.

And her scent ...

Gods above and below, her scent.

It was unlike anything I'd ever known, unlike the cloying sweetness of the forge or the sharp tang of battle. It was warm and intoxicating, like the first breath of air after emerging from the river's icy depths.

It filled my lungs and settled deep in my chest, igniting some part of me I'd never known before. My fangs burned, sharp twinges sparking along my gums. My tongue ... it ached, hypersensitive, as though begging to taste her, to confirm what my senses already screamed at me.

Mine.

Though she was an otherworldly figure surrounded by destruction, my every instinct roared with certainty. This stranger drenched in firelight and shadow belonged to me, and I ...

I belonged to her.

The sureness was maddening.

I wanted her, not with the fleeting yearning of warrior lust but with something infinitely deeper, something that clawed at the core of my being. My claws flexed involuntarily, tips scraping against the rocky surface beneath my feet.

"Who are you?" The question tore from my lips though she was too far away to hear.

She looked at me as though she'd heard the words, understood them—felt them. Her lips parted, and though I could hear no sound, her voice resonated in my very blood. A single word formed in her breath—just one. I couldn't make it out, but it vibrated through me, carving itself deep into my soul.

She raised her hand, pale against the encroaching flames, and reached toward me. My wings instinctively flared, as though they could bridge the impossible distance.

Mine.

The word burned through my mind again, sharpening as the air around me wavered, turning unbearably hot, even for someone born of fire and heat. My scales—hardened and scarred from countless battles—tingled unbearably, as though anticipating her touch, her claim. My battle-worn body, carved and unyielding, ached for her in a way that made no sense.

This was no battle. This was no war. And yet I felt as though I'd fought for lifetimes, bled and burned, just for this moment.

For her.

The dream shifted.

She was closer now. Her scent crushed me, heady and over-whelming, setting every nerve in my body aflame. Her finger-tips brushed against my chest, tracing the deepest of my scars with an intimacy that made me growl. Her touch was firm.

Possessive.

My head dipped, her breath mingled with mine, and all I craved was—

Light. Blinding, burning light.

No, pain—searing, unbearable pain lancing through my fangs, my claws, my tongue—all the parts of me born to claim and devour. I snarled as the dream unraveled, her form dissolving before I could catch her, and then, abruptly, the world tilted, and I was falling.

Falling into shadows. Into silence. Into ...

My eyes snapped open with a sharp inhale, the echo of her touch still sizzling beneath my skin.

The glow of the heat crystals embedded in my chamber walls did little to stave off the pounding in my chest. My breaths came ragged, uneven. I shot upright, my claws gripping at the carved edges of the obsidian slab I called a sleeping plat-form. I stared down at my hands, the tremors running through them utterly foreign to me.

Darrokar, Warrior Lord of Scalvaris, did not shake.

But my fangs burned.

Closing my mouth did little to soothe the fiery ache in my jaw. I flexed my tongue, wincing as the faintest motion sent unbearable hypersensitivity ricocheting across my senses. My wings, half-unfurled, curled protectively around me.

Damned dreams.

I growled low, the sound vibrating through my chest, but it put no distance between me and the sensations clawing at me. The tingling along my claws, the phantom press of her fingers over my skin, the maddening scent that lingered in the air, entwining with the faint freshness of the river below.

I couldn't dismiss it—not as a trick of the mind, not as a warrior's exhaustion or the effects of a poor night's rest. This was something deeper. I'd known of the fated bond only through stories and ritual, through the words of others. I'd never dreamed of it for myself.

And yet. She was real. *Somewhere*, she was real.

I rose from the slab, dragging my claws over its cool surface as though that might cure the chaos within me. It didn't help. My clawed feet touched the smooth volcanic rock of the chamber floor, and my wings drew close to my body, their membranes taut with tension.

Moving toward the sky tunnel carved into the ceiling, I narrowed my eyes to the faint stream of light streaking down from the twin suns. It was dim now. The sun shafts would soon burn brighter, but for now, this slice of sky was cool enough for reflection.

Reflection. The word felt weak, and the fire ravaging my senses left no room for hesitation.

I braced my hands against the angular edges of the tunnel's opening, letting the external heat press against my scales. My claws scraped at the volcanic stone, seeking some purchase, but there was no escaping the torrent within. It gnawed at me, simmering low in my gut and coiling tighter with every moment. I wanted to howl into the void, to demand the gods of my ancestors explain this madness.

Instead, I tilted my head back toward the narrow view of the heavens. Somewhere, far above this labyrinth of obsidian halls and warrior chambers, was the source of my agony—and my salvation. The dream ... it hadn't been my imagination. It was a call.

I didn't understand how or why. Or how to answer it.

It didn't matter.

I would find her. I would tear through realms known and unknown if that's what it took. Just as the scar across my chest was earned and worn with pride, I would bleed for this bond. I bared my teeth in a wild grin.

Whatever gods had decided this woman was mine had better prepare for what they'd unleashed.

My fangs ached again, sharper this time. My claws flexed, and the scent of her ghosted through my senses once more, dragging foreign sweetness through the heat of Volcaryth. My mate waited ... somewhere.

"Mine," I murmured to the silence of my chamber, the word taking an unfamiliar softness atop the granite edges of my voice.

1

DARROKAR

THE ANCIENT STORIES spoke of beings from far away worlds. That dream hanging heavy over my thoughts put those stories at the forefront of my mind.

But it was the dark streaks of smoke in the sky that showed me something truly otherworldly had come to visit.

The crash was a speck on the horizon, smoke curling upward to stain the crimson of Volcaryth's sky. The suns hung heavy above, their fiery rays bearing down on us in judgement. I led the flight, my wings carving smooth arcs through the scalding air. Behind me, the shadows of my warriors mirrored me—loyal, deadly, unshakable.

"The wreckage reeks of foreign metal," Rath growled, his ruby-red scales catching a glint of light. "We should scour it clean before it festers."

I shot him a look over my shoulder. "Have you forgotten the difference between fear and reward?" My words cut sharp, a blade honed by years of command. "We don't eliminate the unknown until we understand it."

Rath huffed but said no more. He knew better than to push me, though the way the veins along his neck pulsed betrayed his simmering impatience. It was his strength and his flaw—an explosive temper that mirrored his namesake, a heart of flame forever on the verge of inferno.

Vyne glided closer to my left flank. His deep green scales shimmered faintly in the glare of the suns, his voice as steady as the flow of the sacred river. "Whatever fell from the sky wasn't designed for Volcaryth. It can't endure this heat. Whatever, or whoever, survived that crash might need aid." His gaze flicked toward Rath. "We should at least assess before we destroy."

"Romantics and fools," Rath muttered, just loud enough for Vyne to hear. Vyne ignored it, his focus locked on the blackened trail of destruction ahead.

My vision narrowed as we drew closer, the chaotic debris field growing more distinct. Twisted shards of unfamiliar metal jutted at jagged angles from the scorched earth, smoke curling like gnarled claws over the broken landscape. Steam geysers erupted sporadically around the crash site, their lethal hiss lending a sense of unease to the already chaotic scene. And amid it all—movement. Subtle, cautious, but definitely there.

"Scatter formation," I commanded. "Sweep the perimeter. Observe, but do not engage."

They obeyed without question, each veering off with practiced precision. Seeing them move as extensions of my will stoked my pride, though it was short-lived as I descended toward the heart of the wreckage. My instincts roared in my ears—both the calculated reasoning of a seasoned leader and the maddening pulse of something far older than violence or strategy.

Her.

The scent struck me like a blade to the chest, ripping through the stale heat of molten metal and burned earth. Sweet, rich, and intoxicating, it cut through everything to brand itself into my senses.

My wings stuttered mid-beat, and I barely corrected in

time to avoid a graceless landing. My claws hit the rock with more force than I intended, the impact jarring up my legs and grounding me for the moment.

Where was she?

My fangs burned, an insistent throb that radiated straight to the base of my skull, and my tongue scraped against the roof of my mouth, extra sensitive in anticipation of the taste of her. A growl bubbled at the back of my throat, low and possessive. I forced it back, barely. This was no time for instinct to override reason—though I felt the tenuous grip I had on my control fraying with every breath.

Movement to my right. I snapped my head toward it, wings flaring wide in an automatic show of dominance. The motion was fleeting, barely a flicker—a shadow disappearing behind a jagged chunk of the fallen craft. But it was enough. My claws flexed against the scorched ground.

I advanced slowly, my frame tight and ready. This wasn't the erratic shift of lesser wildlife fleeing the chaos—it was calculated. Intelligent. And if the foreign scent mingling with hers was any indication, I wouldn't face her alone.

The first attack came swift and silent—a jagged hunk of metal hurtling toward me, spinning wildly like an improvised blade. I sidestepped easily, pivoting as it clanged against the stone behind me. My lips curled into a savage grin. Stealth had its merits, but it could only take you so far against a Drakarn warrior.

Another projectile, this time from my left. I ducked, twisting my wings to shield my vulnerable flank as the air hummed with its passing. Rath and Vyne were watching now; I felt their shadows circling above, waiting to see how I handled the ambush. I gave no order, not yet. This was my moment to assess, to understand the enemy before deciding its fate.

A hiss tore through the air as a figure emerged—a woman,

fierce and unrelenting, holding what looked like a metal staff stripped from the wreckage. Her hair, a cascade of molten red, caught the light, turning her into a living flame. Scars of soot streaked across her skin, evidence of her battle to survive the crash. Despite her apparent injuries, her stance was solid, her resolve unwavering.

She had no claws. No wings. No scales. Nothing but fragile skin and a tight-fitting, torn outfit made of some dark material that had to be soaking up the heat of the day.

Her eyes—emeralds sharper than any dagger—fixed on me like a predator assessing its prey.

I froze.

It was her.

A moment stretched into eternity as our gazes locked, the world shrinking until it contained only her. The scent of her overwhelmed me. My fangs pulsed in time with my thundering heartbeat. My wings flared wider unconsciously, a declaration I couldn't suppress.

She was magnificent.

And she was terrified.

Her grip tightened on the staff, and I recognized the emotion in her eyes—it was defiance, strength honed under unimaginable duress. She would fight, not because she believed she could win but because the act itself was all she had, a refusal to yield.

Behind her, a second woman emerged, slighter but no less fierce. Her makeshift weapon mirrored her companion's, though her stance was more defensive, her weight shifting subtly as she kept a wary eye on the skies.

"I'll give you one chance to stand down." My voice cut through the oppressive heat. I shifted my weight forward, claws digging into the rock, my intent clear. "You are not in a position to threaten, let alone win."

The copper-haired woman snarled—an admirable mimicry of an actual predator. She spoke then, her voice sharp and foreign, the language unfamiliar and edged with desperation. I didn't understand the words, but the meaning was clear enough: she would not surrender.

Beside me, Rath landed with a heavy thud, his laugh booming. "They don't even have claws, Darrokar. Let me handle this," he said, hefting his lavaforged blade as though the mere act of drawing it ended all debates. "Two strikes, and they'll scatter like ash."

"No," I growled, the single word laced with steel. My gaze never left her, the connection between us tightening like a noose. "She's mine."

Rath froze, startled into silence by the force of my claim. Good. He didn't need to understand the depths of it, not now. Recognition burned through me, raw and undeniable. I would not allow anyone else to interfere in what was written into my very bones.

She stepped forward, her courage foolish yet compelling, and the impossibility of it all struck me anew. How could someone so fragile stand her ground against creatures born of fire and war? How could she stir something within me I'd long thought missing?

But she did, and I was powerless against it.

"Mine," I murmured again, the word barely audible but thrumming with intent.

And she flinched. Not visibly—not to anyone who wasn't watching her as closely as I was—but I felt it. A flicker of something in her challenging gaze.

Recognition? Fear?

Impossible. The distance between our worlds was greater than the void of stars she must have crossed to fall here.

Yet ... she knew me.

I was certain of it.

I stepped closer, ignoring the warning hiss of her blade scraping against the stone. The air between us crackled, alive with tension. The heat of Volcaryth paled in comparison to the fire she ignited within me. Still, I curved my claws inward, forced my wings to lower slightly. Despite everything, I didn't want to frighten her more than I already had.

"Who. Are. You?" I demanded, my voice a low rumble that trembled with the weight of a thousand battles fought and won. This was a different kind of war—one I wasn't sure even I could win.

Even as her staff rose in defiance and her companion shouted something unintelligible, I prayed she wasn't an enemy I'd have to put down.

Because killing her would destroy me.

2

TERRA

THIS WAS BAD. Really bad.

Worse than any of us could have imagined.

The feral roar of the alien's voice rumbled through the air just as Vega ducked a perfectly timed swing of a serrated, glowing blade. I could barely hear myself think over the clanging of makeshift weapons and the reverberation of Vega's curses alongside Kira's sharp orders.

Every fiber of my body told me to keep fighting—to plant my boots firmly in this hellscape of molten debris and give everything I had to protect the others. And yet ...

I couldn't.

Not because my body felt weak—it didn't. Despite our ship's crash and the oppressive heat and the boiling haze of this hell planet threatening to pull me under, I had strength left in my hands, surging through my muscles like a coiled snake ready to strike.

But when the alien male stalked toward me, his massive wings flaring wide like a predator closing in on cornered prey, I hesitated.

My chest burned as though something fiery and alive had been ignited beneath my ribs. My mouth felt as dry as this red desert while, weirdly, watering at the same time, a sensation that left a metallic tang on the back of my tongue.

And then, there was the scent.

Hot, sharp, masculine—it seared through the chaos, cutting through the smoke and sweat. It should have terrified me, should have sent me scrambling backward in retreat. Instead, every nerve in my body tightened in reckless, traitorous awareness, dragging me forward toward *him*.

This wasn't just a *what the hell is going on* moment. This was an entire *what the hell is wrong with me*.

"Terra, move!" Vega's sharp voice yanked me back to reality. My head whipped around just in time to see her block a blow with what was left of a metallic railing, the impact sending sparks skittering across the heated stone.

Adrenaline surged.

"Vega, fall back!" I barked, my voice hoarse but steady, even as my gaze slid traitorously back toward him.

He wasn't just watching me—I could swear he was freaking *claiming* me with just his eyes.

Golden irises pinned me in place, holding me as solidly as if his claws had already locked around my neck. The intensity there didn't match the mess of the scene around us. This was something else entirely.

Something wild.

A flash of movement had me pivoting, avoiding a sidelong blow. Another alien, large but leaner than mine—no, not *mine*, what the hell—angled in my direction with his blade raised. His scales shimmered faintly with the planet's fiery light, but I barely had time to register his features beyond the immediate recognition of him not being *him*.

Hawk's sharp whistle drew his attention just long enough for me to swivel behind him, a desperate swing of my improvised weapon enough to knock his blade off course. The ground beneath us groaned, steam rising in violent hisses as nearby geysers threatened another eruption.

"Terra!" Kira shouted, her panic-tinged voice cutting through the haze. "We're outnumbered! Selene and Lexa have the civilians covered, but if we don't—"

I cut her off with a harsh gesture because I already knew her point deep inside, the same way I recognized no number of clever maneuvers were going to help us now.

We'd drawn our line in the sand, but this hell planet's blistering winds had long since erased it.

"Stand down!" I ordered, my voice firm, clearer than I felt inside. My gaze swung to Vega next, who was already cornered closer to where Hawk tried to angle yet another hurl of debris. "*Stand. Down.*"

The reluctance in Vega's eyes mirrored my own internal struggle, but she nodded stiffly before stepping closer. As the others abandoned their positions one by one, scrambling for what little cover the terrain allowed, the shame of surrender twisted through me like jagged glass.

I *hated* this. Hated every fiber of my body for even considering it. And yet ...

Some part of me was oddly at peace with the decision, if only to prevent more harm.

I dropped my weapon and raised my hands, slow and deliberate, forcing myself not to meet the infernal heat of his gaze as he approached. Before I could speak—or gesture more clearly— he rumbled something low in his impossibly deep voice.

The sound carved its way through every level of my being, sinking into places I didn't know existed.

A wild flush rose to my throat before spreading upward, the betrayal of my own reaction coloring my complexion as my knees hit the ground.

The scorch-pain that had radiated dully in my chest spiked.

Then, he touched me.

It was a grip—not gentle but restrained power, claws not bared, hand unyielding but careful. His warmth enveloped me even through those reinforced tactical fibers of my cryo gear.

Except warmth was wrong. Wrong and far from describing the molten flush centered just below my ribcage.

The growl he gave then—alien threats or promises—I didn't know nor care which. Everything about those tonal complexities was vivid and sent heat straight to my core.

I had to be going crazy.

His voice was a brand, searing itself onto me. I couldn't understand the word he spoke, but its intention carried through the air like heat off the lava banks. It resonated with something primordial in me, silencing even the rippling hiss of geysers and shouts of my people.

I swallowed hard, my mouth watering in a way that was distinctly unnatural given the situation. His scent—the fiery, predatory warmth of it—fanned the flames of my confusion, nudging my focus away from my team's safety toward something far more personal, far more dangerous.

The alien squatted lower, his physicality looming over me like something I could feel. Those golden eyes, their slitted vertical irises narrowing slightly as though in calculation, locked onto my face.

"Stop," I bit out, my voice cracking but firm. Around us, the sounds of Vega growling her defiance and Hawk and Kira shifting to regroup were a distant murmur, as if the two suns above had dipped closer and drawn the alien and me into our own private storm.

He tilted his head at my outburst, his wings shifting behind him in a cascade of webbed black and faint sparks of glowing orange veins, like magma running beneath the surface. It should have been the stuff of nightmares, a predator crouched above me without the barest hint of human softness.

Instead, the burn within my chest pulsed, an undeniable urge to lean closer to him—which was precisely why I grit my teeth and tightened every muscle in defiance.

"I said *stop!*" I barked again, emphasizing the words with a shove against his hand where it gripped my arm. It didn't move; his strength was absolute. He could have crushed the bone beneath his hold, but I could feel the control.

Instead of retreating, I met his gaze with every ounce of fury and confusion swirling inside of me, forcing the trembling of my fingers to still.

He murmured something again, softer this time, as though coaxing a wild animal out of hiding. There were no harsh consonants in his alien tongue, just a series of low, rolling syllables that wrapped around my senses like a smoldering caress.

And then—oh god, *then*—his claws brushed along the bare skin of my wrist, light enough to skirt the surface but heavy enough to light up every nerve beneath it.

Heat rippled down my spine, a supernova of sensation erupting unseen between us. My lips parted in a quick inhale, the air thick with heat, sweat, and *him*. My body betrayed me again, shifting forward as though drawn, even as my brain screamed at me to *pull away, now, before it's too late.*

"Get your hands off her!" Vega's voice shattered the narrowing fog, sharp as shattered glass and laced with rage. My head snapped toward her in time to see her jerking a metal shard upward, but she was too close to one of the other warriors —a scarlet-scaled beast whose fangs bared at the threat.

"No! No, wait—stand *down!* I've got this!" My voice tore out of me again, this time larger than just the alien and me. It broke Vega's motion with a half-second pause, long enough that when the blade-armored tip of my assailant's *tail* flicked toward her, the alien didn't run her through.

The alien never took his eyes off me. His golden stare narrowed slightly, the predator in him assessing *me*—not for my fragile position on my knees, not as prey, but as something else.

Something I was scared to examine too deeply.

I didn't know what I expected—some grand gesture of violence, a moment where he would crush me beneath his power and leave no doubt about where his people and mine stood in this bizarre standoff.

Instead, his grip softened even more, claws grazing my skin in a way that felt uncomfortably ... intimate. It was as though he had heard the unspoken plea for control in my voice and answered with a show of restraint so deliberate it made my breath hitch.

His mouth moved again, the alien syllables wrapping around each other like molten metal. I couldn't make sense of the words, but something burned through the language barrier, something deeper than intent. It wasn't just *what* he said—it was *how*. The way it traveled through the humid air between us and curled itself into my subconscious.

I tried to yank my arm back, but his fingers tightened just enough to hold me still. His scent hit me again, wild and fiery, dragging my attention back to him.

"You don't understand what surrender means, do you?" I hissed, my voice low enough for only him to hear. Anger laced my words, but it wasn't the pure fury I'd leaned on for survival before. This was too tangled—too infused with something else to be simple rage.

His slitted gaze flicked over my face, calculating. He tilted his head to the side, lips pulling into something that wasn't quite a snarl but wasn't entirely neutral either. The motion distracted me for one dangerous second, enough for Vega's voice to cut through the heated haze between us.

"Terra, let me fucking fight!" she snapped, her ragged breath giving away how close to the edge her own reserves were. I could feel her tension radiating even as Hawk moved in beside her, both of them too battered and too smart not to know the inevitable conclusion if this dragged out.

But I couldn't let their lives end here.

"Stop it," I said again, louder this time, feeling the weight of every word grind against the raw edges of my pride. My jaw clenched as I spoke, as though physically forcing the surrender from my throat. "All of you. Now."

Hawk, Kira, and Vega hesitated, unsure, searching my expression for answers. And why wouldn't they? I hadn't exactly briefed them on "kneeling in front of fiery alien dragon men" as part of our survival strategy. But they *had* been in enough impossible situations with me to recognize that this wasn't a bluff—they just didn't have to like it.

The alien male made a deep sound in the back of his throat, almost a purr, as his gaze lingered on my face. It wasn't a kind sound—not quite mocking, but close. As though he saw that moment—my humility, my defiance, and my desperation—and enjoyed how it tasted.

"What?" I snapped at him, my own patience wearing thin under the weight of his attention. "You think this is funny?"

His response was to move even closer. I barely registered the shift before I felt the heat of his breath on my cheek. His other hand, the one not firmly locked around my arm, hovered near my face for the briefest of moments before withdrawing again.

The sharp tang of his scent—the alien fire and molten embers—deepened, igniting that physical insanity that had taken root inside me. The pulse beneath my ribs burned hotter.

My teeth and tongue ached again, and for one horrifying second, I jerked my lips shut as though that would keep whatever was happening to me at bay.

His rumble deepened, the vibration crawling into my chest and settling there like an inferno. He wasn't laughing. There was no mockery there, not really. What I heard in that sound—what I *felt* in it—was darker.

Hungrier.

And I hated that some part of me was hungry too.

"Terra," Hawk called again, the concern in her voice sharpening. She wasn't used to seeing me like this—none of them were. And why would they be? Leadership, decisiveness, composure—that was what they knew of me. That was who I *was*. I didn't lose myself. Not in combat, not in isolation, not even kneeling on a battlefield under dual alien suns while some hulking predator branded my soul with his gaze.

Except right now, I wasn't sure that was entirely true.

The alien tilted his head, considering me—or maybe simply savoring whatever curse-bound connection had glued me to him. His wings fanned wide with a slow, deliberate stretch that made their sheer size unavoidable. In any other context, I might have called them magnificent, the veins glowing faintly in the hell planet's heat. But all I could focus on was the fact that his body had shifted to block me further from the others.

Possession.

The thought made me shiver in a way I hated. Not just because it felt accurate, but because it didn't feel entirely unwelcome—and that terrified me.

As though sensing the shift in my thoughts, his claws flexed lightly around my arm, a silent acknowledgment that sent another unwelcome flush of heat coursing through my body. I yanked harder this time, pulling back with everything I had, but his grip didn't waver. It didn't tighten, either.

He rumbled something else, those alien words rumbling in his chest more than his throat, and leaned just a fraction closer. This time, his scent overwhelmed me completely, leaving no room for coherent thoughts beyond my own confused, traitorous reactions.

"I don't know what you want," I hissed, my voice sharp but uneven thanks to the inexplicable sensation building inside me. "But I'll make this real simple: The others? They're not part of this. You deal with me and *only* me."

Behind me, I could hear my team shifting uneasily. I didn't dare try to meet their gazes, not when I couldn't guarantee the calm façade I always wore would hold. Letting them see would be worse than whatever these creatures decided to do with us.

The alien didn't move at first. His eyes burned into me, searching, weighing something I couldn't see. Words slipped through his lips again—low, deliberate, foreign—and his claws eased, if only just.

Then, without warning, he pulled me closer. Not roughly, but with the kind of demand that left no room for negotiation. His presence dwarfed mine, even without the physical reality of his size towering over me.

And then, he spoke the first word I understood—not from language, but from the resonance in my very bones.

"*Luvae.*"

Mine.

3

TERRA

VEGA CURSED every step of the way for the first mile or so. If she had slightly less discipline, she might have made a run for it. But we had six women hiding in a hidden cave not far from the crash site.

We might have been captured, but they were still free. I wasn't sure that would actually be any help. Most of them were civilians, and they'd rip through supplies fast.

Figuring out what this planet was, who these aliens were, had to be the top priority.

Was there even the slightest chance of sending out a distress signal? How far were we from Earth? I had so many questions and no hope for answers. Not now.

The aliens marched us through the hot sand to a barely seen cave entrance and led us down beneath the surface, past twisting tunnels and rushing rivers that carved their way through walls of volcanic rock.

I breathed in thankful gulps of the underground air. It wasn't cool, not really, but the moisture and the shade made it feel like paradise.

The scale of it was overwhelming at first—colossal stone archways leading to cavernous halls that thrummed with life.

The sharp, rhythmic clang of weapons echoed in the background, accompanied by commanding voices in the alien tongue. Even beneath their guarded stares, I found myself wanting to look at it all, to memorize every detail.

For survival, I told myself. But part of me couldn't help but feel a connection to the raw power of this place.

And now, we were there. Trapped. Hard, uneven stone underfoot, cool despite the heat of the planet. A single, heavy metal door secured us within. No windows. No clear way out. Alone with my team and too many unanswered questions.

Hawk paced a short distance near the far wall, keeping her eyes sharp on the door. Kira was crouched next to her pack, which she'd tucked behind what little cover the room provided, her fingers deft as she rummaged through it. Vega sat with her back to a wall, legs folded under her, her expression sharp and calculating.

She was studying everything, cataloging it like she always did. And me? I stood quietly near the door, rubbing at the faint ache on my arm where that alien had grabbed me. No bruising. No break in the skin. Yet I could still feel the heat of his claws there, like a brand.

Or maybe it was his presence that left that mark.

I was ashamed of how vivid the memory was. His golden eyes had burned through me with an intensity I couldn't shake. That deep voice, unfamiliar but alive with meaning, haunted me. And worst of all was the word he said—or more accurately, the way it felt.

That single syllable reverberated in my chest long after he'd pulled away.

Luvae.

I clenched my fists against the thought, forcing my feet to brace wide as if that would steady me entirely. My tongue connected briefly with the roof of my mouth, and I immediately regretted the action when that now-familiar tingling sensation kicked in again, traveling the length of my jaw like a warning. Or a threat.

God, I hated this.

Hawk's voice broke through the tense silence, sharp and practical, "What's the plan, Captain?"

She always said "Captain" like that, as if I needed the reminder. Like she knew my mind was racing, that I needed the weight of authority to stop me from spiraling into personal doubts. And damn if she wasn't right. Again.

There was no need to remind her that we'd left our ranks behind back on Earth before climbing onto the generation ship. We'd all signed on to be security forces at the new colony when we woke up.

This place? Definitely not part of the plan.

I inhaled deeply, forcing myself to meet her gaze. "We need to take stock," I said, my voice steadier than I felt. "Assess resources. What do we have? What do we know?"

"Kira?" Vega prompted.

"Still got my pack," Kira confirmed, her voice low but colored with quiet triumph as she pulled out something small and black. "They didn't stop me from bringing it. Either they underestimated us, or they don't fully understand human tech."

There were aliens back on Earth, but none like this. The travelers who had made it to us had never hinted at a place like this. These aliens, these monsters reminded me of dragons in a way I couldn't quite explain, and I was worried we were about to become their hoard.

Or dinner.

"What's that?" Vega moved closer as Kira turned the device over in her hands, inspecting it.

"Basic translators," Kira said, offering a faint smile. "They're not perfect—more like a rough filter of language patterns—but they should let us listen in. With some quick tweaks, I might even get them working both ways, but it might take some time."

Vega was immediately wary. "We don't want them to know we can understand them. That gives away our only advantage. Better to keep it one-sided, use it to gather intel."

Kira frowned but didn't argue, her focus dropping back to the device in her hands. She knew Vega rarely argued unless she was absolutely certain she was right. She handed out the thin slips of metal and showed us how to attach them to the skin behind our ears where they'd be hidden by hair. Even if the aliens caught sight of them, they sort of looked like scars. They wouldn't know we could understand them.

"They're powered by bioelectricity," said Kira. "No need for a power source."

When the translator powered on, I heard a faint buzzing in my ear, and my head ached for a second before the pain faded.

"We need to figure out what they want from us," Vega said, leaning back against the wall again. "And then if escape becomes viable, we act."

"Escape?" Hawk crossed her arms. "In case you didn't notice, this place is built like an actual fortress. And even if we made it to the surface, this whole damn planet's trying to kill us."

"So?" Vega shot back sharply. Her gray eyes narrowed in the eerie glow, steel and fire beneath her calm, collected surface. "We've got people out there who have no idea what happened to us. Do you want to just leave them?"

"No," Hawk's tone was grim, "I'm suggesting we don't act out of desperation. Until we know what we're dealing with, laying low is the safer play."

"Enough," I said, raising my voice just enough to halt the back-and-forth. "Both of you are right." My gaze flicked between them, making sure they were listening. "We keep track of what options are on the table. If an opportunity presents itself, we take it. But until then, we stay alive by keeping our heads down, assessing the situation, and not drawing unnecessary attention."

Hawk's shoulders eased slightly, and Vega gave a begrudging nod. It wasn't perfect, but it would hold. For now.

Kira's voice, softer but no less certain, drew my attention next. "For what it's worth, I don't think they're going to kill us," she said. "If they wanted us dead, they had plenty of chances already."

None of us disagreed, though the unspoken doubt hung heavy in the air. Wanting something from us didn't mean we were safe. It just meant we weren't expendable. Yet.

The door groaned suddenly, massive and heavy as it swung inward. The sound reverberated through the room. My heart climbed straight to my throat, my senses sharpening as I braced for whatever entered next.

Him.

The heat I'd struggled to push down earlier rose again, coiling deep within me. His frame filled the entryway, larger-than-life and impossibly commanding.

Obsidian-black scales gleamed faintly in the light, touched with crimson undertones that practically glowed. His wings took up the space around him like he owned it, folding close enough to brush the edges of his imposing shoulders. Behind him, three others followed in silence—two of them vaguely familiar from the crash site, though I barely spared them a glance.

No, my focus was locked entirely on him.

He stepped forward, steady and purposeful, and though the chamber wasn't small by any means, it immediately felt too tight. Like he was sucking all the air from the room with his presence alone.

My pulse quickened, my body tense and alert for reasons I couldn't fully explain. It was beyond just survival instincts now. This was something else.

His golden eyes found mine without hesitation. No scanning the room, no split-second hesitation. Just ... me. Always me.

I hated the way that softened edge of his gaze hit me, vibrating down to my bones. I clenched my fists at my sides and forced myself not to step back—to hold my ground despite the almost suffocating pull of whatever unnatural gravity seemed to bind him and me closer.

One word fell from his mouth, low and resonant.

"Come."

Even without the translator, the tone carried a layered command I felt as much as heard. There was no mistaking who he meant—even without the sharp, obvious shift of his golden stare boring into mine.

The others bristled immediately, their instincts screaming at them to protect me. Hawk rose to her feet fully, her jaw tight and her body stiff as a board. Vega stiffened, but wisely said nothing, though her dangerously calculating eyes flicked quickly toward me for a barely noticeable second. Kira tensed, balancing protectiveness with obscuring the translator still in her hands.

"You can't expect us to let her—"

I cut Hawk off with a sharp motion, tilting my head just slightly in warning. She quieted but didn't move, and I adjusted my focus back to the towering figure in the room. He hadn't spoken again yet, nor moved much closer, but the weight of his expectant presence left room for little else.

I didn't have the luxury to argue—not with them, not with

him. It wasn't about surrender. It was about survival. Every choice I made had to balance the survival of the team against the unknown variables of what came next.

So I lifted my chin, squared my shoulders, and forced every ounce of confidence into my voice when I spoke.

"Fine," I said, keeping it clipped, sharp, and neutral. "Just me." He couldn't understand me, I knew, but I pointed at my chest and hoped he got the idea.

He tilted his head slightly, those brilliant golden eyes narrowing just a fraction—and for a moment, I felt the weight of his scrutiny like a burning ember pressed against raw nerve endings. Then he simply inclined his head, an almost unnervingly deliberate acknowledgment.

"Captain, you don't have to—" Hawk started again, stepping forward.

"I do," I cut her off again, softer this time. I didn't look at her—not because I didn't care, but because meeting her eyes would only crack the carefully constructed weight of authority I was clinging to right now. "Stay with the others. Watch. Listen. And *wait.*"

The last word was for all of them, though it hung heavier on Hawk's shoulders than mine. Her jaw tightened visibly, but she nodded ever so slightly. I knew her well enough to sense the storm she was holding back.

Drawing one deep, steadying breath, I stepped toward the massive alien looming near the chamber's entrance. My legs were steady, though every instinct screamed at me to stop, to fight.

But I couldn't. Not yet.

His gaze burned over me, intense and searing as molten fire, as he turned and led me wordlessly out into the dim glow of the underground city.

4

TERRA

THE ALIEN—MY alien, I guess—said something quietly to the others. Despite my translator, I couldn't pick up on it. I just had to hope he wasn't telling them to do anything nasty towards my team.

If they got hurt, I'd never forgive myself.

I followed my alien through winding caverns that towered high overhead, high enough that some of the aliens were flying rather than walking.

The cavern was so high it was almost possible to forget we were in a cave.

We walked through a courtyard where aliens fought and drilled. It was strange that it was so bright even though we were underground. High above, there were breaks in the ceiling, allowing light in.

He led me to a building and opened a door. I stepped into a room, my boots scraping lightly against the smooth stone floor as the door groaned shut behind me. The sound was final, a low, resonant thud that ricocheted through my chest.

I didn't flinch—wouldn't let myself—but it took effort. I breathed deep, but it didn't push out the taut, simmering unease curling under my ribs.

The first thing I noticed was the heat. Not stifling or oppressive like the planet's surface, but a different kind of warmth, radiating in waves as if the room pulsed with life. Crystals embedded in the walls glowed faintly, their golden and red hues shifting like flickering embers. They bathed everything in a soft, otherworldly glow, making the space feel both cavernous and intimate.

He stepped into my peripheral vision, and I held my ground. His movements were purposeful, a predator's grace that drew my eyes against my will. The leather-like material of the fitted armor over his dark scales caught the light, and my fingers ached to touch.

Stupid, traitorous fingers.

His wings shifted subtly, brushing the edges of the room as if claiming the space, and by extension, me.

Focus, Terra.

"Darrokar," he said, his voice a low rumble that commanded attention. He pointed at his chest, his sharp, clawed hand resting there for a beat before he locked his golden eyes on mine. I felt the gravity of his presence pull at me, like standing too close to the edge of a cliff.

Two could play that game. I straightened, a thin smile carving across my face—unflinching, even though my pulse pounded against my ribs. I pointed at myself. "Terra," I told him evenly, my voice steady despite the low hum of apprehension under my skin.

His head tilted, just slightly, as he studied me. The sharp contours of his face softened for a moment, some flicker of recognition crossing his features. It faded quickly, replaced by the same unreadable expression that had unsettled me earlier.

"Terra," he echoed, voice rolling over the syllables like thunder. The way he said it felt unfamiliar, yet *right*, and I actively tamped down the strange heat unfurling in my chest.

Pull it together, soldier.

Satisfied, he turned away and gestured toward the far side of the room, where steam drifted lazily from the surface of a massive stone tub set into the floor. Water—not molten rock or some alien equivalent—but clear, bubbling water filled it, the surface shimmering faintly in the light.

Tub was an understatement. It was basically a pool.

I stared at it, momentarily caught off guard. He wanted me to ... What, take a bath? After being marched across the desert, imprisoned, and dragged down here like a prisoner—or worse? He expected me to relax like it was some grand spa day?

"You've got to be fucking kidding me," I muttered. His eyebrows twitched, but his expression remained unchanged.

I'd be lying if I said a bath didn't sound amazing. I was covered in a week's worth of desert filth and who knew how many years of stale air from the cryo-sleep chamber. The stone bath looked like something out of a dream. But I had a feeling that every time I took something from the alien—from Darrokar —there'd be a price to pay.

He gestured again, this time more insistently, his clawed hand slicing through the air toward the tub before his gaze flicked back to me. I could feel the weight of the command, even if the words weren't there.

I narrowed my eyes, forcing myself to stay calm, though the urge to snap rose hot and fast. My options were limited. If I flat-out refused, he might force me or worse. I didn't know what it would cost me—or my team—and I sure as hell wasn't about to start something I wasn't prepared to finish.

But.

He didn't get to just make me to do a striptease right in front of him. That wasn't how this worked. Survival didn't mean submission.

Independence intact, but acting dumb, I tilted my head and

feigned ignorance, gesturing toward myself with exaggerated confusion as if to say: *What do you want from me?*

He clearly didn't buy it, the tightening of his jaw proved that much. Without breaking stride, he strode toward a chaise carved from obsidian and covered in silky pillows situated near the room's center and lowered himself onto it, every move calculated.

The tension in my muscles coiled tighter as I watched him recline, propping an arm on the back of the chaise as if this were a casual negotiation rather than ... whatever the hell it was. His golden eyes remained locked on me, unyielding, and damned if I didn't feel cornered in this vast room.

The door creaked open then, and two figures entered, slim and silent. They moved gracefully—quiet servants who carried a large tray between them. They had wings but didn't have claws.

No, that wasn't it.

Their claws had been filed down to barely anything, and their hands looked almost like mine, if bonier. Was that something these aliens did to keep their servants from rebelling? Or was it their choice?

It wasn't like I could ask. And even if he could understand me, I doubted Darrokar would answer.

My stomach clenched sharply at the sight of food arranged in vivid, unfamiliar splashes of color. Fruits that shimmered like gemstones, steaming pieces of cooked meat glistening with glaze, and a pitcher of liquid that glittered faintly in the dim light. The smell, rich and inviting, hit me with an intensity I wasn't prepared for.

I hadn't realized how long it had been since I'd eaten properly until then. Rations from the crash site only went so far, and saving water was becoming a brutal necessity. My body screamed to lunge for the tray, but I froze when Darrokar shifted.

He made a harsh sound—commanding, territorial. His clawed hand extended outward, palm flat toward the food, before it gestured again toward the tub. The meaning didn't require translation.

Not until you bathe.

Seriously?

Anger burned hot in my chest and sharper than my hunger. My first instinct was to refuse outright, to make a stand then and there. But survival whispered caution. Picking a fight over food I couldn't secure for myself was a losing battle.

Watching him closely, I took a slow step forward, then another, my eyes flicking deliberately between him and the tray.

He didn't move, his expression impassive, but as soon as I stretched a hand toward what looked like a caramelized piece of meat, his clawed grip shot out lightning fast. Before I could react, my wrist was enclosed in heat and strength, dragged upward just enough to make me stumble closer to him.

"Wash yourself," he hissed, my translator having no problem at picking up his words.

My heartbeat spiked violently. I wanted to pull back on instinct, but his grip was firm, holding me steady as he rose in one smooth, fluid motion that had him towering over me again. The world narrowed alarmingly.

My brain scrambled to control the interaction, to tip the balance back to neutral ground, but Darrokar had other plans. Slowly, deliberately, his other hand rose to point once more at the steaming bath behind us, his command clear.

Fuck.

"Fine," I bit out, not caring that he wouldn't understand the sarcasm laced in my tone.

He'd get the message in my posture, in the way I refused to look away as I wrenched my wrist from his grip. My skin tingled where his claws had pressed—not hard enough to pierce, but firm enough to leave an impression that was more than just physical.

Heat burned in my veins now, distinct and unwelcome. A little too familiar.

I turned sharply on my heel and stalked toward the tub, determined to do this my way if I was doing it at all. Rebellion was futile in the grander sense, but there was power to be found in the smaller victories.

Without pausing, I stepped directly into the steaming water, my boots sinking into its depths with a faint splash that echoed in the silent room. The fabric of my pants clung to my skin, the sensation cloying and uncomfortable as I lowered myself fully into the bath, clothes and all.

When I leaned back against the edge, crossing my arms defensively over my chest, I finally let myself look his way. His expression was ... unexpected.

No anger. No disappointment.

Amusement flickered faintly at the edges of his golden gaze, and the sight of it made me press my teeth together in frustration.

Then he tilted his head back and laughed.

5

DARROKAR

THE SIGHT OF HER, drenched and defiant in my bath, sent a blade of desire straight through me.

She didn't cower. She didn't plead. Instead, she faced me with those striking green eyes, her chin tilted in a warrior's challenge, shoulders squared as if daring me to push her further.

Water streamed from her soaked clothes, rippling around her, but she gave no sign of discomfort. She was magnificent—a contradiction of softness and steel, fragility and stubborn defiance.

I couldn't stop the grin before I let a low, rumbling laugh escape, filling the chamber with its echo. It wasn't a sound I often made, and it caught even me off guard. Her head tilted slightly at the sound, her eyes narrowing, but not before I caught a flicker of something—confusion? Surprise? Perhaps something deeper that she hadn't meant to show.

Desire warred with my warrior-strong self-control. Everything about her—her scent, her defiance, her very presence—tested my patience in ways nothing had before.

It wasn't just the mate-bond roaring beneath my skin, demanding I claim what was mine. She wove herself into my senses, made me hyper-aware of every breath, every subtle change in her expression.

This was a battle, but not one I could fight with claws or sword.

I turned away, stalking toward the massive window that overlooked my city, my back to her now. The pull she had on me was maddening, but I needed the distance to collect myself. My wings flexed as I drew a breath that seared hotter than molten rock, willing my control back into place.

Below us, Scalvaris sprawled out in all its harsh beauty. The rushing river snaked through the city, our lifeline and what made Scalvaris habitable. Great towers of obsidian rose high, their jagged spires glistening in the glow from the water and sky shafts that let in the light. Warriors trained in the combat pits, the sound of steel cutting through the air even faintly audible here.

I pointed out the window. "Scalvaris," I said firmly, the weight of the word sharp in the chamber. It fell heavy between us, and I stopped myself from glancing back at her, curious to see if she would recognize the significance of the gesture.

She'd shifted in the bath, her eyes now fixed on the scene beyond the window. Something shifted in her expression—curiosity, maybe even wonder—as her gaze swept over the city. I could tell she tried to suppress it, but the faint parting of her lips, the way her brow softened for just a moment, betrayed her. And then it was gone, neutral steel replacing it once more.

"Scalvaris," I repeated, louder now, drawing her attention away from the view. Her eyes darted to me, wary again as if she thought I might try something. I lifted an arm to gesture toward the city and held her gaze. When I spoke the word a third time, her eyes narrowed slightly, as if realizing my intent. And then, slowly, she attempted to repeat it.

It wasn't a perfect approximation. Her voice rounded the

edges, softened the harsh crack of the "v" sound. But it was enough to make the mate-bond snap taut within me, the word sparking something dark and deep. It didn't matter how far she'd come, how different her people might be.

There she was, speaking *my* language, standing in *my* city. Nowhere in all the stars could fate weave something more potent.

I nodded slightly, encouraging her.

"Scalvaris," she said again, more force this time. My chest rumbled with satisfaction. The mate-bond burned brighter, tighter. My mate. My future. All I had to do now was convince her to accept what I already knew.

I crouched low beside the edge of the bath, close enough to feel the tension radiating from her body. That scent—wariness tinged with fear—hit me again, sharp and unwelcome. It was a knife pressed against my warrior's instincts, demanding I tread carefully when every fiber of my being told me to act. My claws scraped against the stone tiles beneath me, but I forced my hands to remain steady, curved inward to show that, for now, I meant no harm.

The bond howled within me, insistent and unrelenting. Soothe her, it demanded, shield her, claim her.

My instincts roared their agreement in a frenzy, but I smothered them the way I had hundreds of times in battle—as a leader, not a beast. This wasn't the moment for dominance or possession. Not yet. Not until I could strip the fear from her gaze and replace it with something far more potent.

My eyes drifted to the tray of food one of the servants had brought earlier. Crystal fruit, redclaw meat, lava-crusted bread —sustenance meant for warriors, each piece glistening and steaming in its fresh preparation.

Her eyes darted to the meal, then back to me. I saw it then, flickering just beneath her defiance—a flash of carefully guarded hunger. She wanted it, needed it, though she wouldn't dare reach for it. Not yet. There was too much uncertainty between us, too much unknown.

And still, she watched me, her jaw tight, her battered resolve holding firm even as her body betrayed her needs.

Magnificent.

But my control was wearing thin. The weight of her closeness, her scent, and the heat of her presence soaked into me like magma against stone. She didn't yet understand who—or what—I was.

Without a word, I stood, shrugging off the leather armor with practiced ease. My tail curled behind me as the heat in the room licked at my exposed scales, every inch of me unrepentant and bare. I didn't look away from her as the last piece fell. Her wide eyes snapped to me. Lower, to the thick cords of muscles across my chest. Lower still as her gaze followed the long, scaled length of my tail ... the hilt of my cock beneath my abdomen.

Her attention lingered, her pupils dilating, and for a single beat, every shield in her expression fractured. Surprise. Curiosity. Something darker that made the mate-bond growl with triumph. And then she realized I was watching her. Her head jerked back up, her cheeks flushing a deeper shade. She threw her gaze back towards the city.

I let my wings unfurl slightly, the movement calm and deliberate as I stepped into the bath beside her, silent except for the faint lap of the water against stone.

She stilled completely, her shoulders locking tight, her breathing quick but shallow. I could see the tension in her frame, the churning war inside her between fear and something she likely couldn't name.

"Relax," I murmured, though I knew the word was foreign to her. My voice came softer than intended, a low rumble that settled into the space between us. She didn't flinch—good—but those brilliant green eyes tracked my every move.

I sank into the water, the temperature comfortably warm, not as scalding as I preferred. My wings folded inward, creating a faint ripple that reached her side, and I settled just close enough that we mirrored each other's height. She had no claws, no scales, her skin bare and fragile-looking in comparison, and still, she met my presence with an obstinate boldness that made the mate-bond pull even tighter.

I reached out slowly, careful not to startle her as I took her arm in my hand. Her skin was alarmingly smooth, so warm and delicate under my touch it felt like the barest whisper of sensation against my clawed fingers.

She stiffened but didn't pull away. That was a start.

With quiet precision, I lifted her hand and gestured out the expansive window overlooking the city. "Scalvaris," I said clearly, annunciating each syllable. I pointed across the vista of molten rivers and obsidian towers, my tone firm but unthreatening. "My city. Your new home."

Her eyes followed my gesture, her focus drawn to the pulsing life of Scalvaris below. For just a moment, awe replaced the fear and tension, softening her expression into something unguarded and raw. My chest swelled at the sight. My mate, alien and utterly foreign to my people, was looking at the city I ruled with the wonder of discovery. I would show her all of it.

But for now, simple gestures and intention would suffice. I pointed again to the training yards where warrior-screams echoed faintly through the haze of heat rising over stone and steel. "The combat pits," I rumbled. Then, I shifted my hand to the obsidian tower glinting just shy of the cavern roof's reach. "Our council."

Each word was deliberate, shared slowly, my tone even and unthreatening. She didn't understand the meaning, not fully, but her attention never wavered, her focus locked on both my gestures and my expression as though committing every detail to memory.

She was observant. That was all I could ask for now.

When I shifted to gesture again, her attention caught on the movement, and I felt her gaze dip—briefly but clearly—to my tail.

Ah.

Her frightened posture twitched like a flame. Not with pure terror. Something instinctual flared in her gaze, carefully muted by fear, but noticeable to someone as attuned to her every breath as I was.

No shame, no coy retreat. That tension I'd noticed, the fire buried under that vulnerable surface, promised far more than mere resistance. It brought an ache to my groin, a patient, steady throb I longed to sink into her softness. But not yet. Not until she understood what she'd awakened.

I turned my head toward her again, leaning just a breath closer, tipping the balance between cautious distance and deliberate proximity. Her eyes snapped back up to mine, startled—the connection immediate.

My lips curved into a slow smile, and I felt a flicker of power shift between us.

"For now," I murmured, my tone quiet but heavy with intent, "you'll learn."

She wouldn't understand the words—but her gut instincts might. Those flashes of curiosity, the way her body reacted but didn't fully retreat, whispered to me of possibilities far greater than whatever distant stars birthed her.

One step at a time, my beautiful, fragile mate. I would teach her. About language, about trust, about belonging. About me.

I reached for the crystal fruit first, its translucent, glistening flesh catching the chamber's dim light. I held it in my claws and said the word clearly. "Krysfruit." Turning to her slowly, I brought it to my mouth, taking a quick bite while keeping my eyes locked with hers.

She watched silently, her hands wrapped defensively around herself. I held the half-eaten fruit out to her, no words this time, just the offering. This was no trick. I didn't speak for her benefit, but for mine: "Krysfruit."

She didn't move at first. The tension between us lingered, thick as the heat of molten rock.

But after a long moment, she reached out slowly for the fruit, her wet fingers brushing the hard planes of my claws as if testing if I'd snap them closed like a trap. The soft contact of her skin against mine was electric and devastating. It stripped the air from my lungs, leaving only fire and smoke behind.

Mate. *Mine.*

Her lips parted slightly as she inspected the fruit, her mouth moving as though trying to form its name again. And then, without warning, she bit into it. Her breath hitched, and her eyes widened at the burst of flavor. Surprise colored her face, quickly replaced with something deeper—pleasure? Gratitude? It was fleeting, but I caught it. She inhaled deeply and finished it in two bites.

"Here," I growled softly, reaching for something else to distract from my rising instincts. "Redclaw," I explained, pulling it slowly from the tray. She mimicked the word, though her accent mangled it more than the last. I didn't care. Each broken syllable warmed me in ways I didn't think possible.

Piece by piece, she sampled the foods I handed her, every repetition of my language satisfyingly imperfect and wholly hers. The tension in her posture eased, her guard dropping under the weight of small kindnesses she clearly hadn't expected.

So when I reached to wipe the juice from her lower lip, the act surprised us both.

The angle of her jaw fit perfectly in my palm as I brushed the pad of my thumb against her skin, careful not to scratch her with my claw. Soft. Too soft for a warrior and yet utterly captivating. Warmth sparked across her flesh and into mine, lighting a fire that demanded to be fed.

Her lips trembled almost imperceptibly, her body leaning forward ever so slightly, a conflict she likely couldn't name flickering in those eyes.

She was aroused. And afraid.

I withdrew my hand before she could pull away, ripping my palm from her jaw with such force it was as if I were severing the bond itself. She blinked, the moment broken as confusion colored her features once more. The mate-bond screamed at the distance. My discipline howled at the thought of pushing her too fast. I exhaled heavily, standing with my wings slightly mantled in frustration.

"Rest," I said gruffly, motioning to the food cart before kicking the impulse down further into silence. My gaze lingered just a second longer before I climbed out of the tub and stalked toward the adjoining chamber.

6

TERRA

AFTER FIVE FREAKING days of captivity that was unlike anything I'd ever encountered, I was going crazy. Darrokar kept me in his rooms. He fed me, sometimes *by hand*, and looked at me with desire clear enough to cross the galactic boundary of our species.

But he didn't try to touch me.

The bar was so low if I was thankful my alien captor wasn't a rapist.

I needed to get out of his rooms and do *something*. And, finally, the opportunity presented itself when Darrokar was called away by one of his men in a flurry of wings and weapons. It didn't look like he'd be back soon.

I'd been in plenty of hostile environments in my time. Cities brought to ruin by coordinated strikes. Desert strongholds besieged by the enemy. Forests turned death traps by insurgents who knew the terrain better than they knew their own names.

But Scalvaris? This place was something else entirely.

It wasn't just the eerie beauty of it that unsettled me—or the fact that it was alien in every conceivable way. It was the pulse of the place, the way the underground river moved with purpose, the jagged obsidian towers looming like silent sentries, the faint vibration underfoot that hummed with a life of its own. The city wasn't just alive; it was watching.

So was he.

Even with Darrokar gone, I felt him everywhere. In the heavy air, the flicker of heat crystals set into the walls, the faint scent of something smoky and dark that clung to my skin after we'd shared that damned bath days ago. Distraction was a luxury I couldn't afford, and yet, there he was, burrowed under my skin.

I shook the thought loose, tightening the sash of the thin, draping garment Darrokar had left for me in the wardrobe. It felt too delicate on my skin, like I ought to be lounging in a palace and being hand fed grapes rather than skulking through this fortress of stone. The fabric shifted with every movement, whispering against my legs in infuriating contrast to the thick combat gear I was used to. But there wasn't time to curse my outfit.

I had a team to find.

Slipping out of Darrokar's private quarters had been easier than expected, though the tendrils of unease in the back of my mind warned me not to trust that. Doorways gave way to dark passageways, and I clung to those shadows like a thief, moving soundlessly as I'd been trained to do.

This wasn't just about survival. This was about Hawk, Kira, and the rest of the women who had trusted me with their lives. I hadn't heard from them since Darrokar dragged me into his world. Were they even alive?

I swallowed that thought before it could take root.

My boots—dry now, thankfully, after my stunt in the bath—muffled against the stone floor as I moved. Scalvaris unfolded around me, a labyrinth of volcanic beauty and alien architecture, no corner of it offering even the faintest illusion of safety.

The corridors opened onto a busy thoroughfare. Drakarn guards with pierced wings and painted claws stalked the perimeters while warriors sparred in open courtyards. Merchants bartered and bickered under glowing banners of some strange kind of fabric that shimmered like the skin of an oil slick. The air was thick—hot and metallic, tinged with the scent of scorched earth and something faintly sweet that might've been food.

I slipped into the crowd, keeping my head low and shoulders square, projecting an air of purpose. If you looked like you belonged somewhere, you could avoid most questions. It was a trick that worked for just about any Earth city. Alien strongholds, though? I had to hope it was a universal concept.

The Drakarn were taller than me—and broader—and their movements carried an innate predatory grace. I avoided their gazes as best I could, though I sensed the curiosity trailing me like a weighted cloak. No matter how I acted, I didn't look like I belonged.

Human female.

Alien.

I clenched my jaw against the wave of unease that followed.

Focus, Terra. Find your team.

I wasn't sure what we were going to do after that. It wasn't like we could repair our ship and go home, but I refused to remain a prisoner if there was anything I could do to fight back.

The buzz of voices around me rose and fell in smooth rhythmic tones, words trading quick ownership between merchants and customers, guards and warriors, but the meaning filtered into my understanding with startling clarity. It was almost scary how smoothly my translator worked.

"What's that thing?" a rough voice murmured nearby, low but sharp enough to cut through my thoughts.

I shifted subtly to glance at the source: two Drakarn warriors standing at a corner, their wings partially unfurled as though asserting dominance even in casual conversation. One of them tilted his head my way, just slightly, and I cursed silently.

"I've never seen anything like it," his companion said. "Who captured her? She isn't marked." There was an undertone of satisfaction that shot ice up my spine.

Just as the first warrior's eyes met mine, I stepped behind a passing merchant cart loaded with cloths and tools. *Remain calm. Keep moving.*

I ducked down an adjoining path, the atmosphere darkening with every step. The path sloped downward, leading me into a narrower corridor lit only by faint, intermittent glows from embedded crystals high above.

The din of the thoroughfare softened into echoes, each step magnified in the enclosing walls. A mistake. I knew it almost immediately. I should've stayed in the open, however dangerous, rather than isolate myself in this predator's tunnel where sound carried but there was no easy road to escape if I was cornered.

A second footfall—definitely not mine—echoed faintly behind me.

I didn't react, forcing my heartbeat to steady even as adrenaline spiked painfully through my veins. Years of training distilled into each step, light and deliberate, drawing him closer without betraying my awareness.

If you run, you'll be prey.

The sound of claws scraping lightly against stone rippled down my spine. Guttural laughter followed, bouncing off the walls around me—a low, sinister chuckle that spoke of confidence, power, and the kind of cruelty that was clear despite the galactic distance.

I pivoted sharply, my fists already curling as I planted my feet. The Drakarn male—a hulking figure with slate-gray scales streaked in gold and crimson—saw my movement and paused just long enough to flash a smile that showed too many rows of jagged teeth.

"You shouldn't roam alone, little one," he said, his words rolling over me. The confidence in his tone made my skin prickle.

I straightened, letting my stance widen slightly. "I don't want trouble," I said, as if this were home; as if he could understand me.

The amusement in his gaze deepened. He unfurled his wings slowly, the leathery expanse brushing faintly against the walls of the corridor. "It gibbers." He stalked closer, each step deliberate. "You've strayed far, creature. Mine to take."

Take. The word hung in the air between us.

He lunged.

I pivoted on instinct, the move fast and sharp enough to sidestep him as his claws sliced through empty air. My fist shot out—fast and unforgiving—and collided with the side of his jaw. His scales absorbed the blow with far less impact than I hoped, but it was enough to stagger him for half a second.

Damn, that hurt my hand.

I couldn't hesitate. My heel slammed into the side of his knee, forcing his weight down, and I darted backward, aiming for distance.

He recovered too quickly. Wings moving like weapons in their own right, folding toward me as he surged upward in a flurry of movement. His claws caught the edge of my garment, tearing fabric as I twisted out of his grasp.

There was no way I could outmatch him in terms of strength. I had to be faster, smarter. My body moved on autopilot, muscle memory from years of training guiding me as I rolled beneath his second strike, the heat of his breath brushing my shoulder as I narrowly avoided his grip.

Pivot. Duck. Strike.

But his relentless speed sliced away any advantage I might have found. The narrow corridor funneled his larger frame directly toward me. He was built for this—pure, unyielding, ruthless. His claws slashed the air where I'd just been, close enough to stir the fine hairs on the back of my neck. I twisted away, only to have his tail snap outward, knocking my legs from under me. I hit the ground hard, air forced from my lungs in a sharp gasp.

Before I could recover, he was on me.

"So sweet, little morsel," he snarled, his voice as heavy and cloying as the heat pressing down on us. His claws dug into the stone on either side of me, trapping me between him and the coarse ground. His wings arched wide, cutting off the faint light above, bathing us both in shadow. "And I'll enjoy every—"

I bucked upward, slamming my knee into his side. It wasn't much, but it made him grunt and shift his weight just enough for me to twist free—almost. His claws snatched at my wrist, his grip unrelenting as I struggled to wrench myself loose. I lashed out with my free hand, drove the edge of my palm toward his jaw, but he dodged it, the motion fluid, snake-like.

"Clever," he rumbled, flicking my arm aside with a calculated twist. He moved in a blur, pinning both of my wrists above my head in a vice grip that made my fingers go numb. With one hand, he immobilized me completely, his other trailing the torn edge of my garment. "But clever won't save you."

I thrashed against him, my breathing ragged as I pushed against his hold, but his strength was absolute, each attempt to get free like throwing myself against a wall of volcanic rock.

Panic threatened to bubble to the surface, but I shoved it down, my mind racing for an opening.

He lowered his face toward mine, his fangs glinting faintly in the dim light. His breath was hot against my cheek, carrying the metallic tang of battle. "So fragile," he murmured, as though the revelation mystified him. His claws flexed slightly around my wrists, his intent a dark, coiling promise. "And yet your fire ... intoxicating."

Every nerve in my body screamed for action—for escape—but I was out of options. My muscles strained against the weight of him, fury and desperation coursing through me like a fever. His golden eyes glimmered with cruel amusement, drunk with the power imbalance.

"You will yield," he said, his voice dropping to a whisper, low and insidious.

"No," I spat, defiance laced into every fiber of my being. I didn't care if I couldn't win—I refused to let this bastard think he could break me. My teeth clenched in determination as I drove my knee into his stomach again. This time, he caught it with his own thigh, absorbing the impact fully. Shit.

He chuckled low, the sound vibrating through my bones. "Fight all you like, little one—"

His words ended in a choked gasp as something massive collided with him from above—a blur of obsidian scales and crimson eyes.

Darrokar.

7

DARROKAR

HER SCENT HIT me and everything else—the noise of the city, the heat of the air, the weight of duty—blurred into nothing but static.

Burning, intoxicating, *mine*.

The metallic tang of fear laced with the innate heat of her essence twisted through the corridor, jolting through my veins like a spark setting dry kindling ablaze. My claws flexed as I swooped down.

Every sense turned razor-sharp, every instinct narrowing down to a singular truth: someone had dared touch what was mine.

The crackle of my wings carried me forward, each beat concise, lethal. I didn't need to hear the snarl of a rival or the scrape of claws against stone; the bond searing hot in my chest was enough. The scent of her fear pulling me deeper only hardened my resolve.

When I found him, whoever he was, I wouldn't leave enough of him behind to even be recognized.

The corridor opened below me, narrow and dim, like the throat of a predator swallowing prey. There she was—my woman. My mate. Pinned, pressed beneath the hulking frame of a fool whose arrogance would cost him his life.

The world stilled. Terra's red hair flashed in the dull glow of the crystals above, her eyes burning with anger even as her frame strained against the brute's grip. The torn fabric of her robe clung to her curves, a delicate temptation sharpened by the ferocious will radiating from her battered form. She wasn't broken.

Even now, caught in a moment where lesser creatures would yield, she fought.

I was moving before thought could catch up. My claws raked across the warrior's back as I descended. The satisfying crunch of impact and the guttural snarl torn from his throat barely registered—he flew forward and away from her like refuse cast aside. His body slammed into the opposite wall with a force that cracked the stone, but it wasn't enough.

Not nearly enough.

I was on him before he hit the ground, talons biting into his chest as I drove him down. My tail lashed, the sharp end snapping against him like a whip. His hiss of pain fed the storm inside me, an ember igniting into an unquenchable blaze.

"You touch what is mine," I growled, every word a vow of retribution. "You dare lay your filthy hands on her?"

The coward sputtered nonsense, claws scrambling at my grip, but he was drowning in the tide of my rage.

I struck him again—a clean, direct blow that shattered his jaw and muffled whatever plea he might've been foolish enough to voice. Blood spattered hot across the corridor floor, and still, he fought weakly against me, wings flapping once before falling limp.

More. The burning ran deeper than anger, deeper than instinct. This wasn't just about the affront to me—it was the threat to her. My mate. The risk he'd dared to take, the harm she might've suffered, and worse, the damage he'd already dealt, all fueled the fire ravaging me.

The tip of my claw trailed the hollow of his throat, and for a fraction of a moment, I weighed the balance of his life. It would be so easy—just a flick of my wrist, a casual slice, and any insult he'd ever dared breathe would vanish in the pool of his own lifeblood.

"Darrokar."

The steady voice was ice over flame.

I stiffened, my head snapping up. Rath stood at the end of the corridor, his ruby-red scales darkened by the dim light, his golden eyes steady and unfaltering in their appraisal.

"Enough," he said, his voice low, firm. "You're not a feral beast to fight over scraps."

Scraps?

I let out a snarl that vibrated through the floor beneath us. But behind the instinctual anger was the truth of his words cutting deep.

I shouldn't be standing over this pathetic excuse for a warrior like an enraged adolescent. Every action, every blow, every breath I took had repercussions—ones that extended far beyond my own satisfaction. Rath was not just one of my trusted lieutenants; he was one of the few who dared speak sense to me when I needed it most.

Sucking in a breath, I reined in the fire still snarling at the edges of my control. My claws retracted slowly, the scent of blood cooling.

But it wasn't over.

I snarled down at the crumpled pile beneath me. "You'll answer for this." The threat in my tone was marked not by an immediate promise of death, but by something colder—and far worse.

I straightened, chest heaving, and turned toward her.

Terra.

Her name branded itself in my mind even before my eyes found hers. She was on her feet now, leaning slightly against the wall for balance, but her stance was still as strong as before. Despite the reddening mark on her wrist, the tear in her robe, the undeniable evidence of her struggle, she didn't cower.

Her eyes blazed, filled with an emotion I couldn't quite place—fear? Fury? Something else entirely?

I closed the distance between us in two strides, folding my wings tight to keep from brushing against the jagged walls. My shadow spilled across her as I approached, and some treacherous part of me ... paused.

What would I find? Gratitude? Hatred?

The beast inside me wanted her caged against my chest, nestled beneath my wings, breathing my scent until she knew without doubt that I would annihilate anyone who dared come near her. The man within me—the leader, the lord—hesitated. The expression in her eyes didn't have a hint of submission.

It never had, not from the moment we'd first locked gazes back on the surface.

"Are you hurt?" The question left my lips before I'd meant it to, edged with more anger than worry. Not at her—at myself, for failing to stop this. She was still grasping my language, but she was learning almost unnaturally quickly. Perhaps a quirk of her alien species.

Her chin lifted. "Sivanae." *I'm fine.*

Spirit.

Heat roared to life beneath my scales once more, but this time, it wasn't anger. My claws curled slightly, the urge to soothe her quieting the violent edge lingering in my veins. I studied her wrist and stepped closer, my fingers grazing the images already burned into my mind—scents, textures, the heat that pulsed just below the surface of her human skin.

She didn't pull away. Didn't flinch. If anything, the awareness crackling between us deepened.

If Rath wasn't still somewhere nearby, I'd be tempted to take her against the stone wall.

"You shouldn't have left my quarters," I said, my voice low, restrained.

She arched a brow and opened her mouth, sucking in a breath. But she closed her lips and let the breath out without saying a word.

The tension between us was a living thing. Her gaze didn't waver, defiant even in the face of the heat building between us.

My fangs ached again, my wings radiated heat from unused energy, and most unsettling of all, I could feel her—*truly* feel her—in a way that went beyond the physical. It was as if her bravery, her fire, was threading itself into me, entwining with instincts I'd thought I could control.

She wasn't just a flame; she was an inferno, and I wanted to be consumed.

But now was not the time.

"Rath," I growled without turning away from her. My voice carried through the corridor, echoing with the sliver of authority I'd fought to recapture after my outburst. "Take care of him."

Rath stepped forward, his heavy claws clicking against the stone. The glow of his pupils shifted toward the crumpled warrior still struggling to rise from the floor. Rath didn't need to say anything. His gaze alone promised the kind of reckoning that would leave both scars and stories.

The injured male coughed, blood speckling his lips, and attempted to spit out a few words. Whatever pathetic excuse or plea he hoped to offer never left his mouth. Rath seized him by the arm, wrenching him upright with a strength that belied his calm demeanor.

"Your orders?" Rath asked me, his tone neutral, but his eyes glinted with the expectation of blood.

"Banishment," I said, the words clipped, deliberate. I would have flayed the skin from his bones for what he tried, but Rath was right. We had rules here. Laws. And I had my duty. "If he sets foot here again, his life is forfeit."

Rath nodded once. He knew as well as I did that this couldn't be about my personal vengeance or the insult to Terra—this had to be about Scalvaris, the council, the laws that bound us.

Still, the beast inside me seethed, unhappy to let the matter go so easily.

Rath dragged the warrior down the corridor, his claws digging into his captive's shoulder with enough force to make him limp. The sounds of their retreat faded, leaving only the faint vibration of my breathing and the subtle crackle of heat crystals above.

I turned back to Terra.

She stood there, her shoulders squared, her chin tilted up in that infuriatingly stubborn way that made it impossible to look away. Her fire was undimmed, even after what she'd endured. Perhaps even because of it. The faint tear in her robe revealed a sliver of thigh, her skin marred by a scrape that sent a fresh wave of fury surging through me.

My claws flexed involuntarily at my sides, aching for some-thing—someone—to shred, but there was no one left to punish.

Not here. Not now.

She stared up at me, unflinching. She was a strange, frag-ile-looking creature by Drakarn standards, but in that moment, she felt as indomitable as the crystal peaks of Volcaryth. My mate.

"Why?" I demanded, the single word cutting through the silence like the edge of my blade. My voice came out rough, still jagged with the remnants of my rage. I repeated one of the few words she had learned in my tongue. "Why?"

She folded her arms across her chest, her movements tight and deliberate, as if shielding herself from the weight of my anger. She didn't answer, not in words.

Instead, she looked past me, her jaw tight, her throat working as she swallowed. Anger flared in me, unbidden and illogical. She wouldn't even meet my eyes. After all I'd just done—after I'd torn apart that bastard for daring to touch her— she stood there, defiant and distant.

I stepped closer, the heat from my body radiating between us. I wanted her to look at me. Needed it. For all her fire, her courage, her maddening refusal to submit, there was something about her silence that was ... unbearable.

I lifted my hand to her cheek, my claws careful not to hurt her delicate skin. She was warm beneath my touch, nothing like the rage simmering in me. She flinched, just barely, but didn't pull away. That defiance of hers again—burning, stubborn, and maddeningly intoxicating. She hadn't submitted to the bastard who had dared to touch her, and she wouldn't submit to me, either. Not without a fight.

Good.

"Why?" I repeated, softer this time, but no less demanding. My thumb traced the line of her jaw, brushing against the faint smudge of blood that wasn't hers. The sight of it made my wings twitch.

My mate—my woman—had been hurt in my city, under my watch. The guilt clawed at me as fiercely as the rage had moments ago.

Her eyes finally snapped to mine, sharp and unrelenting as a blade's edge. She said nothing, but the tension in her posture spoke volumes. She was angry—at me, at this place, at the circumstances that had forced her into this position.

"Do you seek to test me, fierce one?" I asked, my voice low, a dangerous rumble that carried more than a hint of warning. "I've already had to restrain myself once today. Do not tempt me to lose control again."

Her lips pressed into a thin line, but I saw the spark in her eyes—the spark that told me she was on the verge of spitting something back at me. She didn't, though. Instead, she tore her gaze from mine and yanked her arm free of my touch, turning her back to me in a deliberate act of rebellion.

The air between us crackled with tension, thick and suffocating. My claws twitched at my sides, and my wings unfurled slightly, the instinct to dominate, to claim, warring with the rationality that told me *not now*.

"You think you're strong enough to walk these halls alone?" I growled, stepping around her to block her path. "You think your ferocity will protect you from men like him?"

Her eyebrows scrunched together, and she opened her mouth again, hesitating over the words. "Warrior. Me. Fight."

It took me a moment to understand, and everything within me rebelled at the thought. I didn't want a weak mate. I'd always assumed my heart would one day belong to another warrior.

But Terra had no claws to slash, no scales to protect her, no wings. She was more helpless than the lowliest servant.

And had a warrior's fire in her heart.

Could I really deny her this?

"You want to fight, luvae?" I let the word slip before I could stop myself. *Luvae.* Not just "woman." Not just "mine." Something far more intimate. A word reserved for a bond so deep it was carved into a Drakarn's very bones.

A mate. *My* mate.

Her eyes narrowed, the sharp green of them cutting through the dim light like a blade. She didn't understand the word fully—she couldn't. But she recognized the weight of it, the way it lingered between us like the heat hanging in the thick air of Scalvaris.

"I fight," she said, her voice hard, clipped. She jabbed a finger against her chest, her meaning clear despite the fractured language. "Me. Warrior."

My wings flared slightly, a reflexive response to her audacity. The fire in her words made my blood simmer, equal parts frustration and something darker, hotter. I stepped closer, towering over her, forcing her to tilt her chin up to meet my gaze.

"You think you understand what it means to be a warrior?" My voice rumbled low, the cavern amplifying the menace woven into my words.

"Training begins tomorrow."

8

TERRA

THE TRAINING AREA was everything I'd come to expect from the Drakarn: brutal, functional, and entirely unforgiving. Rough stone walls glimmered faintly in the light cast by heat crystals embedded in the ceiling. Their glow painted the cavern in molten oranges and reds, making the space look like it had been carved directly out of a volcano. The floor was worn smooth in some places, jagged in others, as if even the ground here would punish the unsteady.

A place like this didn't care about mercy. And neither did the man pacing in front of me.

Darrokar moved with all the lethal grace I'd come to associate with him: dark wings half-unfurled, casting jagged shadows that danced along the walls. His tail lashed in sharp, deliberate arcs, its spiked tip threatening to slice through the air between us. His claws flexed and curled as though itching for violence.

But it was his eyes—those molten gold, slit-pupiled eyes—that held me captive. Anger blazed within them like a forge stoked too hot, but there was something more, something darker writhing just beneath the surface.

"Disgrace," he snarled, his voice a low rumble that

resonated through the cavern. The word ricocheted off the stone walls, its weight as sharp as his claws. "To attack one not marked as warrior. No honor."

I watched him, forcing myself to remain still. Observing. Calculating. If I was going to survive there, I needed to understand these people—their rules, their fragile egos, their ideology. And right then, I was learning a lot about what made Darrokar tick.

He wasn't just angry about my unsanctioned expedition into the lower tunnels. No, this was something deeper. Personal.

"The punishment is exile," he continued, the words more to himself than to me. His tail slammed once against the ground, sending a vibration through the floor strong enough to rattle my teeth. "But it should have been death. It *would* have been death —if—" He cut himself off, his teeth clicking together audibly.

That barely reigned fury of his could've suffocated weaker prey. But I wasn't prey. Not his. Not anyone's.

"Why did you leave?" he snapped suddenly, spinning to face me. His wings flared wide, nearly brushing the walls on either side of us. It was a deliberately intimidating display, but I refused to flinch. "Why risk—why go?" His words were clipped, as though speaking simply, hoping I would understand, cost him effort. His control was slipping by the second, and I couldn't shake how those seething remnants of anger lingered alongside something far less definable.

I pulled in a breath, readying myself for what I was about to say. My mask of control was thin, but I wore it like armor. "Because I needed to," I said evenly. With the translator's help, I'd picked up a lot of his language, even if it wasn't programmed to help me speak. "And I'm not helpless."

His eyes widened, a flicker of surprise cracking through his glowering mask.

"I won't let you cage me."

The resulting silence was deafening. He froze mid-breath, tension coiling through his massive frame like an earthquake gearing up to strike. Slowly, deliberately, his wings folded back against his spine, and his gaze locked onto mine with renewed intensity.

"You speak our words," he said, the syllables slow and measured. His breath hitched, almost imperceptibly, as though he'd walked into an ambush deeper than he could have anticipated. "All this time, you understood?"

"Long enough," I replied, meeting his stare head-on. "I wanted to hear what you'd say when you didn't think I could understand."

"Clever," he bit out. The word dripped with distaste. And yet, beneath the disapproval, there was something dangerously close to admiration. "You should've stayed inside," he said finally, his voice losing some of its heat but none of its growl. "You are—" He paused, seeking the translation in his mind. "—too valuable to risk. Reckless."

"I don't need your protection," I said. The sharpness of my words sliced between us. "I'm a soldier—a warrior. Back on Earth, I led people into battles you couldn't begin to imagine. I *protected* them when no one else would. My people. My team. That's who I am. Not some ... fragile ornament you get to keep locked in a room."

Golden eyes narrowed. He stepped closer, enough for the heat radiating from his body to waft over my skin. "You think this is about keeping you? Claiming you?" His voice dropped lower, a throaty growl that somehow vibrated against the hollow of my chest. "If I wanted to 'keep you,' little warrior, you'd already be mine."

The way those words lingered—low and rough and laced with something that burned hotter than anger—made my blood ignite in a way I didn't entirely welcome. I swallowed hard, refusing to let him see even an inch of ground. "Then *prove it.* Train me."

He stilled. For one tense moment, he seemed to loom even taller, darker, his shadow stretching long across the cavern floor. "Train you?" he repeated, a new note invading his voice. His wings shifted, sharp-edged feathers rustling faintly as his head tilted to study me again. "You hope to challenge me, human?"

"No," I said, the word delivered with pointed clarity. "I hope to survive. And if there's anyone in this goddamned cavern who knows how to fight like one of you, it's you."

Darrokar exhaled sharply through his nose. "Arrogant," he muttered, though there was almost ... approval in his tone. "But not wrong."

I'd barely registered the shift in his stance before he moved. One heartbeat he was standing several feet away, the next he was face-to-face with me, so close I could see the faint, bluish veins that webbed through the black scales along his collarbone's jagged ridges. His heat washed over me again, molten and all-consuming, dragging my pulse into dangerous territory.

"Then fight for it," he rumbled, his voice raw. "There is no training without pain. No victory without blood."

Good.

Darrokar didn't give me time to reply. A blur of black scales and wings filled my vision as his tail whipped toward my legs. I leapt back, barely missing the strike that would've sent me sprawling. His movements were fluid, natural—as if each muscle in his body answered to some ancient rhythm. There was no hesitation, no pause to predict his next move. He was testing me, and I knew damn well he wasn't going to make this easy.

Good. I didn't want easy.

He lunged again, faster this time, and I dropped low, rolling under one of his outstretched wings. My shoulder scraped the rough stone of the floor, sending a spike of pain up my arm, but I ignored it, springing to my feet. Before I could fully regain my stance, he was already moving, his claws slicing through the charged air in a controlled strike—not close enough to hit me, but close enough to remind me how sharp they were.

"Your instincts ... they are not entirely pathetic," he growled, circling me. His tail lashed behind him, coiled energy barely held in check. "But instincts alone will not save you. Not here."

I matched his steps, refusing to let him hem me in. "Then maybe you should stop showing off and actually teach me something," I shot back, my breath coming faster than I would've liked. He wasn't even winded. Of course he wasn't.

The corner of his mouth curved upward, a flash of fangs against his obsidian-black scales. "A warrior should never beg for knowledge. Take it." There was a challenge in his voice, low and electric, and I hated how much it set my nerves on fire.

"I'm not begging," I said, narrowing my eyes. "I'm demanding."

Darrokar stopped, wings unfurling just enough to shadow me as he leaned forward, closing the distance between. His golden eyes glowed in the dim light, molten and unwavering as they fixed on mine. "Then demand it with more than words, *Terra.*"

The sound of my name on his tongue hit me harder than any blow. It wrapped around me, resonating in a way that made my stomach tighten and my chest ache. But I shoved that feeling aside.

He moved again, and this time I was ready. As his hand came toward me, claws curving just enough to hook, I stepped inside his reach, deflecting the strike with my forearm. The impact jolted through me, and it became startlingly clear just how solid he was. Like striking steel wrapped in scales. But I didn't back down—I pivoted, grabbing for the ridges along his arm to use his momentum against him.

It almost worked.

Almost.

But then his tail snapped against my calf, throwing me off-balance. I stumbled, and in an instant, he had me pinned. One massive arm locked around my waist, yanking me flush against his chest while his other hand braced my forearm, holding it immobile. His heat seared into my back, and when he leaned close, the low, rumbling vibration of his growl buzzed through my skin like static electricity.

"You rely too much on technique without understanding your opponent," he murmured into my ear, his breath hot and smoky against my neck. His voice was calm now, almost uncomfortably so. "You fight to win. My kind fight to dominate."

"As if there's a difference," I said through gritted teeth, twisting in his grip. I managed to free one arm and jab my elbow back, aiming for what I assumed was a pressure point just below his ribs.

It didn't have the effect I wanted.

Instead of releasing me, Darrokar laughed—a low, predatory sound that sent a flicker of warning through my gut. "So you do have claws after all," he said, and then, so quickly I couldn't counter, he spun me around and pressed me back against one of the cavern walls. His wings flared, closing in like walls on either side of me, boxing me in. "But they're dull. You'd be dead before drawing blood."

The worst part wasn't the position—it was the way his gaze raked over me, a mixture of challenge and something far more dangerous. He wasn't just testing my combat skills anymore. He was testing *me*. Every nerve in my body felt strung tight, as if this wasn't a fight but a negotiation happening on some deeper, unspoken level.

"You think I'm done?" I spat, defiance burning away the unwanted heat pooling low in my stomach. "This was round one."

Darrokar's fanged smile widened, and a pulse of something fierce flickered in his expression. "*Now* you sound like a warrior."

Using anger as fuel, I shoved at his chest. He allowed the motion to unbalance him, only slightly, but it was enough for me to duck beneath his arm and put distance between us again. My breaths became ragged, and I tightened my stance, forcing my body to obey even while my senses screamed at how *close* he still was.

"Faster," he said and then lunged, dropping to a crouch as he swiped low with his tail. I jumped to avoid it, but the movement shifted my balance just enough for him to catch me mid-air, claws skimming my side as he spun me around and pinned me again. This time, when his chest pressed to mine, the rough stone of the wall dug into my back, grounding me in an intimacy that felt explosive rather than suffocating.

His head dipped low, and for one impossible moment, I swore his lips were close enough to graze mine.

"What are you waiting for?" he whispered, a low rumble laced with maddening satisfaction. "Prove me wrong, *Terra*. Show me you are more."

I was breathing too hard to answer, every muscle coiled and trembling beneath his unrelenting heat. And then—then he looked at me, really looked, and something unspoken passed between us. His hand, still braced against my arm, loosened slightly, his claws careful as if remembering how breakable I was. His tail, still coiled near my ankle, stilled.

The air between us was electric, charged not only with

tension but something far deeper and infinitely more potent. My pulse thundered in my ears, drowning out the weight of unasked questions lingering between us.

"Fuck it," I muttered.

And then, like a dam breaking, I grabbed the back of his neck and yanked him forward, slamming my lips up to his in a kiss that tasted like battle and surrender all at once.

At first, Darrokar froze, a flash of surprise breaking through his storm-like intensity. But the hesitation lasted less than a heartbeat. Then he was kissing me back—ferociously, flawlessly, with a heat that burned away reason. His claws bit into the stone at my side, fingers caging me even as his wings swept forward, shielding me completely from the outside world.

A growl rose from deep in his throat, vibrating through his chest and into mine. His lips were hot and firm against mine, his fangs grazing the edge of my bottom lip just enough to make me pull him closer, tighter, like gravity wasn't strong enough to hold us together.

When I finally broke the kiss to breathe, we were both panting, bodies pressed so tightly there wasn't space for air between us.

"Little warrior," he rumbled, his voice laced with something I couldn't pin down.

"Time for round two."

9

TERRA

I SNAKED my hand around his neck and pulled him close, crushing our mouths together. This time, there was no hesitation—just pure, unadulterated need colliding between us.

Darrokar's arms wrapped around me, one sliding low along my spine to pull me against him while the other tangled in my hair. The sharp tips of his claws scratched lightly at my scalp, sending a shiver rippling down my body that had nothing to do with fear and everything to do with lust.

I arched into him, relishing how hard he felt beneath his thin training pants.

A growl escaped him as I nipped at his bottom lip, catching it gently between my teeth before soothing the sting with a swipe of my tongue. He groaned, a low rumble from deep within his chest. It vibrated against my ribs and sent bolts of energy sparking through my veins.

He released his grip on my waist only to bring both hands up, cupping either side of my face. His thumbs stroked across my jawline, tracing its contours reverently. The touch was surprisingly tender considering that he had claws that could tear me to shreds with one wrong move.

"I've never wanted anything more than you," he murmured

against my lips before dipping his head lower. His tongue traced a scorching path along my throat and collarbone while his fingers slid down over my shoulders until they reached the neckline of my borrowed armor top.

I sucked in a deep breath as those razor-sharp points trailed delicately across my skin. Even through the haze of desire, some distant corner of my brain marveled at how careful he was being with me.

There was only the hot stone of the training floor, and though this was Darrokar's private quarters, it wasn't exactly secluded. Anyone could walk in on us.

I couldn't care.

The world had narrowed to this moment: me, him, and his hands peeling away my clothes.

He tugged impatiently at the straps holding my armor together, fumbling clumsily with the fastenings in his haste to remove them from me entirely. Until, with a sexy growl, he tore through the straps with his claws, slicing them to ribbons.

If I had any survival instincts left, I'd be running right now. But it was too late. My pulse thundered against his lips.

"Terra ..." He whispered my name like a prayer as he pulled back far enough for our eyes to meet once more—and what I saw burning within their depths took my breath away completely.

It wasn't just lust or desire—it ran deeper than that somehow—older and wilder than anything I'd ever felt before in my life.

And it scared me how much I wanted it too.

His claws trailed down my sides, leaving goosebumps in their wake as he traced every curve and dip of my body before finally coming to rest upon my hips. He gripped them firmly, possessively, drawing me even closer until there wasn't so much as an inch separating us.

"*Luvae,*" he growled, lips pressing against my neck.

I didn't know exactly what it meant, even with the translator, even after he'd used it so many times, but the word sent a shiver down my spine. I tilted my head back, offering him better access. His tongue traced patterns across my skin, leaving trails of fire wherever it touched.

I was on the ground before I realized he was laying me down, my legs spread and his hips nestled between them, his heavy weight pinning me in place. I could feel the hard length of his cock straining against the fabric of his pants and pressing insistently between my thighs.

The stone of the training floor was hot against my naked back, and the heat of Darrokar above me only intensified the sensation. It should've been uncomfortable, maybe even painful, but instead, I found myself arching into it, craving more of the delicious friction that was building between us.

He shifted slightly, angling himself so that his hips rubbed against mine in a way that made stars burst behind my eyes. "More," I panted, reaching up to tangle my fingers in his thick, dark hair. He obliged, grinding against me, his movements slow and deliberate and utterly intoxicating.

His tail curled around one of my ankles, locking it in place while his claws hooked under my knee, lifting it higher, allowing him to tear my pants off until I was completely nude. His wings flared wide, casting shadows over us both.

Then he curled them in tight and grinned. "I want to devour you, *luvae.*" He leaned down, and his lips captured one of my nipples. I gasped, arching against him as he teased it with his tongue, flicking and circling the sensitive peak until it hardened beneath his touch.

His tail flicked up between my thighs, caressing the slick folds there until it found my clit. The contact sent sparks dancing through me, making me buck helplessly against him.

He made a rumbly sound in his chest that vibrated against me, and I moaned shamelessly in response.

My breasts ached for him to pay attention to them, and he must've sensed it because his tongue licked a hot line from one nipple to the other before his teeth scraped across them, sending shivers of pleasure racing through my body. He sucked on one, then the other, drawing each tip between his fangs until they were swollen and sensitive.

I never thought I could come from just that, but he had me close.

His tail continued stroking my sex, coiling itself between my thighs before plunging its smooth, scaled tip into me. It thrust in and out slowly, methodically, building the pressure inside me with every stroke. I was dripping with need, aching for more.

Holy fucking shit.

It was beyond unreal. And from the tone of Darrokar's dark, sensual laugh, it was only beginning.

Darrokar's tail withdrew from me, leaving me panting and reeling. I barely caught my breath before his hands were on me again, lifting and turning me onto my side. His powerful body moved with a graceful, predatory fluidity that captivated me.

"Look at me," he commanded in a voice rough with desire. His golden eyes glowed intensely, reflecting the dim, fiery light of the cavern. I obeyed, turning slightly to see him kneeling beside me, his wings arched behind him like dark, menacing arches.

He was an impressive sight—black scales gleaming with a reddish tint, muscles dancing under his skin as he moved, his erection straining against the now-far-too-tight fabric of his combat trousers.

He stripped them away, revealing his cock in all its alien perfection.

I was mesmerized by the sight, my earlier curiosity now a blazing inferno of fascination. His penis was unlike anything human, with its base covered in black and red scales, transitioning into red flesh with thick, dark veins that throbbed. The tip was uncut, surrounded by a fleshy, tongue-like structure that moved independently, twitching in anticipation, as if inviting me closer.

A bead of liquid pearled at the tip, and without thinking, I reached out to touch it. My fingers brushed against the smooth, velvety surface, and his entire body shuddered. His whole cock was covered in a warm and slick fluid, nearly as wet as I was, and carrying his unique, intoxicating scent that made my head spin with desire.

"Terra ...," Darrokar murmured, his voice a mix of reverence and raw need.

I brought my hand to my lips, tasting him. The flavor was unexpected, musky and potent, laced with an aroma that seemed to seep into my very bones. My tongue, already overly sensitive, tingled with the contact, sending a wave of arousal straight through me.

"This is part of my pheromones," he said, watching me closely, his eyes dark with lust. "The more we do this, the more intense our arousal will grow. The harder it will be to stop."

There was no way I was stopping. Darrokar's gaze never left mine as he guided my hand to his erection, his cock already leaking pre-cum in anticipation. I wrapped my fingers around it, marveling at the unique texture. It was warm to the touch, almost hot, and I could feel the pulse of his heartbeat in the thick veins. The scales along the base were surprisingly smooth, a subtle contrast to the ridged flesh above them.

As I began to stroke him, my thumb brushed over the intriguing tongue-like tip, sending a shiver down my spine. Darrokar's low growl vibrated through his body, his hips reflexively jerking into my touch with urgency. I teased the sensitive flesh, circling and stroking it in a rhythm that seemed to drive him wild, the obsidian scales at the base of his cock glinting in the dim light.

His pre-cum drooled steadily, smearing between my fingers and soaking into my palm, leaving a sticky trail. I leaned in, capturing the tip of his cock between my lips, and swirled my tongue around it to taste more of those intoxicating pheromones. They had a sharp, musky flavor, both familiar and unknown, fueling my own growing arousal.

Darrokar's fingers tangled in my hair, guiding my head as I lavished attention on his cock. His hips rocked into my mouth, using my rhythm to fuck himself against my tongue. The blunt, tongue-like tip bumped against the roof of my mouth, sending sparks through me with each touch.

I sucked harder, determined to wring every drop of pleasure from him.

His tail was between my legs again, stroking my folds until I was practically shaking. I moaned, the dual sensations of his cock in my mouth and his touch on my sex driving me wild.

Darrokar's wings flared, the shadows cast by their dark membrane dancing across the stone floor as he exhaled a ragged breath. His claws scraped against my shoulders, the slight pain mixing with the pleasure as I continued to explore him with my lips and tongue. I could feel the heat building between us, the air thick with the scent of us.

"Terra, your mouth ... fuck," he groaned. "I need to be inside you, *luvae.*"

My body ached for it.

With a grunt of effort, Darrokar flipped me onto my back, his powerful form pinning me to the stone floor. I wrapped my legs around his hips, feeling the thick head of his cock nudge against my entrance.

"Yes, please," I whispered, grinding against him desperately. The heat of his body enveloped me, his scales rough against my sensitive skin.

His eyes blazed with an intense golden light as he gazed down at me, his pupils dilated to slits. The air between us was alive with raw, unbridled lust, the heat from his skin radiating against my own. "You're so wet for me, luvae," he panted, his deep, gravelly voice sending shivers down my spine. His tail curled possessively around my thigh, the tip dragging lightly over my sensitive skin, eliciting a whimper of pleasure from my lips.

I nodded frantically, unable to form words as my hands gripped his forearms, anchoring myself to him. I was lost in the hunger of the moment, drowning in my own desire that seemed to mirror his. The musky scent of his arousal filled my nostrils, a heady mix of male pheromones and something uniquely his that made my head spin and my core clench around emptiness.

With a low, vicious growl, Darrokar pushed forward, the thick, sensitive head of his cock breaching my slick entrance. I gasped, my back arching off the ground as he stretched me open with a deliberate, almost brutal slowness.

"Darrokar!" I cried out, and he sank deeper. He paused, his hips still, giving me a moment to adjust to his size.

A wave of dizzying pleasure rippled through me as Darrokar's full length finally filled me, his cock pulsing with each beat of his heart. I was stuffed to the brim, every inch of him embedded deep within my core, his base pressed firmly against my sensitive clit.

The sensation of being so completely claimed by him, of his immense cock stretching me open in a way no human ever had, was overwhelming. It was like nothing I'd ever experienced, and my body responded with a desperate, primal urge to move, to take him even deeper.

Darrokar held himself there, buried inside me, the veins on his neck corded with tension as he fought for control. I wanted to feel him moving within me, the heavy thrusts I knew he was capable of, but instead, he stayed utterly still, as if giving me time to adjust to his overwhelming presence.

"Move ... please," I begged, my voice breaking on a desperate moan. "I need to feel you."

With a sharp, guttural growl, Darrokar surged forward, his hips snapping against mine in a relentless rhythm that stole my breath and shattered my control. He pounded into me with brutal efficiency, each thrust driving me deeper into the stone floor, the force of his movements rattling my bones.

The pleasure was intense, a blinding, all-consuming fire that ravaged my senses and left me mindless in its wake. I wrapped my legs tighter around his waist, using the leverage to meet his thrusts, to take him as deep as he could go. My nails raked down his back, leaving scored trails on his scales as I gripped him, holding on for dear life as he ravished me.

The sound of skin slapping against skin, punctuated by my ragged gasps and moans, filled the cavern. Darrokar's cock throbbed inside me, his thickness stretching me in ways that bordered on pain, but the pleasure far outweighed any discomfort. My inner walls clenched around him, milking his length as he pounded into me, the friction building with each merciless stroke.

"*Luvae*, I can feel you ... so close," Darrokar panted, his voice a rough growl. His golden eyes flickered with a feral glow, his gaze feverish and possessive as he watched me.

I could only moan incoherently, my body moving in time with his, seeking that exquisite release that eluded me. The pressure inside me built to a crescendo, my walls pulsing around his cock as he drove into me harder, faster.

And then, with a keening cry, I shattered. My orgasm

ripped through me like a wildfire, consuming everything in its path. Wave after wave of bliss crashed over me, leaving me gasping and trembling in Darrokar's passionate grasp.

Darrokar's powerful body tensed, his muscles rippling beneath his scales as he buried himself to the hilt inside me. He groaned, a deep, carnal sound that vibrated past his chest and into mine. His cock throbbed, pulsating with a rhythmic intensity that seemed to synchronize with my own clenching release.

"I'm going to come," he warned, his voice strained with the effort of holding back. "Hold on, *luvae*."

With a guttural roar, he released, his hips jerking with each violent spasm as he emptied himself inside me. His hot seed flooded my core, coating my inner walls with a thick, viscous warmth. I felt every pulse, every tremor of his climax, the sensation almost unbearably intense as he filled me to the brim.

The heat of his release seared through me, intensifying the pleasure already coursing through my veins. I was helpless to do anything but surrender to the overwhelming sensations, my body wracked with the aftershocks of my own orgasm.

Darrokar nuzzled into my neck, repeating one word over and over. "*Luvae. Luvae. Luvae.*"

And something in me finally understood. It didn't mean *mine*. Not exactly.

It meant mate.

10

DARROKAR

THE AIR WAS heavy with her scent.

It wasn't just there in my chambers—it clung to my skin, my wings, my very senses. Sweet, wild, and utterly intoxicating, it overpowered the tang of molten stone and heat crystals embedded in the walls. It blurred the dividing lines of my thoughts, drowning out every instinct except the unshakable knowledge that she was mine.

Terra Drake. Human. Warrior.

Mate.

My bond to her was no longer an unfulfilled ache—it was real now, visceral, carved into the marrow of my bones. Every beat of my heart pulsed with it, this connection between us, fierce as fire and as unrelenting as the world outside these walls.

She had fought me—challenged me—and I had claimed her.

But even now, as she lay curled against me, her breaths steady and deep with sleep, I knew this bond was not so simple. She was no fragile thing, no docile creature content to be tamed. No, she burned with a fire that refused to be extinguished.

And it was that fire that both drew me to her and unsettled me more than I cared to admit.

I stretched across the smooth, heat-warmed stone of my sleeping platform, my wings draping over its edges like smoldering shadows. Its surface, carved from volcanic rock, radiated the comforting warmth of my people's fire-born home. Around me, my chambers glowed faintly with light from the heat crystals, their molten orange veins crawling through the blackened stone like living things. Shadows flickered across the ceiling, the dance of firelight a reflection of the restless energy pulsing through me.

She stirred beside me, her copper hair spilling across my obsidian scales in a cascade of molten light. Her hand rested against my ribcage, delicate fingers curling as if she sought to anchor herself to me even in sleep. Her warmth sank into me, more potent than the heat that surrounded us.

I should have let her rest. Should have allowed her this brief reprieve from the chaos of this world that was not her own. But responsibilities loomed beyond these walls—duties that would not wait, threats that would not yield. My people. My enemies. The council. All of them circled like carrion birds, waiting for any sign of weakness, any crack in my armor. And Terra ... Terra was no ordinary crack. She was a blaze, wild and beautiful, and I knew it would take all my strength to shield her from what was to come.

A faint shift in the chamber's light caught my attention. The massive doors at the far end, carved with the sigils of my house, groaned open with deliberate slowness. A figure stepped inside, silhouetted against the low glow of the hall beyond. Tall, crimson-scaled, and exuding the confidence of a predator who knew his place in the hierarchy.

Rath.

He entered without hesitation, his wings tucked neatly

against his back and his molten ruby-red scales shimmering faintly in the light. His sharp amber eyes swept the room, lingering briefly on the sleeping form of Terra before meeting mine. His mouth curved into a smirk—the kind that had earned him more than one scar in his years as my subordinate.

"Darrokar," he greeted, his voice low and rough. "I see you've been ... busy."

I rose slowly, careful not to disturb Terra. Her hand slipped from my chest as I shifted, and though her warmth lingered, the absence left a quiet ache in its wake. She murmured something soft, a garbled word that I couldn't quite catch, before settling once more into stillness.

"Speak," I ordered Rath, my voice low and clipped. My wings flared slightly as I stepped away from the platform, the movement stirring the heavy air of the chamber. "And make it quick."

Rath's smirk widened as he came closer, his taloned feet clicking softly against the stone floor. "The exile is done," he said simply, his tone casual. "The *kervash* won't find shelter in the wastes. And if he does, it won't last long."

A growl rumbled deep in my chest at the memory of that bastard's audacity. His hands on Terra, his challenge to my claim—it had taken more restraint than I cared to admit not to end him myself. My claws flexed, scraping against the stone. "Good," I said darkly. "If he values his life, he'll stay gone."

Rath nodded, though the gleam in his eyes told me he hoped to meet the *kervash* again. "And if he doesn't, I'll gladly remind him why that was a mistake."

The words might have been a joke, but his gaze drifted again to Terra, and though there was no malice in his curiosity, it still set my instincts on edge. I stepped closer, my wings flaring wider in a reflexive show of dominance.

"She's ... different," Rath said at last, tilting his head as he regarded her. His tone was cautious, but not entirely free of judgment. "Not what I expected."

"You expected nothing," I snapped, my voice sharp as the edge of a blade. "You know nothing of her."

Rath raised his hands in mock surrender, the smirk fading from his face. "The council will want to know more," he said carefully. "You know they'll question this. Question her."

"Let them," I growled, stepping closer. The heat of my anger flared in the air between us. "I have no interest in their doubts or their traditions. Terra is mine, and no council, no law, will take her from me."

Rath studied me for a long moment, his amber eyes narrowing slightly. "Traditions run deep, Darrokar," he said quietly. "You've always walked the line between honoring and defying them. Just be certain which side you stand on."

I didn't respond. I held Rath's gaze, the weight of his words settling uneasily in my chest. Loyalty was etched into his bones, but his caution was not without merit. The council would not let this go unchallenged. They would see Terra as a disruption, an unknown, perhaps even a threat. And to them, threats were meant to be eliminated.

But the fire that burned within me—the bond that tethered us—was unshakable. Terra was no threat. She was strength. Resilience. Defiance. And she was mine.

Rath must have sensed the resolve in my silence, for he shifted, his wings folding more tightly against his back. "For what it's worth," he said, tilting his head, "I've never seen you like this. It's ... unsettling."

I narrowed my eyes. "Unsettling?"

He nodded, his smirk returning, though it lacked its earlier edge. "You're quieter. Less ... predictable. Whatever she's done, it's making the rest of us nervous."

"Good," I said, my voice low and deliberate. "You should be nervous."

Rath gave a short laugh, more breath than sound, and inclined his head. "As you say, Warrior Lord. But nervous warriors make rash decisions. Keep an eye on your council—they'll be watching."

Without another word, he turned and strode toward the door, the click of his talons echoing off the chamber walls. His wings brushed lightly against the frame, and the heavy door groaned shut behind him, leaving me alone with my mate once more.

I stood there for a moment, staring at the closed door, my thoughts uneasy. Rath's words were an unwelcome specter in the back of my mind. He was right—nervous warriors did make rash choices. And the council was nothing if not a collection of nervous old fools.

But I would deal with them if and when they became a problem. For now, my priority was here—beside me, stretched across the sleeping platform like she belonged in this world carved from fire and stone.

"Who was that?" Terra's voice startled me, soft but steady, tinged with curiosity.

She was propped up on one elbow. The red waves of her hair framed her face, and her green eyes glinted with humor. She was watching me closely, her gaze as sharp as ever. She was my mate; I should have expected nothing less.

"Rath," I said simply, crossing the room to stand beside her. "A warrior. And a nuisance."

She laughed softly, a sound that sent a pleasant hum through my chest. "I figured as much," she said, stretching languidly. "He came to poke the bear."

I tilted my head, frowning. "What? What is a bear?"

Her lips twitched into a grin that was part teasing and part affection. "Large, furry predator. Very grumpy. Not unlike you."

A low growl rumbled in my throat, but there was no heat behind it. I leaned closer, bracing one hand on the platform beside her, my wings shifting slightly to block out the faint glow of the heat crystals. "Grumpy?" I murmured, my voice a dangerous purr. "You think I am grumpy, little warrior?"

Her smile widened, unafraid of the dark promise in my tone. If anything, she seemed to enjoy provoking me. "Absolutely," she said, her voice laced with humor. "Don't worry—I like it. In a terrifying, 'don't-mess-with-me-or-I'll-breathe-fire' kind of way."

I couldn't help the faint smirk that tugged at my lips. Her courage, her sharp wit—it never failed to catch me off guard. "I don't breathe fire."

She reached up, her fingers brushing lightly against my jaw, her touch soft yet electrifying. "No?" she asked.

The air between us crackled, charged with something stronger than the mating bond. The heat of the room, the glow of the crystals, the distant hum of the geothermal currents—it all faded into the background.

There was only her. Her fire. Her defiance.

I caught her hand in mine, my claws brushing against her smaller, softer fingers. The difference between us—her fragility, my strength—should have been stark. Irreconcilable. And yet, it didn't matter. Because in that moment, she wasn't fragile. She was unshakable.

"You are a menace," I muttered, though the words held no bite.

"And you love it," she countered without missing a beat, her grin widening.

I didn't respond, but the look in her eyes told me she already knew the answer. She always seemed to know.

She shifted slightly, pulling herself up to sit cross-legged on the platform. Her copper hair caught the flickering light, turning it into a halo of flame. "So," she said, her tone more serious now. "What's the plan?"

I raised an eyebrow. "The plan?"

"Yes, Darrokar, the plan," she said, rolling her eyes. "You don't strike me as the kind of guy to just wing it."

I flicked my wings just enough to let them catch the light. "Winging it has worked well enough for you so far."

She smirked. "Of course."

I growled softly, though the corners of my mouth twitched. "I make no promises."

Her expression softened, and the humor faded, replaced by something quieter. "I'm serious," she said, her voice quieter now. "This bond between us—it's ... intense. And I can see it in your eyes. Is there something I'm missing here?"

"It's my responsibility to protect you," I said simply, as if that could encompass the depth of what I felt.

She shook her head, her expression firm. "I can take care of myself."

"You are mine, *luvae.*"

Before she could start to argue, I captured her lips and lowered her back to the sleeping platform. We had no need for more words.

TERRA

IF THERE WAS one good thing about dating—could you call it dating? —the scary Drakarn leader, it was that I no longer had to sneak around to find my people. I just had to ask.

But as one of Darrokar's warrior trainees lead me through narrow passages and down deep into the caverns of Scalvaris, my wariness grew. It wasn't just because of the attack. After training sessions with Darrokar, I had more than one way to get away from an attacker, but my brain still had to catch up with that.

It was dark down there, the crystals in the walls glowing so dim I had to squint to see, and I didn't spot the door until my guide came to a halt.

I stepped inside, expecting the worst.

This wasn't where they'd kept us before, and once I was through the door, it wasn't *that* bad. It was brighter, for one, and there was furniture.

The room was carved entirely from stone, the furniture sleek and functional, with chairs and low tables molded from the same obsidian-like material. A larger table in the corner hosted scattered supplies—rations, some clothing, and a few unfamiliar tools. Despite the relative comfort, it was clear that while this wasn't a dungeon, it wasn't exactly freedom either.

Hawk was the first to notice me. She rose quickly from her seat at the corner table, her tall frame unmistakable even in the dim light. The sharp intake of her breath was followed by a burst of motion as Kira and Vega turned toward the door. The flickering light cast their expressions in shifting shadows—relief, disbelief, and something sharper beneath the surface.

"Captain," Hawk said, her voice tight with suppressed emotion. She didn't need to call me that, but she must have been shaken if it slipped out. It wasn't a title we used for familiarity there, but hearing it made my stomach twist into knots. "You're not dead."

I couldn't help the smallest, hollow smile. "Not quite," I said, keeping my tone light to mask the weight beneath it. As I stepped farther into the room, the atmosphere shifted. Where there had been relief, suspicion began to take root. One by one, they straightened, their eyes narrowing as they took me in.

"Where the hell have you been?" Vega's voice broke the silence, a low growl of frustration barely restrained. Her arms were crossed tightly over her chest, her muscular frame rigid with tension. Her eyes shone with accusation as they met mine.

"I wasn't exactly able to move around the city," I said firmly, though their reactions were fair; I would've felt the same. My voice was even, commanding, but my own guilt clawed at the edges of my composure. "It's complicated—the Drakarn don't trust us."

She raised an eyebrow, the faintest smirk lifting one corner of her mouth, but it wasn't amusement—it was cold calculation. "Complicated? That's an impressive way to describe leaving your team stranded," she said, her words deliberately measured, barbed just enough to land their hit but not too much to be insubordinate.

My grip tightened on the edge of one of the stone chairs as I stepped fully into the room and allowed the heavy door to close behind me. "Stranded? As if I had a choice to leave you! I've been trying to find you guys for two weeks."

"That's rich," Hawk muttered sharply, coming to stand beside Vega. The two loomed like a united front, their solidarity almost tangible. "We've been dragged around this place like cattle, interrogated repeatedly despite the fact it's clear we don't speak the language, and watched day and night by freaking alien dragon-monsters who act like we're a zoo exhibit. Where the hell have you been?"

I flinched, my soldier's mask cracking just a fraction.

"I didn't have a choice." My reply came softer than I intended, and that was a mistake. Hawk seized on it immediately.

"No choice? Or did you just find a cozy place with a bit less stone and a bit more ..." Her words trailed off, her expression darkening. Her gaze flickered to the leather vambrace around my arm.

Vega pounced on Hawk's unspoken insinuation. "Yeah, you look remarkably ... well-fed. Well-rested." Her eyes flicked between me and the door, as though expecting someone to burst in after me uninvited. "And those clothes ..."

My team looked clean enough; clearly, they'd managed to bathe at some point, and their clothes weren't as ragged as you'd expect after two weeks, so they might have been washed. But they weren't in the borrowed warrior leathers I was wearing.

"Don't," I snapped sharply, my voice ringing out in a way that silenced them all. The effect was momentary, but the words had done their job. I drew in a slow breath and composed myself before continuing. "This place isn't what we could have expected. Darrokar—"

A collective groan interrupted me the moment I'd spoken

his name. Hawk threw up her hands, and Vega's smirk turned positively venomous. "Oh, here it is," she muttered. "She's dicknotized."

"I'm not dicknotized!" I said, louder than I should have. My voice momentarily startled even me, echoing faintly against the walls. My cheeks burned with a blush, and I wanted to bury my face in my hands.

Hawk's jaw dropped slightly, her dark eyes narrowing with something a lot like realization—and betrayal. "Oh my God," she said flatly. "Are you really ... How do you even with the claws?"

Heat bloomed in my chest. "Carefully. Guys, it's not what it sounds like. Darrokar is—"

"Different?" Vega scoffed. Her cold, gray eyes sparkled with disbelief. "You've got to be kidding me, Terra."

"You don't understand," I snapped, rounding on her sharply enough that even Vega seemed taken aback. "I've been learning all I can about this place. It's not like we have any other place to go. We need to figure out how to make a life here."

"So are we all shacking up with scary aliens?" Kira muttered from her seat near the window. Unlike the others, her tone lacked venom, but her quiet detachment was worse.

I turned to her sharply, hoping for an opening to better understand her uncharacteristic demeanor, but the rest of the team wasn't about to let the conversation die.

"Men don't just help powerless women for free, Captain. I don't think it matters what planet you're on," Hawk said evenly, pointedly using the title again with all the weight of an accusation.

I couldn't respond—not the way they wanted me to. The truth was too tangled, too raw to share without unraveling it completely. "We're alive," I said flatly. "That's what matters."

The tension in the room thickened with every second of

silence that followed. They didn't trust me—not completely. I couldn't blame them, but that didn't mean I had the luxury of indulging their doubts. We didn't have time for division.

"We need a plan," Vega said suddenly, breaking the stalemate with her usual pragmatism. She straightened, stepping forward just enough to draw attention back to her. "This situation, whatever arrangement you think you've made—it's a temporary solution at best. We need to take control of our circumstances before we lose any chance."

Hawk nodded in agreement, but Kira remained silent. Her focus seemed fixed on some invisible point beyond the barred window, her body language distant and closed. I filed it away for later—something was definitely off.

"And what do you propose we do?" I asked, crossing my arms and tilting my head expectantly.

Vega's lips curved upward into a faint smile, but there was no humor in it. "We need to be in a less secure location, for one."

"I think I can get you moved to better quarters." No matter what Vega was planning, it was on my list. My team shouldn't be prisoners.

"That's step one," Vega continued. "Then I slip out and find the others. It's all well and good that you've found a boyfriend, but have you forgotten the civilians we're supposed to be protecting?"

"I have not," I said, my tone sharp. "But we need to stop acting hostile. If you let me tell Darrokar—"

"Absolutely not!"

"No way."

"Are you crazy?"

It was a unanimous no.

"You're assuming we're not already considered threats," Vega countered, holding my gaze without flinching. "Do you really think they'll let us move freely?" She tilted her head towards the door where my escort was waiting outside.

Kira finally spoke, her voice cutting through Vega's as if on cue. "And if the others are dead?"

The bluntness of her words struck the room like a blade, silencing everyone. Even Vega faltered, her mouth closing into a thin line.

"They're not dead," I said firmly, though the knot in my chest tightened at the thought. "We can't think like that. If there's even a chance—"

"If they're gone, Terra. What then?" Kira pressed. She still wasn't looking at me directly, but her words carried an edge I wasn't used to hearing from her.

"Then we mourn but keep going," I said forcefully. "And we need to remain together to do that."

"Are we together?" Hawk asked quietly but pointedly. Her words weren't loud, yet they landed with the weight of an avalanche. The unspoken question hung in the air: *Are you with us, or are you with **him**?*

I drew a breath, my gaze sweeping over each of them before returning to Kira's still-guarded expression. I didn't have the answer they wanted—but maybe I could give them something else.

"I am still with you," I said finally, my voice quiet but firm. "And I swear, I will find a way to get us out of this hell. But if we screw this up and Darrokar—"

"What are his intentions exactly?" Hawk pressed, her tone skeptical. "As far as I can tell, all we've earned for two weeks of patience is this room and a lot of unanswered questions."

The truth burned at the back of my throat, but I couldn't give them that yet. Instead, I kept my voice calm, even. "Give me time."

Vega shook her head but didn't argue further. She turned

toward the table, busying herself with organizing supplies. Hawk followed Vega's lead, rummaging through the makeshift inventory with ill-concealed frustration.

Only Kira lingered near the narrow window, her distant gaze unreadable.

As my team settled reluctantly into tense silence, I stepped closer to her, my expression softening just enough to pass as nonchalant. "Kira," I said softly. "What's going on?"

She hesitated before answering, her shoulders stiffening slightly. "Nothing. Just thinking."

"Anything I should know?"

Her eyes flicked toward me briefly, but she didn't hold my gaze. "No," she replied quickly—too quickly.

I studied her for a moment longer, debating whether to push harder. But something in her posture warned me against it. Kira wasn't ready to talk, and forcing the issue would only make it worse.

"Alright," I said finally, stepping back and allowing her the space she clearly wanted. But as I turned away, her quiet urgency echoed in my mind, along with Vega's cold practicality and Hawk's frustrated skepticism.

They were my team, my people—and I'd never felt more separate from them.

I had walked into this room expecting to reunite with familiar camaraderie, with strength forged in shared struggle. But all I'd found were fault lines, cracks that spiderwebbed deeper than any one conversation could bridge.

I had to fix this.

Somehow.

12

TERRA

EVERYONE MADE SACRIFICES FOR SURVIVAL—
SOMETIMES it was dignity, sometimes it was trust. I wasn't sure which I was losing more of lately. The echo of my team's words from earlier still rang in my ears, sharp as a combat knife.

It didn't matter that I understood their frustrations or that some part of me even agreed with them. Hearing the doubt in their voices—*their doubt in me*—was like having skin carved away piece by piece.

Could I lead when my own team barely trusted me anymore?

My fingers traced the leather cords of my vambrace absently as I waited in Darrokar's chambers, the faint orange glow of heat crystals reflecting off the volcanic glass walls. The space felt unbearably stifling today, every minute a reminder that I had a million unanswered questions and no sense of where to even begin.

The groan of the chamber doors sliding open made me tense, though the familiar scent that accompanied it eased some of the tautness from my shoulders. Darrokar strode in like a storm contained, wings folding neatly behind him.

"*Luvae,*" he greeted, his deep voice wrapping around me in a comfort it felt almost wrong to accept.

"Darrokar," I replied, straightening where I stood.

I had to start standing up for my people, and that was going to start now. But before I could say anything, he stopped in front of me, holding out a bundle wrapped in dark material. "For you," he said simply.

I blinked, then took it from him carefully. It was heavier than I expected, the texture pliable but sturdy beneath my fingers. A closer look revealed that it wasn't just any material—they were Drakarn warrior leathers. But there were no slits for wings in the back. These were custom.

For a human.

"For me?" I asked, even though the evidence was staring me in the face. The design wasn't purely Drakarn; it had elements of my Earth uniform woven through it—the reinforced plates, the utilitarian cut meant for ease of motion. More importantly, it was unmistakably mine, from the precise tailoring to the weight beneath the shoulder straps.

Darrokar stepped closer, his golden eyes shimmering. "You cannot fight as one of us if you are not dressed as one of us. Does it not please you?"

I ran my fingers over the intricate detailing along the neckline. "I—no, I mean yes." I shook my head, struggling to find the words. Whatever confidence I'd bolstered before his arrival was unraveling rapidly under his focused attention. "It's perfect."

And nothing I expected.

Before I could muster more than that, Darrokar's claws brushed my hand. It wasn't a gesture I would've noticed before meeting him, but now I couldn't miss it—not the faint scrape of his black scales against my skin, nor the way his touch sent an illicit ripple of something unbearably warm up my arm.

"Let me help you," he said, his voice quieter now, more intimate.

It wasn't a question; it wasn't entirely an order either. My throat tightened as I nodded.

He lifted the armored chest plate, stepping in closer to secure it over my torso. I could feel the heat of him radiating outward even before his claws brushed my sides, buckling a strap here, adjusting a fastening there. There was nothing casual about his movements—they were deliberate and precise.

"You were unhappy when you returned today," he murmured, resting his hands against my shoulders as he adjusted the pauldrons.

I tensed, tilting my head up at him. "How do you—?"

His golden eyes flashed with that knowing look that drove me insane, a faint glimmer of amusement curling at the edge of his mouth. His claws ghosted along my collarbone as he stepped back, admiring his handiwork like a craftsman inspecting their masterpiece. "*Luvae,* I see too much to remain ignorant, even when you keep it silent."

"They need better quarters." My voice was sharper than I intended, but I was too raw to smooth it out.

He heard what I wasn't saying. "Whatever mistrust your people hold, it will not endure."

I stared at him, crossing my arms protectively over the newly donned armor. His unwavering confidence—his ability to just *decide* something would be fixed—was still something I couldn't entirely reconcile. "They've been locked up for weeks while I've—"

He arched an obsidian brow at that, the smirk softening into something irritatingly tender. "Shall I invite them all here into our bed?"

Our bed.

Aliens didn't seem to exactly be the type for a *define the relationship* talk, but everything Darrokar did, everything he said, let me know that this thing between us wasn't just some passing fascination with the new species in town.

He wanted to keep me.

Without waiting for my response, he moved toward the chamber's exit, inclining his head for me to follow. Despite my lingering doubts, it didn't feel like a request.

The training grounds were blisteringly alive when we arrived, a chaotic melee of roaring warriors, swiping claws, and clashing lavaforged blades.

Darrokar's presence silenced the chaos almost immediately, his warriors bowing their heads briefly in acknowledgment before shifting focus to me.

I could feel their judgment rippling across the space, tinged with curiosity, disdain, and something else I couldn't name.

I stepped closer to Darrokar's side instinctively, though I regretted letting that self-consciousness fear show a second later. He noticed, of course—his sharp gaze had an infuriating ability to catch things I barely let myself register.

"This is your chance," he said, his voice quiet but firm, pitched low enough for only me to hear. "Do not shy away. Strength does not require familiar words."

Easy for him to say—he had wings, claws, and all the fiery charisma of a walking inferno. I had ... stubbornness and a never-ending list of self-doubts.

"Choose your opponent," he said aloud, this time ensuring every Drakarn present could hear.

The weight of hundreds of eyes turned to me immediately, an almost physical force. I swallowed hard, my heart hammering against the new armor like it, too, didn't trust its protection.

"Her," I said finally, pointing toward a red-scaled, towering warrior standing near the edge of the circle. She was nearly twice my size, her well-toned muscles betraying years of combat experience. If I was going to do this—if I had to *prove* anything—it wouldn't be by taking the easy route.

The arena fell dead silent as we stepped into one of the designated rings. My opponent didn't bother with introductions or a nod—she simply snarled, wings flaring wide as her talons flexed against the blackened stone.

I forced the nerves out of my body, focusing instead on the steadiness of my stance. I wasn't there to die—I was there to learn.

The first blow came swiftly, a wide arc of claws that had more force than calculation behind it. I ducked, twisting my body sharply enough that her wing flap almost pulled me off-balance. Almost.

She didn't give me the chance to recover, lunging forward before I could right myself. Her claws raked downward, and I barely avoided taking the full brunt by pivoting my weight and rolling to the side. The ground beneath my palm burned—a cruel reminder that this wasn't just training. This was the proving ground, and failure wasn't just embarrassing—it was dangerous.

Darrokar stood at the edge of the ring, his presence a dark shadow that drew my awareness despite the chaos of the fight. I didn't need to look to know his eyes were fixed on me, golden and unreadable. Was he watching to see if I could keep up or to see how quickly I'd fall?

Either way, my body moved differently knowing he was there—more desperate to succeed, even as my muscles trembled with the effort.

The warrior snarled again, her claws slashing out at me in a series of calculated strikes, each one driving me back toward the edge of the ring. My feet scrambled against the blackened stone as I blocked her blows with the training blade Darrokar had handed me moments earlier—a blade that suddenly felt absurdly small in my grip.

She wasn't just using brute force anymore; she was toying with me, her attacks designed to keep me defensive and off-balance. I gritted my teeth, frustration simmering with every blow I barely deflected. My breathing was labored, sweat beading on my forehead despite the cool edge of the leathers.

"Is that all you've got, *luvae*?" Darrokar's voice sliced through the tension like the edge of a blade, seemingly mild but deceptively sharp.

I didn't dare look at him, but I could feel the weight of his words. It wasn't mockery—not entirely—but it was enough to provoke the anger simmering just beneath my skin to a boil.

Focusing on my opponent, I lunged forward, feinting to her right before pivoting on my heel and aiming low at her exposed flank. She moved faster than I anticipated—a flash of red scales and the sharp crack of claw against blade as she parried the strike and thrust her wings outward for an additional push. The force knocked me off-balance, and I stumbled backward, my back perilously close to the molten edge of the ring's boundary.

The crowd of warriors surrounding the arena let out a low, collective rumble—an almost animalistic sound that made me shiver. I couldn't tell if they were impressed or disappointed.

Get it together, Terra.

I swallowed hard and zoomed in on her next move. Her claws lashed out again, and this time, I dropped low before spinning behind her, raising the blade toward her exposed back.

The strike landed.

A shallow cut formed just above her hips—nothing debilitating, but enough to draw a sharp hiss of pain. She flared her wings again, spinning to face me with renewed anger, her stance widening as she prepared to attack.

But I had no intention of waiting.

Before she could regain the advantage, I surged forward, blade poised for another strike. I wasn't foolish enough to think I could overpower her, so I put every ounce of focus into speed and precision, trying to anticipate her reactions.

"Enough."

Darrokar's voice reverberated across the arena, commanding immediate stillness.

My opponent straightened, casting a wary glance toward Darrokar before stepping back and lowering her wings in submission. I didn't know if I imagined the faint smirk tugging at her lips or if it was genuine.

Darrokar strode into the ring with the ease of someone who had never doubted their place in it. His golden eyes met mine, scanning the dirt smeared along my jaw, the faint trembling of my hand where I clutched the hilt of the blade.

"You did not win," he said evenly, his voice firm but lacking malice.

I lifted my chin, willing myself not to flinch beneath the weight of his gaze. "No, but I didn't lose."

His mouth quirked—the barest hint of something that might have been approval. "A draw is not a victory, *luvae*. But it is not a failure either."

One of the warriors behind him chuckled—a low, rumbling sound full of amusement. My cheeks flushed, but Darrokar silenced them with a sharp glance. His authority over them was absolute, even when it appeared effortless.

"You rely too much on your human instincts," he continued, stepping closer until the scent of smoke and molten stone curled between us. His wings cast a wide, imposing shadow that swallowed the flickering light of the arena's veins. "Speed is not your only weapon, but neither can you abandon it entirely."

I gritted my teeth. I could feel my pride aching under the weight of his critique, but I nodded curtly. "Then teach me."

The mutter of murmurs that rippled through the gathered warriors at my words was barely audible, but I caught it. Those closest to the ring exchanged glances, their pupils narrowing into slits, revealing too much interest in the exchange.

The air between us crackled, thick with implications neither of us fully wanted to voice.

Darrokar stepped closer again, his clawed hand reaching out to turn the hilt of the blade in my grasp just slightly. His touch wasn't rough—more curious, as though he were examining a fragment of a puzzle. "You harbor a fire," he murmured, his gaze slipping back up to meet mine. "But you suffocate it out of fear it will burn too brightly."

"I don't have the luxury," I replied, the words leaving my mouth before I could stop them.

"Nor did I," he said, so quietly it nearly went unheard over the faint hiss of molten stone.

It wasn't the response I had expected, not from him. For just a moment, the walls that so often surrounded him cracked, and something raw and unguarded slipped through.

I should have stepped back—I should have said something, done *something* to break the spell that suddenly bound the air between us. But I didn't.

Instead, I held his gaze. And something in me wondered if, maybe, the thing that bound us wasn't a chain at all.

"Tomorrow," Darrokar said at last, his voice once again the commanding rumble I'd come to recognize. "You will return here. The training will be harder."

I straightened, forcing a smile to mask the exhaustion already settling over me. "I'd be disappointed if it wasn't."

His lips curved just faintly. "Good."

"OUCH, OUCH, OUCH." My mate limped into our quarters, careful to put her training sword on the hook where it belonged before she collapsed down onto the chaise, dust from the training field blanketing the silk pillows.

She carried herself well on the battlefield. Shalyn was one of the toughest warriors in her training group, and Terra had held her own.

Her red hair, bound in a braid for training, had long ago started unraveling, and now her curls fanned out behind her head like blood upon the rock of our world.

She looked magnificent.

"I'm going to be sore tomorrow," she groaned, rubbing her legs.

"You look sore now." I leaned back in the tub, the warm water steaming around me. "Come soak. Soothe your muscles."

"I think you have ulterior motives." She grinned, stripping off her chest protector. Her silken undershirt clung to her sweat-slicked body.

"Maybe." I grinned, my fangs flashing. "Or maybe I want to take care of you after such a brutal beating."

She laughed, dropping her pants and kicking them aside. "Brutal? I held my own."

"That you did. Don't sully the water with your filthy clothes." I watched her undress, admiring her curves, her strength, her determination. She was unlike any other female I had ever met.

"You deserved that." She gave me a pointed look.

Perhaps I did. I wouldn't admit it.

She slid into the tub, settling between my legs and leaning back against my chest. I wrapped my arms around her waist, pulling her close. "Better?"

"Much." She sighed, relaxing against me. "I haven't trained like that in ages. Not since before we left Earth."

"We'll make a warrior of you yet." I nuzzled her neck, inhaling her scent. It was stronger than usual, making my tongue tingle. "Why did you leave? Where were you going?" She'd told me of her home, this Earth, but it still sounded unreal to my ears.

"To make a new life. Ours wasn't the only ship to leave. There's been so much discovery, so many planets just waiting for us. The settlement company said we'd all have plenty of space, ample opportunities ... Saying it now, it sounds like a con. I don't know if it was just the te—," she cleared her throat, "the team with me that crashed or if the whole ship came down. There were thousands of people. Do you think we're the only survivors?"

I hadn't lured my mate into the pool to make her morose. I pulled her close. "I'll send out scouts. If there's news of other ships, we'll find them."

She twisted, looking up at me. "You would do that? Why?"

"Because you are my mate." It was simple, instinctual.

"But we barely know each other." She frowned, her brows furrowing.

"I know enough. You are strong and determined. Loyal. Brave. You fight with honor and skill, and you have a fire inside you that burns bright." I let my claws trail over her stomach until she shivered under my touch. "Let me show you."

She turned in my arms, straddling me. Her breasts pressed against my chest, her nipples hardening against my scales. "I tell you how sore I am from training, and you want to fuck?"

I might have thought she was serious if not for the glint in her eye. "Yes. I want to fuck you." I growled, nipping her bottom lip. "I want to taste you, to fill you, to mark you as mine."

"Then what are you waiting for?" She wrapped her arms around my neck and kissed me. Her lips were soft, her mouth warm, and her tongue eager. She tasted of sweet spices and something else that made my cock throb.

I groaned, pulling her close and deepening the kiss. She arched into me, grinding against my hard length.

I broke away, trailing my mouth down her neck and sucking on her pulse point. "Tell me you're mine."

She shuddered, her fingers digging into my shoulders. "Yours."

I pinned her to the side of the tub. Water splashed around us, hot and steamy. She gazed up at me, her green eyes shining with desire.

My mouth claimed hers again, drinking in her sweet essence as my hands roamed her body, relearning every curve and dip. Her skin was warm and slick from the water, waiting for my exploration. I deepened the kiss, my tongue diving in to dance with hers.

She moaned, arching against me, her nails raking down my back.

I trailed kisses along her jawline, her neck, her collarbone, tasting the salt of her sweat and the unique flavor that was Terra. Her heartbeat pulsed against my tongue as I licked her skin, each beat an echo of her life force. I growled low in my throat.

My fangs throbbed with the need to mark her, to claim her fully as my mate.

"Darrokar," she gasped, her voice husky with desire. "Please, I need you."

Her words were my undoing. I hefted her up onto the edge of the pool and spread her legs.

She trembled as I settled between them, my broad shoulders and wings pushing her thighs wider. She was exposed, open, and utterly vulnerable to me. I felt a surge of possession, my mate bared for my pleasure. Her scent filled my nostrils, musky and sweet, driving me wild.

I traced the sensitive flesh of her inner thigh with the sharp tips of my fangs, a low rumble building in my chest. She shuddered, her fingers spearing through my hair, urging me closer. I chuckled, and the vibrations sent gooseflesh rippling across her skin.

"I need your mouth." Her voice was ragged with desire.

I trailed my tongue along her seam, a line of fire in its wake. She gasped, her hips lifting to meet me. Her folds were slick with arousal; her taste made my cock ache. I delved deeper, my tongue exploring every fold, every sensitive inch of her.

She was swollen, a hard little pearl begging for attention. I lavished it with my tongue, circling the sensitive bud, sucking gently until she was writhing beneath me. The heat of her pressed against my tongue, her hips grinding against my face as I devoured her.

"Darrokar," she moaned, her voice echoing through the chamber, a symphony of pleasure and need.

My name on her lips fanned the flames of my desire, each syllable pushing me closer to the edge.

I growled against her, the vibrations sending shockwaves

through her core. My tongue plunged into her, mimicking the thrusts I longed to give her with my cock. She was close, her inner walls clenching around me, her breath coming in short, sharp gasps.

I pulled back, leaving her panting and desperate. She whimpered, her fingers tangling in my hair, trying to pull me back. But I had other plans. I wanted to savor this moment, to draw out her pleasure and my own.

I looked up at her. Her lids were heavy, her pupils dilated, cheeks flushed with desire and exertion. She was a breathtaking sight—my mate, laid bare and eager before me. The air was thick with the scent of her arousal and the steam from the tub, creating an intoxicating atmosphere that only amplified my hunger for her.

"Darrokar, please," she begged, her voice shattered from her need.

A slow, sensual smile curved my lips. "Patience, *luvae*," I murmured, my thumbs tracing idle patterns on her inner thighs.

With deliberate slowness, I reached for the flask of oil resting on the tub's edge. The dark glass glowed with the heat of our world. I poured the oil into my palms, watching as it shimmered in the dim light, reflecting the dance of flames from the heat crystals around us.

The warmth radiated from my hands as I massaged the oil into her skin, starting at her ankles and working my way up her calves, her knees, her thighs. With my claws, I had to be careful, and for the first time in my life, I envied the servants who filed theirs down to nothing but nubs.

Each touch elicited a shiver, a gasp, a soft moan from her lips. Her muscles tensed beneath my fingers, her legs quivering with anticipation as I neared her core.

Once I reached her inner thighs, I paused, the pads of my

thumbs dancing along the sensitive flesh just inches from her sex. She writhed, her hips lifting in a silent plea. But I held back, maintaining a steady rhythm that kept her teetering on the edge but never pushing her over.

"You're torturing me," she panted, her hands fisting beneath her.

A dark chuckle rumbled in my chest. "Do you want me to stop, *luvae?*"

Her eyes flashed with defiance, but her body betrayed her, arching into my hands, seeking more contact. "Don't you dare."

A bolt of desire shot through me.

With my claws in the way, I couldn't dip my fingers inside, couldn't spread her open. But I was a Drakarn and would not be so easily cowed. My tail flicked up and teased her entrance, the thick, muscled limb pressing against her slick heat. Her body reacted, clenching around the mere suggestion of penetration.

I smoothed my tail along her folds, coating it with her arousal before pressing forward. The first push of my tail inside was a delicious stretch, her inner walls unyielding but creamy with need. I withdrew, a low growl rumbling in my chest at the sight of her pink, core flesh glistening.

"Darrokar, please," she begged, her hips jerking in a futile attempt to impale herself on my tail.

I captured her mouth in a searing kiss, claiming her moans and whimpers as our tongues tangled. My tail delved deeper, filling her to the hilt, and she screamed into my mouth. Her muscles rippled and clenched around me, milking the sensitive scales.

My cock throbbed. My tail was normally a weapon of war, not pleasure, but the things her body was doing to me sent pulses of desire straight through me.

I withdrew, then plunged back in, a rhythm as relentless as

the twin suns. Each thrust dragged a guttural moan from her throat, each withdrawal leaving her crying for me to return. I varied my pace, stoking the flames of her desire, teasing her to the brink then backing off, determined to prolong this delicious torture. Her internal stimulations were adding an extra layer of connection and enjoyment—the pulsing of her heart, the subtle rhythms of her breathing, the heady taste of her pleasure all added to the sensory delight.

"You're so deep," she gasped, her hips bucking wildly, trying to take me as deep as possible. "I need more."

I grinned against her mouth. "Patience, little warrior. I have only just begun."

I adjusted my grip, using my claws to fondle and tease her breasts alongside the relentless thrusts of my tail. I loved the way her nipples hardened into points, begging for attention as she writhed beneath me. My own cock throbbed in time with my pulse, aching to be buried inside her, to fill her completely. But this, this was about her pleasure, about claiming her as mine, body and soul.

"Don't tease me anymore," she pleaded, her voice breaking on a sob. "Please, I need to come."

My response was a deep, rumbling growl and a flex of my tail inside her. That growl turned into a snarl as I finally relented, my tail moving in a wild, frantic rhythm, slamming into her with abandon. Her scream ripped through the chamber as her orgasm crashed over her, her inner walls clamping down on me like a vise. I could feel every pulse, every spasm, her body milking my length for all it was worth.

The sound of her release and the sight of her face contorted in ecstasy pushed me over the edge. I yanked my tail out of her and replaced it with my cock, thrusting like a Drakarn possessed.

I buried myself as deep as possible inside her, my cock

throbbing and pulsing as I emptied myself into her waiting body.

We stayed locked together, chest to chest, her legs wrapped around my waist, her breath coming in ragged gasps as we rode out the aftershocks of our passion. My claws held her hips carefully, holding her in place, our hearts thundering against each other.

After what felt like an eternity, I gradually pulled out, my cock glistening with our combined fluids. Terra made an unhappy sound at the loss, her legs falling limp around my waist.

I pulled her back down into the warm water, cradling her against my chest.

I could never have imagined that someone like her would be my mate. But now that I had her, I would fight every force on Volcaryth and anyone from her Earth before I let her go.

14

TERRA

MY FIRST THOUGHT WAS *FIRE.*

Then tornado.

A horn sounded the alarm all through Darrokar's quarters, making my heart pound and jerking him out of a sound sleep beside me.

"What's that? What's going on?" It could have been some sort of drill, but from the tension in Darrokar's form, it was real.

And serious.

"Security has been breached." He scooped up my shirt from where it had fallen on the floor. "Get dressed. Someone will be here soon with a report."

"I need to check on my team." I'd just managed to get them moved to actual rooms in Darrokar's dwelling, though they were all still angry at me for whatever it was I was doing with Darrokar.

Mate.

It was what he called me. It felt right. And if I looked deeper, I might have words of my own I could use, but I was too much of a coward to think too hard about it.

I threw on my shirt and pants quickly, ignoring the lingering soreness from my training the day before. My team—

Hawk, Kira, and Vega—might hate me right now, but they were still my responsibility. My people. Whatever was happening, my first priority was making sure they were safe.

Darrokar was already at the door, his broad silhouette framed by the faint orange glow of the crystals embedded in the walls. His golden eyes were hard and focused, slits narrowing as though he were preparing for a battle. When he turned back to face me, there was an edge to his expression that made the air between us feel charged.

Before I could take a step toward the hallway, the door groaned open, and Rath stormed in, his ruby-red scales glinting in the dim light. His wings, half-furled, twitched with tension. He didn't bother with formalities.

"The human, Vega Cross, is missing," he growled, his voice deep and grating.

I froze. "What?"

Darrokar's wings flared, his talons flexing against the stone. "Explain."

"Her quarters were empty when the security check was conducted," Rath said, his gaze flicking briefly to me before locking back on Darrokar. "The guards stationed near her rooms failed to notice her departure. Either she evaded them on foot, or ..." He paused grimly. "Or she was taken."

The words were a punch to the gut. "No," I said immediately, shaking my head. "Vega wouldn't just let herself be taken." And I remembered the conversation we'd had a few days ago. She wanted to escape, to go find the others. Then my mind caught up to the rest of what he said. "Guards? I thought we agreed my people were guests."

I gave Darrokar a pointed look.

"Guests," Darrokar repeated, his voice a low rumble that sent an involuntary shiver down my spine. "Guests do not vanish in the dead of night without explanation." His golden eyes bore into mine, molten and sharp as obsidian, daring me to challenge him further.

"She may have left on her own and then been taken," Rath suggested, his tail lashing with agitation. "Her trail vanishes abruptly in the crimson deserts. The pattern suggests an aerial attack."

My blood ran cold. If Vega had been taken by air ... "I need to see."

"No." Darrokar's response was immediate, his wings mantling protectively. "The crimson deserts are treacherous enough for those born to them. You will remain here where it's safe."

"Like hell I will." I stepped forward, squaring my shoulders. "Vega is my responsibility. I'm going."

"You do not understand the dangers—"

"Then explain them to me," I cut him off, my voice sharp with frustration. "Because right now, all I see is one of my people missing and you trying to keep me from finding her."

The room crackled with tension. Darrokar's golden eyes blazed, his massive frame seeming to fill the space between us. "The rival clans would consider you a prize beyond measure. My mate, defenseless, different. They would use you to strike at me, at Scalvaris."

"Defenseless? I thought we covered that. I can take care of myself."

"Can you?" He moved closer, his heat radiating against my skin. "Can you fight warriors who have spent their lives perfecting aerial combat? Can you survive the desert's heat storms or navigate the thermal updrafts?"

"No," I admitted, my heart hammering. "But I know Vega. If she left willingly, I might know where she's headed. If she was taken, I can help predict her actions."

Rath shifted uncomfortably, clearly wanting to speak but waiting for Darrokar's response.

Darrokar's jaw clenched, the muscles in his neck tightening. "You know more than you're telling me."

It wasn't a question. I swallowed hard, guilt and necessity warring in my heart. I'd promised to keep the others a secret, but with Vega gone and a group of Drakarn ready to scour the desert to find her, how long could they stay hidden?

"Tell me what you know," my mate demanded.

The accusation hung between us, heavy as molten stone. I met his gaze steadily, even as my heart threatened to beat out of my chest. "I know Vega. I know she's smart, capable, and wouldn't leave without a reason."

"A reason you won't share." His voice was dangerously quiet now, a rumble that seemed to vibrate through my bones.

"It doesn't matter." The words tasted bitter. "Let me help you find her."

Darrokar's tail lashed, his frustration evident in every line of his powerful frame. "You ask me to trust you while you keep secrets that could endanger us all."

"My lord," Rath interrupted, his expression grim. "The longer we delay, the colder the trail grows. If rival clans have her ..."

"Prepare the search party," Darrokar ordered, not taking his eyes off me. "I want our fastest warriors ready to fly within the hour."

Rath nodded sharply and left, the door hissing shut behind him.

As soon as we were alone, Darrokar closed the distance between us. His claws ghosted along my arm, a touch that was both possessive and questioning. "Why do you resist telling me the truth? Do you not trust me to protect your people?"

"Some secrets aren't mine to share." I fought the urge to lean into his touch.

His other hand cupped my face, forcing me to look up at him. "And if those secrets get someone killed? What then, *luvae?*"

The endearment, spoken with such raw emotion, made my chest ache. "That's why I need to go with you. I can help."

"You could die." His thumb traced my cheekbone. "The desert shows no mercy, and neither do our enemies."

"I'm not asking for mercy." I covered his claws with mine, feeling the rough texture of his scales against my palm. "I'm asking for a chance to protect my own."

Something shifted in his expression—pride mixed with fear, anger with understanding. "You will follow my orders without question. If I tell you to retreat, you retreat. If I tell you to hide, you hide. No arguments."

"Not a one."

I would keep my word. And somehow figure out how to untangle this knot before it ruined everything.

When I found Vega, I was going to *kill* her.

15

DARROKAR

TERRA'S ARMS were a vise around my neck, her body a surprising weight pressed against my chest as we knifed through the wind's violent bursts. Below, the crimson sands unspooled, an endless landscape warped by waves of ferocious heat.

The wind, thick with the grit of the wasteland, delivered the faint tang of her—fear, sharp and undeniable, a core of determination, and beneath it, something furtive. Something that tightened the skin around my fangs with gnawing suspicion.

She was hiding something.

A thermal punched at my wings, and I corrected our course automatically, my gaze raking the merciless terrain. The desert was a predator, even to those of my blood. For humans? It was death.

Ten of my fiercest warriors shadowed us, their flight a testament to years of honed discipline. Rath was among them, his ruby scales flashing beneath the brutal sunlight. The volatile temper that usually simmered beneath his surface was notably absent, replaced by a focused intensity I knew intimately.

He, too, was on the hunt.

"There!" Terra's voice, thin but clear, sliced through the wind's roar. Her finger jabbed toward a jagged obsidian spire, a black fang tearing at the horizon. "That rock formation. It's the only shade for miles."

My wings stiffened, a prickle of unease tracing my spine. She was right, a certainty in her tone that scraped against my senses. It spoke of experience, of a familiarity that shouldn't exist. Unless ...

"You know this place." It wasn't a question.

Her body's stillness against mine was an answer in itself. "No, but it's where I'd hide out if I needed to disappear."

The word hung between us, heavy with unspoken implications. From whom? From me?

Banking sharply, I angled towards the spire, a silent command for the others to maintain altitude, circle wide. As we closed the distance, the scent hit me, acrid and unmistakable—Drakarn. A significant number. And beneath that reek, the faint, metallic tang of humans.

Plural.

Involuntarily, my grip around Terra tightened, my talons flexing against her back. She gasped, a sharp intake of breath, but I couldn't force my hold to ease. Every instinct screamed that she knew. Had known all along that more of her kind were out there.

She'd spoken of her ship, of the thousands aboard. Had she truly been ignorant of their fate? Or had even that been a carefully constructed lie?

We landed on a thin ridge, the twisted obsidian shielding us from immediate view. Below, nestled within a natural amphitheater carved by the wind, sprawled a rival clan's encampment. Sentries patrolled the perimeter, their wings held half-spread, struggling against the scorching air. And there, tethered within a sheltered alcove …

"Six," I growled, the sound a low reverberation in my chest. "There are six more of your kind with your Vega."

Terra's heart hammered against my scales, a frantic drumbeat against my own. She offered no denial, her silence a damning indictment.

"You knew." I released her, the physical act mirroring the desperate need to put space between us. The betrayal burned, sharper and more insidious than any desert sun. "All this time, you knew there were others."

"Darrokar—"

"Don't." My tail lashed, a swift, violent flick that sent a spray of crimson sand arcing through the air. "Did you imagine I wouldn't protect them? That I would ever bring them harm?"

Her green eyes locked onto mine, unwavering, laced with a fierce defiance that offered no apology. "I couldn't risk it. Not with their lives on the line."

Her words struck with the force of a physical blow, leaving me winded. My chest constricted, but it was the dull ache beneath the surge of anger that truly unraveled me. "But you could risk *us*? Risk severing the bond between us? The trust we've bled to build?" My voice dropped, the raw edges of my hurt scraping against the air. "I am your mate, Terra."

"And they're my responsibility." Her tone was clipped, every syllable precise, but a tremor ran beneath the surface. She took a step closer and lifted her hand.

Even as her scent—spiced earth and something uniquely hers, something that burrowed deep—enveloped me, my instincts screamed a warning. I recoiled, a deliberate step back that widened into a full extension of my wings, stirring the dust into a swirling vortex between us. Her hand froze mid-air, a fleeting flicker of something akin to pain crossing her features before her jaw tightened, snapping into that familiar soldier's resolve I both loathed and admired.

"Don't," I repeated, my voice a low, guttural rumble, barely leashed. My wings curved inward for a heartbeat, shielding me in an involuntary gesture before settling against my back. "You lied to me. Do you understand what you've done? Every fiber of my being is designed to protect you, to trust your word as law. You are *mine*."

Her lips parted, but before either of us could plunge deeper into this chasm of fractured trust, a shadow swept over us. I snapped my gaze skyward, recognizing the unmistakable shift of Rath's broad wings, a stark silhouette against the harsh light, signaling movement within the camp below. A brutal reminder that our enemies remained, even as the world between Terra and me felt as though it was imploding.

I turned back to her, my muscles coiled, every nerve ending screaming. The urge to drag her close, to reassure myself of her physical presence, warred violently with the equally powerful need to thrust her away, to create distance. But beneath the consuming anger, the relentless hum of the bond persisted, an invisible tether binding me to her in ways I couldn't sever, even if I desired it.

"Stay here," I commanded, the order sharper than intended. "Those *kervash* won't hesitate to use you against me if they see you."

Her shoulders squared, her entire demeanor coiling like a struck serpent. "I can fight," she spat, each word laced with iron and defiance.

I leaned in close, my words a near-snarl, the raw fury a mask for the agonizing vulnerability she'd exposed. "Do you think I question your strength, Terra? Do you believe me blind to it? But down there, strength alone is insufficient. I will not risk losing you."

Her gaze flickered for a fraction of a heartbeat, a raw, untamed emotion breaching the surface before she ruthlessly suppressed it, drawing down those impenetrable walls she so easily erected.

I wanted to grab her, shake her until the facade crumbled, until she dropped that damnable guard—for once, for me. But Rath's signal flashed again, more urgent now, pulling my attention away before the unspoken could be said. Before I could confess the chilling realization: her betrayal cut so deep not because it revealed weakness, but because it illuminated the terrifying extent to which I had already surrendered my heart.

"That wasn't a suggestion." I spread my wings, the membranes stretching taut, catching the harsh light. "You've proven you can't be trusted. Don't compound your error."

The raw hurt that flashed across her features nearly shattered my resolve. But the lie, however delivered, remained. And now, we plunged into battle with compromised trust and unknown threats.

I launched myself into the air before she could retort, catching a thermal that lifted me higher. Below, the camp stirred, a disturbed nest of vipers. They'd seen us.

Good.

Let them come.

Rath fell into formation beside me, his voice a rumble carried on the wind. "Movement to the east. They're attempting to move the humans."

A snarl tore from my throat, baring my fangs. "Take the others. Cut off their escape route. I'll engage their warriors."

He hesitated, his gaze flicking toward the alcove where the humans were held captive. "If they resist?"

"Subdue. No fatalities." I met his gaze, the command

leaving no room for interpretation. "These humans are under my protection now. All of them."

A sharp nod acknowledged the order. He peeled away, leading the others in a wide arc to intercept the enemy clan attempting to flee with their captives. I tucked my wings, plummeting towards the cluster of rival warriors spilling from their makeshift shelters.

The first Drakarn never registered my approach. My talons ripped across his wing membranes, the tearing sound sickeningly satisfying as he cartwheeled into the sand. The second managed to gain altitude, but a brutal sweep of my tail sent him spiraling back to earth.

More swarmed to meet me, their scales a harsh variety of colors under the blazing sun. They fought with a practiced savagery, but I hadn't earned the title of Warrior Lord of Scalvaris through chance. My claws found the vulnerable gaps between their scales, my wings a blur of motion, deflecting their clumsy attacks.

A flicker of movement at the edge of my vision snagged my attention—Terra, disregarding my direct order and on the move. Fury and a chilling spike of fear warred within me.

The distraction was costly. Claws raked across my shoulder, a searing line of pain drawing blood. I roared, spinning to face my assailant, when Rath's voice, laced with urgency, ripped through the din.

"Darrokar!"

His warning arrived too late. A hulking warrior, his scales the color of a gathering storm, positioned himself above me, preparing a dive that would have shredded my wings. But then, a flash of red hair erupted between us.

Terra.

She'd scaled the treacherous obsidian spire and launched herself at my attacker, her smaller form colliding with his far larger one. They tumbled through the air, a tangled mass of limbs and scales, and for a terrifying heartbeat, I thought she would fall.

But she was a whirlwind of controlled chaos. Using his momentum against him, she twisted, redirecting his descent into the jagged face of the spire. The impact reverberated through the rock, showering us with black glass shards.

I caught her before she hit the ground, the frantic rhythm of my heart slamming against my ribs. "I ordered you to stay back."

"Yeah, well, you're welcome," she shot back, her grip tight on my shoulders, her eyes blazing with adrenaline. "Now put me down. They need help."

They. Always others.

But she was correct. The battle's focus had shifted to where Rath and my warriors were locked in a brutal melee, struggling to shield the humans. I set Terra down behind a fallen boulder, ignoring her immediate protests.

"Stay. Here." My growl was a promise of violence. "Or I'll chain you to it myself."

Her mouth opened in protest, but I was already airborne, my wings slicing through the humid, smoke-tinged air as I hurtled towards the heart of the conflict.

The battlefield was a riot of guttural snarls, desperate shouts, and the brutal clash of honed steel against obsidian-hard claws. Rath stood as a bulwark between the cluster of humans and the relentless assault, his massive crimson form a living shield. But his stance was off—his weight unevenly distributed, his wings trembling with subtle, unnatural spasms. His gaze kept flicking towards one human woman, her face pale but resolute, clutching a makeshift weapon with surprising ferocity.

I banked low, the rush of displaced air churning grit and blood-soaked sand as I targeted the largest of the remaining rival Drakarn. His scales were a dull, mottled gray and covered in scars, a testament to countless battles. He raised a jagged blade, poised to strike down a fallen warrior who lay clutching his wounded side, blood blooming in the sand beneath him.

The subtle tightening of the air, the near-silent intake of breath from the human woman—her eyes wide with horror—told me she saw it too. I could almost hear her gasp as my talons raked across the enforcer's back, sending a shower of blood and splintered goethite scales flying. He roared in pain and fury as his weapon spun from his grasp, landing with a muffled thud in the sand-soaked ground.

His head snapped towards me as I landed heavily, my wings flaring for balance, the impact jarring my legs. My fighters roared their approval, the sight of their Warrior Lord bolstering their resolve.

The enforcer staggered to his feet, his back a ruin, his movements sluggish. He lunged, more out of desperation than skill. It didn't matter. I sidestepped with a fluid grace, my tail whipping around, catching him mid-charge. Bone crunched against bone, a sickening sound, and he was airborne for a fleeting moment before slamming into a jagged outcrop. He didn't rise. The fight drained from his eyes, leaving them vacant.

The tide of the battle shifted. I tracked Rath's movements, a brief assessment of his position and the threat he posed. More of the humans were upright than I'd anticipated, their crude weapons wielded with a surprising amount of fierce determination.

Whatever fear or burning anger fueled them, it bought the precious seconds my warriors needed to gain the upper hand.

My focus snapped back to the remaining rival Drakarn, their attempts to regroup failing miserably. Their scattered formation reeked of panic; their leader was either dead or had fled.

Fools.

I surged forward again, claws crunching on fragments of scale and bone as I slammed into another straggler. His yelp was abruptly cut short beneath my weight, the air expelled from his lungs as I drove him into the sand. His body convulsed once, then went still. A feral snarl tightened my lips, though I suppressed the surge of satisfaction. Such indulgence was a waste of energy, a luxury I couldn't afford.

"Press the attack! Leave no survivors!" I bellowed, my voice a weapon that cut through the chaos. The commanding tone galvanized my warriors. Discipline, precision, overwhelming force—it yielded the same brutal efficiency as always. The rival Drakarn faltered, their resistance fracturing. Instincts for self-preservation eclipsed any semblance of strategy.

Their retreat was a disorganized rout. My warriors pursued relentlessly, each strike precise, aimed to incapacitate or kill. The sands drank deeply of fresh blood, the air thick with the metallic tang and the acrid smell of scorched flesh. The wounded were abandoned, left to writhe in pools of their own lifeblood under the pitiless suns. A grimly familiar sight.

The battle's frenzy subsided, leaving an echoing silence. The heady scent of victory, usually exhilarating, left a bitter taste on my tongue. I planted my claws firmly, wings folding against my back as I surveyed the remnants of the carnage.

My gaze snagged on Rath. He stood unmoving, his bulk still shielding the huddled humans. His breathing was ragged, a low, rhythmic rasp against the backdrop of fading battle cries.

I landed beside the alcove, the humans shrinking back, their faces etched with fear and a fragile defiance. Vega stood at the forefront, her posture protective despite her obvious exhaustion.

She inclined her head, a subtle gesture of acknowledgement. Her gaze swept over the fallen Drakarn. "This didn't exactly go as planned. Some asshole grabbed me as soon as I left the city."

"You speak our words." Was this another human trick?

Vega shrugged. "I'm a quick study."

I had to leave it aside for now. "Terra is unharmed." I glanced over my shoulder, seeing my mate approaching, disregarding my earlier command.

Of course.

The two women exchanged a brief, assessing look, a silent communication passing between them. I recognized the subtle narrowing of Terra's eyes, the telltale sign she was calculating which truths to reveal.

Rath approached, his wings held tight against his back. "The area is secure."

I studied the humans, noting their reactions. One in particular drew my attention—a slight female with vibrant purple hair who couldn't seem to tear her gaze away from Rath. That was a problem for later.

"We return to Scalvaris," I announced, spreading my wings, my shadow falling across them. "All of us. Arrangements will be made for these women."

If my mate had any objection, she kept it to herself.

The flight back was taut with unspoken tensions, the air thick with simmering emotions and unasked questions. Terra rode with me again, but the familiar warmth of her was absent, replaced by a rigid stiffness that felt like a physical wound.

I watched my warriors pair off with the rescued humans, noting the careful way Rath positioned himself to carry the purple-haired female to the medical cavern.

The twin suns disappeared as we descended into Scalvaris. I landed on my private balcony, setting Terra down with a force harder than intended.

She stumbled, catching herself, her green eyes meeting

mine. They held a turbulent mix of defiance and something I couldn't decipher. Regret? Fear? The clarity I once possessed was gone.

Only one question mattered, the one that had clawed at me since the battle had begun. My voice was stripped bare, raw with need in the fading light.

"Will you ever trust me?"

16

TERRA

OH GOD, I'd fucked up. Big time.

My hands were still shaky from the less-than-smooth flights to and from that dust-choked excuse for a hideout. Darrokar's gaze felt like a physical blow, and honestly? I deserved every ounce of the accusation radiating off him.

Instinct screamed I should've laid everything bare from the start, trusted him, consequences be damned. But the *others*. I couldn't ignore the responsibility I had to them.

The steady rhythm of the underground river in the distance did nothing to slow the frantic hammering of my pulse. Darrokar remained a towering silhouette against the soft glow of heat crystals embedded in the walls. Every line of his body screamed tension, his golden eyes, those vertical slits, burning twin holes right through me.

Words were inadequate, clumsy shields against the raw emotion crackling between us.

"Why?" The weight of his question settled on my chest, heavy and suffocating. "You lied. About everything."

"Not everything," I managed, my voice low, strained. It sounded weak, even to my own ears. My hands betrayed my inner turmoil as my thumbs rubbed agitated circles against the worn fabric of my borrowed pants. "When we woke up ... it was chaos. They're mostly civilians, Darrokar. My job is to protect them. When we saw you, your warriors coming for us ... I told Selene and Lexa to hide them. We couldn't risk—" My voice hitched, the lie sticking in my throat like grit.

"Couldn't risk what?" He loomed, his sheer size filling my vision, stealing the air from my lungs. "Risk trusting me?"

"Yes." The word burst out, sharper than intended, the blunt admission tasting like ash.

His wings flared, the membranes shifting, and I saw the subtle flex of the claws at his sides. But I pushed on, the need to explain, however poorly, eclipsing my worry.

"Yes, I couldn't risk trusting you *yet*. You don't understand what it was like. We went to sleep on a ship, expecting ... Earth. We woke up to *this*. Fucking sand lizards attacked us before some of us were even fully out of the cryo-pods. This whole damn planet has tried to kill us since we opened our eyes. How could I trust *anything*?"

The crystalline light in the room did nothing to soften the harsh planes of his face, the molten fury still simmering in his gaze. That anger wasn't foreign—some emotions transcended galaxies. But this was different. This wasn't directed at some faceless enemy; this was aimed squarely at *me*.

"That might hold if we were speaking of the first days," he said finally, his voice dangerously soft, the quiet menace more cutting than any roar. "But you thought I would allow them ... allow *you* ... to suffer within my city? Despite every breath within me screaming to protect you?"

Guilt twisted in my gut, a sharp, sickening lurch. "That wasn't my intention."

"Then clarify it for me, *luvae*." He stalked closer, until there was barely a breath between us, trapping me in the inferno of his gaze. "Tell me why you withheld the truth."

The room felt smaller. I needed a moment, a breath, to gather the scattered pieces of my rationale. "I didn't ..." My breath hitched as I met his unwavering gaze, the raw hurt there a far sharper torment than any outward rage. "I do trust you. I *wanted* to trust you. But they were my responsibility."

His expression didn't soften, but something behind the gold flickered, a flicker of ... understanding? "And now?"

"Now?" I blew out a frustrated breath, the sound ragged. "Now, I don't know what the hell I'm doing anymore." I pressed two fingers hard against my temple, the gesture more forceful than necessary. "My head and my heart are a damn mess because of you."

"You speak as if it is a curse," he murmured, though the underlying tension in his voice hadn't fully dissipated. His golden eyes narrowed, dissecting my defenses like a surgeon's blade.

"Because it feels like one," I admitted, the words leaving a bitter taste. "Because I'm terrified of trusting it. Of trusting *you*."

His wings lifted slightly, the movement subtle but significant, eclipsing the faint light filtering from a high crevice, making him seem impossibly vast, impossibly *other*.

Because he is, that traitorous voice whispered in my mind, the one I'd ruthlessly silenced with every lie, every deflection, every self-deceptive argument that this connection couldn't possibly be as profound as it felt.

"And yet," he said, his voice dropping, becoming a low thrum that vibrated through me, "you do."

My breath hitched. His proximity was overwhelming, too close, yet utterly necessary, a grounding force in the swirling chaos of my emotions. I didn't understand it, not completely. But I was beginning to understand *us*, and that realization was more terrifying than any alien predator.

"I ..." The words caught, snagged by a sudden surge of panic, my pride a stubborn knot in my throat. I couldn't articulate it, couldn't give voice to the gaping void inside me that only his presence seemed to fill. But my body betrayed me, a subtle shift bringing me closer, erasing the inches between us until I could feel the radiating heat of his scales against my skin, his scent, that intoxicating mix of spice and something uniquely Darrokar, engulfing me.

"Tell me," he commanded softly, the word a quiet insistence, not a roared demand. It was a steady anchor in the storm raging within me. "Do you love me?"

Every muscle locked tight.

The question, stripped bare of any artifice, hit with brutal force. My towering, formidable Warrior Lord, demanding nothing less than the unvarnished truth of my heart—a truth I'd barely dared to whisper to myself.

"I don't know how to do this," I breathed, the confession barely audible, trembling in the charged air. "I've been trained for a thousand things, Darrokar. But not this. Not *you*."

"That is not an answer, *luvae*." His voice deepened, becoming impossibly intimate, laced with a raw thread I couldn't quite decipher—hope, perhaps, though he guarded it fiercely.

I could have lied. Deflected. Offered some carefully crafted response to sidestep the core of his question. But the desire to shield myself, to maintain that brittle control, had fractured.

The realization struck with sudden, undeniable force, the words tumbling out like a dam had broken. "I love you." The admission was a raw whisper, choked with the unfamiliar burn of unshed tears prickling at the back of my eyes. It was a fragile offering, terrified and utterly sincere. "I'm so sorry. I—"

His large, clawed hands cupped my face, the unexpected gentleness of his touch in contrast to his imposing strength. My words faltered, dying the moment his golden gaze locked onto mine, holding me captive. My chest rose and fell too quickly, my heart a frantic drum against the deafening silence stretching between us, but his touch remained steady, anchoring.

"You are my mate," he breathed, the words a fierce whisper, quieter than I'd ever heard him, but undeniably powerful. His thumbs brushed over my cheeks, a subtle caress erasing the tears I hadn't even realized were falling. "That means I have already forgiven you."

"But I—"

"You are mine, Terra," he stated, his voice still soft, but edged with steel. "Always. There is nothing to forgive."

And before I could argue, before I could even think to resist —as if resistance was a possibility I truly entertained—his lips claimed mine.

His kiss was firm, insistent, and imbued with a surprising tenderness. I met his urgency, my hands fisting in the rough fabric of his tunic, fighting the instinctive urge to drag him closer, to meld our bodies into one. The quiet intensity of the moment was overwhelming, a raw vulnerability that compelled me to pull away and to hold on tighter all at the same time.

His tongue slipped past my lips, a silent invitation that I accepted without hesitation. The taste of him was intoxicating, a heady mix of something uniquely his and the lingering heat of the Volcaryth suns. A shiver danced down my spine, and I pressed closer, the solid warmth of his body an anchor.

His hands moved from my face, one tracing the curve of my back, pressing me against him, the other cupping the nape of my neck, tilting my head to deepen the kiss. I felt the subtle scrape of his claws against my skin, a reminder of the untamed power he held, even in this tender embrace.

Fear should have been my first reaction, but all I felt was a surge of excitement, a thrill that chased away the lingering shadows of guilt and doubt.

A low growl rumbled in his chest, against my mouth, sending a delicious tremor through me, a silent challenge I had no desire to refuse. My heart hammered, a frantic rhythm echoing the possessive urgency of his kiss. My fingers tightened in his tunic, pulling him closer, unwilling to cede even a millimeter of space.

He broke the kiss, just long enough for his gaze to lock with mine. His pupils were dilated, the gold of his irises burning with an intensity that stole my breath. "You are mine, Terra," he murmured, his voice a rough caress.

"Yes. Yours." The words were out before I consciously formed them, a raw response that earned me a fierce, possessive smile, a flash of predatory satisfaction that sent a fresh wave of shivers down my spine. His wings shifted behind him, the leathery whisper of their movement filling the brief silence before he lowered his head to kiss me again.

My hands, freed from their grip on his tunic, traced the hard line of his chest, feeling the thick muscles beneath the fabric. He tensed subtly as my fingers brushed over a scar, deeper than the others, his claws at the small of my back twitching almost imperceptibly. I paused, my fingertips tracing the uneven edges of the faded mark. "What's this from?" I murmured, pulling back slightly to meet his gaze.

He hesitated, his eyes flicking away for second before returning to mine. "A long time ago," he began, his voice suddenly thick with the weight of buried memories. "When I was young. Foolish. I underestimated an opponent." He shrugged, a dismissive gesture that didn't quite reach his eyes. "A lesson learned in blood and pain." His hand covered mine, pressing my palm firmly against his chest. "It does not matter now."

Before I could question further, he swept me off my feet, my legs wrapping around his hips just below the curve of his wings as he stalked towards the sleeping platform. My clothing seemed to vanish in a flurry of frantic movement, impatient hands stripping away the barriers until it was skin against heated scale.

He laid me on the soft silks of the platform, his gaze never leaving mine as he loomed above me, a magnificent predator claiming his prize. His body was a breathtaking blend of muscle and sharp angles, the obsidian scales gleaming in the gentle light filtering through the crystalline formations, and a surge of lust pulsed through me.

This formidable creature, this alien warrior, was mine, and I devoured him with my eyes, tracing the powerful lines of his wings, the intricate patterns of his scales. His golden eyes burned into me, reflecting a raw, possessive intensity that mirrored my own desire.

"You're beautiful," I whispered, the words barely audible, yet they seemed to echo in the stillness of the cavern. His wings flared at the simple declaration.

His lips curved into a slow, predatory smile that sent a shiver of anticipation down my spine. "So are you, *luvae*." His voice was a low purr, a vibration against my skin that ignited a firestorm within me. He leaned down, his wings partially unfurling, enveloping us in a private cocoon of shadow and heat. "I want to hear you say it again," he murmured against my lips, his breath warm and heavy.

My heart pounded against my ribs, my stomach flipping with a potent cocktail of anticipation and nervous excitement. I felt exposed, vulnerable, yet the familiar tremor of fear was absent, replaced by an overwhelming sense of rightness. "I love you, Darrokar."

A growl rumbled in his chest, a sound of pure pleasure and

possession as his lips claimed mine again, the kiss fierce, demanding, leaving no doubt of his claim. His mouth moved to the sensitive skin of my neck, his tongue tracing a tantalizing path, sending shivers cascading down my spine. The subtle scratch of his fangs against my flesh was a thrilling reminder of the predator lurking beneath the surface, and I shuddered, my nails digging into the solid muscle of his back, urging him closer.

"More," I gasped, my voice a breathy plea, and it was enough.

He pulled back, his gaze burning into mine, his lips curled into a wickedly seductive smile. "Anything for you, *luvae.*"

My hips arched instinctively, my body begging for the contact only he could provide. A deep laugh vibrated through his chest as he shifted, his movements fluid and deliberate. In one swift motion, he rolled us over, pinning me beneath him, his weight a welcome pressure.

His cock, thick and pulsing with anticipation, pressed against my entrance, and a sharp gasp escaped my lips as he slowly, deliberately, pushed inside me. It was everything I remembered, every time before, only amplified, the molten heat of him filling me, stretching me in ways I hadn't thought possible.

He moved slowly at first, his hips grinding against mine in a wild rhythm. I urged him deeper, wanting to lose myself completely within him. He obliged with a low growl, his cock throbbing inside me, each pulse sending shockwaves of pleasure through my core. The sensation was almost too intense, the raw heat of him, the satisfying stretch, the profound sense of being utterly consumed. I arched my back, pressing my breasts against his scaled chest, and he groaned, the sharp tips of his fangs grazing my neck.

"Darrokar," I gasped, my voice a ragged whisper, but he

offered no verbal response, only a deeper growl as his hips began to move faster, driving into me with a dark, relentless intensity that left me breathless and trembling beneath him.

His pace quickened, each thrust hitting that elusive sweet spot deep within me, blurring my vision, silencing the frantic chatter of my mind. I clung to him, my nails digging into the unyielding strength of his scales as I met his every movement, my hips rising to take him even deeper, craving the exquisite friction.

The air thickened with the sound of our ragged breathing, the slick slap of skin against scale, and the low, guttural sounds of pleasure that escaped his lips with each powerful thrust.

I felt the coil of pleasure building within me, tightening, intensifying with each pass of his cock, until it was a living thing, humming with unbearable tension just beneath my skin. His lips found mine again, the kiss fierce, possessive, a primal claiming that left no room for doubt. I met his urgency with equal fervor, my body moving in perfect sync with his, meeting every thrust with a desperate hunger that bordered on madness.

The coil inside me snapped, and a cry tore from my throat, swallowed by the intensity of his kiss. My inner muscles clenched around him, milking his cock as wave after wave of mind-shattering pleasure crashed over me, pulling me under. He groaned, his hips stuttering, his movements becoming ragged as he followed me over the precipice, his seed pulsing into me in hot, rhythmic bursts. We clung to each other, our bodies slick with sweat, trembling with the aftershocks of our shared climax, the heat of our skin melded together, our hearts hammering in unison.

The silence that followed was profound, grounding. I lay nestled against him, the steady rise and fall of his chest beneath my cheek a reassuring anchor—breathing, alive, *real*. My fingers traced the warmth of his scaled abdomen absently, the soft glow from the crystal formations painting us in flickering firelight.

Darrokar's arm lay possessively across my waist, his long tail draped loosely over the edge of the platform. His warmth enveloped me, and for a fleeting, precious moment, the restless storm in my mind finally quieted.

"I've spent my whole life trying to do everything on my own," I said quietly, the words a soft crack in the stillness. His claws, tracing lazy patterns on my arm, paused briefly.

"You do not have to anymore." His voice was low, molten with a certainty that resonated deep within me, stealing my breath.

"I'm scared," I whispered, pressing my forehead against his chest, unsure if I wanted him to acknowledge the vulnerability or pretend he hadn't heard. Admitting fear was a luxury I rarely afforded myself—not openly, not even internally. But there, cocooned in his warmth, the words spilled out, unchecked. "Scared of what I'll become if I let this ... let *us* ... take me. I'm afraid of losing control."

His wing shifted then, wrapping around me like a shield, and his lips brushed against my temple, the lingering warmth sending a wave of sensation rippling through me. The cavern air smelled of heat, of sweat, of him—so distinctly Drakarn, so undeniably Darrokar.

"You will not lose yourself," he murmured, his voice fierce yet achingly gentle, as if I were as fragile as I was flawed. "If you are afraid, then I will carry that fear as my own, just as I will carry any burden that challenges you. Your strength is your own, Terra, but it belongs to me now as well."

Something wrenched in my chest then, not the sharp sting of shame or the friction of anger, but a quiet shift, a slow surrender. A gradual loosening of tension I hadn't even realized I'd been carrying.

I didn't respond, the sudden weight of his words a heavy lump in my throat. But I felt his hand tighten against my back, his warmth a tangible reassurance that he wasn't going anywhere, and the frantic rhythm of my pulse began to slow. Quietly, perhaps with more desperation than I intended, I pressed my fingers against his warm abdomen and closed my eyes.

This place, this life, wasn't the plan. But I'd take the alien beside me over any plan I'd ever imagined.

And I'd thank fate every night I slept in his arms.

RATH

THE BURNING in my chest felt like I'd swallowed a piece of the lava that runs through this cursed planet. It wasn't the ache of a battle wound, or the sharp stab of betrayal. No, this was different.

Fucked up, even by my standards.

It clawed, not at my flesh, but at the very core of me, a hollow ache that echoed, a desperate need that whispered, *her*.

I could still taste the subtle sweetness in the air, faint but undeniable. The scent I had caught in the battle against those damned *kervash*, now tinged with something else.

It wasn't just a scent. It was an invasion that was tearing through my carefully constructed wall of self-control. My internal fires seemed to burn hotter, threatening to set my ruby scales ablaze. I had left, stomped through protocol and practically begged information from healers like a fledgling but got nothing. Then I'd snarled and still got nothing, but she was there.

I knew it in my blood.

My claws scraped against the stone walls as I pushed open the oversized door of the healer's cavern. It was always too bright in there, the heat crystals pulsating an irritating light that made my scales itch. The scent of crushed herbs and scented oils filled my nostrils, a sickly sweet smell that normally did nothing, but now, it was layered with something else, *her* scent that I had tracked through the air, even faint.

My wings twitched with an energy I couldn't place—part anticipation, part rage at the waiting.

"Rath!" The sharp voice of the Mysha cut through the thick air. Her golden scales flickered as she turned, her yellow slit pupils narrowed in annoyance. She was old, ancient even, her voice edged with an authority that only age and skill could grant. Most of my warriors flinched under her gaze.

Even I felt a prickle of unease.

"What in the twin suns do you think you're doing? This is a place of healing, not the war council." Her tone was clipped, practical. She never failed to remind me I was a walking, breathing inferno.

"I need to see the humans." My tone was low, a rumble in my chest. My need to get closer to *her* burned so hot that I only managed to maintain a modicum of civility.

She huffed, a sound like pressurized steam venting. "For what purpose? They are all various levels of heat sick and need to recover."

"It's important. Council business." I was on the war council. It was my business. A technical truth, but the words felt like lies. "One of them had purple in her hair."

Mysha's head tilted back, amusement flickered inside her dark eyes, as though I had just told a rather poor joke. "They are half-dead from the heat and covered in enough dust and sand to choke a *dranith*." She gestured with a clawed hand towards the rows of beds carved into the rock walls, each occupied by a listless human. "None of them is in any shape to speak to the council. They are being medically contained."

My claws tightened. I wanted to roar my frustration, to demand she bring *her* forth now. But I held back. Her dismissal stoked the fires in my chest, a constant burning that threatened to burst out, not that she would care. "I shall decide whether she can speak."

"You will not. Leave, go back to the training grounds, and work your rage out." Her voice was firm, absolute. "You disturb the healing." She waved her hand as if swatting away an insect.

I fought to contain the roaring in my ears. My wings pushed against the confines of the cavern walls, restless, itching for flight. It was there, faint but unmistakable. Mixed with the sickly herbs and oils, I caught a trace, her aroma. Like a desert flower, sweet, delicate, but with a hint of something wild underneath ... *mine.*

It twisted inside me, an undeniable, visceral pull. It clawed at my throat and settled in my stomach, both painful and enticing, the promise of something more.

I took a step toward the beds, my gaze sweeping over figures hidden under white sheets and only the occasional limb visible, looking for a specific face and scent combination. The scent grew stronger as I moved closer, a magnetic pull. I wanted to touch, to inhale, to press my nose to her skin and confirm what my body told me was true. My fangs tingled, a sensation that ignited a deeper fire inside me, an urge I'd never truly expected to feel.

"Leave this place, Fire Heart." Her yellow eyes could see my intentions, piercing through my attempts at discretion with a knowing sharpness that bordered on irritation. "I will not let you disturb these patients."

I balled my fist, claws digging into my palm. "You cannot deny me this, elder; I have a *right.*" The words hissed past my teeth.

"Your right ends where your tantrums begin." She glared

with a look that could burn an entire forest. "If you continue this nonsense, I will summon the guards to escort you out. Consider yourself warned."

I knew from her tone the threat wasn't idle. She would make good on her word. And I still couldn't see. I took a deep breath. It was not worth an all-out battle. I had to be smart. Patient. She was my mate. If the bond was what I felt, then she was more important than anything. "Fine," I ground out, "but I'll be back."

Once in the open air, I finally felt the flames inside me simmering down. I needed to think. The sky was ablaze, Volcaryth's twin suns a painful reminder of the heat that had nearly killed *her*. I couldn't stand the thought of that happening again.

Mate.

The word echoed in my mind. This wasn't some fleeting desire. This was a bond, a connection that defied logic and tradition. My heart thrummed in my chest as I let the weight of the situation settle upon me.

A human ... How could I possibly ...

Doubt twisted around my heart, a snake trying to kill my future. What if the connection was false? What if she found me repulsive? What if she didn't want me? Despite all my rage and power, the thought made me flinch.

I was Rath Flame Heart. I commanded legions; I had faced down the greatest warriors of our time; I was the fire in our clan, yet the possibility of her rejection was more terrifying than anything. The uncertainty made me want to roar, to shake the world until reality shifted.

I pushed past the fear, the self-doubt, the uncertainty. My scales glinted as my wings snapped open, and I took to the sky, ready and determined. The ground rushed away under me as my muscles worked, propelling me upward. A plan was forming.

I needed to see her, to touch her, to mark her as mine. And nothing—especially not a stubborn old healer—would stop me.

My roar echoed through the air, a promise written in flames.

———

ECHOES OF FIRE

RATH

The burning in my chest felt like I'd swallowed a piece of the lava that runs through this cursed planet. It wasn't the ache of a battle wound, or the sharp stab of betrayal. No, this was different. Fucked up, even by my standards. It clawed, not at my flesh, but at the very core of me, a hollow ache that echoed, a desperate need that whispered, *her*.

I could still taste the subtle sweetness in the air, faint but undeniable. The scent I had caught in the battle against those damned *kervash*, now tinged with something else ... *hers*.

It wasn't just a scent. It was an invasion that was tearing through my carefully constructed wall of control. My internal fires seemed to burn hotter, threatening to set my ruby scales ablaze. I had left, stomped through protocol, and practically begged information from healers like a hatchling but got nothing. Then I'd snarled and still got nothing, but she was there. I *knew* it.

My claws scraped against the stone walls as I pushed open the oversized door of the healer's cavern. It was always too bright in there, the heat crystals pulsating with an irritating light that made my scales itch. The scent of crushed herbs and scented oils filled my nostrils, sickly sweet, it was layered with something else, *her* scent that I had tracked through the air, no matter how faint.

My wings twitched with an energy I couldn't place—part anticipation, part rage at the waiting.

"Rath!" The sharp voice of the head healer, Mysha, cut through the thick air. Her gold scales twitched as she turned, her slit pupils narrowed in annoyance. She was old, ancient even, her voice edged with an authority that only age and skill could grant. Most of my warriors flinched under her gaze.

Even I felt a prickle of unease.

"What in the twin suns do you think you're doing? This is a place of healing, not the war council." Her tone was clipped, practical. She never failed to remind me I was a walking, breathing inferno.

"I need to see the humans." My tone was a low rumble in my chest. My need to get closer to *her* burned so hot that I only managed to maintain a modicum of civility.

She huffed like pressurized steam venting. "For what purpose? They are all various levels of heat sick and need to recover."

"It's important. Council business." I was on the Blade Council. It was *my* business. A technical truth, but the words felt like lies. "One of them had purple in her hair."

Mysha's head tilted back, amusement flickered inside her dark eyes, as though I had just told a rather poor joke. "They are half-dead from the heat and covered in enough dust and sand to choke a *dranith*." She gestured with a clawed hand towards the rows of beds carved into the rock walls, each occupied by a listless human. "None of them is in any shape to speak to the council. They are being medically contained."

My claws curled into fists, sharp points pricking my palms. I wanted to roar my frustration, to demand she bring *her* forth now. But I held back. Mysha's dismissal stoked the fires in my chest, not that she would care. "I shall decide whether she can speak."

"You will not. Leave, go back to the training grounds and work your rage out." Her voice was firm. "You disturb the healing." She waved her hand as if swatting away an insect.

I fought to contain the roaring in my ears. My wings pushed against the confines of the cavern wall behind me, restless, itching for flight. It was there, faint but unmistakable. Mixed with the sickly herbs and oils, I caught a trace, her aroma. Like a desert flower, sweet, delicate, but with a hint of something wild underneath ... *mine.*

It twisted inside me, an undeniable, visceral pull. It clawed at my throat and settled in my stomach, painful and enticing, the promise of something more.

I took a step toward the beds, my gaze sweeping over figures hidden under white sheets and only the occasional limb visible, looking for a specific face and scent combination. The scent grew stronger as I moved closer.

I wanted to touch, to inhale, to press my nose to her skin and confirm what my body told me was true. My fangs tingled, a sensation that ignited a deeper fire inside me, an ancient urge I'd never truly expected to feel.

"Leave this place, Fire Heart," Mysha's yellow eyes could see my intentions, piercing through my attempts at discretion with a knowing sharpness that bordered on irritation. "I will not let you disturb these patients."

I balled my fist, claws digging into my palm. "You cannot deny me this, elder; I have a *right*." The words hissed past my teeth.

"Your right ends where your tantrums begin." She glared with a look that could burn an entire forest. "If you continue this nonsense, I will summon the guards to escort you out. Consider yourself warned."

I knew from her tone the threat wasn't idle. Mysha would make good on her word. And I still couldn't see *her*. I took a deep breath. It was not worth an all-out battle. I had to be smart. Patient. My mate was there. If the bond was true, then she was more important than anything. "Fine," I ground out, "but I'll be back." Leaving the healing cavern was harder than abandoning an injured soldier on the battlefield.

Once outside, I finally felt the flames inside me simmering down. I needed to think. The sky was ablaze, Volcaryth's suns a painful reminder of the heat that had nearly killed *her*. I couldn't stand the thought of that happening again.

Mate.

The word echoed in my mind. This wasn't some fleeting desire. This was a bond, a connection that defied logic and tradition. My heart thumped in my chest as I let the weight of the situation settle upon me.

A human ... How could I possibly ...

Doubt twisted around my heart, a snake trying to kill my future. What if the connection was false? What if she found me repulsive? What if she didn't want me? Despite all my rage and power, the thought made me flinch.

I was Rath Flame Heart. I commanded legions, I had faced down the greatest warriors and beasts of our time, I was the fire in our clan, yet the possibility of her rejection was more terrifying than anything. The uncertainty made me want to roar, to shake the world until reality shifted.

I looked out over the horizon, at the lights of the suns that shone like two burning eyes, watching me. She would be mine.

I pushed past the fear, the self-doubt, the uncertainty. My

wings snapped open, and I took to the sky, ready and determined. The ground rushed away under me as my muscles worked, propelling me upward. A plan was forming.

I needed to see her, to touch her, to mark her as mine. And nothing—especially not a stubborn old healer—would stop me. My roar echoed through the air; a promise written in flames.

1

ORLA

THE WALLS BREATHED.

I pressed my palm flat against the warm stone of one of Scalvaris's cavernous corridors, feeling the faint vibration beneath my fingertips—a rhythmic hum, like the planet itself was pulsing. The rock walls arched above me, their surfaces etched with glowing crystal inlays that spiraled in fractal patterns. My eyes traced the designs, recognizing the deliberate engineering: the veins of heat-resistant mineral branching like capillaries, channeling thermal energy away from inhabited spaces.

Brilliant. A passive cooling system.

"You're doing that thing again," Selene's voice echoed slightly in the vastness around us.

I blinked, lowering my hand. "What thing?"

"The *I'm-about-to-dissect-a-moonrock* stare." She adjusted the strap of the medical kit she had slung over one shoulder, her dark eyes sharp. "You forget to breathe when you're geeking out."

"I'm breathing." I tapped the journal tucked under my arm, its pages already crammed with sketches of the Drakarn's metallic-bark trees—their root systems siphoning groundwater from aquifers even deeper than this underground city. "This isn't just architecture, Selene. It's a *biome*. They've integrated their ecosystem into every structural choice. The heat redistribution alone—"

"Isn't going to matter if you collapse from dehydration." She thrust a canteen into my hands. "Drink. I don't want you falling to heat sickness again."

I grimaced but obeyed, the lukewarm water bitter with electrolyte tablets. Two weeks in that cave after the crash had left all of us humans frayed, but my body still hadn't forgiven me for sprinting through 120-degree winds during our subsequent capture.

The scar along my ribs throbbed faintly as I moved, a reminder of giant claws. It had been nearly a month since I was released from the medical caverns, but my body was still recovering.

Selene watched me swallow, her medic's gaze dissecting every micro-expression. "You're favoring your left side."

"It's a *habit*, not a limp. The muscle's healed." Mostly. I pivoted to distract her, gesturing toward a nearby archway where Drakarn artisans welded alloy into the stone. "Look at those joints—we don't have anything like that back home. The thermal expansion coefficient must be *exactly* matched to the surrounding rock." My fingers itched to take a sample.

She sighed, knowing she couldn't win this. "Just ... don't vanish into another magma vent. Terra'll skin me if I lose you."

"Noted." I smirked, scribbling a hypothesis about the crystal inlays' refractive index. "But if I *do* fall into a lava tube, prioritize saving the journal. It's got a month of soil pH readings."

Selene rolled her eyes but lingered as I crouched to examine a fissure in the floor. Thin tendrils of steam curled upward, carrying a mineral tang that made my sinuses burn.

My thumb brushed the tattoo on my wrist—a DNA helix entwined with oak leaves, inked the day I'd defended my thesis.

Adapt or die, my mother's voice whispered in memory. *Life persists where logic says it shouldn't.*

The Drakarn had taken that mantra to staggering heights. Above us, massive roots from the surface trees plunged through the cavern ceiling, their metallic sheen shimmering under bioluminescent fungi. I sketched frantically, labeling the symbiotic relationship: *Fungal networks neutralize soil toxins; roots stabilize subterranean chambers. Mutualism evolved under extreme pressure.*

"Orla." Selene's tone shifted, the playful edge replaced by steel. "You're swaying."

"I'm *balancing.*" The lie tasted stale. My vision blurred at the edges as I straightened, the cavern tilting like a ship in a storm.

Her palm gripped my elbow to steady me. "You need rest. Actual rest, not ... whatever this is."

I pulled away gently, nodding toward a distant bridge fortress. Its obsidian spans glittered with embedded heat crystals, their prismatic light fracturing into rainbows across the river below. "I need to *understand.* How they've sustained a civilization here—it's everything I've studied. Everything I ..." *Wanted to prove I could achieve.*

Her gaze softened. "You can't unlock the secrets to the planet in a single day. Maybe one of us could help?"

The words prickled. I adjusted my grip on the journal, its leather cover worn smooth from years of use. "I work better alone. You know that."

A beat passed. Selene's jaw tightened, but she nodded. "Fine. But if you're not back by nightfall, I'm sending Kira with a tracking beacon. And she'll bring the handcuffs."

I saluted half-heartedly, already turning toward a shadowed

tunnel where the walls pulsed with unfamiliar glyphs. "Tell her to bring the scanner on my table. I'll want spectrographic readings."

Her exasperated groan faded behind me as I slipped into the gloom, my boots crunching over gravel that shimmered with flecks of pyrite. The air grew cooler, drier—*climate zones segmented by airflow*, my mind catalogued. A low, resonant chanting vibrated through the stone, harmonizing with the distant rush of the underground river.

I paused, pressing my palm to the wall again. The vibrations sharpened, resolving into a melody that raised the hair on my neck.

Somewhere ahead, the Drakarn were *singing*.

My bruised ribs protested as I quickened my pace, but I ignored them. The scientists who'd laughed at my proposals for Martian biodomes hadn't understood this thirst either—the need to *see*, to map the uncharted edges where theory bled into wonder.

Volcaryth's secrets tempted every part of me, and I'd unravel them one layer at a time.

The chanting thickened like honey, each harmonic layering until the air seemed to vibrate with intent. I followed the sound through a narrowing passage, my boots scuffing against stone worn smooth by centuries of footsteps.

The fungi there glowed cobalt instead of orange, their light catching on glyphs carved into the walls—angular, urgent slashes that my translator couldn't parse. With my subdermal translator I could understand spoken text, but I'd have to learn to read their language the old-fashioned way.

I paused to sketch them, noting how the symbols clustered near ventilation shafts. A prayer? Warning markers? My pencil hovered.

Unknown semantic function. Further study required.

A gust of superheated air rushed from an overhead shaft, carrying the acrid tang of sulfur and something sweeter—burnt amber resin, maybe. My fading purple braid stuck to the sweat-dampened collar of my shirt as I climbed a spiral ramp, each step sending dull fire through my healing ribs. *Idiot. Should've taken Selene's painkillers.* But pharmaceuticals fogged observation, and I needed every synapse sharp.

The ramp ended at a wall about ten feet high. I didn't see a door or any of the chanting Drakarn. At this point, a normal person would have turned away, or maybe just stood to listen.

They didn't have my drive.

Or my climbing skills.

It was one of those things I'd done for fun back on Earth, the precision and risk focusing my mind until all that mattered was the next handhold, the next summit. And ten feet? That was nothing.

I was halfway up the wall before I wondered if this was, *perhaps,* not the smartest move. My side protested every stretch, and my vision was a bit hazy around the edges again. I wouldn't say no to Selene's canteen, but she'd taken it with her.

Maybe the wall was there for a reason.

But I was already halfway up, and the chanting was growing more intense. I just wanted a peek.

The wall ended in a broad walkway that looked out over an amphitheater full of Drakarn. My eyes had to adjust to the eerie twilight. Below me stretched terraces, concentric rings descending toward a central dais where obsidian monoliths speared upward like shattered teeth.

Dozens of Drakarn knelt between them, their winged backs rippling in unison as the chant reached its peak. My breath caught.

I crouched behind a pillar, journal open to a fresh page. The warriors' tails flicked as they moved, their wing membranes taut with precision. Two figures emerged from the shadows—a male with onyx scales threaded with gold, a female who wore a beaded crimson headdress that trembled with each step. They circled the dais, claws scraping grooves into stone already scarred by generations.

Not combat. Too synchronized.

The female lashed her tail, the tip whistling centimeters from the male's throat. He pivoted, wings flaring to buffet her with heated air.

The female reared back, her throat pulsing as she unleashed a roar that made my molars ache. The male responded by dragging his claws through a trough of black sand, sending up a plume that swirled into patterns. Symbols. The same glyphs from the tunnel walls.

My translator implant buzzed uselessly against my skull as the crowd's chanting shifted in tone, their voices splintering into dissonant harmonies that prickled my skin.

A warm trickle slid from my nose. I swiped at it absently, fingers coming away smeared with crimson. *Damn dry air.* The blood droplet hit the stone with a soft *tick.*

Every Drakarn head snapped toward my hiding place.

For three excruciating heartbeats, the cavern held its breath.

Then two hundred pairs of vertical pupils contracted as one, their sulfur-yellow and orange irises fixing on my hiding place. The chanting died mid-syllable, leaving a silence so complete I heard the creak of leathery wing membranes adjusting.

The female's wings fanned into a jagged corona, her snarl revealing twin rows of fangs. The monoliths behind her began to thrum, their surfaces bleeding veins of crimson light that pulsed in time with my rabbit-quick pulse.

Wrong. This is all wrong.

The onyx-scaled male moved first. His wings snapped open with a crack like splitting stone, the gold filaments in his membranes catching the monoliths' hellish glow. Claws longer than hunting knives scored the rock as he ascended the terraces in liquid surges, each lunge closing twenty feet. The air around him shimmered like a living mirage.

"Wait—" My voice was strangled, drowned by the sudden dissonant hissing. A dozen warriors flanked him, tails lashing. Their collective heat hit me in a wave, parching my throat, searing my already sweat-slicked skin.

The female priestess barked a guttural command. My translator spat static, then a mangled phrase: *"... profane ... she defiles the sacrament ..."*

Think. Breathe.

My heel found empty air as I reeled back—the ledge of the wall behind me. Journal pages fluttered as I windmilled my arms, pain screaming through my ribs. The male's talons missed my shoulder by millimeters, shredding my sleeve.

"Please!" I rasped, fingers scrabbling at a fissure in the rock. "I didn't mean—"

A chorus of shrieks answered. Warriors fanned out along the upper ledges, tails coiling to strike. The priestess mounted the dais, her claws raised high. In them glinted a curved blade forged from the same devilish light as the monoliths—a weapon that hurt to look at, its edge warping the air with the threat of pain.

Move. Now. Run.

I lunged for a narrow cleft in the cavern wall—too slow. A spiked tail wrapped my ankle, yanking me onto my back. The impact knocked the breath from my lungs, my vision blurring as scaled hands pinned my wrists. Hot drool splattered my cheek, the male's sulfur-tinged breath scalding my face as he snarled words my translator finally deciphered:

"The defiler must die."

Somewhere in the roaring dark, my mother's voice whispered: *Adapt.*

I twisted my wrist, jabbing a rock sample pick hidden in my sleeve. The male howled as the tungsten spike found the soft junction between his thumb scales. His grip faltered—just enough to roll sideways as the priestess's strike fell.

The sacred blade shattered the stone where my heart had been.

Warriors descended in a storm of claws and blades. I scrambled like a crab over the uneven stone, side screaming in agony, lungs burning with every gasp.

There.

A ventilation shaft—narrow, glowing faintly with the same cobalt fungi from the tunnels. I dove headfirst for the claustrophobic passage as another tail yanked at my heels.

"After the defiler!" The priestess's cry chased me as I tried to scramble into darkness. "Let the magma cleanse her sacrilege!"

The shaft walls closed around me, sharp mineral edges tearing skin as I crawled toward faint distant light. Behind, the scrape of claws on stone multiplied.

They were faster.

They were everywhere.

They were *hungry.*

"Wait—I can explain—" My voice drowned in the ruckus.

A clawed hand locked around my bicep, talons piercing fabric and skin. I cried out, journal slipping from my grasp as the male yanked me forward. His breath seared my face, smelling of charred meat and bitter spice. The female stalked closer, her headdress clicking as she spat a word I didn't need my translator to define.

"Execution."

2

RATH

THE *DRANITH'S* severed claw still smoked in my grip, its jagged edge glowing faintly with residual venom. Knees deep in the ash-choked moat of Scalvaris's eastern gate, I sucked in air thick with the stench of scorched scales and sulfur.

Battle-lust burned through my veins like ore, my scales slick with blood that hissed where it dripped onto smoldering stone. My warriors-in-training panted behind me, their labored breaths echoing the distant wail of steam geysers. The raid had been messy, desperate—dranith weren't usually this bold. It should've made me cautious.

It didn't.

I crushed the claw to powder. "Double patrols on the lava trenches," I growled at Voskath, my voice raw from inhaling cinders. The younger warrior's green scales were dulled by soot, his blade notched from parrying serrated pincers. "The next swarm that tries crawling up our walls, burn their wings off before they—"

Her.

The scent punched through the stink of charred flesh and sulfur—sweet, sharp, *human.* Ozone and damp stone, ink and something floral, cutting through the haze like a blade through smoke. My nostrils flared. My cock stirred.

Fuck.

I spun, wings snapping open with a crack that sent ash devils swirling. The crowded plaza blurred—artisans hauling cracked shields toward the forges, healers hurrying past with stretchers dripping blood, younglings darting between legs to scavenge discarded arrowheads.

No purple-haired human. No delicate throat to mark. But the scent lingered, tendrils of it coiling around me, whispering promises that made my fire churn.

"Rath?" Voskath's blade hovered near my arm, its edge still steaming from dranith blood. "Your eyes are doing the ... flame thing."

I clawed a boulder, relishing the crack of stone. Sparks skittered across my knuckles. "Tend your patrols."

The temple bell tolled—three jagged peals that meant sacrilege. My pulse roared louder than the geyser fields.

Move. Find. Protect.

I lunged toward the sound, boots crushing discarded weaponry into the ashen soil. The scent thickened near the forge district, where smoke coiled from the chimneys in lazy spirals. My blood boiled hotter with every step. Scales along my ribs flushed crimson—a mating flush, the kind hatchlings giggled about in training caves. Pathetic. Weak.

Unbecoming of a council warrior.

A scream tore through the acrid air. Female. *Hers.*

I was sprinting before the echo died, shoving Drakarn aside. A youngling carrying ore baskets went sprawling, black crystals scattering across the stones. An elder cursed my lineage, her graveled voice lost in the thunder of my pulse. I didn't care. The forge's heat slapped my face as I rounded the final corner and launched, wings pumping as I vaulted the wall surrounding the Forge Temple and landed into ...

Chaos.

Warriors formed a snarling ring around the central dais, their tails lashing in unison like a nest of vipers. Karyseth's priestess cadre chanted, their claws dripping blackened oil into the sacred flame pit. The air reeked of burnt myrrh and something fouler—congealed rage. And in the center ...

Orla.

Two warriors dragged her forward by her absurdly fragile arms, her boots carving furrows through the ash. Blood streaked her temple, matting that violet braid she never tied properly. The frayed ends glinted with tiny metal clasps.

Her shirt hung torn at the shoulder, revealing a lattice of old scars. These *kervash* had dared to touch her.

I would end them all.

Karyseth loomed over the flame pit. "Defiler of the Forge!" The High Priestess's voice slithered through my marrow, colder than the void between stars. "You trespass where fire births honor! You steal sacred sight with ... *this.*"

She held up Orla's journal, pages fluttering like a wounded bird. My mate's—*no, not mate, never claimed*—lips moved silently, calculating something only her clever human mind could fathom. Always thinking, even in the jaws of death.

The priestess hurled the journal into the flames.

Orla jerked against her captors, muscles straining. "Wait! Those were just—"

Karyseth backhanded her.

The crack of flesh on flesh snapped my last thread.

Heat surged through my veins, primal and possessive. My vision tinted red, flames licking at the edges of my sight. The warriors nearest me stumbled back, clutching scaled faces as if seared by my aura. Good. Let them burn.

"Enough."

The word rolled out as a growl, low enough to make the stone underfoot tremble. The crowd stilled. Even the sacred flames bent toward me, the light warping around my smoldering form.

Karyseth's pupils narrowed to dagger points. "Warrior Rath. This doesn't concern the Blade Council."

Orla's gaze locked with mine. Blood welled along her split lip, a crimson bead trembling at the edge before falling. Her pulse rabbited at her throat, a fragile, rapid beat that called to the fire in my blood.

Mine to guard. Mine to claim.

I stepped into the circle.

"It does now."

The priestess's claws gleamed wet with Orla's blood. I counted three drops hitting the dais before my vision cleared enough to see details—the way my mate's left wrist bent at a wrong angle, the charred edge of her journal's cover peeking from beneath Karyseth's scaled foot. My fire surged hotter.

"This *human* scribbled our sacred glyphs," Karyseth hissed, grinding the journal deeper into ash. The stench of burning parchment mixed with Orla's coppery blood. "Stole secrets from the Forge Master's own sanctum. The penalty is—"

"Death by molten ore," the crowd chanted, tails thumping stone in rhythm. Always eager for blood, these zealots. The less faithful Drakarn were smart enough to stay away. But the humans? They were too new here to know better.

Orla coughed, shoulders shaking. Not from fear—from rage. I knew that tremor. Had felt it in my own bones when Ignarath butchers took my sister. Her voice rasped raw but precise. "How could I?" She lifted her chin, blood smearing across that delicate human throat. "This is ridiculous."

Laughter rippled through the warriors, harsh and guttural.

Karyseth's tail lashed, sending a burning brazier crashing to the stones. Embers skittered toward Orla's boots. "The Defiler speaks nonsense!"

I stepped closer. Heat radiated off me in visible waves now, making the nearest Drakarn stumble back. My focus narrowed to vital points—the warrior on Orla's left, Krazath, had a weak grip, his thumb joint still swollen from last week's sparring session. The one on her right favored his scarred leg, the old wound from the siege of Ignarath.

It would take nothing to end them now.

Then she looked at me.

Fuck.

Her pupils swallowed the irises—pain or terror, maybe both. But beneath the split lip and bruising, her gaze burned with the same stubborn fire that had let her remain standing after her starbound vehicle crashed on the fiery desert and all that came after that. My claws flexed. She'd nearly died. Would've, if I hadn't—

No. Not now.

Karyseth's scowled. "This is our right, warrior. Leave it."

The crowd parted as Darrokar emerged from the smoke, his human mate, Terra, a shadow at his side. The warlord's obsidian scales glinted with cooling battle filth, his expression unreadable. News must have traveled fast for him to be here already. Farther back in the crowd, I spotted other council members, Mektar and Zarvash. I didn't know if they'd followed the rumors or if they'd been there for the start of the ceremony.

Orla had no position, no hope of making these zealots see sense. Darrokar could claim her as a concubine, but he was so newly mated and devoted to his human that all would see past the ruse and challenge the claim here and now.

And, having seen his mate's fire, I feared she might strip off his scales one by one for trying.

I met his gaze, trying to come up with some kind of plan that would save Orla. I could only think of one thing. It was all I had thought of for the past month, waiting for the moment to be perfect.

And this moment was as far from perfect as it got.

His fist clenched—once, twice—the old signal. *Proceed. But it'll be your mess to clean up.*

Karyseth caught the gesture. Her snarl revealed cracked fangs. "The human dies. By law. By fire."

Orla's breath hitched. A sound like glass shattering in my ribs.

I moved.

My wing buffeted the left warrior into the flame pit, his scream cut short as he scrambled to safety. My tail snapped the right one's knee before he could react, the wet crunch drowned by the crowd's collective hiss. Orla collapsed forward, and I caught her against my chest, her body shockingly cold against my burning scales.

"She is mine!"

My roar shook the cavern. Cracks splintered up the sanctum walls, dust raining from the ceiling.

The words seared my throat, hotter than any battle cry.

Karyseth recoiled, her robes billowing at the hem. The crowd's snarls died mid-breath. Even Darrokar went statue-still, his wingtip twitching once before stilling.

Fuck tradition. Fuck the laws.

Orla trembled against me, her heartbeat thrumming against my scales like a caged songbird. I tightened my grip, claws careful not to pierce her soft flesh.

Mine to shield. Mine to claim.

The truth of it scorched through my veins, leaving no room for doubt.

Orla's bloodied lip beckoned like a flame. My tongue

throbbed. Fangs ached with phantom pressure—not a battle-urge, but the need to bite, to brand. My claws flexed against her ribs, the points burning where they dented her shirt's already torn fabric.

Her scent coiled tighter around me with each ragged breath she took—ozone sharpening to lightning-struck stone, floral notes blooming into midnight orchids that only grew in sacred burial caves. My nostrils flared. The priestess's rancid myrrh couldn't mask it now. Couldn't drown what my blood recognized.

"Lies!" Karyseth shrieked again, spittle flying. Her claws slashed the air, etching sigils that made her supplicants recoil. "I see no bond-mark! There has been no vow! This is blasphemy!"

The crowd rippled, warriors hissing, tails lashing. I felt the moment the balance tipped—zealots reaching for blades, acolytes edging closer with hooked chains.

Now.

I flung my wings wide, the membranes casting crimson shadows across the dais. Heat rolled off me in visible waves, warping the air. "You question my honor, Priestess?" my voice boomed, rattling loose stones. "You dare deny the bond?"

The ancient word silenced them. Even Karyseth froze.

Orla's breath hitched. "What's—?"

I unsheathed the heat-crystal dagger at my belt—ceremonial, rarely used, its edge dull but the hilt carved with my clan's fire runes. The blade glowed faintly, responding to my touch.

Hold steady, human.

"Kneel," I commanded, voice steel-edged.

Orla's knees buckled—part shock, part my tail's gentle press behind her knees to make sure she did it. I dropped with her, wings mantling around us both. The dagger's hilt pressed into her palm, her fingers ice-cold against mine.

"Grip it," I growled low so only she could hear. "Tighter. They need to see."

She obeyed, knuckles whitening even as her hand trembled. Good. Smart.

Karyseth lunged forward. "This farce insults the Forge!"

I ignored her, leaning close until my fangs grazed Orla's ear. Her scent flooded me—fear-sweat and ink, sharpening my focus. "When I let go," I murmured, "you put this blade to my throat, *shyrarva*. Understand?"

Her eyes widened, but she nodded. Brave little human.

I released the dagger and threw my head back, baring my throat. My vow shook the sanctum. "By flame and claw, I claim her!"

Orla's arm trembled as she pressed the blade's edge to my pulse. The crowd gasped. Even Darrokar leaned forward, wings half-spread.

Karyseth's tail lashed. "A trick! The human doesn't know our ways!"

"She holds my fire," I snarled. The dagger's glow intensified, reacting to Orla's touch—my soul recognizing her. The sacred crystals embedded in the hilt ignited, casting her face in a golden glow.

The crowd murmured, claws pulling back.

Almost.

The priestess's claws scraped stone as she stepped closer. "Fire cannot lie," she sneered. "Let the human speak the vow. Let her blood mingle with yours in the sacred flame. Then we'll see this ... *bond.*"

My flames dimmed. *Fuck.* The full ritual required marks, blood, fire—things that would break her. I'd seen initiates scream during bonding ceremonies, and they were Drakarn. No one but the zealots performed the ritual or did something insane like subject themselves to a mating challenge. The gods didn't care, and I would not risk my mate.

Orla was still holding the blade to my throat. Her whisper barely reached me. "What do I—?"

"Silence!" Karyseth's tail cracked.

The dagger trembled in Orla's grip. Her wide eyes reflected my smoldering scales. So fragile. So mortal. One wrong move, and they'd scorch her to bone.

No.

Instinct surged—fangs aching to pierce, claws itching to claim. My tongue dragged across sharp teeth, tasting the ghost of her blood from when I'd carried her half-dead from the sands a month ago. Sweet. Addictive.

Too much.

I gripped her waist, scales hissing against her shirt's synthetic fabric. Her breath hitched, and she pulled the knife back. Every instinct roared to bite, to brand, to make my claim the truth. But her fragile neck ...

"Trust me," I growled low, the words more plea than command.

Her nod was barely perceptible.

I struck.

My tongue dragged up the salt-damp hollow beneath her ear, every ridge and tastebud igniting as her scent exploded across my senses. Her pulse beat against the flat of my tongue—wild, human-quick, a rhythm that made my cock throb against my battle harness.

Fuck, she was soft. Softer than silk, her skin like gold under my slow, possessive stroke.

A whimper escaped her—high, reedy, cut short by clenched teeth. Her hips jerked against my thigh, seeking friction. My scales flared hotter there, granting her the barest hint of warmth.

Let her burn.

"Steady," I rumbled against her jaw, though my own tail lashed uncontrollably, like I was some unblooded warrior. Her hands fisted against my shoulders, tugging the sensitive roots of my scales in a way that sent fire coiling down my spine. I groaned, the sound traveling from my chest to where our bodies pressed together.

Her answering gasp tasted like victory.

I licked lower, following the tendon straining in her neck. Her blood sang here—spiced fear and burgeoning want, a cocktail that made my fangs ache to pierce. My claws flexed into her hips, pricking through fabric as I hauled her harder against me. Her scent deepened, ozone sharpening to storm-air, damp stone blooming with the musk only a roused mate could shed.

"Mine," I snarled into her skin, lapping at the sweat beading along her collarbone. My wings mantled tighter around us, shielding her from their stares as my tail coiled around her ankle. Let them see her flush. Let them smell her arousal.

Let every fool here know this fire was mine alone to stoke.

Her moan when I reached the scar below her ear nearly undid me—husky, unbidden, a sound that made my cock harden even further.

Fire surged lower. The dagger clattered as her grip slackened, her other hand fisting into my battle harness.

Karyseth's roar shattered the moment. "Enough! Your theatrics insult the Forge!"

I whirled, shielding Orla with my wings. Flames licked my vision. "You doubt the scent-bond? Come closer then, Priestess. See what fire I've kindled."

The challenge hung smoking around us.

No Drakarn moved.

Orla's whisper tickled my ear. "Your scales ... they're glowing."

I glanced down. My ribs shone crimson through ash-streaked plating—mating flush in full blaze. *Fuck.*

Darrokar's wingtip brushed my shoulder. "The bond is ... unexpected," he rumbled, "but evident."

His mate stepped up beside him, human eyes sharp. "She's marked," Terra said smoothly. "By your laws, that's binding."

Karyseth's tail lashed, but warriors began bowing—first Krazath, then others, until only the priestess stood seething.

Orla's fingers flexed against my chest. "Marked?"

I crushed her closer. "Later."

I locked eyes with Karyseth, letting flames lick across my teeth. "Challenge the bond, Priestess. I'll burn this sanctum to ash before she bleeds."

Silence.

Darrokar stepped forward, his own recent mating scar glinting. "Enough. This is done." His gaze cut to me, unreadable. "The council will discuss this further."

The crowd erupted—outrage, awe, the hungry buzz of scandal. Karyseth's shriek pierced the din, but the warriors were already dispersing, casting wary glances at Orla.

At my mate.

I didn't move. Couldn't.

Orla's whisper tickled my jaw. "Your pulse is racing."

"So it is," I breathed. I couldn't look away from her.

Fuck. I'm doomed.

THE BIG HULKING alien who claimed me as his mate had his claws on my arm the whole way back to his chambers. I stumbled once before he slowed his pace, silently adjusting for my shorter legs.

We practically crossed all of Scalvaris until we entered a building I'd never seen before and he took me down a winding staircase, the air growing warmer with each step.

Frankly, I'd had enough of unfamiliar buildings for one day, or for a lifetime. Every time I closed my eyes, I imagined those Drakarn, their claws slashing at me as they called for my blood, my life.

I shivered, despite the heat.

My shirt was in tatters, and I could use a month-long soak in a tub, but I needed to know what the hell was going on. "Where—"

"Hush," he said. "Wait."

I bristled, but there were other Drakarn watching us, hungry eyes taking in the scene. Questions had to wait until we were behind closed doors.

And what mighty doors they were.

The stone door sealed behind us with a resonant thud, and

suddenly it was just the two of us in a chamber that smelled of smoldering embers and something darker—smoke and aged leather. Rath released my arm like I'd scalded him. I pressed my back against the door, its engraved runes biting into my shoulder blades as I cataloged the room with frantic precision.

The air tasted like licking a battery. I cataloged the chamber's dimensions through shaky breaths—twenty by thirty paces, hexagonal basalt walls striated with bands of volcanic rock. Heat crystals pulsed yellowish light from recessed niches, their fractal patterns mirroring the city's cooling system I'd observed earlier. It felt like a lifetime ago. Had it been more than an hour? A bed platform dominated the far wall, hewn from a single slab of stone and layered with shimmery silks.

Rath moved to an alcove, his tail trailing behind him. My traitorous eyes tracked the play of firelight across his scaled shoulders—ruby plates shifting from blood-black to fiery crimson with each breath.

"You'll stay here." He tossed a clay pitcher onto the table. Water sloshed, beading instantly on the heated surface. "I do not trust Karyseth to respect my claim."

I pressed harder against the door, its carvings mapping constellations against my spine. "Your claim? What does that make me exactly? A prisoner? A pet?" The words came out sharper than intended. Adrenaline still sang in my veins, mixing dangerously with the tang of his proximity.

I knew what he'd said in the moment, and a desperate need for survival had me following his lead. But now? When there weren't angry Drakarn breathing down my neck? Things didn't feel so clear.

The pitcher's glaze caught the light as it settled—a ceramic so glassy it could've been forged in Volcaryth's core. My fingers twitched with the urge to test its thermal conductivity.

Anything to anchor myself in data instead of this ... this *thing* coiling under my ribs.

Rath's wings flexed. "You are neither prisoner nor pet." He didn't turn as he spoke, claws methodically stripping off his battle harness. Each piece hit the table with a clatter that made my pulse skip. "The claim grants protection." He paused. "It was the only thing I could think to do in the moment."

The laugh scraped my throat. I gestured to the bed's silks—translucent layers in scarlet. "And *that*? Part of the protection package?"

His spine stiffened. Scales along his shoulders flared, revealing the softer, opalescent hide beneath. My traitorous brain noted the biological purpose—perhaps thermoregulation during threatening displays.

Stop it. He's not—

"I did not plan to claim a mate today. I apologize for not making my bed. Sleep where you wish." Rath finally turned, and god, the full force of him nearly buckled my knees.

Firelight sculpted the planes of his chest, catching on piercings that glinted along the ridges of his scales. A silver ring through one nipple. Another through the soft flesh beneath a clavicle plate. Two more in his ears. Where else was he pierced?

My mouth went dust dry. "The silks are heat-regulated," he continued, oblivious to my internal combustion. "The bathing pool recirculates through geothermal filters. Do not touch the weapons."

I forced my gaze to the arsenal lining the far wall—blades with crystalline cores, their edges shimmering with residual energy. "Charming decor."

"Practical." He stepped closer, and the air thickened with his scent—ember resin and something muskier. My lungs constricted. "The zealots won't challenge my claim openly. Not tonight, but this affront won't go unanswered."

"How was I supposed to—" I cut myself off, edging along the table, putting its bulk between us. You couldn't argue with zealots. I supposed that was true on any planet.

The journal's loss ached like a phantom limb.

"They don't care about mercy." Rath's tail lashed, sending a stool skittering. "They want blood for their burnt god."

"So you just, what, claimed me? Without even knowing my name?" The words cracked.

"I know your name, Orla Mitchell." Rath stood motionless by the weapons wall, his silhouette haloed in crystal-light. Moonlight from a sky tunnel shaft cut across his scales, turning them to liquid mercury. I counted seven blades within his reach, each more lethal than the last.

"Right." My voice was too loud in the hollow space. "So this ... *claim*. It's a loophole in your laws? Why would claiming me do anything?"

He turned slowly. "Death is the penalty for outsiders who witness the sacred rites. The claim binds your life to mine; as my mate you are ... mine. They cannot harm you without challenging me."

"And if we don't ... click?" Me and relationships hadn't exactly gone places back on Earth. I couldn't see how it would work out between me and someone who wasn't even human.

His nostrils flared, the heat-crystals dimming as if the room itself held its breath. "That is not an option. The zealots are patient hunters."

A shiver skated down my spine. I stepped toward the table, like it could act as some sort of shield. "You didn't answer my question. What am I to you now?"

The silence stretched, thick with the creak of leathery wings adjusting.

"A problem," he said at last.

I barked a laugh. "Charming."

"One I will solve." He moved closer, claws still glinting. My pulse stuttered—an autonomic response, I told myself. Nothing more. "You will stay here. Keep out of trouble. When the threat passes …"

"You'll unclaim me?" My thumb rubbed the DNA helix tattoo on my wrist, the ink gritty with ash. "How convenient." Was I angry about that? Wasn't it what I wanted? I was still shaking with residual fear and couldn't get control of my feelings.

His growl vibrated in my molars. "There is no *unclaiming*. The bond is … permanent."

The word buzzed between us like a live wire.

I gripped the table's edge. "You didn't think to mention that before tongue-bathing me in front of your entire cult?"

"Would you have preferred the pyre?"

Yes, part of me wanted to snap. The part that still smelled burning journal pages. But the larger part—not the scientist, but the woman—was blisteringly grateful to be saved. And curious.

What did Rath look like under those leathers?

I *did not* look back to the sleeping slab.

Rath stepped closer, each footfall thundering through the volcanic stone. The heat radiating from him intensified, warping the air between us. My traitorous pulse quickened as his shadow engulfed me, the ridges of his scales catching the firelight in fractal patterns that danced across my skin.

"Convenience and survival are often at odds," he rumbled, his voice lower than the geothermal hum in the walls. His claw traced the table's edge beside my hand, black talon scoring a hairline fracture in the stone. "You'll adapt."

"Adaptation requires time. You've given me nothing but

vague threats and ..." My gaze flicked to the bed platform, its silks shimmering with invitation. *Damn it.* "Theatrics."

His nostrils flared, the piercings along his brow ridge glinting as he leaned in. "You want data, scientist?" His breath scorched my temple. "Your pulse is elevated. You're sweating. And your scent ..." A low growl rumbled through my shoulder where his claw brushed my tattered sleeve. "Betrays more than your words."

I jerked back, the table's edge biting into my thighs. "It's about a thousand degrees in here."

"Liar." His tail lashed. "You reek of ..." His tongue flickered out, tip grazing my collarbone. My knees almost buckled at the sensation—a thousand nerve endings igniting under that brief contact. "Curiosity."

An echoing knock shattered the charged silence like a stone through glass. Rath's growl vibrated through me once more as he stalked toward the door, his tail lashing a warning pattern against the tiles. I sagged against the table, my fingers trembling as I pressed them to the spot his tongue had touched—skin still buzzing as though he'd branded me with electricity.

He wrenched the door open with a snarl. "This is not—"

Terra stood framed in the archway, her green eyes sharp as broken bottle glass. She didn't flinch at Rath's bared fangs, her gaze sliding past him to lock onto me before she pushed past him and entered the room. "You're alive. Good."

I straightened, tugging my shredded sleeve over the scratch marks on my arm. "Mostly."

Rath tried to further block her path, wings flaring. "Leave."

"I just spent a half hour listening to my mate describe *in detail* what he plans to do to you. Do not test me right now." Terra cocked her hip, hand resting near the plasma pistol at her thigh. "We need to talk."

The standoff crackled—two predators sizing each other up.

I edged around the table, hyper aware of Rath's scales flushing crimson along his spine.

"It's fine," I said.

His claws flexed. "She's—"

"My friend. Let her in."

Rath's pupils narrowed to slits, but he stepped aside with a hiss that made the heat crystals dim. Terra strode in, her boots leaving ashen prints on the polished stone.

"Cute love nest," she said, surveying the weapon-lined walls. "Very ... dungeon-core chic."

I choked back a laugh. "He's going for murderous hermit aesthetic."

Rath made a rumbling sound in the back of his throat. "As I said, this mating was unplanned."

I looked over at my ... mate. The word felt strange in my head. "Can we have some privacy?"

He opened his mouth, and I could almost hear the denial. Then he nodded. "Anything for you, *shyrarva*. I shall go see that your things are moved here."

"Don't call me that." But I was speaking to his retreating wings and then the closed door.

That left Terra and I alone.

"So they're all like that," she muttered. "Karyseth's work?" she asked, nodding towards my torn shirt. Her voice stayed neutral, but the set of her jaw betrayed her anger.

"Priestly hospitality." I forced a smile, leaning into the familiar routine of banter—Terra's no-nonsense words, the faint citrus scent of her soap. Grounding. Human.

She clicked her tongue. "I expect Selene will be breaking down that door as soon as she hears. You've still got cracked ribs that never fully healed. And this—" Her fingers brushed the crescent marks on my wrist where Rath's claws had gripped too tight. "The Drakarn aren't gentle, even when they try. I don't like this."

I stared at the wall of weapons, their edges catching the light in prismatic shards. "It kept me breathing."

"For now." Terra stepped back, her gaze sharp as a scalpel. "It wasn't just Rath that Darrokar was yelling about. This situation with the Forge Temple could get bad. Some on the council are far more sympathetic than they are to us." Her tone softened. "He called you *shyrarva*. That's a mating name; he spent time thinking about it. Whatever's going on with him—"

The alien word prickled my skin like sunburn. "It's just part of the act."

"You think this is an act? Is that what he said?" She launched herself up so she was sitting on Rath's—our?—table.

"You think he's for real?"

There is no unclaiming.

"Drakarn don't fake bond-marks. That tongue thing he did?" She fanned herself exaggeratedly. "Hot damn."

I hated how my cheeks flamed.

Terra's boots swung inches above the floor, the casual motion at odds with the tension in her voice. "The Blade Council tolerates us because Darrokar's mate-bond gives me standing. But Karyseth's faction?" She tapped her fingernails against the table, each click echoing like a gunshot. "They've been itching for an excuse to purge 'weakness' from Scalvaris. You just handed them a flamethrower."

I traced a fracture in the stone, my nail catching on micro-crystalline edges. "So the solution is ... what? Let Rath keep pretending we're soulmates?" The word tasted absurd, like trying to swallow a neutron star. "There have to be protocols for cultural misunderstandings. Mediated dialogues—"

"This isn't a UN summit." Terra hopped down, boots

scraping against the floor. "This is their holy law. Either the bond's real, or it's heresy. No third option." She gripped my shoulders, her callouses catching on torn fabric. "If the Forge Temple can prove this is a sham? They'll execute you. Then they'll come for the rest of us, arguing humans corrupt their warriors' honor."

"Rath said the claim was permanent. That there's no undoing it."

"Because there isn't." Terra's gaze drifted to the silks pooled on the sleeping slab. "Drakarn bonds aren't human. Darrokar nearly ripped a warrior's throat out for brushing against me during the monsoon feasts." Her eyes raked over the fresh scab on my lip. "When Rath tasted you ..."

Heat flooded my cheeks again. "It was nothing."

"Bullshit." She released me to pace past Rath's arsenal, fingers trailing over a curved blade.

The memory of his tongue flicking my collarbone ignited phantom static across my skin. "He called me a problem."

"And stared at you like you're a damned supernova." Terra spun a dagger, the edge catching firelight. "Bond-marks are ... physical. Biological. Believe me; I know. The council could demand proof." Her gaze dropped to my neck, where Rath's tongue had left invisible burns. "If they test you—"

"*Test?*" The word curdled in my stomach. I pressed a hand to the scar below my ear, still humming with phantom heat. "What kind of test?"

The door groaned before she could answer. Rath filled the archway, his scales dulled to burnt umber in the low light. A leather satchel hung from his claw, spilling familiar items—my scanner, a bundle of rock samples, the cracked remains of my field goggles. And some clothes. He set it down with surprising care, the contents clinking.

"Your possessions," he rumbled. "Including this." From his

belt, he produced my journal—singed but intact, its pages warped from fire.

I lunged forward, snatching it before logic intervened. The leather cover was a bit scorched. "You stole this from the pyre?"

His tail twitched. "Salvaged. Before the final blaze."

The admission startled me. I flipped through crackling pages—sketches of ventilation shafts intact, soil pH tables legible beneath soot stains. My throat tightened. "Thank you."

Rath inclined his head, the gesture almost courtly. "Of course, *shyrarva.*"

The alien word pricked like a splinter. "I have a name."

"We'll talk about this more later," Terra said before Rath and I could get into it. "Just stay strong. Sell this bond." She turned toward the door and paused before looking back. "If you need someone to talk this out, you know where I live."

"My mate can speak with me," Rath growled.

Terra and I both rolled our eyes.

"Thanks," I told her. "I'll think about what you said."

As if I could think about anything else.

———

I needed to sit. The adrenaline crash had settled into an ache in my skull. I crossed the room, wanting distance from him, and dropped onto the corner stone bench. The basalt was cold beneath me despite the warmth radiating off the chamber walls.

I gripped the edge of the bench and pressed my palms tight against its rough surface. My mind played the scene from the temple again, unspooling every scream and snarl until I winced. The memory of Karyseth's claws swiping inches from my chest made my pulse race. My body ached from running, from falling, from everything.

"You should take the bed," Rath's voice broke the silence. It carried low and steady, like the rumble of distant magma.

I looked up. He was standing near the platform, his tail coiled tightly behind him, his claws flexing in and out. The lines of his face were rigid—the air of a creature used to commanding obedience—but his tone had softened. "You need rest."

I shook my head, trying for a semblance of control. "I'll make do here."

"You aren't fine." He stepped closer, his broad shoulders tense. The weight of his presence filled the room like a flame creeping closer, heating everything in its path. "You're bruised."

I laughed, bitter and quiet. "Don't worry about me. You've done enough already."

He looked startled at my words, like I'd struck him. His chest expanded with a sharp inhale, faint embers lighting beneath his scales. "Do not mistake necessity for—" He stopped, his tail lashing against the floor. "The claim was to save your life. But it is my responsibility now to see to your health."

"I didn't ask for that."

"No," he admitted, the single word scraped raw. "But you are." He stepped closer still, heat rolling off him in waves. "And I protect what is mine."

The word *mine* sent a shiver through me. I tried to suppress it. Failed. I stood, the aching protests of my body ignored, and faced him—one hand gripping the edge of the bench for steadiness, the other clenched into a fist by my side. "I am not *yours*. I am my own person. And I can take care of myself." Not that I was doing very well at that right now.

If my defiance rattled him, he didn't show it. His slitted pupils narrowed further, the faintest growl vibrating from deep within his chest. "You can barely stand."

I glared at him. "Yeah? Whose fault is that?"

The growl cut off, his jaw tightening as heat flared briefly along his scales. He didn't respond.

I forced myself to break eye contact, grabbing the nearest folded blanket from edge of the sleeping platform. "I'll sleep over here tonight," I said, my voice sharp but quieter now. "I've crashed on a couch before." Of course, those couches had cushions. But the Drakarn were not soft. Apparently, they didn't care about comfort.

"You're being stubborn," he replied.

"And you're being overbearing."

A long pause stretched between us. Eventually, Rath exhaled a sharp breath. It came out like a hiss, his tail flicking the edge of the floor. "Fine." His voice was cold, the diplomacy gone. "Do what you want."

The space between us rippled with tension. I sat heavily on the couch, wrapping the blanket around myself stubbornly. My ribs flared a fresh complaint, but I ignored it.

Rath settled onto the stone platform across the room. His movements weren't loud, but every scrape of claw against obsidian battered my senses. He sat rigidly, his broad back facing me. The glow of the heat crystals cast faint, pulsing patterns over his wings, which drooped slightly now, less tension in the sinewed muscles around them.

We didn't say anything else. I pulled the blanket tightly around my shoulders and propped a pillow between the wall and my aching ribs. My body begged for stillness, but my mind wouldn't quiet.

The events of the day looped through my thoughts like a jagged-edged film reel. Karyseth's accusing snarl, the hissing crowd, the sensation of Rath's claws tearing through the zealots' ranks to claim me—each memory spiraled into the next. My fingers drifted to my neck where his tongue had left an invisible brand, heat still radiating beneath the skin every time I thought of the phrase, *"She is mine."*

I squeezed my eyes closed, trying to focus on the pain—more tangible sensations. My ribs, still tender, resisted when I shifted positions. My palms stung where I'd scraped against jagged rock while fleeing. My shoulders cried out from hours of tension. The couch was too hard to offer relief, no matter how I contorted myself.

Sleep didn't come easily. My mind stayed alert, cataloging every sensation, every flicker of uncertainty crawling over my skin. The warmth of the chamber wrapped around me like a smothering blanket, layering atop the press of Rath's invisible gaze. I doubted he'd turned to look, but I could still feel him—could hear his steady breaths above the ambient noise of the city. There was something about his proximity that made it impossible for me to relax, no matter what position I shifted into.

My ribs rebelled again, a sharp ache cutting through my chest. I groaned and bit back a curse.

"You're still awake." His voice broke the quiet, startling me.

"I'll sleep eventually."

I didn't.

4

RATH

THE RIVER MARKET roared with life as we entered, its heartbeat pulsing alongside the river winding through the city's core. Reflections from the water and heat crystals played across market stalls and stone ceilings, casting moving shadows.

Voices rose and fell in waves: merchants hawking fire-etched jewelry, farmers shouting over crates of krysfruit, and warriors exchanging boasts while sharpening their lava-forged blades. The heat radiating from the stones beneath our feet pressed upward, intensifying with the crush of bodies.

Orla walked at my side, her eyes darting across the crowd with equal parts curiosity and unease. I let my wing brush against her, and she gave me a wavering smile. My tail flicked once, irritated—not at her, but at the stares and whispers that followed us, and the way her shoulders drew tight under their weight.

Let them stare. Let them see my claim and understand the price of disrespect.

It had been two days since the claiming, since she'd held a blade to my throat, and I'd tasted her pulse under my tongue. Two days of torture where she kept her distance but hadn't left my quarters. Two days of her sleeping in a little burrow against one wall made of scavenged silks and pillows as if I hadn't offered her sole use of the bed.

So close, and yet I was not invited to touch.

Not yet.

She'd wrapped herself in one of my spare tunics, cinching the fabric at her waist with a belt she'd found in her satchel.

My mate. *Mine.*

That truth burned beneath my ribs, stronger than the voices around us.

The problem was obvious. My bond with Orla—a human, an outsider—would be challenged. The priestess had made her doubts clear, and already the rumors were taking hold. This walk wasn't just for her safety.

Scalvaris thrived on appearances. If they saw us together, if they saw her protected and claimed, perhaps the whispers would quiet—or at least recede to the darkest shadows where they would eventually die.

But her discomfort was a persistent stress against my instincts. It was as real as the storm-salt scent that clung to her. Her pulse stayed steady, not spiked with fear, but the tension in her jaw and the press of her lips said enough.

I reached down and brushed the back of my hand against hers. She blinked, her sharp chin tilting toward me. She drew in a quick breath, and the faint color blooming in her cheeks sparked something in my chest I didn't fully understand.

"Are we here to get something in particular?" she asked, her gaze shifting to a vendor selling polished stone carvings.

"I thought you would like to see the market," I lied.

Her thin brows rose, disbelief plain. I tightened my wings against my back, though their membranes itched to flare in denial. She was clever, my Orla. Too clever.

"This has nothing to do with flexing your wings at everyone

here?" Her tone was dry, though a flicker of curiosity lurked behind her words.

"Nothing," I said evenly.

Her snort was quiet but unmistakable. "Sure. I'll play along. Show me the market, which I have definitely not walked through almost every day since I got here."

We passed a group of younglings crouched near a tiled fountain, their eyes darting toward Orla before flicking away. She stiffened at their scrutiny, and I swallowed the growl that threatened to rise. My scales felt hot against the back of my neck, but I forced myself to stay composed.

"Drakarn diplomacy at its finest," Orla muttered, crossing her arms over her chest.

I stopped at a stall displaying stylized carvings made from heat crystals. Orla paused beside me, her eyes narrowing as she studied the goods. I reached for a hand-sized crystal shaped like a flowing wave, its edges pulsing faintly with gold light.

Her brow furrowed. "What are you doing?"

"They call this enlightenment stone," I said, avoiding her question. "It's said to reflect the holder's true emotions."

"We have something like that on Earth," she said, her fingers twitching toward the edge of the table. I knew the habit —her engineer's instincts itching to take things apart, to understand their workings. "They're called mood rings. They just react to body heat."

The merchant, a gray-scaled artisan with worn claws, grunted. "Pretty. For a pretty lady."

I stiffened at his tone, but Orla only shrugged, her lips tilting in faint humor. "Pretty's not bad."

I placed the crystal in her palm, ignoring the merchant's sharp intake of breath. Drakarn didn't give gifts lightly, not without meaning. But I wanted her to feel something other than the weight of this unfamiliar world.

Her fingers curled around the crystal, her lashes lowering as she examined the glow. I held my breath as she murmured, "Fascinating," the word so soft it barely carried above the noise. The crystal's gold hue deepened to fiery orange where her fingers pressed into its surface.

My tail curled instinctively, satisfaction simmering low in my chest. Just as quickly, her hand hovered, the crystal held out in silent offering to return it. "It's beautiful, but I—"

"Keep it," I said sharply enough that the merchant flinched. "It's yours."

She hesitated, her lips parting in protest. But when her eyes met mine, I saw the shift. Her resistance softened, something unspoken lingering in its place.

"Alright," she said at last, the word carrying no edge.

I felt the tension in my shoulders ease as I handed over a few coins and we moved on.

The market's edge opened into a quieter stretch, where the crowd thinned and the noise faded to scattered conversations. The cobblestones beneath our feet gleamed faintly, their grooves worn smooth by countless years of footsteps. Here, the air didn't press as heavily, though Orla's posture stayed stiff.

"This ..." Her voice broke the silence, hesitant. "All of it. It's a little overwhelming. I feel like everyone's staring at me. Even more than usual."

I fell into step beside her. "It will calm down. I'm sure some warrior will make a spectacle of himself, and all eyes will turn to him."

She let out a short laugh. "Like he'll claim a human in the middle of a crowded temple to save her from certain death?"

I considered her for a moment before speaking. "When you put it like that, I concede it may take a little more time."

"Great."

Dwelling on possibilities would do us no good. "Come," I said finally, gesturing to an alcove ahead. Its sloped ramp curved upward, a decent launch point.

She glanced at the entrance, her lips pressing into a thin line. "Where—"

"Not far. Trust me."

Her brow arched, skepticism plain. "The last time I trusted you ..."

I smiled faintly and held out a hand.

She walked with me. Each step carried us higher, the market noise getting fainter. I glanced back once, checking her footing, but she moved steadily, her gaze focused.

She squinted at the view, her hands braced on her hips. "Is this ... a vent? You really know how to show a girl a good time."

I barked a laugh. "A vent? No, this is a launch point. From here, the air will carry us above the city." My wings flexed slightly. "Would you like to see it?"

Her brows furrowed, her lips parting in what I guessed was an objection. "Wait— You— What are you suggesting?"

I stepped closer, letting my wings spread to catch the air. "Fly with me."

Her gaze darted to the cave ceiling high above, then back to me, her hesitation clear. But there was something else, something fragile that flickered behind her sharp exterior. She was a scientist, a curious woman, and fearless enough to wonder. She bit her lip, and I could see the moment curiosity won out.

She stepped close. "If you drop me, I swear—"

I grinned, something warm unfurling beneath my ribs. "I wouldn't dare."

She stiffened as I wrapped an arm around her waist, my claws brushing the fabric of her tunic to steady her. My tail curled lightly around her knees, ensuring her balance, and she made a surprised sound that went straight through me. I had to clench my jaw as blood rushed to my cock. The warmth of her seeped through the thin layers of clothing, her scent filling the space between us.

"Relax," I murmured when her hands clutched reflexively at my shoulders. Her tension rippled through me, though it was matched by a steady courage I couldn't help but admire. "I have you."

Without giving her time to second-guess, I crouched slightly and leapt, wings snapping open to catch the warm spirals of air. The force of the launch pressed her tighter against me, her gasp muffled as the currents caught us, my wings lifting us effortlessly into the sky.

Below, the ledge and the narrow shaft vanished, swallowed by the shimmering cityscape of Scalvaris. The river wound through the volcanic architecture like glass, its glow constant against the dark stone. The spires of the city stretched high to where they brushed the edges of our cavernous home in some places.

Orla clung to me, her arms locked tightly around my shoulders. Her breath came in quick bursts against my neck, but her fear began to ebb as she tilted her head to take in the view.

"This is," she started, her words faltering. She leaned slightly, her gaze sweeping over the expanse below us. "This is incredible."

I banked slightly, adjusting my wings to glide along the natural updrafts. "The city looks different from above. No busybodies."

"It's ..." Her voice trailed off again, her brow furrowing as if searching for the right words. Finally, she shook her head. "I don't even know how to describe it."

Her reaction stirred something deep in my chest. I couldn't explain why her awe mattered to me, but it did.

Her grip loosened slightly, and the tension in her shoulders melted away as she adjusted to the rhythm of the air. For the first time in days, she looked at peace.

I angled us toward the higher cavers, their jagged entrances almost invisible against all the rock. An even narrower fissure came into view, its entrance obscured by shadows. I guided us inside, the currents shifting as we dipped into the hidden space. The air cooled slightly, the light dimming as we flew through a shaft barely large enough for my wings until the cavern opened up around us, and a large skyshaft illuminated the room around us in natural light.

Luminous heat crystals lined the walls, their glow pulsating in vibrant waves of red, orange, and blue. Pools of water teeming with life shimmered across the cavern floor, their surfaces reflecting the light in rippling patterns.

I landed softly on a ledge near the cavern's center, releasing Orla carefully. Her feet found solid ground, but she didn't move immediately. Her head tilted back as her eyes widened, taking in the light and color that surrounded us.

"This," she said, her voice barely above a whisper. "This is..."

There were no words. I stepped back and let her take it all in.

She turned in a slow circle, her fingers brushing the stone walls. The light danced across her skin, painting her in shifting hues. "It's like nothing I've ever seen. How is this here? Untouched?"

"This is a sanctuary," I said simply. "Few know of it. I discovered it when I was a boy."

Her gaze flicked to me, questioning. "And you brought me here."

"Yes," I said, my tone steady. "Because I wanted you to see it."

She hesitated, her fingers pausing over a crystal vein that pulsed faintly under her touch. "Why?"

The question hung between us, heavier than I'd expected. I could have given her a hundred reasons—about trust, about showing her my world—but the truth felt too raw, too unformed to articulate. She was my mate. All that I was belonged to her.

"Because you should," I said at last. "This place is ... it's what Scalvaris is beyond the fire and ash. It's what matters."

She studied me for a moment, her expression unreadable. Then she turned back to the crystals, her hand tracing the patterns with a softness I hadn't seen in her before.

"It's beautiful," she murmured.

I didn't respond, letting her take it in. Her presence here felt right in a way I couldn't explain, like the cavern itself welcomed her. Watching her, I felt something settle deep in my chest—something dangerous; something I couldn't yet name.

She moved toward one of the pools, crouching at its edge. The liquid shimmered faintly, its surface undisturbed. Her reflection wavered as she leaned closer, her curiosity pulling her into the moment.

But then, her footing shifted. A loose stone cracked under her weight, and she wobbled, her arms flailing for balance.

I lunged, my wings flaring as my tail wrapped around her waist. She yelped softly as I pulled her back, her feet dangling briefly above the edge before I set her down, steadying her with both hands.

Her chest rose and fell rapidly, her pulse a beat against my palms. "Um ... thanks," she muttered, her cheeks a charming shade of red.

"Be careful," I said, my voice low. My grip on her tightened briefly, the edge creeping in despite myself. "This place isn't forgiving."

She looked up at me, her face inches from mine. Her breath was warm against my jaw, and for a moment, the cavern seemed to shrink around us, the air thick with something unspoken.

"It's just a pool of water," she reconsidered. "Right? It's not acid or filled with some sort of flesh-eating bacteria, is it?"

"It's water," I confirmed. But I hadn't let her go.

I didn't move, my gaze locked on hers. The urge to close the distance, to claim what was mine, burned through me, sharp and insistent. But I held back, the weight of the moment balanced on a fragile edge.

Her eyes—so green they put the finest gems of Scalvaris to shame—held mine with an intensity that made the cavern feel smaller, the air between us warmer. She was breathing a little faster now, her chest brushing lightly against me with each inhale. The moment was pressing in on her too.

Good. She felt it.

Everything about her drew me in—her stubborn tilt of the chin, the faint smudge of krysfruit still on her cheek from earlier, the way her hair caught the flickering light and haloed her head in fire.

My mate. Everything in me roared with the truth of that word.

I shifted closer, just a fraction. Her gaze dropped to my lips, then shot back to my eyes, a quick flicker that didn't escape me. She was thinking about it. I had to choke back a groan as her tongue darted out, wetting her lips.

Orla, my storm-salt human, had no idea the ruinous effect that small action had on me.

Her lips were full, softly curved, and I imagined how they'd feel against mine—how they'd taste. The memory of her pulse beneath my tongue still haunted me, that intoxicating warmth lingering in my senses long after we'd pulled apart. Giving her a mark, a claim she couldn't ignore, had been the only thing that quelled my lust that night.

For now.

I angled my body closer, allowing my wing to brush against her. Her quiet intake of breath told me she wasn't entirely unaffected. The tension in her shoulders had loosened, her weight shifting ever so slightly toward me.

The cavern echoed around us, the water's soft lap against the stones providing a rhythmic beat. She tilted her head up just a fraction, presenting that delicate curve of her neck, and my mind spun with the images of my teeth grazing her soft flesh, of her moans vibrating through me as I worshipped her body.

Calm down.

Patience.

"I—" she began, her voice barely a whisper, but she didn't continue.

My tail, still possessively curled around her lower body, loosened its grip just enough to let her feel the tension coiled in me. She looked down, surprised by the delicate hold I had, then back at my face, her eyes wide and unguarded.

That thought alone stoked the fire within me. My lips twitched in a half-smile as I imagined her, hair wild and flushed, biting her lip as she hovered over me in our bed. *Ours.*

She caught her lip between her teeth—and there it was again. That small action, that sliver of vulnerability that threatened to rip what little control I had left to shreds. I leaned in just a breath more, my mouth a breath from hers, the heat between us undeniable.

But she stepped back, her hand brushing against her waist where my tail had been. "You're right," she said, her tone lighter now, almost teasing. "I should be more careful."

I exhaled, the tension in my chest easing just enough to speak. "You certainly keep me on edge."

Her lips quirked faintly, the barest hint of a smile. "I'll take that as a compliment."

If I wasn't careful, this human would be the end of me.

5

ORLA

RATH'S QUARTERS FELT CRAMPED, and not because of the walls. The space itself was more than large enough—ample room for his oversized bed platform, his towering racks of weapons, and his peculiar collection of volcanic relics that sat arranged with obsessive neatness. Even the row of silken tunics in his closet space that I hesitated to touch hung spaced precisely apart.

Despite the size, the air seemed to press in on me, heavy and unrelenting.

I didn't care if the temperature-controlled sheets were some engineering marvel or if Rath thought my scanner and rock samples from my satchel should be displayed like trophies. None of that mattered—not when every surface of the room exuded *him*.

His heat clung to the walls. His scent—the faint aroma of charred air and metal—saturated the space. His essence lingered like those wings of his, wrapping around me even in his absence.

I could only take so much before I went crazy.

Two days after that ... *moment* in the hidden cavern, and I needed an escape.

Rath had left early in the morning, mumbling something about council meetings and an overdue conversation with Darrokar. For someone so usually direct, his reluctance to step away had been blatant.

His gaze had lingered over me, eyes gleaming with an unshakable intensity that seemed to bypass verbal barriers. He'd stopped masking it. That heat, that quiet certainty—it was everywhere now. And it filled the chamber to the brim, a threat ... or a promise.

I pulled one of his tunics tighter around myself, its fabric absurdly light but efficient against the wind in the tunnels. My usual work shirt hadn't seen the light of day since the temple disaster, shredded into something unwearable. I had other clothes I could wear, but if I was being honest—with myself, at least—I liked the way the tunic faintly carried his scent.

Pathetic, Orla.

I slipped out of the room before my thoughts could spiral deeper. His chambers sat deep enough within Scalvaris that wandering unnoticed wasn't hard—except for the prickling sense that I was doing something wrong.

Whether it was a paranoid trick of the mind or those zealots lurking just out of sight, I didn't know. But it didn't stop me from pressing forward. My boots echoed against the carved stone floor as I threaded through corridors, the veins of heat crystals casting faint orange light along my path.

The carved arteries of the city felt alive, their high-ceilinged passages whispering with the pulse of steam vents and rushing water systems below. Crossing busier intersections felt overwhelming—hissing pipes venting heat, Drakarn warriors sharpening blades, and artisans hauling crates of glimmering crystals. Bits of guttural words reached me in clipped fragments, their consonants rippled with unmistakable curiosity whenever I passed. I kept my head down.

By the time I veered into the quieter halls leading toward the human quarters, I felt brittle. Like one wrong breath would snap me in two.

The enclave for the crew had been carved into an alcove smaller and plainer than any Drakarn living space that I'd seen —not that I'd seen many, but I welcomed the dimmer atmosphere. The air felt cooler here, soothing the perpetual flush lingering on my skin.

I hesitated near the edge of the communal space, listening. Kira was murmuring to someone, possibly baking if she had the supplies, and Eden's habitual humming—no surprises there. But when I heard Selene's voice—a calm, familiar low timbre edged with her usual combat-medic steadiness—I knew exactly where I was headed.

Knocking softly at her door, I leaned into the cool stone wall.

"Come in," she called easily, warmth coating her voice.

Selene's quarters weren't much bigger than mine had been, yet she'd managed to make the small space her own. Every piece of equipment—medical or otherwise—sat in perfect order on her table. The faint scent of antiseptic mixed with something floral, maybe herbal tea. She glanced up as I stepped inside, a roll of bandages still in her hands, her braid shifting over one shoulder.

"Big, red, and broody let you sneak away?" she teased, setting the bandages down with a flourish.

I snorted, slumping into one of the stiff-backed chairs she'd tucked against the wall. "Not exactly. He's in a meeting. I got away before he could do anything about it. Talk about suffocating." The words tasted wrong on my tongue. Not quite a lie but definitely not the truth. Rath had been accommodating, kind, without pressing for anything I wasn't ready to give.

Her brows quirked, a wry smile tugging at her lips.

"Could've fooled me. Kaiya saw you two in the market. She said it was *quite* the sight."

I groaned, my hands flying to cover my face. "Please. Just don't." My voice was half-laugh, half-groan.

Selene laughed softly, leaning against the table, arms folded. "Sorry, sorry. No teasing. Not right now, at least." She gave me a sympathetic look. "For real, how is it?"

Before I could answer, a familiar figure filled the doorframe briefly, tray in hand, likely on her way to the communal oven. Kira caught neither my gaze nor Selene's, murmured something apologetic, and disappeared down the corridor again before I could even finish my frown.

"Is she okay?" I asked. She'd seemed depressed ever since I woke up there. But maybe that was just how she was; it wasn't like I'd known her before all of *this*.

Selene's sigh was deep and slow. "She's hanging on, but she's not okay. Her sister was on the other side of the ship before the crash. The uncertainty is worse than grief; it's a wound she can't stop picking at."

My stomach twisted, guilt mixing uncomfortably with weariness. "That's terrible," I muttered, staring blankly at the polished surface of the table. It was bad enough knowing I'd never see Earth again, but I'd made that decision when I signed up to leave. Volcaryth wasn't the intended destination, but I was starting to adjust, at least a little. To lose a sister, though?

Selene's voice softened again. "We're all dealing with something," she said, her careful gaze settling on me. "Which brings us back to you and your Drakarn shadow. I want details. How did this happen?"

I hesitated, fumbling for words that didn't all sound hysterical. "I ... have no freaking clue," I finally said, picking absently at one loose thread in my borrowed tunic sleeve. "I'm stuck with him—and part of me, god ... I think part of me might actually ..."

"You're allowed to like him, Orla." Her smile was faintly amused but far from cruel. "No one back on Earth is going to chastise you for caring about someone. Even fire-breathing aliens."

"They don't breathe fire," I said, as if that was the important part. "I don't even *know* him. And this mating thing? This ... supposed mystical, permanent 'bond'? It feels absurd. We're from different planets. How can there be something ... meant to be?"

She didn't laugh this time. "Terra's figured it out with Darrokar." Her voice held a quiet steadiness, the kind reserved for those who'd already pieced together the advice you weren't ready to hear. "Might not hurt to ask her."

"There's nothing *to* figure out," I countered, wrapping my arms around myself. "I didn't ask for any of this." The memory clawed its way back—zealots surrounding me, Karyseth's venomous words, blood slipping down my skin onto that damned altar. A shudder rippled through me, bone deep. I crossed my arms tighter. It wasn't enough to hold the memories at bay.

Selene's gaze softened, but she didn't argue. Her elbows rested on the table as she watched me in that unnervingly steady way medics had. Like she wasn't just treating wounds but cataloging whatever might linger beneath. When she finally spoke, her words cut straight through my defenses. "And yet, here you are, sitting in his tunic, spilling over with more anger about liking him than the fact he nearly tore a priestess to shreds to keep you safe."

The floor felt suddenly unstable beneath me. I opened my mouth to deny it, but no words came out.

Damn her and that disarming precision.

"Look ... I'm not saying you need to declare your undying devotion after four days. But maybe instead of running from what's happening as fast as you can, sit with it. Decide what you actually want, not just what's easiest."

I leaned back, wary. "You think this is easy?"

"It's easier than admitting he matters." She nodded toward the tunic I was fidgeting with, a faint, teasing smile brushing her lips. "He's right there, on your skin, and you're fighting him tooth and nail."

I groaned, pressing both hands to my forehead. "He's not just overwhelming. He's ... consuming. He looks at me, and ..." My voice broke slightly, the heat rising to my cheeks as I remembered how Rath's eyes blazed when he called me *shyrarva*—like I was the center of everything his world revolved around. "He's so sure, like he knew this was inevitable. And I— I don't *get* how that feels real."

She stood quietly, her fingers returning to sort through folded bandages. "If this is going to be your reality, you'll need to decide sooner or later if Rath is part of your plan. Because from what I've seen?" She smirked faintly. "He's already made his choice."

Her words hit me harder than I wanted to admit. I slouched deeper into the chair, stubbornly tracing the carved heat veins lining the wall. Despite my hesitation—and outright denial—something kept pulling me toward him, as inevitable as a current in rushing water. But I refused to put that into words. Refused to let her see my hesitation grow roots.

"I should get going. Kira's probably five loaves deep into baking mode," I said, forcing a weak laugh as I stood, brushing off the details too big to face directly.

"You mean before Rath realizes you're gone and goes scorched earth on the city to find you?" Selene quipped smoothly, already stacking supplies back onto her shelves.

Her comment stopped just short of teasing, but it still nudged too close to reality. I waved her off and let myself out, the door clicking softly shut behind me.

The tunnels were quieter now, the soundscape reduced to the occasional hiss of steam vents far above. The market district lights had probably dimmed by now, and I imagined the bustling trade had slowed to murmur and flicker.

But Selene's questions still churned. What role did I want Rath to have in my life? *Did* I want Rath in my life? Did any of it even matter? The bond couldn't be broken. We were stuck on this planet. What choice did I even have?

My thoughts spiraled violently as I walked. Time moved strangely in Scalvaris with the suns blotted out by so much rock, it was difficult to keep track. When I reached the tighter corridors leading to Rath's quarters, the silence weighed too heavy. Something chafed against my instincts, the kind of subtle wrongness that set alarms I couldn't ignore.

The corridor felt empty—but not the kind of empty that invited peace. The eerie sort, like the silence of predators just before striking. Heat crystal veins faintly lit the walls, painting jagged shadows across the passage floor, their occasional flickers betraying any movement.

My heart thudded faster. Each step felt heavier. My fingers flexed reflexively at my sides, searching for something to anchor to as the unease crawled across my skin. If someone was following me, I didn't want to confirm it by turning.

Then, just ahead, the shadows wavered unnaturally before solidifying into a hulking figure.

Drakarn.

I stopped breathing for half a heartbeat. Dark scales glistened against the crystal's dim light, their edges marked with dark red burns that'd fused them jagged near the warrior's left jawline. His wings hung poised, their membranes catching barely enough light to seem like a predator fanning them before striking. All menace. His slitted eyes warmed with barely contained hostility as his snout lifted to fix me under his unwavering scrutiny.

I knew him. One of Karyseth's zealots—Krazath. Those burns hadn't been there the last time I'd seen him.

The hate in his eyes? It had only grown stronger.

This was *so* not good.

6

ORLA

MY FEET WERE LEAD.

My fight-or-flight reflex leaned toward panic in both directions, but escaping through the narrow passage the towering Drakarn now filled wasn't an option.

If Krazath wanted me dead, running wouldn't do me any good.

I couldn't let him think I was weak. If the Drakarn were one thing, it was brazen. I couldn't be a meek little human. My voice came low, steady enough—though too sharp-edged to be safe. "Nice burns. Someone cooking a little too close to the lava vents?"

His sneer widened, with fangs catching the faint light. "Foul human," he rasped, his voice scraping like charred stones grinding against each other. His claws flexed as he crept forward, his tail dragging along the floor. "You crawl among us, stinking, frail ... You should be extinguished like vermin."

I squared myself, forcing calm into my stance even though I doubted it would last. "You're wasting my time." Stupid. Taunting a zealot was idiotic, reckless even.

But something hot inside me couldn't be cautious. Not right now.

I think I really hate this guy.

Krazath's eyes narrowed, his yellow pupils contracting into sharp slits. Heat radiated from him, thick and stifling. His tail struck the ground with a crack that rolled through the stone like thunder.

"You, and all your kind, pollute this place," he spat. "Soft, brittle things who scavenge at the feet of real power. You stand here because one of us allows it. Because the warrior lord is too blind to see what filth he's bathed himself in."

"Funny," I said, my voice steadier than I expected. "Considering you're spending your time cornering one of us *weaklings*, I'd say you're the one dragging down the honor of your people. Picking on me doesn't make you powerful. It makes you pathetic."

Real smart, Orla. Poke the dragon some more.

Krazath's lips curled into a snarl. "Watch your tongue, *mokral*," he said, his claws raking across the stone wall. My translator couldn't handle that last word, but the tone was clear that it was an insult. "Rath's protection won't last forever. It's made a mockery of everything. No Drakarn worthy of their name allows himself to—" His sneer deepened, the next word practically spat from his mouth. "*Mate* with prey."

The insult hit me harder than it should have. I clenched my fists at my sides, the urge to lash out bubbling in my chest. My rational mind screamed at me to shut my mouth, to stay quiet, to de-escalate. But another part of me, that deep-seated fire Rath had somehow stoked, refused to back down.

"He doesn't seem ashamed to me," I bit out. "But if you have such a problem with him, why not take it up with Rath directly? Oh, that's right—you won't, because you'd lose. Badly."

The words left my mouth before I could weigh them, and the reaction was immediate. Krazath's eyes flared with rage, his tail slamming against the wall with enough force to send tiny fractures racing across the surface. It was getting hotter with every passing second, like a freaking furnace.

"You frail, arrogant worm," he hissed, taking a step forward. His wings flared slightly, casting long shadows down the passage. "You think you're untouchable because he chose you? Tell me, human, what will you do when this bond proves false? When the council strips him of his honor for this shame he's branded on himself?"

I gritted my teeth, taking an instinctive step back. The passage behind me was narrow, the walls rough against my fingertips, but there was no escape route. Krazath kept advancing, his hulking frame growing larger with every moment.

His tail lashed out again, brushing against the stone near my leg, close enough to send pebbles flying. My breath caught in my chest, panic dangerously close to winning out, but I refused to give him the satisfaction of showing it. My instincts screamed for help, but there was no one to hear me—not here. Not now.

The roar came like an eruption, not just loud but thick and guttural, shaking the air around us. The sound hit me in the chest, a physical force that reverberated down the passage.

Rath.

His shadow spread over us, massive, looming, impossibly huge. Krazath froze, his snarling confidence melting into something almost comically scared. Rath landed between us, wings unfurled, claws flexing at his sides with deliberate menace. His yellow eyes blazed, locking entirely on Krazath.

"Do you value your life so little that you'd dare threaten her?" Rath growled, the words a rough snarl that carried more weight than any shout could. Each syllable carved itself into the air, vibrating with intensity.

Krazath's wings twitched, retreating closer to his body. His composure cracked, though his own snarl remained, however dimmed. "I've done nothing to your human." His voice carried an edge of defiance. "But I will not hold my tongue. She doesn't belong here."

Rath's tail lashed sharply. He took a step closer, each movement deliberate, his wings brushing the walls as his presence swelled to fill the corridor. "She belongs where I say," he rumbled. "You've overstepped."

Under other circumstances I might have felt bad for Krazath.

Almost.

The tension between the two Drakarn was tangible. Rath's fury was a living, breathing thing, so heavy in the air I felt it pressing against my skin.

But Krazath wasn't done yet. He straightened, baring his fangs in a last-ditch show of bravado. "Your bond is a disgrace," his voice rose dangerously. "You weaken yourself by clinging to a creature so far beneath us. The council will not let this stand forever. Even you cannot—"

The motion was faster than I could track. In a blink, Rath's claws were at Krazath's throat, his tail coiled sharply around one of the other warrior's legs to keep him pinned. The force of his movement sent heat crystals shuddering.

Krazath froze, his wings pinned awkwardly against the stone as Rath pressed him into the wall. The tips of Rath's claws barely dented Krazath's scales, but it was enough. The promise of what they could do lingered in the air.

"You forget yourself," Rath snarled. "I have claimed her. The bond has been witnessed. Speak against it again, and you won't walk away."

Krazath stiffened, refusing to flinch despite the claws hovering near the vulnerable seam of his throat. "Kill me here, and you lose what little respect you still have." He had to strain to speak.

Rath didn't move, the menace radiating from him crackling in the air like charged embers. His claws flexed ever so slightly, enough to make Krazath's neck strain even harder against the pressure. Every muscle in Rath's body screamed restraint about to snap, held in place by a force of will barely tethered.

He wasn't going to back down. I wasn't sure he *could*. But I had a sinking suspicion Krazath was right.

"Rath."

The single syllable breached the suffocating silence. He didn't turn immediately, his wings still flared, chest rising and falling in bursts. But my voice had reached him. Slowly, his head shifted, eyes now more orange than yellow locking onto mine. They burned sharply, though beneath the fury ran something deeper—conflicted, something raw.

I took a cautious step closer, my pulse beating so fast and uneven it was dizzying. "Don't," I said, my voice quieter this time. "He's not worth it."

Rath's tail remained coiled, his claws unmoving. Then, with a deliberate exhale, Rath shoved Krazath back against the wall and released him.

Krazath stumbled, quickly regaining his footing, though his entire body bristled with humiliation. He glared at Rath, his wings twitching, itching for retaliation. But he didn't dare make a move.

"You forget yourself, Flame Heart," Krazath muttered, voice dripping with venom. His gaze flicked to me, the disdain in his expression twisting my stomach. "This will not end well for you. Or her."

Rath's growl vibrated through the stone floor beneath me. "Leave. Now."

Krazath's eyes narrowed, but he held his tongue. Slowly, he

retreated into the shadows, his claws scraping along the basalt wall until his shape dissolved into the distant gloom.

Silence filled the corridor again. The weight of everything hung around us, choking away the air as my pulse thudded in my ears. Rath still hadn't moved. His wings remained half-spread, his shoulders locked and tense, even as Krazath's form grew distant and then disappeared entirely.

All at once, my knees felt weak, and I leaned against the cooler wall for balance, dragging in sharp breaths. The corridor shrank around me—heat, emotions, fear, everything collapsing inward. But it wasn't *just* fear. I looked at Rath, at every line of tension in his frame, and saw something more than rage.

I found my voice, barely a whisper. "He's gone."

Rath didn't react immediately. His tail snapped behind him, short, tightly controlled arcs that betrayed his lingering agitation. It wasn't until I took a hesitant step closer, this time letting my fingers hover inches from him, that his focus shifted. He looked at me, and the edges of that predator's fire softened just a little.

"You're shaking," he said, his voice rough—hoarse, almost tender in its uneven delivery.

My whole body trembled, from adrenaline, from everything that had just happened. One hand clasped the fabric of my tunic. I was breathing too fast, too shallow. I was trying to ground myself, but the room still felt unsteady.

Without a word, Rath moved. Fluid. Deliberate.

In a single step, he closed the space between us, his massive hand landing softly against the small of my back while his tail wrapped securely around my legs. For a creature so imposing, his touch was shockingly careful, almost reverent. He pulled me toward him, the heat of his chest pressing into me like a shield against the world. His claws shifted, hesitant, before curving over the back of my head.

"You're safe," he murmured, his voice brittle, like the words were more for himself than for me. "No one will touch you. Not while I breathe."

The dam inside me broke. Hot tears spilled over before I could push them down, frustration and relief colliding in a way that was too much to hold in.

My fingers gripped the loose fabric of his tunic as my forehead rested lightly against his chest. There was no fighting it—no pushing him away even though some part of me insisted I should. I hated the comfort I found in his presence, hated that it settled me better than anything else.

Hated that I didn't pull away.

The tears came harder, and Rath didn't try to stop me. He held me close, his tail tightening just slightly to anchor me. His thumb brushed gently over my shoulder.

"Let it go," he said.

I shook my head weakly, voice muffled against the smooth scales of his chest. "I didn't ask for this."

"Neither did I." He was quieter now, laced with a kind of rawness that caught me off guard. His words hung there, heavy and unshielded.

I tilted my head to meet his gaze, expecting deflection or annoyance, something calculated. Instead, I found that same flicker of vulnerability—the crack running under all the searing confidence he projected. It did something to me, tugged at threads in my chest I didn't realize were tied so tightly.

"Why do you care so much?" The question escaped before I could stop it, more honest than I intended. I regretted it instantly. Surely, he wouldn't—

"You're mine," he said simply, like the answer was carved deep into his bones. His gaze burned, unrelenting in its certainty. "No one will touch you. Not Krazath. Not anyone."

I blinked, the weight of his words pressing into the space

between us. His voice carried no hesitation—just absolute conviction. It terrified me. Not because of the possessiveness, but because something in me wanted to believe him.

I snorted unsteadily, trying to mask the twisting warmth in my chest with something sarcastic. "Humans don't exactly subscribe to this 'fate-bonded forever' thing, you know."

Rath tilted his head. "Maybe that's why you shatter so easily," he said, not cruelly, but with a faint edge borne of an observation he couldn't possibly have made. "You're too quick to let go."

It should've annoyed me. It didn't. Instead, it settled somewhere deep, pulling at parts of myself I didn't want to examine.

Finally, I sighed, wiping the last of my tears with the back of my hand. "This won't stop them, you know," I said quietly. "The zealots, the council, Karyseth. They're not just going to let this slide." My voice faltered slightly, gesturing toward the corridor where Krazath had disappeared.

Rath's wings folded at last, his body slowly losing its tension. He stepped back half an inch—but only half. "Then let them come." His voice crackled with the threatening promise.

I groaned, thumping my head against his chest. "That's not an actual solution."

His lips twitched—not quite a smirk but enough to send that sharp curve of a fang glinting faintly. "It's the only one they'll understand."

I shook my head, torn between exasperation and something dangerously close to trust. "You're impossible."

His tail brushed briefly against my back before curling faintly near my feet again. "So are you."

The faintest, reluctant smile tugged at my lips. Maybe impossible wasn't so bad.

7

RATH

THE BLADE COUNCIL'S private chambers were near-silent, punctuated only by my claws drumming against the polished table. The room was cavernous and foreboding. No flames burned in the sconces—just the cool glow of heat crystals embedded in ancient walls. Normally, I found purpose in the hush, its weight sharpening thought and honing words. But now, all I could focus on were the whispers.

"... your bond is a disgrace ..."

Krazath's taunt clung to me, acid and unshakable. The effort it took not to rip his throat out still thrummed in my veins. I'd lost my temper before, but never so closely to losing full control. The memory of Orla's voice cutting through that red haze—steady, soft—kept me from digging my claws into the stone right now.

"If you scowl any harder, Rath, your face might stick that way."

Vyne's voice shattered the silence. He reclined in his chair, green scales catching the dim light. That smirk of his was always too wide, the gleam in his gaze constantly daring someone to test him.

"Careful," I warned. "You might tempt me to see how quick you really are."

His smirk only grew. "Bold words. Aren't mates supposed to mellow old warriors? You sure you shouldn't be off romancing your human instead of sulking like a fledgling?"

Heat crawled into my chest, roughening my tone. "And what would you know about mates, besides imaginary ones you put into terrible poems?"

A loud crack cut me off—Khorlar's fist crashing down on the table. His granite-gray scales looked dull, but that glare of his had enough force to still anyone.

"Enough," he said, voice like grinding stone. "If you wish to quarrel, do it elsewhere."

Vyne raised his hands in mock surrender, though mischief still danced in his eyes. I tamped down my anger with effort. He wasn't entirely wrong—my mind had been wandering all morning, and I hated that fact.

Darrokar finally spoke from the head of the table, where he'd sat in silent observation. Faint red pulses played across his black scales as he tapped his claws on the armrest. His voice held the weight of both his status and his role as my oldest ally and friend.

"We don't have time for squabbles," he said. "Your bond with Orla has thrown the council off-balance. Half see it as a betrayal of our ways. The others view it as proof of your strength in taming a wild creature. Either way, the whispers aren't stopping."

I bared my teeth, the tension building in my chest. "Let them whisper. Krazath, Karyseth—whoever challenges me will regret it. Besides, you have a human mate. They accepted her."

Darrokar's brow arched. "You've already nearly taken Krazath's head off, if the rumors are accurate. News of that is everywhere. And as for my mate, you were out on scout duty when I made my case. This new match has reignited all the resistance I faced."

Khorlar folded his broad arms, drawing my attention. "He's right. You may not have killed Krazath, but you almost did—and that's enough to stir trouble."

My anger flared again. "I won't hold back if someone threatens my mate. And Krazath is telling tales. I barely touched him."

"Be that as it may," Khorlar said calmly. "Your actions have fallout. Krazath is nobody, but his allies wait for you to lose control."

Every detail of last night was etched into my mind: Krazath cornering Orla, how her fear laced the air, how rage nearly consumed me. Only her voice had kept me from ripping his throat out.

Darrokar's deep tones cut in, "You're on a blade's edge, Rath. The council was wary enough of letting the humans stay. There are plenty who respect the Forge more than you, even if they are not adherents."

I usually would have argued, but Darrokar's words held too much truth to dismiss. I could feel the weight of them like a blade pressed to my neck.

"I will not let her go," I said, voice edged.

"Of course not," Darrokar snapped. "You need to be smarter. You built your place here through victories; win this battle the same way."

Khorlar nodded. "The people remember your strength in the River Trials, and how we took care of those lava beasts the Narvix tried to unleash on us. You can sway opinions, but not if you act like a mindless brute whenever your mate's involved."

I hated agreeing with them, but a seasoned part of my mind recognized the logic. The fire inside me, though—the one that began the moment Orla entered my life—raged at the thought of placating anyone who'd undermine her.

Vyne's drawl cut in again. "Maybe spend a little less time in bed with her and a little more time proving you're not going soft."

I shot him a glare that made his grin waver. He would never stop laughing if he knew I did all of this for a mate I had yet to even kiss. One taste had made me *this*.

When she finally opened herself fully to me ...

I couldn't think of that here, especially not now.

Darrokar rose, his towering shape casting a long shadow. "No one doubts a bonded warrior who makes his mate's protection part of his strength," he said, "but you must prove it isn't a weakness. The River's Run Festival is coming up," he said. "The timing couldn't be better."

"For what?" I asked, wary.

He met my gaze without flinching even though his words were a knife. "For you and Orla to participate in the Mating Challenge."

The tension in the chamber thickened so much I could barely breathe. Vyne whistled softly. Khorlar's stony brow furrowed, but he remained silent.

I stared at Darrokar, anger igniting behind my ribs. "Absolutely not. No one's done that in years. Surely you jest."

He shook his head. "Never about this. You know the festival's importance; they still speak of your success at the warrior trials all those years ago. The Mating Challenge is revered—our people treat it as the ultimate test of bonded pairs."

I felt my wings twitch, my pulse hammering. "It's insane. Warriors spend years preparing to face it together. She's a civilian. And a human. You think I'll throw her into a crucible meant to break the strongest among us? I don't see you offering to throw your human in beside mine."

"Tread carefully now," Darrokar warned, the beginnings of a growl under his words. "If you can't find some way to prove the bond to the doubters, this will not end. Zealots corner her while your back is turned. Word spreads that your human mate weakens you. Is that safer?"

I let out a long breath, claws curling into the table. "You think risking her life solves this?"

"I think showing the council—and all of Scalvaris—that your bond is more than a ploy to protect her is the only way. The River's Run draws every eye. If they see your mate stand at your side, if they see what she's made of, they'll have no choice but to accept her."

"She's human," I said in a low rasp. "You expect her to pass a challenge designed for trained warriors, ones who can brush off wounds she cannot?"

Darrokar's expression didn't shift. "I've seen what these humans can do. They're stronger than many care to admit—and you know it too, or you wouldn't have claimed her."

That truth sank like a hot coal in my gut. Orla was fierce in ways few understood. But she hadn't chosen this life. It had chosen her. I couldn't make her face such trials purely to appease the old guard. Yet ... I saw Darrokar's point. Too well.

I forced my shoulders to relax. "And if I refuse?"

Darrokar's gaze hardened. "The doubt will continue to spread until Karyseth finds a way to truly challenge you in council."

Drakarn traditions were harsh. A mate bond was supposed to be sacrosanct. Lying about it would dishonor a warrior beyond nearly all else. I wasn't lying, but a small part of me could understand why it might look that way.

Vyne's voice drifted back into the stalemate. "You could always make another public declaration. Challenge someone for her honor, take her right there in the marketplace—very dramatic. The city will love it."

I turned on him with a snarl, tail whipping the air. "Try me, Vyne."

Khorlar broke in. "He may be a fool, but he's not entirely wrong. Your woman must know the stakes. If she accepts, at least the council won't treat her as a human outsider—they'll treat her as your mate."

A brittle kind of hope mingled with dread in my chest. Orla wouldn't shy from a confrontation. She'd meet it head-on, even if it tore at her. The thought of exposing her to the Mating Challenge, though, made my blood chill.

"Let me talk to her," I ground out, not hiding my reluctance. "She deserves a choice. I have taken enough from her already."

Darrokar nodded. "Good."

I pivoted sharply toward the exit, wings fluttering in frustration, tension climbing my spine. I'd had enough of this.

Khorlar's rumbling voice stopped me mid-stride. "Don't forget why you chose her."

I didn't turn around. Couldn't. The memory of that primal pull, the way her scent sliced through me and stirred something feral, flashed again in my mind. Conviction and fear tangled in my throat.

One false step and I'd pay in Orla's blood.

The corridors outside felt stifling, the veins of heat crystals pulsing along the dark walls. My steps echoed louder than normal, each stride a release of pent-up energy I couldn't unleash in the council room.

Then I saw that piece of filth—Krazath. He smirked as he spoke in hushed tones with Zarvash, another councilor and a follower of the Forge Temple. Krazath's wings were partially unfurled in an agitated stance, while Zarvash's calm expression gave nothing away. When they noticed me, their voices dropped even lower.

I let my steps slow, eyes narrowed. Their posture—leaning in, wings tense—reeked of plotting. I caught a stray sentence from Zarvash: something about opportunists and precarious positions. Typical.

Zarvash stepped away from Krazath and inclined his head as he passed me. "It seems I cannot go a day without hearing about you."

I grunted. "And you believe it all?"

His bronze eyes flicked over me, unreadable. "I merely follow the truth. Wherever it may lead."

He moved on, leaving Krazath to glower at me from the edge of the passage. I stared back, letting him see the warning in my eyes.

If he tried coming near Orla again, I'd finish what I started.

My tail lashed behind me as I marched on, refusing to engage. Whispers were turning to poison, the wind in Scalvaris carrying rumors that sharpened like blades. If I stayed idle, they'd come for Orla the moment they sensed weakness.

I wasn't slow or soft. I'd walk straight through a wall of flame for her.

But the Mating Challenge? That might be a step too far.

Something would break soon, and I'd damn well make sure it wasn't her.

8

ORLA

THE COMBAT ARENA vibrated with an energy that sank into my bones, an undercurrent of heat and expectation that made the air feel electric. It wasn't just noise or movement—it was this pulsing vitality, as if the cavern was alive, fueled by the clash of blades and the rhythmic pacing of trained warriors.

I leaned forward on the rough-hewn stone bench in the observation area, the grit beneath me scraping against the thin fabric of my tunic. My presence here felt wrong—a guest in a moment that wasn't mine—but I was too curious to resist.

That, and Rath had asked.

"Here, try this," Eden said, pressing closer to my side as she handed me something wrapped in foil. "Earth candy. Save me before I scarf it all down myself."

The cheerful, fluorescent colors on the wrapper were almost outrageous in this environment—like smuggling daylight into shadows. I lifted an eyebrow at her, but her grin was irrepressible, her dark brown eyes bright with the kind of humor that disarmed you before you knew it. Eden's energy was like standing too close to a sparkler, irritating and charming all at once.

"Your heroism knows no bounds," I replied dryly, taking

the candy. The foil crinkled as I unwrapped it. The candy hit my tongue like a slap of concentrated sweetness, the fake fruitiness coating everything in a way that felt nearly alien after weeks of consuming krysfruit and slabs of burnt meat.

"You're welcome," Eden said, popping a second piece into her mouth with a dramatic snap. She leaned forward, her elbows resting on her knees as her gaze swept over the warriors below. "Which one's Rath?"

I scanned the pit, my eyes darting from winged figures to shimmering scales, searching for that particular sharpness that had become so familiar. Swaying tails twitched, claws glinted, and blades thick with heat refracted dim light until finding him in the crowd felt impossible.

Then it wasn't.

That moment when I spotted Rath was like swinging a door open too fast and catching a blade of sunlight. My thoughts snagged because this wasn't the Rath I was used to—not the watchful, tightly-coiled man who spoke with clipped words and calm truths. No, this figure moved with an effortless swagger that made something deep inside of me tighten with want.

Oh, hell.

"How could you miss him?" I heard myself mumbling. His imposing frame cut through the chaos. Other warriors were strong, brutal even, but Rath's presence was something distinct, an unfamiliar language of danger and grace—power in its rawest form. His scales reflected light like shards of glass, catching every flicker of motion in a way that created a halo of shimmering, restless energy around him. His wings unfolded slightly; not wide, but calculated, like a wolf showing just enough teeth to let you know it wasn't interested in playing nice.

"Never mind," Eden said in awe, her voice breaking my

spell as she zeroed in on him. "Found him. Seriously, though, your guy could probably walk into a room and set it on fire just by existing."

Heat crept up my throat, uncomfortable and unwelcome. "He's not my guy." I wasn't sure if the words were meant to rebuff her or convince myself. Feeling Eden's sidelong glance, I sighed and forced a casual shrug, but the movement felt unnatural, wrong. "He just ... knows how to make himself seen. That's all."

Eden turned her half-smirk my way for just a second too long. "Sure," she said, her voice dripping with disbelief. Her posture instantly melted back into something more casual as she leaned forward again, resting her chin on one hand. "But seriously, that presence. Like, if someone so much as looked at me the way Rath looks at you ..."

I groaned, cutting her off as she dragged the words out like each one had worth in its own right. "Eden. Please."

She smiled, lifting her hands in a playful gesture of surrender. "Fine. Commentary off. But the fact that you're still red? Not my fault."

In the arena below, Rath advanced on his sparring partner—a warrior whose movements began with confidence but quickly transformed to hesitation. Rath's blade didn't move like the others, didn't try to impress. It sought efficiency.

Watching him was like watching the beach grind down stone: violent and inevitable but removed from petty emotion. Even the air around him seemed different, a slight stillness in the invisible space between moves that put spectators on their heels.

It wasn't theatrical. It was purpose built for destruction.

"Doesn't hold back, does he?" Eden asked. Her earlier levity had dimmed, replaced by something quieter.

"No," I replied, swallowing hard. My hands clutched the edge of the bench. "He never does."

The arena's collective breath sharpened, a break in the rhythm below turning all focus toward the latest fight. A new challenger stepped forward, taller and sharper-edged than the others—his scales jagged and mismatched, singed in a way that made him seem more like something built imperfectly than born.

Krazath.

Eden stiffened at my shoulder instantly, her fingers curling into fists. "*Him*," she hissed before exhaling sharply. "That asshole."

I knew. Recognized him from the corridor, from the temple, from the tension Rath had worn like armor since. My pulse stuttered, uncertainty and rage colliding somewhere too deep for me to untangle. Despite myself, I leaned forward.

"No," I breathed, watching Rath turn to meet Krazath's gaze—a fire already sparking in his eyes. He didn't hesitate, didn't flinch. He entered the space of Krazath's challenge like it was inevitable, like this confrontation had always lived in their bad blood.

Krazath's first move was a sweeping strike, the kind meant to intimidate and overwhelm—a predator testing the weak points of his prey. His blade arced through the air, but Rath was already moving, his form a blur of red and shadow, slipping to the side with a fluidity that made Krazath's lunge look clumsy by comparison.

Rath's counterattack came swiftly, his blade slicing upward in a motion so precise it seemed choreographed. Krazath twisted away just in time, the edge nicking one of his jagged scales instead of cleaving through flesh. The sound of it—a sharp, metallic scrape—sent a shiver down my spine, and I gripped the bench under me so hard my knuckles ached. Or maybe it was the fight itself, the suffocating tension coiling tighter with every traded blow.

Eden's voice dropped lower. "He's claiming you. That's what this is, right? Showing everyone that you and him ...?"

Her words knocked against me sideways, almost disorienting. "That's ... insane." Part denial, part something that sounded a bit too much like hope.

"Isn't it?" she said, but her focus was unwavering. "And yet, here we are."

Rath's style was deliberate, measured—a predator who wasted no energy. Every flick of his claws, every step forward or back seemed calculated to expose Krazath's weaknesses. Krazath fought like a storm, wild and frantic, each strike more aggression instead of strategy. His scales caught the dim light, flashing like broken glass as he swung again and again, trying to break past Rath's cold precision.

When Rath ducked beneath a violent downswing, his wings snapped outward in a sudden motion. It was a feint, but Krazath took the bait, stepping left where Rath's foot was already planted. Rath spun, low and fast, his tail whipping around to strike Krazath's shin with bone-cracking force. Krazath stumbled, snarling in frustration and pain as he caught himself on one knee.

"Come on, Rath," I whispered under my breath, my voice lost in the roar of the arena.

I hated this. I hated watching what looked like a car crash. My throat felt raw already, like I'd been screaming even though I'd been biting those yells back as hard as I could. But beneath my concern, there was a dark, treacherous part of me that wanted Rath to humiliate Krazath, to crush him so completely that whatever thread of malice still tied him to Rath would snap. I wanted—I needed Rath to win, because losing wasn't an option. Not here. Not with Krazath.

Krazath recovered with a roar, his jagged claws swiping at Rath in a wide arc that forced him back a step. But Rath immediately surged forward again, blade aimed for Krazath's ribs. The two were locked in close combat now, claws and fangs snapping as their bodies twisted in a brutal struggle. Rath locked one of Krazath's wrists in a vice-like grip, twisting with a sharp motion that forced his opponent to drop the secondary blade he'd been brandishing. It clattered to the ground and skidded away into the dirt.

For a heartbeat, Rath's face tilted upward, and our eyes met.

It was only for a fraction of a second, but the ferocity in his gaze hit me like a tidal wave. It wasn't hesitation or desperation —no, Rath wasn't just here to survive. He was here to finish this, to make an example of Krazath.

I couldn't look away even as my hands trembled, my nails digging into the stone beneath.

"Damn," Eden's voice was almost inaudible. "He's ... something else."

But my attention was back on the pit, my chest tight as Krazath fought back with a vicious headbutt, the crown of his jagged scales slamming into Rath's cheek. Rath staggered, and Krazath surged forward like a wounded beast sensing weakness. My heart jumped into my throat as Krazath's blade lashed out, aiming for Rath's unguarded side.

Rath's wings flared wide at the last possible moment, snapping him back and away from the attack. Krazath's blade sliced only air as Rath rose into the space above their clash, hanging there like some radiant, damnable god of war. Then he dove, his descent like a meteor aimed directly at Krazath's chest. The impact landed with a deafening crack as Rath's claws wrenched Krazath's weapon from his hands and sent it spiraling away.

The crowd roared, their voices blending into a singular chaos as Rath's blade pressed to Krazath's throat.

The fight was over. Everyone knew it. Even Krazath.

It took another few minutes for Rath and Krazath to observe the formalities. Krazath limped away towards a bronze scaled Drakarn who was glaring at Rath. But I couldn't care about that. Not right now.

I jumped out of my seat and scrambled down the steps towards the floor of the arena like I was some fan at a hockey game back on Earth.

"Rath!" My voice rang out, rebounding faintly off the stone walls of the arena.

Ahead of me, his steps faltered. I watched his tail dip in its usually measured sway, the movement slower now, as though the storm of emotions from the fight below was still rattling inside him. His shoulders remained stiff, wings tucked tightly against him, but tension rolled off him in waves.

I pushed forward, quickening my steps until I'd almost caught him. My fingers brushed the dark fabric of his sleeve—a fleeting touch that made him freeze instantly. His wings twitched, the faint, sharp motion betraying that coiled energy he barely contained.

Slowly, he turned to face me.

And then there were his eyes.

I wasn't sure what I'd expected—anger maybe. But when Rath looked at me, it wasn't fury I found crackling behind his gaze. It was something softer, quieter, but no less powerful. A tension of a different sort tightened across the planes of his face, his jaw locked like he was holding back a torrent of words he couldn't quite put to shape. The intensity of it sent a surge of heat traveling up my spine.

"You were ..." I faltered, shoving the words around in my head before one finally fell out into the silence. "Incredible."

I felt the weight of the admission as soon as it left me—a truth I couldn't take back even if I wanted to. My face burned under his scrutiny, the heat of my words hanging awkwardly between us. But I held his gaze, hoping somehow my honesty would cut through whatever wall he was throwing up right now.

Rath watched me like he was studying every fragment of my face, looking for cracks in my reasoning. Then, slowly, his expression softened—not a lot, but enough that the hard lines of his features eased, and the tension in his shoulders bled away just a fraction. His hand moved—just slightly—as though he wasn't sure whether to reach for me or retreat, claws flexing faintly before settling by his side.

"You are unharmed?" he asked at last, his voice rasping like sandpaper scraping over stone.

The question caught me off guard. "I—you're the one who was fighting! Not me."

His jaw twitched as he exhaled slowly through his nose, a dark and indecipherable flicker passing behind his eyes. But then he shifted slightly closer—a small movement, enough that I could feel the faint warmth of his skin, even through the layers that separated us.

"It was for you," he said simply. "They needed to see."

Something inside me wavered. The world felt too small all of a sudden. The sharp edge in Rath's voice didn't match the softness of his gaze as he studied me. His quiet admission— words that rang with pure honesty, untempered and raw— coiled in my chest, making breathing inexplicably difficult.

"I—" Words failed me as my thoughts got all tied up. My lips parted in an attempt to say something—anything—but before coherent language could rally itself, some shared thread between us tightened and snapped clean through.

I kissed him.

IT WAS INSTINCTUAL—MESSY and unplanned, like something breaking through a dam you'd ignored was cracking all along. My hands had moved without permission to brace against his chest, my fingertips instinctively brushing the heat rolling beneath his tunic. His skin, warm like heated stone, burned against me in a way that made my stomach twist.

I barely registered the way his breath stopped short, the faint hitch of it ghosting across my cheek. And still, I couldn't stop.

Everything ground to a halt. Rath didn't move, caught mid-instinct and undecided about which way to fall. His hands hovered in that uncertain space between grasping and retreating, claws curling tight against his palms. For a second, I wasn't sure if I'd gone too far, crossed a line I didn't fully understand, until—

Until he moved.

Slowly, deliberately, Rath leaned into the moment with a care that bordered adoration. If the kiss was meant to break him open, it did so in increments—his lips firm but measured, like he was unlearning and relearning the world in the span of seconds. He tilted his head faintly, matching me, and just when

I thought the storm between us was only a distant rumble, his hand found my waist.

The sharp heat of his claws, even through the protective layers of fabric, sent a shiver racing across my body. His grip was firm but careful, aware that the strength he carried so effortlessly could crush if miscalculated. The other hand came up too, fingers grazing my jaw with a touch so tender it left a trail of fire.

For all his capacity for destruction on the field, Rath kissed like he was holding something fragile. It undid me completely.

An involuntary sound escaped me—a quiet tremble fought and failed to be smothered. Rath stilled for only a heartbeat before a low hum rumbled deep in his chest, that faint growl a visceral reaction that spoke more than words ever could. The weight of it pressed against me, made every small tether anchoring me to reality snap.

There was no disguising the hunger threaded into his kiss— the way his lips moved more firmly now, with just enough edged desperation to make my heart stutter and spiral all at once. His grip tightened against my waist as his other thumb grazed just along the edge of my face. The warmth radiating from his skin enveloped me completely.

Time didn't exist between us. There was no measured counting of breaths, no acknowledgment of anything beyond the persistent, magnetic pull binding me irreversibly to him.

When Rath finally pulled away just enough to breathe, the space between us felt fragile, the air charged with something that hadn't yet settled. His forehead brushed lightly against mine, unwilling to pull back completely, and for a fleeting moment, we both stood frozen in that sizzle. His eyes burned with something unreadable, raw and unguarded in a way that tightened and softened my chest all at once.

He exhaled, the hint of warmth in his breath lingering

against my lips. "*Shyrarva*," he rasped, that word catching somewhere low in his throat, vulnerable and rough-edged.

I couldn't respond. Couldn't move. Because the look he gave me wasn't just intense—it was exposing Rath's inner soul, daring me to step into the chasm I'd just forced open.

"I—" The syllable was barely audible; a ghost of a word that dissolved the moment I uttered it.

My voice had betrayed me, my thoughts racing too fast to form anything coherent. I tried again, but the tightness in my chest stifled any clarity, leaving me breathless and trembling in a way I couldn't control. My hands slipped from where they'd been clutching at his tunic, retreating awkwardly to my sides.

Rath didn't speak. He stood motionless for a moment, caught between moving closer and pulling away entirely. His gaze dropped to my lips again before sweeping back upward, catching and holding mine with the same intensity that had turned my pulse inside out moments ago. When he finally stirred, his hand didn't fall away. Instead, his thumb lingered at the edge of my cheekbone, brushing the curve of my skin with an unexpected gentleness that made my core clench.

He leaned in slightly—just enough for his lips to ghost across my temple in a gesture so soft it was almost imperceptible. The whisper of contact was there and gone, but it left a weight in its place. His claws flexed once at his side before stilling again.

"You ..." His voice, rough and deliberate, dropped low. "Taste sweet."

It wasn't flirtation, not really. Rath wasn't posturing—he was simply delivering an unfiltered truth. A fact, delivered the way one might observe a shift in the wind or the steady glow of a distant star. And yet, those three words sunk their claws into me with far more force than anything practiced or contrived ever could. They left me reeling, tangled in sensations I hadn't quite found the nerve to name.

I swallowed hard, helpless against the flush that crept up my neck. My head dipped slightly, instinct pulling me away from the direct line of his gaze in a feeble attempt to collect myself. "It's the candy," I muttered, the excuse spilling out too quickly, too obviously, as if the absurdity of it could dissolve the gravity of what had just happened.

"The candy," Rath repeated, his tone edged with faint amusement, but it wasn't dismissive. If anything, his voice sounded lighter now, less hesitant. He watched me steadily, his head tilting slightly to the side. A faint curve played at the corner of his mouth, subtle but unmistakable—less a grin and more the shadow of something that might've been softness, had it belonged to anyone else.

"Yes, the candy," I insisted like it mattered. "Artificial sugar, weird additives. Science, or ... something." My hands gestured vaguely, but even I didn't believe the excuse as it left me.

His breath left him in a quiet huff—not an outright laugh, but close enough to trail warmth through the space between us. He took a step back, the movement so measured it felt less like retreat and more like careful consideration. His eyes didn't stray from mine, still holding steady in that way that sent sparks tracing along my nerves, even as the distance afforded me some scrap of relief.

The return of the background noises—whispered murmurs from lingering Drakarn nearby—felt abrupt, like the outside world had forced itself back into focus before either of us was ready for it. I wasn't sure what was worse: the crowd's judgement-lined gazes or the lingering hum in the air from Rath's proximity, charged despite the subtle distance now between us.

"Let's get out of here," Rath said, voice quiet but resolute. "The stares will only grow heavier." His hand, still steady even as mine trembled faintly by comparison, extended forward—an invitation rather than an assumption. "Away from this."

For all my hesitation, my fingers brushed against his without thinking, drawn forward more by the weight of his presence than any conscious decision on my part. His touch was steadying, a quiet guide away from the turmoil still echoing through the arena.

In a swift motion, Rath stepped closer, his arms and tail wrapping securely around me as his wings spread wide. The rush of movement that followed—the leap into the air—stole my breath as the ground disappeared below us. His strength, the sheer solidity of him beneath and around me, was grounding in a way I hadn't expected.

As the city's sprawling depths gave way to the open expanse of sky, a new kind of quiet settled around us—thicker, calmer, where the muted roar of the wind carried no judgment or expectation. I leaned into him, the warmth of his scales blocking out the cool bite of the wind, and my stomach flipped in a way that had nothing to do with the flight.

It wasn't until we began aiming for the soft, glowing light of a familiar space nestled high above the city that I understood where he was taking me.

"Your sanctuary," I murmured, my voice tinged with something quieter than awe but no less full of wonder.

Rath tilted his head slightly, glancing back at me just as the sanctuary's crystalline shimmer began to catch and reflect the light. "Yes," he said softly, matter-of-fact as always, but with a deeper purpose stitched into the single word. "It is what you need." His wings flexed once as we descended fully, slowing to land gracefully on the secluded cliffs below.

When my feet found solid ground again, he didn't step away, not immediately. Instead, his gaze lingered, searching for something—I wasn't sure what—but finding some answer all the same.

I didn't look away.

The air in the sanctuary shifted the moment we landed inside. It looked the same as before—the light filtering delicately through the overhead openings, scattering soft reflections across the pools dotting the cavern floor. But there was something different about it now, some newfound weight in the silence, heavier and more profound than the first time I'd been there. I stood just past the entrance, my fingers skimming the rough stone, and let the space breathe around me. The tension in my chest eased.

Rath moved farther inside, his wings pulling tight against his back, steps uncharacteristically careful. He didn't look back at me, at least not right away. Instead, he let out a breath, the sound carried away by the quiet.

Here, in this place, his usual sharpness seemed muted. Not absent—Rath was never truly at ease—but less rigid, his presence more thoughtful and drawn inward. He paused near one of the pools, his back to me, his head tilting slightly in the way it did when he was weighing something unspoken.

I hovered near the entrance, reluctant to disturb the fragile peace unfolding before me. My hand lingered on the stone for a moment longer before I forced myself to step forward, movements slower than his, less sure. The sanctuary's beauty pressed softly into my awareness, an ache of something I couldn't quite name settling beneath my ribs.

"Rath," I murmured, his name slipping through the quiet.

At the sound, he turned to face me. He didn't speak immediately, studying me with that unyielding intensity that seemed to see too much. His tail flicked slightly against the ground, a motion that betrayed whatever storm lingered beneath the surface. When the silence stretched just enough to become awkward, I forced myself to step closer, drawn forward as much by the heat of his gaze as by some need to fill the void.

I stopped a few paces away, my arms crossing over my chest as I tried to steady the unease knotting between my lungs. "I don't understand why you're doing this," I admitted, the words emerging unpolished, trembling slightly on their way out. "Why you care so much."

Rath's posture shifted, but his expression didn't falter. If anything, his gaze softened slightly, though it carried the same depth. He said nothing for a long moment, his head tilting faintly, weighing whether I was truly ready to understand the answer.

His claws flexed absently at his sides before his voice broke the stillness. "Your world," he began, his words deliberate, unhurried. "Your people. You've lost much. I see it in you. The way you carry it."

His honesty sliced through me, sharp and unavoidable. My breath hitched slightly, and I tightened my arms across myself. Rath had always been direct, but this felt different—less like an observation and more like a confession.

"I know what it means to lose," he continued, his tone quieter, a faint roughness creeping into its edges. His gaze shifted, no longer fixed rigidly on me but staring somewhere past the pools that flickered faintly with light. "My sister ... she was fierce. Brilliant. Everything I was not." A pause lingered between his words, thick and heavy as memory pressed against them. "And then she was gone."

My throat tightened. Rath was standing there, unraveling pieces of himself in a way that left me breathless. My voice was thready when I found it again. "I'm sorry."

He shifted his gaze back to me then. "Sorry won't bring anything back," he said softly, though there was no anger in the words—only a quiet kind of resignation. "But I am sorry too, for what you carry."

The rawness in his voice undid something in me. In the span of heartbeats, the carefully constructed barriers I'd built around my grief wavered, threatening to collapse entirely. I took a small step closer, unsure of what I was reaching for but needing to close the gap between us all the same.

"You don't have to shoulder that alone," I said, surprising even myself with the quiet conviction in my voice. The words felt foreign on my tongue, unfamiliar but true.

Rath's claws flexed again—a small motion, but one I recognized now as a sign of his restraint cracking. "I will not lose this," he said finally, his voice rough, his gaze steady as it pinned me in place. "Do you understand?"

I swallowed hard, his words—and the meaning behind them—settling heavy in my chest. "Rath," I started, the syllables too small for the enormity of what surrounded us. "I—"

But Rath shook his head, cutting me off with a look rather than words. "Stop running," he commanded, the simplicity of it unraveling me in ways I hadn't thought possible.

My heart twisted painfully at the honesty etched across his face.

How long had I been doing just that—running? From losing my future, from the shattered remains of what I'd left behind, from the truth of what existed between us now? The enormity of it settled around me, and I didn't know how to answer; didn't know how to step into the space he'd so carefully made for me. But I wanted to try.

Rath's hand found its way to my waist again, not gripping but resting there in a way that tethered me to him, grounding me when my thoughts threatened to spiral. It was steady, solid, and patient. "May I?" he murmured, voice low and edged with hesitation as his eyes flickered briefly downward, lingering on my lips before meeting my gaze once more.

"I want to kiss you now. When no one else is looking."

I nodded, a small motion that sent everything else tumbling out of the way.

When his lips found mine again, it wasn't with the same urgency as before. His warmth spilled into me as his claws skimmed along my side, careful and reverent. I let him in, let the storm of everything that had bound me up dissipate in the face of quiet, unrelenting truth.

Whatever this was, I wasn't running anymore.

ORLA

I SAT cross-legged on the edge of Rath's bed, my fingers tracing the intricate weave of heat-resistant silk beneath me, when the door slid open with a quiet scrape. Things had changed since the cave, since the kiss. Kisses.

I was starting to feel more comfortable in Rath's rooms. Our rooms. I didn't shy away when he looked at me like he wanted to devour me. And I cherished the few stolen kisses we'd shared since then. It wasn't some seismic shift in our relationship.

But things were different. Maybe even better.

Rath clutched a small cloth pouch in one clawed hand. The scent hit me first—sweet, floral, *rich*—cutting through the room's usual musk of charred stone and spice. My stomach betrayed me with a low growl.

Rath's nostrils flared, a flicker of satisfaction tightening his jaw as he stepped inside. "You're hungry," he said, not a question.

"I'm fine," I lied. Old habits.

He grunted, unimpressed, and crossed the room in three strides. The pouch landed on the bed between us with a soft *thud,* its contents shifting like treasure. Up close, the scent was dizzying—caramelized sugar, something nutty, a hint of flowers.

"What is it?" I asked, eyeing the pouch like it might hiss.

His tail flicked impatiently against the floor. "Open it."

I tugged the drawstring loose, and the aroma bloomed fully —honey, hot oil, crisp dough. Nestled inside were six golden brown fritters, their surfaces crackled and glazed, still faintly steaming. My mouth watered.

"You ... got these? For me?" I blinked up at him, surprised.

He shifted, the scales along his neck rippling faintly. "You favor sweets." A statement, blunt as a blade. "The vendor claimed these were ... sufficient."

Sufficient. The word felt too small for the effort. I plucked a fritter from the pouch, the pastry's heat seeping into my fingertips. The first bite was a revelation—crisp shell giving way to airy dough, the honey inside hot and floral, tinged with a smoky aftertaste that could only be Volcaryth. A low, involuntary moan slipped out.

Rath went very still.

I froze, the sound hanging between us like a spark. His pupils narrowed to slits. "You ... approve?"

"It's delicious," I admitted, licking honey from my thumb. His gaze tracked the movement, a muscle twitching in his jaw.

Without warning, he sank onto the slab beside me. His thigh pressed flush against mine, scales warm through the thin fabric of my pants. My breath hitched.

"Here." He plucked the fritter from my hand, claws sheathed as he broke off a piece. His other hand cupped my chin, tilting my face toward him. "Eat."

I parted my lips, and he placed the morsel on my tongue, his thumb lingering to catch a stray drop of honey. The pad of his claw grazed my lower lip, sending a shiver down my spine.

"Good?" he rumbled.

I nodded, swallowing hard. "Why ... why this?"

His thumb swept over my chin again, snaring another

streak I hadn't noticed. "A warrior honors his mate's tastes." The words were rough. "Even ... small ones."

A laugh bubbled up, startled and warm. "Small? There's enough here for three people."

The corner of his mouth twitched—not a smile, but close. His tail rose from the floor to loop loosely around my ankle, a possessive anchor. "Eat," he repeated, offering another piece.

This time, honey dripped down my thumb as I took it. Rath's nostrils flared, his gaze dropping to the sticky trail. Slowly, giving me plenty of time to pull back, he leaned in.

His tongue—long, hotter than human—flicked over my honeyed skin.

I gasped. The sound seemed to fracture something in the air.

Rath froze, his breath a low rasp against my wrist. For a heartbeat, we stayed locked there, the world reduced to the glide of his tongue and the gleam in his eyes. Then, with a growl that vibrated through my bones, he pulled back.

My pulse thundered in my ears as I reached into the pouch with trembling fingers. The fritter's crust crackled under my grip, scattering sugar crystals across Rath's scales. His tail tightened around my ankle—a warning or encouragement, I couldn't tell.

"Here, have a taste," I managed, breaking off a ragged piece.

His nostrils flared at the offering, gaze flicking between my face and the crumbling pastry. For a heartbeat, I thought he'd refuse. Then his lips parted, revealing the faintest glint of fang.

The moment the morsel touched his tongue, his pupils blew wide. A low rumble shook his chest as flavors exploded— honey's floral brightness against Volcaryth's smoky depth. His clawed hand engulfed mine, preventing retreat.

"More."

The command vibrated through my bones. I fed him

another piece, then another, each bite punctuated by the slick heat of his tongue grazing my fingertips. His scales glowed faintly where our skin met, marks blooming under my touch like stars being born.

When the last crumb disappeared, he didn't release my hand. His tongue swept the length of my index finger, rasping over calluses left by rock samples and scanner grips. The sound that escaped me was half gasp, half whimper.

"You taste," his growl deepened, tail coiling higher up my calf, "like sunlight."

His eyes trailed down, snagging on the exposed skin of my upper arm. I usually kept it covered. "What is this?" He traced the inked lines swirling across my inner forearm. The constellation patterns seemed to shimmer under his touch, dormant stars awakening beneath scaled fingertips.

I swallowed. "Cygnus. Lyra. Ursa Major." My throat tightened around the names. "They're constellations."

His clawtip hovered over the swirling colors of the Milky Way. "And this?"

"Home." The word slipped out raw. "Or where home used to be. Before ..." I gestured vaguely toward the ceiling, toward the sky that didn't exist there.

Rath's tail tightened around my thigh, the pressure grounding. "Show me."

One by one, I guided his claws over each cluster of stars tattooed on my arm, my voice gaining strength as I recounted myths half-remembered from childhood datapads.

"This one bled," he observed, talon brushing the faded blue ink.

"My first tattoo." I huffed a laugh. "Twelve-year-old me thought stealing a biogel pen from the medbay was a genius idea."

Rath made a sound deep in his chest—not quite a chuckle,

but something warmer than a grunt. "My Blade-Binding." He turned his forearm, revealing a jagged scar cutting through ruby scales. "Fifteen summers. Stole a magma whip from the forge master." His claw traced the injury with perverse pride. "It took three healers to seal the wound. I kept the whip."

His tail slid higher, scales scraping against my legs as he nosed aside my hair to expose the honey-smeared hollow of my throat.

"Your stories are written in dead light," he murmured against my pulse. "Mine in fire."

The star on my arm felt like it was pulsing faintly, keeping time with the possessive grip of his claws. Somewhere in the heat, a new constellation was being born.

Rath's claw closed around the half-empty pouch with wicked deliberation, his gaze locked on the honey glistening at its torn edge. The low light caught the golden strands stretching between fabric and talon, each thread snapping with a soft *pop* that echoed too loud in the sudden stillness. His nostrils flared —inhaling sugar, heat, *me*—as he leaned in until his breath fanned hot across my jaw.

"This," he rumbled, "belongs here."

The pouch tilted.

"Rath!"

Honey spilled in a ribbon, thick and sticky, painting a warm trail from the hollow of my throat to the slope of my breast under my shirt. I gasped at the heat—not scalding, but alive, like sunlight given liquid form. It pooled in the dip of my collarbone.

Rath's tongue swept over a fang. "Better."

His free hand settled at my hip, claws pricking warning-dimples into flesh as he leaned closer. The honey's floral scent mingled with his own—charred cedar and midnight embers—as the last drops fell. His thumb followed the viscous path upward, smearing it wider, *darker*, until my pulse throbbed where honey and his touch collided.

The empty pouch dropped to the floor. His other hand caged my wrist above my head, scales hissing against stone as he lowered his mouth to the mess he'd made.

"We can't let this go to waste," he said. His slit pupils drank greedily at the honey dripping over me. "Too many layers," he growled against my throat.

The first rend of fabric came without warning. His talon hooked beneath my shirt's neckline, slicing downward in one fluid motion. Cool air rushed over newly bared skin as the garment fell away in forgotten scraps. I arched instinctively, honey-smeared breasts heaving under the hunger blazing in his eyes.

"*Mine.*"

The declaration vibrated through his chest and into mine as he straddled my hips. He tore off his own tunic, ruby scales glinting beneath, nipple piercings catching the crystal's glow. My brain short circuited at that.

The first lick was a brand.

I barely registered the cool air on my exposed stomach before his tongue struck—a hot, flat stroke from collarbone to pulse point that left scorched nerves in its wake. His teeth grazed skin, not breaking flesh but promising consequences.

When his mouth closed over the honey pooled in the hollow of my throat, the vibration of his groan traveled straight to my core.

"It tastes better here," he rumbled against damp skin, that wickedly long tongue flicking the frantic beat beneath my jaw. His hips ground down, the rigid heat beneath his trousers leaving no doubt about his state. The musk pouring off him thickened—smoke and charred amber with an undercurrent of something sweetly metallic.

I had to touch him.

He hissed when my nails caught the black hoops piercing his nipples, the sound sharpening as I rolled one between thumb and forefinger. "You," his claws tore through the remains of his trousers, letting the fabric fall to the floor, "play with fire, *shyrarva.*"

The honey between us grew tacky as he reared back, allowing me to see what I'd uncovered. Thick liquid leaked out of the head of his cock. A barbell through his foreskin glinted wetly, each subtle twitch making the pierced flesh quiver like a living thing.

He was pierced *there* too.

Oh my god.

My breath stuttered. Human anatomy hadn't prepared me for *this*—the way red scales rippled like armor at the base before melting into swollen crimson flesh, dark veins pulsing beneath the surface.

Thick. *Too* thick, my hindbrain whispered even as heat pooled between my thighs. The foreskin didn't just pull back— it *rippled*, a strange lip curling lazily against the glans, glistening with beads of translucent fluid that carried his smoky-sweet scent.

My mouth watered.

The barbell piercing through it all caught the light, swinging faintly with every twitch of that alien flesh.

"It's ..." I swallowed, fingers flexing uselessly at my sides. "Not what I expected."

Rath's tail lashed once, violently, before coiling around my bare calf. "Displeasing?" The growl held an edge I'd never heard—vulnerability masquerading as threat.

"No." My hand moved without permission, hovering inches from where pre-cum slicked the veined shaft. "Not even a little."

A claw caught my wrist. "*Shyarva.*" The word was a lit fuse. When I met his gaze, the hunger there scorched every clinical thought to ash. "Touch me."

It wasn't a command. It was desperation.

The first brush of fingertips against his scaled base drew a hiss from us both. The ridges weren't cold—they thrummed with inner heat, textured enough to tease without tearing. Higher up, the skin turned velvet-soft, the dark veins beneath thickening until they felt like braided cords under my palm. That writhing foreskin lip curled around my thumb when I reached the crown, suckling gently.

Oh god. What would that feel like inside me? My body clenched with curiosity and need.

"*Karynae,*" Rath gritted out, hips jerking. His pierced flesh quivered, more fluid welling around the barbell. The musk intensified—clove and burnt honey now, *claiming* pheromones that made my mouth water even more.

All thoughts of science evaporated. There was only heat, and need, and the terrifying realization that I *wanted* this alien intimacy. That every scale and throbbing vein called to something primal I'd buried under data logs and survival protocols.

His claws sank into the silks around us as I stroked him properly, the tongue-like ridge undulating against my palm in counterpoint to my strokes. "Your science," he rasped, fangs gleaming, "did it prepare you for *this*?"

The barbell grazed my wrist as his hips pistoned, the answer written in my racing pulse.

His tail lashed once before slithering up my inner thigh, the tip leaving ghostly trails of sensation. "This scent," he growled, dragging his nose along my honey-smeared ribs. The motion pulled his cock away from my curious hand. "Your fear. Your hunger. They sing the same note now."

The first lick to my nipple drew a broken sound from us

both. His tongue's ridges pressed almost too hard, the tip curling around the peak in a way no human mouth could replicate. When his cock's fleshy lip brushed my inner thigh—hotter than the rest of him, questing blindly—I arched off the bed with a cry.

"Look," he commanded, pinning my hips as his tail wrenched my leg higher. The glide of his cock's extra tongue circled my clit while the rest of him pressed against my entrance, the barbell's cool metal a shocking contrast to the searing flesh around it. Twin sensations splintered my vision into starbursts. "Watch how you take me."

The world narrowed to points of contact—the searing press of Rath's scaled leg against my inner thighs, the sinful undulation of that alien ridge circling my clit, the cold-warm shock of metal where his barbell kissed my entrance. His claws flexed against my hips, pinning without bruising, as his tail coiled higher to keep my leg in place. It should have felt restraining; instead I felt safe. Every shift of muscle beneath his red scales rippled with lethal grace, a predator holding itself in check.

"Breathe," he growled against my ribs, the command fraying at the edges.

I sucked in air that tasted of honey and him, my fingers scrambling for purchase on the bed's silks. The first breach burned—not with pain, but with obscene fullness, the barbell dragging a slick path inside me as his writhing lip latched onto my clit. My back arched off the slab, a cry catching in my throat as dual sensations collided—deep, stretching pressure below and fluttering suction above.

"*Karys'veth ir,*" Rath snarled, words rumbling through his chest into mine. I had no idea if my translator was malfunctioning or if I was just too lost in sensation to understand what he was saying. I couldn't care.

His hips snapped forward, seating him fully in one sure

thrust. The scaled base of him ground against me as his veined shaft pulsed, his cock's tongue working in counterpoint to each jarring movement. My vision whited out, nerves howling as the tip of his tail traced the outside of my thigh.

"You feel—" He choked off, fangs scraping against my shoulder. The mark walked the knife's edge between pleasure and pain, his tongue lapping at the sting as his pace turned erratic.

The relentless feeling pushed me over. Pleasure crested like lava breaching a vent—a scalding, unstoppable rise that shattered into full-body tremors.

Rath's roar vibrated through my bones as my climax clamped down on him, his tail seizing around my thigh as his own release surged hot and thick. The scent of us—charred amber and honeyed musk—swelled until it coated my tongue, his glands marking my skin where his seed spilled.

He collapsed forward, catching his weight on trembling arms, his forehead pressed to mine as I gasped uselessly at the heated air. His cock still pulsed inside me, milking the last aftershocks as his tail loosened its vise grip.

"*Shyrarva*." That word, his special name only for me, was a prayer and a plea on his lips, his claws gently carding through my sweat-damp hair.

I traced the marks my nails had left on his back—constellations of possession barely marked in his scales. His answering rumble sounded almost like contentment.

Rath's weight pressed me into the silks, his forehead still resting against mine, our shared heat forming a humid little world between our bodies. Honey had dried in sticky trails across my chest, mingling with sweat and other fluids. His tail remained coiled around my thigh, a possessive anchor even now.

His pierced nipples brushed my chest with each labored

breath, the hoops now warm from our friction. "You're trembling," he murmured against my throat, his voice sandpaper rough.

A claw-tipped hand slid beneath my lower back, adjusting our alignment until his softening cock slipped free. I bit back a sound at the loss, suddenly aware of the mess we'd made—his release seeped between my thighs, thick and unnervingly warm, carrying that musky-sweet scent that already felt branded into my skin.

Rath's tongue dragged a slow stripe up my honey-crusted collarbone. "Mine," he growled, the word muffled against my skin. Not a question.

I should've bristled. Instead, my traitorous hands fisted in the silks as his teeth found the juncture of neck and shoulder. Not biting—*testing*.

"You're *smug*," I accused, hating how breathless I sounded.

His answering rumble shook through me, more purr than growl. The tail around my leg tightened fractionally as he nosed aside damp hair to lick the shell of my ear. "You smell like me now."

A shudder went down my spine. "Is that ... a good thing?"

He stilled. Drew back just enough for me to see the way his pupils dilated—black swallowing gold. "It means," he said slowly, claws flexing against my hip, "that even the zealots will think twice before challenging what's etched into your scent."

The implication coiled hot in my gut. *Pheromones as property claim.* I opened my mouth to protest, but Rath's thumb brushed the bite mark on my shoulder—the one that throbbed in time with my heartbeat.

"Hush." His nose traced the honeyed hollow of my throat, inhaling deeply. "Your mind will dissect it later. For now," his hips rolled once, a lazy undulation that made me gasp, "let the fire speak."

I wanted to argue. To dissect the biology of his "scent-marking glands," to question the permanence he implied. But his hand was sliding lower, calloused palm cradling the back of my knee, and the words dissolved into a moan.

Somewhere in the fervent quiet, I realized my fingers were carding through the ridges along his spine, memorizing their topography.

Rath's breath hitched, and his hips bucked.

I stilled. "Did I—?"

"Again," he demanded, voice cracking.

This time, when my nails scraped the sensitive grooves between his scales, his whole body shuddered—a seismic vulnerability that echoed in the broken sound he muffled against my throat.

The fire spoke.

And for once, I listened.

RATH

ORLA'S BREATHING was soft against my chest. The air was thick with the scent of her—my scent now woven into hers, permanent and undeniable. I didn't need my heightened senses to notice how perfectly it clung to her skin.

Even in sleep, her body carried the mark of our bond.

A low hum of satisfaction rumbled in my chest. She was there, pressed against me, her fragile human frame fitting perfectly against mine as if the stars themselves had shaped us for this. For each other. My tail tightened its lazy coil around her bare thigh, and the warmth of contact kept threats and doubts at bay for precious moments longer.

She shifted slightly, and I froze. Her face turned toward me, her lashes brushing her cheeks where the glow from the heat crystals danced faintly against her skin. Even now, grappling with the fragility humans wore so openly, I could feel it beneath the surface—the core of strength she didn't see clearly in herself.

The sight of her like this—unguarded, peaceful—should have soothed me entirely. But as my claws brushed idly over her shoulder, tracing one of the curling tattooed designs etched into her skin, I felt the truth simmer deep inside. It threatened to unseat the quiet victory coiling in my chest.

She was fragile in ways a Drakarn would never be. Soft skin where scales should have grown, bones that lacked the tempered strength of volcanic rock. What would stop the world —the council, the zealots, Karyseth—from taking her away from me? What if ...

I tensed, drawing in a slow breath, too measured to be casual, unwilling to let her feel my unease. Damn it. The thought still lingered, twisting cruelly under the protective satisfaction radiating through me.

It wasn't that I doubted her strength. Quite the opposite— I'd seen it flash like lava-forged steel when she squared her shoulders despite fear, when she spoke truths I didn't want to hear but needed nonetheless. I'd seen it in the fire of her defiance, in the way she'd bled and fought for survival in a world so utterly foreign to her.

No, it wasn't her I doubted. It was the bond—or her perception of it. Did she understand what it meant to me? To us? Or did she still see it as temporary? A convenience? A circumstance she'd never intended to become entangled in?

The thought burned more than I cared to admit.

I rolled onto my side, careful not to disturb her, and propped myself up on one elbow. My gaze swept over her form, soft curves barely concealed by the remnants of the sheet tangled at her waist. Her arm stretched beside her head, bearing lines of ink I now recognized as part of her own fragmented mythology—a map of home, of hope, impossibly distant.

A human thing—this need to carry their past like scars and trophies.

I traced another constellation on her forearm, the faint texture of raised skin under my fingertips a startling contrast to my own hardened scales. Her tattoos spoke of stories written in stars long dead, far from the volcanic flames that forged Drakarn bodies and culture. Both beautiful, but worlds apart.

Possession stirred again, heavy and insistent in my chest. She was mine. The bond was everything, absolute, undeniable in its truths. She belonged in this place, with me, and yet ...

Fear dug its claws in. What if it wasn't enough? What if she didn't want to stay?

I growled low under my breath, the sound rumbling more ferally than intended. Her eyelids fluttered slightly, and I forced myself to still, reigning in the breadth of emotion threatening to spill over.

She shifted against me, her head nuzzling faintly into my chest, lips parting with the softest sigh. One of her hands slipped upward, brushing the side of my rib cage. A simple movement, unconscious even, but it sent a warmth spreading through me sharp enough to drown out the darker thoughts lingering at the edges.

Her breathing shifted, soft sighs turning into faint murmurs as she began to stir. I watched the transition, the way her brows knit slightly before smoothing, how her lips parted in confusion or dream and then settled again as her body woke slowly. Each micro-expression felt like a revelation, a glimpse into the depths of her humanity that both fascinated and confounded me.

The rising heat in my chest softened into something gentle, tender. Adoration claimed me, an urge old as the volcanic rivers of Volcaryth—protect, cherish.

I leaned down, brushing the faintest kiss against her temple. A small shiver rippled through her, but she didn't wake fully, so I pressed another kiss lower, to the delicate line of her jaw, the corner of her mouth. Her soft scent filled my senses, tinged now with the unmistakable marks of me—of us.

She sighed, her lips curling into something that was almost

a smile, her eyes still closed as though resisting wakefulness. My tail tightened its coil faintly, holding her closer, savoring the way her warmth fit perfectly into mine. I trailed my claws lightly along her exposed side, careful not to nick or scratch, though my instincts stirred sharply at the sight of her bare skin.

"You're awake," I murmured, my voice softer than I'd intended, vibrating low against her ear.

She made a noise between a hum and a breathless laugh, her eyelids fluttering open as her eyes found mine. "Barely."

"You sleep heavily," I teased, shifting my head so our foreheads brushed, my horns curving enough to frame her face without touching.

Her lips quirked, though her voice was still heavy with lingering sleep. "Maybe I finally found the right pillow."

I swallowed, my claws stilling against her skin as I searched her half-lidded gaze. I wanted to ask her why this moment, why me, but the weight of the sentiment filled the space between us louder than any words could.

Instead, I let action speak. I dipped my head and kissed her. Not the fire of the night before, but something slower, deeper, a language closer to worship. Her breath hitched in surprise, but she melted into it, her fingers sliding up my chest to rest against one of the ridges glowing faintly at my throat.

I let out a low sound of approval, my palm spreading over her lower back as I pulled her closer. Her body responded instinctively, arching slightly into mine, her warmth soaking into my scales. My tail flexed again, securing her in a loop of heat and pressure that felt more protective than possessive.

She was mine, and everything in me wanted her to know it without question.

Her hands slid higher, grazing the edge of one nipple piercing before meandering up to curve lightly over my shoulders. The fire began to rise again, building as my lips trailed lower, testing the length of her neck to indulge in her pulse there. Every small whimper, every hitch of her breath flared the bond between us tighter, hotter.

"Rath," she said my name softly, her voice somewhere between a warning and an invitation.

I pulled back just enough to meet her gaze, my own breathing heavier now, a faint growl slipping loose before I could leash it. "You taste like sunlight," I rumbled, echoing what I'd told her the night before. A lazy smile tugged at her lips, though it faltered slightly as I traced the side of her throat with my tongue, unwilling to break the connection entirely.

My claws flexed faintly against her waist as I forced my breathing to steady, the bond humming between us taut as a bowstring. She was there, and I would indulge in her forever if it were only up to me—but it wasn't. Not entirely. The council's whispers, the scrutiny of the zealots, Krazath's venomous words—they all lingered like shadows, encroaching on the sanctuary of this moment.

I kissed her forehead softly, lingering just long enough to imprint the gesture into my memory, before pulling back. "There's something we need to talk about."

Her eyes narrowed a fraction, shifting from the sleepy warmth of moments ago to something sharper. "That sounds ominous," she said carefully, her voice tinged with curiosity but underlined by caution.

I sat up slowly, shifting her against me so she remained within my reach, still curled in the protection of my tail. My claws tapped absently against my thigh, weighing words against the storm beginning to churn inside me. "The River's Run Festival begins in four days."

She blinked at the abrupt shift in tone, her brow furrowing faintly. "Okay ... And?"

I met her gaze, letting the weight of my own seriousness

seep into the air between us. "It's one of the most crucial events in Scalvaris," I began, my voice low and steady. "It's not just a celebration; it's tradition, culture, strength. It's ... everything."

Her brows arched at my tone, but she said nothing yet, her full attention now locked on my face. I hadn't lied—she was perceptive, almost frustratingly so. I pressed forward before doubt could creep in.

"There is a ... challenge," I said, the words feeling heavier as they formed. "The Mating Challenge. It's a trial set to prove the strength, the harmony of bonded pairs. Any warrior who has claimed a mate can participate, and to succeed is to remove doubt and silence whispers." The words hissed through my teeth. "Like the ones circling us now."

Her silence stretched just a moment too long for comfort, her expression unreadable. She sat up more fully, drawing the frayed sheet higher against her chest as if the motion could shield her from what I was asking.

Finally, she spoke, each word precise. "You're telling me you want us to compete? Publicly, in front of the entire city?"

I forced myself to stay still, to keep my claws from flexing too visibly. "Yes," I said. "Not just for them. For us. To solidify what we have—to show *everyone*—what this bond means." My voice softened slightly, though I knew my words still carried hard edges.

If this was the way to keep her, then I would do it. I could make sure she was safe. No one would doubt us again.

She exhaled sharply, pushing her wild hair out of her face with one hand. "Rath," she began, her tongue catching her lower lip as it always did when she was preparing to say something uncomfortable. "Do you hear what you're saying? This sounds ... dangerous."

"It is," I admitted, not shying from the truth. "But you're capable. And I would never let anything happen to you."

Her head tilted slightly, her gaze sharpening to an almost surgical precision as she studied me. "This isn't just about proving something to them, is it?" she asked quietly. "You're trying to prove something to yourself."

The words sliced through me. For a moment, I couldn't speak, my throat tightening around the denial that refused to form. She didn't give me the chance to find whatever honesty I could muster.

"Rath," she said again, firmer this time. "I ... I need to think."

And before I could stop her, she slid out of the bed and walked away.

ORLA

MY MIND WAS A FRAGMENTED MESS, thoughts colliding like spent debris in orbit, falling and burning before anything meaningful could take shape. I stayed in Rath's quarters just long enough to dress, my movements sharp and mechanical, as if forcing my body into motion could quiet the storm of my thoughts.

It didn't.

Last night lingered as if it had physically etched itself into me—every touch, every growled vow and promise, every searing kiss. As thrilling as it had been, as natural as it had felt to succumb to the pull between us, the aftermath now beat with heavy uncertainty.

Fated mates.

Bonding.

His claim that I was his. The very idea bristled against every logical bone in my body. It should have felt ridiculous, laughable even.

How was I supposed to reconcile my concept of love and connection, something I'd always believed to be built slowly, steadily, with the Drakarn belief of an instant, primal bond dictated by pheromones and instincts?

Except it wasn't ridiculous—not in the way his eyes had burned into mine last night, like I was all that mattered in his world. Not in the way his presence felt stitched into the air I breathed, as if some invisible string tethered us together whether I wanted it or not. Not in the way I'd felt that crushing pull in my chest when I saw him lock eyes with that bastard Krazath in the arena and knew that he'd stepped into that fight for me.

My hands shook as I laced up my boots. I forced myself to pause and focus, fingers gripping tightly to the leather straps.

What the hell was I doing?

Rath was emotionally ... consuming, that much was obvious. But what shook me was how much of myself I'd already given over in return. Since crashing on this volcanic hellscape, my life had been a string of survival-based decisions: solve the next problem, fix the next broken thing, keep yourself and the team alive.

Somewhere along the way, Rath had become one of those problems—or perhaps he'd convinced me survival meant hiding myself in him like he was my armor.

But now? After last night—after talk of some crazy mating ritual, laid out so plainly this morning—none of this felt simple anymore. The problem wasn't just Rath or me or the bond itself —it was all of it, twisting together in this impossible, dizzying knot of biology and circumstance that no Earth training manual could prepare me for.

"Shit." My knees hurt from kneeling too long, the stone floor unforgiving even through the thin layer of fabric covering my skin. I pressed my palms against my thighs to ground myself, willing my frantic heartbeat to slow.

Rath had given me space. I had no idea when he would return to this room and, frankly, the thought of facing him right now put a lump in my throat—not from fear, but from the unbearable pressure of how much he just ... expected from me.

Not demanded, exactly, but Rath's intensity didn't leave space for half-measures or hesitation. If I stayed, if I said yes to him in every way that mattered, there would be no turning back.

And I wasn't sure if I could live up to that.

I needed more space. I needed time to think—somewhere Rath wouldn't follow. He had to sense my turmoil, I was sure of it, but if I left before he returned, maybe I could buy myself just enough distance to wrestle my thoughts into something coherent.

Outside, the whirr of distant voices and the rush of the river carried on, too ordinary to care about my internal conflict.

How could something so monumental happen, and the world just ... keep turning?

The corridors twisted and opened, the spaces feeling labyrinthine and growingly familiar as I navigated them on autopilot. I wasn't even sure where I was going until the faint sound of rushing water reached me, the humid air thickening as the path sloped downward. My chest ached with too many emotions to name, and instinct guided my steps more than reason.

The baths.

I didn't know why the thought brought the promise of relief, but it was enough to pull me forward. I needed calm, clarity—anything to cut through the riot in my head and heart.

Not to mention, I was still a bit ... sticky.

The baths were one of the few places I'd found since arriving here that still felt ... soft. Even with steam hissing from the walls like the breath of unseen leviathans, and algae casting the water in ghostly hues of green and blue, the space was undeniably alive in a way that soothed the edges of my anxiety.

I stripped my clothes in the small changing area and chose a pool in an alcove where prying eyes were unlikely to watch. The warm air clung to my skin as I slipped into the water, the heat enveloping me immediately and drawing a groan from my throat.

It was hotter than I'd expected, almost scalding, but the sting soothed after a moment, replaced by a deep warmth that seeped into my muscles and began to soften the tension I'd been holding onto for so long.

Steam curled in lazy tendrils around me, drifting toward the stalactites above. The algae-infused light kissed the water's surface, rippling faintly with each exhale I released into the mineral-rich pools. Beneath the surface, the volcanic stone was smooth under my feet.

I closed my eyes and sank lower until the water lapped at my shoulders, letting the heat absorb some of the weight pressing against the walls of my chest. For a moment, just a fleeting moment, I tried to pretend I was anywhere but there. That I was back on Earth, immersed in some sort of secluded hot spring, with no alien trials or fated bonds to unravel and no piercing golden eyes haunting me.

But Volcaryth didn't let me forget itself. The ever-present trace of fire lingered in the air, a sharp reminder that I was far removed from the world I'd called home.

The idea of *home* twisted something in me, a deep, confusing ache that I'd been suppressing since the moment we crash-landed. I had thought I'd come to terms with it, that I'd made my peace with the idea that Earth—my colleagues, my family, the life I'd left behind—was gone. But there, in the quiet of the baths, it all bubbled back up.

Maybe that was what terrified me the most about Rath and everything he represented. I wasn't just fighting against this bond—I was fighting against what it might mean to give up the ghost of the life I used to dream of.

Rath wasn't part of that dream. This world wasn't part of that dream.

And yet, somewhere deep within me—far deeper than science could probe—something in me wanted him anyway.

I pressed my palms to my face, the heat from the water clinging to my skin as I inhaled deeply through my nose. The steam burned slightly on its way into my lungs.

I was startled from my spiraling reflection by an unmistakably human voice, sharp and warm as it pierced through the haze of steam.

"Mind if I join you, or are you hiding?" Selene's voice floated toward me before her figure resolved through the mist, a towel wrapped around her body. Her long black hair was damp, clinging to her skin. She must have just emerged from another pool.

I managed a laugh, though it carried a hollow edge I couldn't quite disguise. "I'm hiding, but not from you. Maybe cowering."

Selene grinned, but the look in her dark eyes was searching. Without waiting for more permission, she sank into the water near me with a soft sigh, the ripples from her entry washing over me.

"You've got that look," she said as she settled in, leaning back against the smooth stone edge casually. "The one that says your whole world just got turned upside down. Or exploded."

Her bluntness sent a derisive snort escaping from me. "Can't it be both?"

"It absolutely can," Selene quipped, offering me an easy smile as she swept her fingers through the water. "I'd argue they tend to go hand in hand. Want to share?"

I hesitated, bracing myself. Selene had always been

disarming in her no-nonsense approach to everything—from patching up wounds to sassing intimidating alien warriors—but I wasn't entirely sure even she could make sense of this.

Still, the words began to tumble out before I could stop them. "I feel like I've stepped into a story I don't understand," I admitted, my voice low and thin against the cavern's hush. "And somehow I've already committed to roles I didn't ask for."

Selene tilted her head, her sharp gaze softening just a fraction. "This about Big Red?"

My laugh cracked this time, barely holding together. "When isn't it about him? And don't call him that."

She huffed, sending a ripple of steam-laden breath across the surface of the water. She nudged my leg with her foot under the water, a gentle prod to pull me from my spiraling doubts. "I'm guessing this is less about Rath the warrior and more about Rath the ... whatever he is to you?"

I swallowed hard, trying and failing to dislodge the knot in my throat. "He thinks I'm his fated mate," I said softly, the words tasting almost bitter on my tongue. "And maybe ... maybe there's something chemical or biological there, something real. But it's all so ... fast. So overwhelming. And I've barely figured myself out here, let alone what I am to him."

Selene was quiet for a moment, her gaze sliding toward the faintly glowing pools farther out in the chamber. Her words were gentle but purposeful.

"I won't pretend to understand it all. Kaiya and I have been trying to wrap our heads around the biology. The pheromone stuff, the bonding rituals, their obsession with biting or whatever weird shit is at play," she said, a faint smirk tugging at her lips for a brief second before sobering again. "But connection— real connection—is never just biology. It's built with choices."

"But what if I didn't get to make those choices? He claimed me in front of everyone without even asking."

"To save your life," she pointed out.

Rudely.

I sank lower into the water, letting the heat slap against my skin as if it could dissolve the tension knotted beneath the surface.

"But now what? What happens if I can't live up to whatever this bond is supposed to mean to him? What happens if this all blows up in my face?" My voice broke slightly on the tail end of the question, the jagged strength of my doubts cutting through what little calm I could scrape together.

Selene arched a single brow, looking entirely unfazed by the outburst. "What happens if it doesn't?" she countered, her tone so maddeningly even it was like she knew how that question would twist inside me.

I opened my mouth only for nothing coherent to come out. I wanted to shout back, insist she hadn't seen Rath, hadn't felt the intensity he carried everywhere with him, hadn't been dragged into the gravitational pull of someone so certain of every step he took that it felt impossible to diverge.

But she just waited, her dark eyes pinning me in place the way only she could.

"It's *so* much," I finally managed, the words weak as they left me. It didn't feel like the truth, at least not the whole of it, but it was the best I could offer. "What if I want time to figure this out first? What if I need time that he can't give me?"

Selene's exhale came soft, gentle with understanding. "Then that's what you tell him. Look, your guy strikes me as this ... overwhelming force of nature. But from what I've seen, he'd rather burn himself alive than force you into something you truly don't want. Unless it's to save your life. In which case, well, we've seen how that goes."

I gave her a flat look. "And what makes you think he'll

understand? Have you *seen* how Drakarn handle emotions? Intensity is kind of their whole thing."

Selene shrugged like I'd just asked her something as simple as where she'd stashed the med kits. "They're intense. But they're not incapable of listening. Remember, you're not the only one in this bond thing. If Rath values you—and clearly he does—then make him hear you. Let him understand the space you need. Building something real doesn't mean submitting to his every whim."

I let her words sit between us, their weight shifting something delicate inside me. My jaw clenched, the burning pull of doubt still smoldering, but she wasn't wrong. Rath wasn't just claiming me in the way the Drakarn did; he was offering something at the core of himself, messy and complicated and raw.

The real question might not have been about Rath and his expectations but about *me*. What part of me was afraid of saying yes—because saying yes meant staying, meant stripping away every excuse I had to leave behind difficult emotions and impossible bonds I hadn't planned for.

"You're thinking," Selene murmured. "Stop trying to solve him like he's a damn equation. You can't science your way through this one, Orla."

That pulled a snort from me, my lips tugging into the first faint smile I'd felt all morning. "Are you seriously accusing me of being too logical?"

"Damn right I am." Her grin was irreverent, but her voice softened beneath it. "Listen, science girl, there's nothing logical about falling for someone—human, Drakarn, whatever. You don't get to control it, but you do get to decide what you'll do with it. So yeah, maybe you're scared. That makes sense—this is wild. But maybe lean into it a little. Give it a chance to prove itself before you shut the door completely."

A spark of laughter slipped out before I could stop it, the

sound catching on the edges of my frayed emotions. "Are you sure you're qualified to play relationship guru?"

"Touché," Selene replied, unfazed. "But for what it's worth, if I had a ridiculously hot, ridiculously devoted alien hanging on my every word, I wouldn't be sitting here overthinking it. Enjoy the ride. And I do mean that literally. Figure the rest out later."

The exaggerated waggle of her eyebrows brought a laugh out of me so unexpectedly I almost startled myself with it. I shook my head as warmth unconnected to the water spread through my chest.

"Thanks. Seriously." I tilted my head back toward the slick volcanic rock, exhaling fully for what felt like the first time in hours.

"No problem." Selene leaned back in turn, her grin softening. "And hey, if you need me to punch him, you know where to find me."

"Pretty sure that'd be the shortest fight in history," I teased, finally letting the tension lose its grip on my chest entirely.

Selene kicked water at me in retaliation, and soon laughter filled the small alcove, turning the soothing peace of the baths into something warmer, something ... human.

Exactly what I needed.

13

ORLA

IN RATH'S QUARTERS AGAIN, the silence felt heavier than it should have. I sat on the edge of the bed, my hands curled into the fabric of my pants, twisting relentlessly as I tried to find the right words. They stayed lodged in my throat.

I'd spent hours in the baths, piecing together the fragments of whatever this was—the bond, the uncertainty, the unfamiliar intensity tying me to Rath. Selene had reminded me that none of it had to make perfect sense. But that didn't mean I was any closer to understanding what I should do next.

What if I said the wrong thing? What if I couldn't give him what he was asking for? What if I fucked this whole thing up?

The door opened, and I startled, my pulse jumping as Rath stepped into the room. His wings filled the entryway like they had every right to bend the space around them. He wasn't wearing his formal armor, just a simple combat tunic that hung unbuttoned at the throat. The red of his scales seemed sharper against the black fabric, his markings glinting faintly.

His eyes snapped to mine instantly, narrowing slightly—not in anger but in that way he always had, like he was trying to gauge every nuance of what I wasn't saying aloud. The door shut behind him, plunging us into an oppressive, expectant silence that made my chest tighten.

"You're back." His voice was low and rough, laced with something unreadable.

I nodded, swallowing hard. "I just needed to think."

Rath inclined his head, though there was a faint edge of tension in his wings—tightened, folded close. "And?"

My hands clenched tighter. "I don't know," I admitted, my voice cracking faintly. "I don't know what I'm supposed to do with ... this." I gestured vaguely at the space between us, the air thick enough to feel tangible. "With you. With ... us."

Rath's jaw tightened, but he stayed eerily still, watching me the way a predator watches prey—not to intimidate, but to understand. To wait until my guard dropped enough for him to move.

"I—" I started and stopped, warring with the hurricane of words swirling in my chest. Finally, I just forced them out. "I don't want to ruin this. Or hurt you. I don't know what you expect—"

"There is no expectation," he said quietly, though the weight of his voice made it sound like a promise. "Not from me. Not from the bond. Only what we choose to give each other."

I stared at him, caught off guard by his directness. When I didn't respond right away, Rath stepped closer—not looming or pressing but moving into my orbit with deliberate care. His tail dragged faintly along the floor behind him, its slow sway at odds with the stillness of his shoulders and wings.

"I want to take you somewhere," he said, his gaze holding mine. "Will you come with me?"

The abrupt shift threw me, but the steadiness in his voice left me with few options for protest. My body moved almost involuntarily, standing before my mind could catch up to what I was agreeing to.

"Where?" I managed, trying to shake off the lingering nerves tightening my spine.

"You'll see," Rath replied, a faint curve brushing the corners of his mouth. This wasn't his usual sharp edge—it was something lighter, easier. The fleeting glimpse of it eased the tension in my chest just enough for me to exhale.

Without waiting for further hesitation, Rath extended his arm. I glanced at it, then back at him. His expression didn't change, but there was something faint and vulnerable in the way he waited. Like stepping back might hurt him more than I realized.

I placed my hand lightly against his arm. Rath's claws flexed against his side, his throat dipping with a slow swallow, and then he turned, leading me wordlessly to the chamber's exit.

The walk was short, the corridors of Scalvaris familiar now, though they always seemed different when he was near— charged by his presence, by the awareness that I could always feel subtly pulling between us like gravity.

When we reached the shaft that led out toward the surface, I hesitated. It wasn't dread or fear exactly—just the unfinished idea of stepping beyond my new normal into something entirely unknown, again.

Rath stopped with me, glancing back, his head tilting just enough to catch me in his unwavering gaze. "Do you trust me?" he asked, as blunt as ever.

The question caught me sideways, throwing me off balance before I managed a simple nod.

"Hold tight," he said, and before I could ask what he meant, he swept me into his arms with effortless strength.

The air shifted sharply as his wings unfurled, the rush of volcanic wind cutting through the cavern's stale heat. Rath crouched briefly, his tail curling behind him for balance, before leaping into the vertical shaft.

I locked my arms around his neck, reflexive fear sparking in my chest, but it evaporated almost immediately. There was no faltering in his movement, no hitch of uncertainty as his wings beat powerfully against the currents, carrying us upward.

We broke through to the surface in a rush of light and heat, twin suns blazing against the horizon, their fiery glow drenching everything in gold and crimson. My breath caught as Rath gained altitude, the molten-red deserts stretching endlessly below, interrupted only by jagged peaks that sparkled like captured lightning.

The view was staggering, beautiful in a way that felt almost violent. I couldn't look away.

Rath angled his wings wide, leveling us into a smooth glide. The two suns cast long shadows against his scales, their reddish glow sharpening the dark tiger stripes that cut across his ruby red skin.

"You never see the sky like this underground, not even from the sky shafts," I said softly, more to myself than to him.

Rath's voice rumbled low, almost thoughtful. "The surface is harsher. Less forgiving. But even here, beauty survives."

I turned my head slightly against his chest, catching the faint shift in his profile as he adjusted for whatever destination we were headed toward. "Where are we going?"

"You'll see," he said simply, the words so heavy with quiet finality they felt like a vow.

It wasn't an answer. But I didn't press him. I watched the alien landscape shift below us—the streams of lava glinting like veins beneath the crust and the peaks that caught fire in the suns' light.

After what felt like an eternity wrapped in wind and alien

light, Rath began to descend, his wings pulling inward as we spiraled toward a break in the terrain I hadn't noticed before. Nestled between spires of heat-resistant flora, an oasis shimmered below—a natural spring enclosed by rock walls streaked with veins of crystal. The pool radiated faint steam, kissed by the twin suns but seemingly untouched by the harshness of Volcaryth.

The sight stole my breath. It was like stepping into a memory of Earth, somehow blooming alive on a world that should have crushed it.

Rath landed gracefully at the edge of the spring. As his feet touched the ground with a solid thud, his arms remained steady, still holding me securely against him. For a moment, I clung to him, my gaze caught between the shimmering spring and the sharp edges of the cliff walls framing it. The contrast of molten hues and soft greens was surreal. The terrain around us was harsh and jagged, yet this place seemed untouched, almost sacred.

"You can let go now," Rath murmured, his voice low and impossibly soft near my ear, cutting through the reverent quiet around us.

I flushed, realizing how tightly I'd been holding onto him, and awkwardly pushed against his chest. He lowered me to the ground slowly, scanning my face for something I couldn't name before finally stepping back. His absence left a sudden, oddly cool space at my side, though his heat still lingered faintly in the air.

I turned in a slow circle, taking in the spring. The water shimmered unnaturally, its surface tinted with soft, iridescent hues—brilliant greens, blues, and purples playing against the sunlight streaming through the crystal-lined walls. Heat seeped up from the stones beneath my feet, and strange flowering plants clung to the crevices, their petals pulsing faintly as though they were alive.

"It's beautiful," I breathed.

Rath's gaze didn't leave me, though he inclined his head slightly in acknowledgment. "Few from Scalvaris come here anymore. It lies far from the usual paths, difficult to find without knowing where to look."

My chest tightened at his words. This was something special to him, something shared just with me. "So why bring me here?"

He didn't answer immediately. Instead, he turned and gestured to one of the rock formations nearby. Nestled against the spring's edge, partially hidden by heat-resistant foliage, was a small structure made of organic material—simply designed but clearly well maintained.

"It's a resting place for travelers," Rath said finally. "Warriors, scholars—any who dare to venture far from their clans, their worlds. I thought you might like to see it."

Rath's hands brushed over the markings carved into the stone near the spring, his claws gentle against the ancient etchings. "This was built long ago, after the fall of the old world but before we founded our cities." His tone dipped slightly, tinged with something unreadable. "It was not meant for claiming territory or power. It was meant to be a place of peace."

I stared at him, the magnitude of his words settling heavily in my chest. "Then why did you bring me here?" I asked again.

He turned to face me fully. His wings shifted behind him, a restless motion that betrayed the otherwise controlled expression on his face. He stood for a moment, saying nothing, and then reached into a pouch he had strapped to his side. When his hand reappeared, he held something small but unmistakable —a dagger.

He stepped closer, holding it out between us. "This," he said, his voice low but powerful, "is for you."

The weapon was stunning. The blade itself gleamed, infused with streaks of the heat crystals I'd seen all around Scalvaris. But its hilt was something else entirely, forged from curved fragments of metal that looked unmistakably human. It must have been recovered from the crashed ship. The two materials were woven together as though they had always belonged as one.

I hesitated to reach for it. "You ... made this?"

"It was not an easy thing to create," Rath admitted. "But for you, it felt ... right."

My mouth went dry. I glanced from the dagger to his face but found no mockery or humor there—only raw, steady emotion reflected in the sharpness of his features. He extended it closer, waiting, unbending in his patience until I reached forward and accepted the weapon.

The weight of it was perfect, the hilt cool beneath my fingers while the blade seemed to hum faintly with residual warmth. I traced a finger lightly along the carved grooves of the handle, my breath catching as I realized what it represented.

"You did this to—" I faltered, struggling to find words that could encompass the enormity of the gesture. "You didn't have to do this."

"I did." Rath's voice was a low rumble, his jaw tightening faintly. "We are ... different, *shyrarva*. Orla. Of two worlds that should never have crossed. But for all our differences, the bond does not lie. You are mine, and I—" He faltered, his claws flexing at his sides before cutting through the hesitation. "I am yours. All that I have—all that I am."

The intensity of his confession pulled at something deep within me, a knot of emotion I hadn't allowed myself to untangle since this all began. I stared at him, my chest tight, the dagger trembling slightly in my grip.

He'd put everything on the table, flayed himself open before me without shame or regret.

I dropped the dagger gently onto the carved stone behind me and crossed the short space between us in two steps. Rath stiffened slightly, caught off guard, but I didn't give him time to recover. I reached up, my hands finding the planes of his face.

And then I kissed him.

14

RATH

HER CLOTHES FELL AWAY like ash from a cooling forge. My claws hovered over the fastenings of her tunic, pulled back to their narrowest points as I worked the stubborn closures. A bead of sweat slid down my spinal ridge—not from heat, but from the excruciating care required not to shred the fragile human flesh.

My talons trembled as they skimmed her collarbone, her breath hitching when the blunted tips caught the strap of her breastband.

Fragile. So fragile.

The garment slithered free. Her breasts rose with her next indrawn breath, rosy peaks tightening under air that suddenly felt too thick. Two emotions warred—the urge to mark and the need to worship. My tongue swept over an ivory-sharp fang, restraining myself against instinct's surge.

Slow.

Orla's fingers grazed my flank with agonizing hesitation, undoing the seals along my combat harness. Her blunt nails caught on an old scar near my hip. My cock throbbed at the sensation, scales flushing hotter where her knuckles brushed them. When the last clasp released, the harness fell with a heavy thud. She didn't flinch.

Her palm met the center of my chest, halting me.

"Let me," she whispered.

Her shirt followed mine to the ground. Moonlight through the steam painted her human curves in silver—soft where I was ridged, vulnerable where I was armored, perfect in all the ways that infuriated and entranced. I traced the line of Cygnus's path along her forearm with a single claw, watching goosebumps flare in its wake. The stars etched into her skin called to me, a language I couldn't parse but desperately wished to claim.

My tongue followed where my talon had traveled.

She shuddered.

Her skin tasted of salt and wild energy, humming with the same charge that gathered before a lightning storm. My lips closed around the faded ink of Ursa Major, suckling the scar tissue beneath with just enough pressure to make her fingers knot in my hair. The groan that tore from me vibrated against her pulse point—a sound I hadn't meant to release, raw and stripped of dignity.

Weakness. Sacred weakness.

Her hands found hair, not gripping but cradling. The contact speared through me—a Drakarn's head in human hands, our most guarded vulnerability. I froze, torn between wrenching away and leaning into the blasphemous intimacy.

Air hissed through my teeth.

"Look at me," she urged.

Reluctance burned like swallowed embers as I lifted my gaze. Her irises held flecks of gold now, mirrored fragments of my own eyes caught in the territory of hers. The world narrowed to that impossible symmetry.

My claws flexed against her hips.

"If I hurt you—"

"You won't."

Her certainty destroyed me.

My tongue mapped her—every constellation, every scar—laving slow, wet stripes across the faded ink of Ursa Minor. Her flesh quivered beneath the broad, flat strokes, each deliberate swipe calculated to draw gasps. When I reached Lyra's curve, I let the tip flick outward, rasping over the sensitive dip between rib and hip. Her hips jerked.

"Fuck—!"

The human curse shattered against the hut's walls as I pressed deeper, the full length of my tongue undulating now—a hot, living blade writing devotion across her abdomen. Drakarn anatomy allowed for precision no human mouth could match—broad enough to span her entire navel, pointed enough to circle a single tightening nipple.

Dragging the tip up her sternum, I paused at the scar above her heart—the one she'd inked over with dots of Andromeda. Here, my tongue softened. Broad, flat laps interspersed with the delicate pierce of its pointed end, tracing every link in the tattooed shackles until her moans turned fractured.

Her hands fisted against my ribs when I reached her throat. "Rath—!"

A warning. A plea.

I consumed both.

My tongue delved into the hollow beneath her jaw, twin points massaging the frantic pulse there. Her back arched violently, breasts brushing my scales as I worked higher—flicking her earlobe, then retreating to swirl around the shell. The vibration of her gasp traveled straight to my throbbing cock.

"You taste ...," my growl hitched as her nails found the gaps between my back plates, "like lightning."

Her thighs framed my face as I knelt—an offering and a conquest. Heat curled around us as my tongue extended to its full length to trace a path up her inner thigh. She gasped, heels digging into the notched scars between my shoulder blades. The musk of her arousal cut through the mineral air, igniting glands beneath my tongue I hadn't known could *burn.*

"Fates' breath—"

Her curse dissolved into a moan as the primary ridge of my tongue pressed against her cleft. I stilled, savoring the shiver that racked her body—the way her human softness yielded to my heat.

There.

Her hips jerked, but my tail coiled tighter around her waist —an unyielding anchor. The tip found her lower back, vibrating faintly with the rhythm of my pulse. Every gasp, every twitch of her abdominal muscles mapped directly to the swollen ridges along my cock. Pre-cum slicked the scaled base where it strained against my stomach, the tongue-like foreskin writhing against empty air.

"Look down," I growled against her thigh. "Watch what you do to me."

Her fingers tightened in my hair as she obeyed. The breath left her in a rush.

My cock arched upward—thick, veined, and glistening—the barbell piercing catching the light. The fleshy lip at its crown undulated hungrily, dripping translucent fluid that steamed where it struck the rocks.

"Rath, I—"

My tongue plunged into her without warning, the tapered tip curling upward to stroke that spongy ridge inside that I'd learned drove her mad. Her scream fractured against the walls as my fingers carefully stroked her clit. The dual assault left her thrashing—a wild thing caught in the jaws of something ancient and ravenous.

My claws found her hips, blunt tips dimpling flesh as I dragged her closer. "Come," I commanded against her quivering skin. "Mark my face with it."

Her orgasm hit like lava erupting through bedrock—a flood that drenched my chin. I drank it greedily, glands beneath my tongue swelling to absorb her essence. The taste *changed* as she peaked—sweetness giving way to something metallic and vital, a flavor that seared itself into my marrow.

Mine.

My cock lashed the air, desperate and slick, as I rose on trembling knees. Her dazed eyes tracked the movement, lips parting as I gripped the base, smearing her release across the weeping crown.

"This," I snarled, guiding that writhing lip to her tender inner thigh, "needs you."

"Stop teasing," she gasped, nails scoring my flank.

A feral grin split my face. "Beg properly."

"Please fuck me. *Now.*"

Her plea hung in the air, and something deep in me surged to meet it. My talons flexed against her hips, the blunt tips pressing just enough to leave faint marks—not to hurt, but to claim. Her breath hitched, her body arching toward mine, and I knew I was lost.

I guided her down onto the soft moss that lined the ground, her back pressing into the warm surface as I positioned myself above her. My wings mantled around us, creating a cocoon of heat and privacy, the membrane catching the faint light filtering around us. Her eyes locked onto mine, wide and trusting, and seeing her like this—open, vulnerable, and utterly mine—sent a shudder through my scales.

"Karys'veth ir," I growled, the endearment slipping from my lips as I bent to kiss her. My tongue swept against hers, hot and demanding, and she moaned into the kiss, her hands sliding up my back to grip the ridges along my spine. The sensation of her blunt nails scraping those sensitive grooves made me shudder, a low, involuntary sound rumbling from my chest.

I broke the kiss, my breath ragged, and trailed my lips down her throat, nipping lightly at the sensitive skin. Her pulse fluttered beneath my tongue, and I couldn't resist marking her there, just once, with the faintest graze of my fangs. She gasped, her hips lifting instinctively, and I growled in approval, my cock throbbing against her thigh.

"You're mine," I murmured against her skin, the words a vow and a warning. "Every part of you."

Her response was a breathless whimper as I positioned myself at her entrance, the tip of my cock pressing against her slick heat. The fleshy lip at the crown undulated eagerly, leaving a glistening trail of pre-cum as I pushed forward, inch by agonizing inch. Her body stretched to accommodate me, the sensation of her tight warmth enveloping me almost too much to bear.

"Rath—" Her voice broke on my name, her nails digging into my back as I seated myself fully inside her. I stilled, giving her a moment to adjust, my breath coming in harsh pants as I fought for control. The urge to move, to claim her completely, was a fire in my veins, but I held back, my claws flexing against her hips.

"Look at me," I commanded, my voice rough with need. Her eyes fluttered open, meeting mine, and the trust I saw there nearly undid me. I began to move, slow and deliberate, each thrust drawing a gasp or moan from her lips. The ridges along my cock dragged against her inner walls, the barbell piercing adding an extra layer of sensation that made her writhe beneath me.

Her hands slid down to grip my forearms, her nails leaving faint marks in my scales as I increased the pace. My wings tightened around us, the membrane vibrating with the force of my thrusts, and I could feel her body tightening around me, her climax building with each movement.

"Come for me," I growled, my voice a low rumble that seemed to vibrate through her. Her back arched, a cry tearing from her throat as her orgasm hit, her inner walls clenching around me in waves. The sensation was too much, and with a roar, I followed her over the edge, my release pulsing deep inside her, the scaled base of my cock throbbing with each spurt.

I collapsed onto my forearms, my breath coming in harsh gasps as I pressed my forehead to hers. Her hands slid up to cradle my face, her thumbs brushing against the scales along my jaw, and I felt something in me shift—something deep and un-nameable.

"*Karys'veth ir,*" I whispered again, the words softer this time, reverent. Her lips curved into a faint smile, and she pulled me down for a kiss, slow and tender, her body still trembling beneath mine.

The world narrowed to the rhythm of her breathing, the faint rise and fall of her chest beneath my palm. My tongue traced the curve of her shoulder, lapping at the residual slickness of our joining. The taste of her—sweet and *mine*, tinged with the smoky musk of my release—was intoxicating. My glands swelled beneath my tongue, absorbing her essence, marking her as mine in a way no Drakarn could deny.

Her fingers carded through the ridges along my spine, the touch sending shivers through my scales. I nearly purred, and she laughed softly, the vibration of it humming against my chest.

"You're trembling," she murmured, her voice still thick with the remnants of pleasure.

I lifted my head to meet her gaze, my eyes narrowing slightly. "Drakarn do not tremble," I said, though the faint quiver in my wings betrayed the lie.

Her lips curved into a knowing smile, and she reached up to brush a strand of hair from my face. The motion was so tender, so human, that it made my chest ache. My tail, still coiled loosely around her waist, tightened reflexively, pulling her closer.

"You're beautiful," she said, her voice soft but unwavering.

The words struck me like a blow, leaving me momentarily speechless. Drakarn were not beautiful—we were fierce, powerful, unyielding. But the way she looked at me, with something akin to reverence, made me feel as though I were something more.

Something worthy of her.

I leaned down to capture her lips in a slow, lingering kiss, my tongue sweeping against hers in a silent promise. When I pulled back, her eyes were half-lidded, her breath coming in shallow pants.

"I am yours," I said, the words a low rumble that vibrated through her.

Her fingers traced the line of my jaw, her touch feather-light but searing. "I know," she whispered.

I shifted slightly, my wings mantling around us as I reached for the dagger I had placed on the stone beside us. The blade gleamed in the light, the heat crystals embedded in its surface casting a soft glow. I held it out to her, the hilt resting in my palm.

"This is yours," I said, my voice rough with emotion. "A symbol of our bond. Of what could be together."

She hesitated for a moment before reaching out to take it, her fingers brushing against mine. The contact sent a jolt of heat through me, and I had to fight the urge to pull her back into my arms.

I reached out to cup her face, my claws gentle against her skin. "You are my heart's eternal flame, *shyrarva*."

Her breath hitched, and she leaned into my touch, her eyes closing briefly. When she opened them again, they were filled with a determination that made my chest swell with pride. "You keep calling me that. What does it mean?"

"It is your mating name. And I just said you are my fire's heart."

How could she not know?

Sweat had plastered some of her fading purple hair to her forehead, and she brushed it away. "And you just had that ready on the tip of your tongue when you, uh," she stumbled over the word, "claimed me?"

I could hide the full truth from her no longer.

"I'd had some time to think of it. I've known you were my mate from the moment I first laid eyes on you. Healer Mysha had to throw me out of the healing caverns when you first came to Scalvaris. I nearly tore the place apart to find you. If I had not been sent out to protect the city, I would have come for you long before that day."

My shyrarva was silent for several beats.

She placed the dagger on the stone beside us, her movements slow and deliberate. Then she reached up to pull me down into another kiss, her lips soft and demanding against mine. My wings tightened around us, shielding her from the world as I lost myself in the taste of her, in the feel of her body pressed against mine.

There was nothing else. Just her. Just us. And the bond that tied us together, unbreakable and finally whole.

THE MARKET'S chaos buzzed against my skin, every scent and shout sharpened by the low thrum of anxiety in my veins. I pressed my back against a stall draped in tapestries, their threads pulsing faintly with captured geothermal energy.

My journal lay open in my lap, half-filled with sketches of festival preparations—flame-blackened meat skewers dripping with alien spices, crystalline lanterns strung between dark pillars, a trio of Drakarn children darting underfoot with stolen sweets clutched in their claws.

I forced my pencil to keep moving, ignoring the way vendors avoided my gaze as I passed. Their slit-pupiled eyes tracked me from behind stalls, whispers hissing through sharp teeth. *Outsider. Human. False-mate.* The words slithered around me, unspoken but unable to ignore.

With Rath, everything felt ... so freaking perfect I thought I might explode. Out here, alone, I was forced to remember everything *else*.

A familiar laugh cut through the noise. My head snapped up. *Selene.* There she was, her braid swinging as she walked beside Vega and Eden, their heads bent in conversation. Relief surged hot and sudden in my chest. I opened my mouth to call out—

They turned a corner, vanishing behind a curtain of smoldering incense.

"Damn it," I muttered, snapping the journal shut. The movement sent a flock of paperwing moths scattering from a nearby fruit cart. I stood, brushing volcanic grit from my pants, when the air shifted.

A shadow fell across my notes.

Three Drakarn warriors blocked the path, their scales dulled with ash deliberately rubbed into the grooves as if they were trying to disguise themselves. The tallest bared his fangs in a mockery of a smile. "The councilor's pet requires an escort."

No chance in hell.

My pulse spiked. "I'm fine."

The one on the left lunged.

My body moved before my mind caught up—rock-climbing reflexes twisting me sideways, fingers scrabbling for purchase on a vendor's stall draped in gorgeous silk. The fabric wrinkled under my grip as I swung around the support beam, sending a cascade of tapestries crashing onto the warrior's head. He roared, temporarily blinded by embroidered chaos.

Sweat stung my eyes as I bolted through the gap between stalls. My boots skidded on spilled spice grains, the air thickening with the reek of singed feathers from a nearby poultry cart. A child's discarded toy nearly sent me to my knees, and I stumbled, the second warrior's claws slicing empty air where my throat had been.

"Run, little leech!" someone jeered, met with jagged laughter.

I vaulted over a crate of melons, their skins bursting under my palms. Sticky juice coated my hands as I hurled a shattered fruit at my pursuer. It exploded against his chest in a sweet spray, buying me two ragged breaths.

The third warrior materialized from the crowd's periphery, net already whirling above his head. I feinted left, then dove right toward a butcher's stall—

Too slow.

A weighted net slammed into my back like a meteor strike. Obsidian shards seared through my shirt, etching lines of fire across my shoulder blades. I hit the ground chin-first, teeth clacking together with the taste of copper. The fibers constricted with almost sentient malice, tightening with every thrash.

"Rath will flay you alive!" I snarled. My knee connected with something soft—a gratifying yelp—before four sets of claws pinned me.

"Your fire-heart's not here," the leader hissed, his breath reeking like fermented lava beetles. He pressed a talon against my windpipe, not quite breaking skin. "Scream again, and I'll gift him your vocal cords in a festival box."

A sack descended—coarse fibers soaked in Volcaryth moss extract. The world dissolved into chemical burn and muffled chaos as they dragged me across sharp gravel. I focused on the pain, mapping turns by the way shards bit into my hipbones. Left at the heated belch of bathhouse vents.

Silent tears cut through the grime on my face. Not from fear.

From fury.

"Don't worry, human," the leader purred, hauling me over his shoulder. "You'll see your mate soon."

Liar.

They dragged me through the city, but with the bag over my head, I had no idea where we were going. Deeper, I thought. I couldn't hear the river, and it was almost overwhelmingly hot.

We finally came to a stop, and I heard the groan of metal before the Drakarn carrying me dumped me unceremoniously on my ass.

The cell door clanged shut with finality, its echo swallowed by walls weeping condensation. I pressed palms to rough volcanic stone, mapping fissures through grit-coated fingertips.

I ripped the bag off my head and took it all in.

Three paces long. Two wide. Ceiling low enough to graze my scalp if I stood straight.

Luminescent fungi smeared the walls in sickly green streaks, their light just enough to reveal the room's cruel geometry. I crouched, cheek pressed to the floor's single air vent. Sulfur and something floral tinged the stale draft.

I tested the bars, the walls, everything, hoping for some sort of weakness. I yelled for help until I was hoarse and then started again once I'd had time to recover. Hours could have passed; I had no way of knowing.

I yelled again.

"Should've gagged her properly," a guard growled beyond the door, his Drakarn consonants sharp as flint. It was too dim in the cell to get a good look at them.

His companion snorted. "Let the leech wheeze. Karyseth wants the human intact, not comfortable."

My nails bit into palms. *Karyseth.* That damned priestess who wanted me dead. This wasn't random hostility—this was politics. And revenge.

Footsteps approached. I scrambled upright, back flattening against the warmest wall—the one vibrating with geothermal currents. One of the guards came into view.

"Still breathing?" The guard's slitted eye glinted with malicious delight. "Pity."

I lunged, slamming my shoulder against reinforced metal. The impact shuddered through my bones. "Tell your coward leader to face me herself!"

Laughter rattled the door. "You're feisty for prey. We'll see if you—"

The insult dissolved into wet choking. Someone new spoke —a voice like smoldering silk. "Run along, pups. The grownups need to chat."

The guards cursed and fled.

A Drakarn I'd never seen before slouched against the frame, his emerald scales catching the fungal glow in a way that made his entire body seem to smolder with a strange green fire. Unlike Rath's warrior-straight posture, this one moved with liquid indolence, a half-eaten fruit skewer dangling from his claws.

"Well," he drawled, eyes raking over me, "you're shorter than I imagined."

I pressed harder against the rumbling wall, fingers curling around a loose stone shard. "Who the hell are you?"

He took a deliberate bite of fruit, juices running down his wrist. "Vyne. Rath's favorite nuisance." The barbell through his tongue glinted as he spoke. "He's currently two sectors away chasing false leads, thanks to Krazath's little friends. Which leaves you with me."

"Bullshit." My grip tightened on the shard. "Prove it."

Vyne sighed dramatically and reached into his tunic. My muscles coiled—until he produced Rath's mating dagger. *My* dagger. He flipped it hilt-first toward me, the blade embedding in the floor between my boots.

"He'll kill me when he finds out I touched that," he said, licking fruit residue from his claws. "His mate's blade shouldn't bear another's scent. Sentimental fool. I nicked it from your quarters before coming to find you."

I wrenched the dagger free. "If you're here to help, get me the fuck out of here."

"You *are* feisty. I see why he likes you. Unfortunately, no can do."

"What?" I surged forward, jerking the knife from the floor and pointing it at him like it would be any help with cell bars between us.

"First, I don't have the keys. The guards were scared, but they're not completely stupid. You'll be let out bright and early tomorrow for the Mating Challenge." He tossed the skewer aside.

My blade trembled in my grip. "The what?" I remembered Rath bringing it up, but I'd forgotten about that completely. And I'd certainly never agreed to it.

Vyne's tail flicked, its tip tracing idle patterns on the floor. "The Mating Challenge. It's the traditional method for weeding out weak bonds. Or disposing of political embarrassments." He leaned closer, the fungus painting his smirk toxic green. "Guess which category you're in?"

I clutched the dagger tighter. "Rath wouldn't agree to this."

"That doesn't matter." Vyne produced a vial from his belt—liquid fire swirling like captured lightning. "The Forge Temple started this; Karyseth is challenging your bond in one of the few ways that can't be denied. Either you both survive the trial tomorrow and prove yourselves, or ..." He mimed an explosion with his free hand.

"So why isn't *he* in a cell?"

Vyne rolled the vial between his claws. "He may be by now. No one's been stupid enough to volunteer for a Mating Challenge in ... a decade? Maybe more. We're all a bit rusty on the formalities. If he finds you before tomorrow, your life and his will be forfeit. But I'm not sure he cares about that right now. I've spoken to some of your friends. They say you're the smart one."

"What are you getting at?" I didn't like this man, and I couldn't trust him. What kind of friend would act this way?

"If you ever want to be accepted in Scalvaris, you need to undergo this challenge and survive. It won't satisfy Karyseth—nothing but your death will—but she's only one woman. The rest of the city will fall in line, especially with Darrokar backing you."

He sounded a lot like Terra had all those weeks ago when this all started. I really wished it was her who was talking to me.

But, damn it all, I saw his point.

My pulse hadn't stopped pounding. "How does it work?"

"Survive until sunrise. Someone will take you to the testing grounds. You and Rath face the dangers of the test—geothermal vents, shadow predators, the usual fun." He slid the vial through the bars. "One drop melts steel. Two?" His pierced tongue flicked over a fang. "Don't be nearby."

I pocketed the acid, noting how his levity didn't reach his eyes. "Why are you helping?"

"Rath's the only one who laughs at my jokes." He turned to leave, scales rippling with false nonchalance. "Oh, and human? Try not to scream when the skin sloughs off your bones. It's undignified."

Alone again, the vial settled against my thigh, its threat as volatile as my thoughts.

Did you know? I silently asked Rath's ghost. *Is this your idea of romance?*

My fingers found the dagger's hilt—Rath's craftsmanship, Vyne's theft. Both Drakarn men leaving scars in different ways. I tested the wall's weak point, volcanic grit raining down as I pried loose a handhold.

I wanted out of this cage more than almost anything else. The vial in my pocket could get me out.

But I hesitated.

The fissure taunted me—a hairline crack weeping steam near the cell's corner. I crouched before it, Vyne's vial burning a hole in my pocket. One drop could fracture the volcanic stone. Two might collapse the entire wall.

My thumb caressed the stopper.

Run.

The survival instinct drilled into me screamed for action. Melt the bars. Slip into the steam vents. Let the acidic reek of Volcaryth's underbelly cloak my escape.

I uncorked the vial.

The liquid fire hissed at exposure to air, its surface swirling with miniature plasma storms. I held it over the fissure, watching light dance across the stone. One trembling tilt would expose the weakness in the rock.

And possibly blow me to bits.

My hand froze.

Coward.

The word slithered through me in a nameless Drakarn's voice, all gravel and disappointed heat. I slammed the stopper back in place.

"Fuck you," I whispered to the phantom judgment.

But the truth coiled tighter than Vyne's acid—escaping wouldn't stop the challenge. It would only prove every sneering Drakarn right.

Human. Weak.

Unworthy.

I retreated, back pressed against the far wall. The dagger's hilt bit into my side as I methodically braided my hair—tight, practical, battle-ready. Every tug of the purple strands filled me with resolve.

Survive until sunrise.

The geothermal hum beneath my shoulders carried whispers of the arena. Vyne's casual horrors—shadow predators, flesh-melting vents—took shape in the condensation dripping down the walls. I imagined hypotheticals, calculating thermal blind spots, drafting escape vectors from half-remembered schematics of Scalvaris' underlevels.

A rasp of claws against stone snapped my head up.

"Final meal, leech."

A guard slid a clay bowl through the slot—lukewarm gruel swimming with unidentifiable protein chunks. My stomach revolted. I ate it anyway, trying to remember those honey fritters Rath had brought me.

Vyne's acid vial went into my left boot. Rath's dagger claimed a spot in the right.

The cell's oppressive heat thickened as night deepened. Sweat glued my tunic to my skin. I counted breaths, trying to meditate.

Three hundred twelve ... three hundred thirteen ...

Eventually, I must have slept.

Metal shrieked.

I jolted upright as the cell door groaned open, revealing silhouettes backlit by blood-orange torchlight.

"The challenge begins when the horn bellows." The guard's smirk dripped venom as shackles snapped around my wrists. "Hope you die quickly."

Somewhere beyond the labyrinth of stone, Rath would be hunting.

And I'd be the prey.

ORLA'S FEAR lingered in the market's choked air like smoke. Vendors scattered as I stormed through the lower districts, my scales burning so violently they cast crimson shadows across the stalls.

"Where is she?" I snarled, slamming a merchant against his own spice cart. Cinnamon pods rained down around us, their sweetness clashing with the ozone stink pouring from my over-heating glands. The Drakarn's yellowish scales grayed at the edges, fear souring his scent.

"I-I swear, my lord, I saw nothing—"

My claws dug into his tunic, singeing the fabric. "Liar." The word came out a growl, my fangs inches from his throat. "Her trail ends here. Who took her? *Krazath's rats? Karyseth's zealots?*"

A child's whimper cut through the tension. I released the merchant, his wares scattering as he fled. The market's usual riot of noise had died to a hush, stall owners barricading themselves behind crates, mothers yanking fledglings into alleyways. Even the river algae's faint glow seemed dimmer, like the city itself feared my wrath.

I followed the fractured traces of Orla's scent—honeyed

panic undercut by an acid tang. My wings twitched, half-unfurled, as I stalked past a butcher's stall. The proprietor froze, cleaver hovering above a lava eel's thrashing body.

"You." I gripped his arm, ignoring the eel's blood dripping down my wrist. "A human. Dragged through here. *Where?*"

The Drakarn's throat worked soundlessly before he managed, "I don't know! They went east."

I was already moving, boots crushing discarded fruit as I sprinted toward the district's eastern edge. The tunnels loomed ahead, their jagged mouths spewing geothermal steam. Orla's scent spiked here—sharp, human sweat cutting through Volcaryth's mineral reek.

Too clean.

I skidded to a halt, nostrils flaring. The trail vanished at a rusted grate, its bars smeared with fresh blood. *Human* blood. My vision hazed red.

My claws found purchase in the grate's hinges, muscles straining as I wrenched it open. Metal screamed, the sound swallowed by the chasm below.

Empty.

No body. No scent. Just a scrap of fabric caught on a rust spike—purple, like the strands she dyed in her hair. I crushed it in my fist, the growl building in my chest shaking the walls.

They'd scrubbed her. Stolen her. *Dared.*

A guard approached, spear trembling in his grip. "Blade Councilor, the protocols demand—"

I backhanded the weapon into the abyss, my claws leaving gashes in his shoulder plates. "Demand *this*," I spat, storming past him. "Find her. Or burn."

I couldn't blindly follow her trail, not when it disappeared. I picked up my pace, heading for a place that might have answers.

The council chambers' doors loomed ahead when *his*

stench hit me—rotten sulfur and ambition. Krazath stepped from a side passage, wings tucked in a mockery of deference, his scales dulled by ash.

"Looking for something, my lord?" His tongue flicked over the fresh scar on his throat—the one *I'd* given him days prior.

I didn't slow. "Move."

He sidestepped, tail lashing. "Or what? You'll burn another market down?" His laughter echoed off the corridor's crystalline veins. "Pathetic. The great Rath brought low by—"

My claws sank into his throat before he finished. I slammed him against the wall, fissures spiderwebbing through volcanic stone. His pupils blew wide, but the smirk stayed.

"Where. Is. She." Spittle hissed against his scales.

Krazath's gills flared, struggling to draw air. "Already in the Pit," he choked. "By dawn, the shadows will peel her soft human flesh while she screams your name. A fitting end for a false mate."

The wall cracked deeper under his skull. Krazath's bravado wavered as heat warped the air between us.

"Kill me," he rasped, "and your human dies slower. The challenge demands *both* participants."

My grip loosened.

He wheezed a laugh, blood flecking his teeth. "The priestess invoked the ancient rites—no bond, no trial. If you're not in the arena at sunrise, they'll feed her to the beasts piece by piece."

I dropped him. He crumpled, gasping, but still sneering.

Krazath's taunts chased me down the corridor—a jagged sound cut short by the click of claws on stone. Zarvash emerged from the council chamber's shadowed archway, flanked by two scribes clutching slates.

"Rash actions won't reclaim your mate," he said. One scribe stepped forward, offering a slate displaying legal script. I smashed it against the wall, shattering the screen into glittering shards.

Zarvash didn't flinch. "The challenge is a mercy. Would you prefer Karyseth's alternative? A public execution by molten immersion?"

One of the scribes shifted, revealing Orla's journal clutched in his claws. My vision tunneled.

"Give. That. To me."

I lunged.

Mektar seemed to materialize from nothingness—a midnight-blue blur—his tail snapping around my throat. Scales bit into my windpipe as he wrenched me backward. My claws scraped stone, leaving furrows in the floor.

"Cease," Mektar hissed, the first word I'd heard him speak in weeks. His spiked tail tightened, forcing me to my knees.

Zarvash plucked the journal from the scribe's grip, flipping through pages filled with Orla's cramped sketches and notes. "Fascinating. She documented our geothermal vents' resonance frequencies. Clever for a primitive."

"Primitive?" I choked out. "She survived all this world has thrown at her."

"Barely."

"She never agreed to this challenge, nor did I," I snarled.

Zarvash shrugged. "Irrelevant. It proceeds at dawn. Fight beside her, and you might both survive. Fight me now," he leaned down, copper eyes reflecting my twisted expression, "and she dies screaming, alone."

Mektar's tail loosened just enough to let me breathe.

"Choose, Flame Heart," Zarvash murmured. "Warrior or fool."

Darrokar appeared in the archway, Nyx at his flank like a steel-scaled shadow. The Warrior Lord's obsidian scales pulsed with restrained energy, his gaze sweeping over my battered state. "Stand down, Rath."

Mektar let me go. He and Zarvash made their escape.

I whirled. "You knew."

Darrokar sidestepped, blocking the entrance with his bulk. "I didn't sanction this."

"Liar!" The word erupted in a shower of sparks from my overheating glands. "Someone on the council had to. You let them drag her into their sick ritual!"

Nyx shifted, his steel-gray scales rasping like drawn blades. "You don't think that councilor just ran out of this room like his scales were on fire? Zarvash is a snake. But the challenge is older than the city; it can't be avoided now that it's begun. You know this."

I rounded on Darrokar, my wings flaring wide enough to brush the corridor's crystal veins. "I don't see you volunteering to prove your bond with a human."

Darrokar's claws flexed, the only betrayal of his anger. "Terra earned her place through combat. You have done nothing to win over the doubters but hide away with your mate as if she's a shameful secret."

The accusation struck like a lava whip. My fist connected with his jaw before I'd fully decided to swing. The crack echoed through the cavern—bone meeting scale, blood meeting fire.

Darrokar staggered, blood welling from a split lip. Nyx moved between us in a blur, his tail slamming into my chest hard enough to bruise. Breath exploded from my lungs as I skidded backward, claws screeching against stone.

"Enough!" Nyx roared, planting himself between us. "Kill each other after the human's safe."

Darrokar wiped his mouth, staring at the blood on his claws in disbelief. "You think I *want* this?" he snarled, advancing on me. "If Orla dies in that pit, *you* unravel. And Scalvaris needs you whole."

I spat at his feet. "Scalvaris can burn."

Nyx's tail snapped out, pinning me against the wall. "You'd abandon thousands for one?"

"Yes." The word left no room for debate. "For her. Absolutely."

Darrokar's nostrils flared, the scent of my conviction thickening the air. For a heartbeat, I saw it—the same recklessness that once made him charge a lava serpent bare-handed. Then it vanished beneath the Warrior Lord's mask.

"Dawn approaches swiftly," he said coldly. "Prepare for your human."

I laughed—a broken, sulfurous sound. "Or what? You'll lock me in a cell too?"

Nyx's tail withdrew. I shoved past him, my claws leaving fresh gouges in the council chamber's doorframe. Darrokar's voice haunted me as I walked away—a growl laced with something that might've been regret. I didn't look back.

The city blurred around me. Drakarn fled into side tunnels as I stormed toward the training grounds, my wings scraping the floor.

The caverns loomed ahead, their arched entrance carved with reliefs of ancient warriors. I remembered the first time I'd walked these halls as a fledgling—pride swelling as my mother's claws rested on my shoulder. Now, the stone faces seemed to sneer.

I seized the nearest combat dummy, its straw guts spilling as I hurled it into a rack of lava-forged spears. Metal clattered like bones. My tail lashed out, shearing through a target post. Splinters rained down, mixing with the acrid stench of my overheating scales.

"False mate!" The dummy's head came off in my hands, its painted eyes mocking. I crushed it to pulp.

A rack of training swords collapsed under a wing strike, blades scattering like teeth. One skittered toward the arena's edge, its hilt catching the faint glow of heat crystals. I stomped it into the gravel, the snap of volcanic steel echoing through the cavern.

"Weakling!" Another dummy met my claws, its torso ribbons fluttering to the bloodstained sand.

Memories surged—Orla's kiss after I'd wiped the floor with the *kervash* I now couldn't kill. I could still taste her on my tongue. Human. Fragile.

Mine.

The last dummy exploded in a shower of splinters. I stood heaving in the wreckage, sulfurous breath fogging the air. Across the arena, my reflection warped in a polished obsidian shield—a crimson-scaled monster haloed by destruction.

I ripped the shield from the wall and hurled it. The crash reverberated around me.

"Had enough?"

Darrokar's voice.

I didn't turn. "Walk away before I do something we'll both regret."

Silence. Then retreating footsteps.

Alone, I sank to my knees, claws buried in sand still damp from yesterday's training bouts. The vents above hissed, their steam carrying the distant roar of the sacred river. Somewhere beneath that sound, Orla waited.

I pressed my forehead to the ground, inhaling the mineral tang of Scalvaris's heart. Her face burned behind my eyelids—not afraid. Never afraid. Defiant. Clever. *Alive.*

When I rose, the training ground's eastern wall bore fresh scars.

"If the city wants a challenge, I'll give them a war."

ORLA

I BARELY HAD time to lurch upright before the guards' claws closed around my arms, dragging me into an opening so violently orange it seared my retinas. My boots skidded across sand still steaming from whatever butchery had occurred here last, and with each step, the heat rose in waves that curled the edges of my vision.

The arena hit me in layers—acrid sweat thick enough to coat my tongue, sulfurous vents belching toxic fumes, the metallic tang of old blood baked into volcanic stone until it reeked like rust and rot.

Cheers erupted from tiered seating writhing with Drakarn spectators, each pair of eyes reflecting a savage hunger. My knees nearly buckled at the sight of them, but the guards jerked me upright, their laughter vibrating through my bones, a cruel counterpoint to the crowd's thunderous roars.

And there, in one tiny section, were my fellow humans. Selene, Eden, Kaiya, Vega, Kira, Lexa, Hawk, Rachel, and on the end was Terra, standing next to her hulking Drakarn mate, Darrokar. None of them were cheering. They looked like they were watching a funeral.

Thanks for the vote of confidence, girls.

"Run fast, leech," a guard hissed, shoving me forward with a push that sent me stumbling across the scorched ground.

The gate slammed shut behind me, a boom louder than the entire crowd. I spun, heart hammering, taking stock through the adrenaline-fueled haze. Jagged pillars rose around me, their shadows crisscrossing over thin crusts of stone hiding lava's glow. To the east, a geothermal vent coughed superheated steam in irregular bursts. My fingers twitched, itching for my journal's grid paper to calculate patterns, to cling to something orderly in this bedlam.

A pebble clattered to my right.

I turned just as the ground erupted, a nightmare uncoiling from the shadows. The monster's maw yawned wide, rows of serrated teeth glowing like filaments in a furnace. Its scales weren't just black—they drank the light, a void edged with ember cracks that pulsed with each thunderous heartbeat. Steaming saliva dripped from its jaws, hissing where it struck the sand and sending up acrid plumes that seared my nostrils.

Acid spit. Great.

The crowd's roar became a distant buzz as the lava lizard's throat rattled. Its tongue lashed out, forked and flickering with actual flames, testing the air. I felt the heat of it from six feet away, a dry slap against my sweat-slicked skin. My thoughts scattered with a single directive: *Survive first. Panic later.*

It lunged.

The world blurred.

I threw myself sideways, shoulder slamming into a jagged pillar as claws the size of steak knives carved through the space where my throat had been. Hot stone tore at my shirt, branding my ribs. The lizard's momentum carried it past me, its spiked tail whipping my thigh hard enough to bruise. A thunderous impact shattered rock behind me, bits of obsidian scattering like glass shards across the steaming sand.

A second predator exploded from a fissure to my left, smaller and faster—a juvenile, maybe, its scales dull gray but eyes burning with the same unending hunger. It scuttled sideways like a crab, claws click-click-clicking on stone, herding me toward the arena's western edge. My pulse pounded in my ears; panic tried to grip my throat. I forced a shaky breath, stuffing that fear to the edges of my mind.

I risked a glance over my shoulder.

Bad move.

A third lizard dropped from a ledge above, all rippling muscle and furnace stink. It landed in a crouch, tail lashing, black claws digging grooves into the sand. This one's scales shimmered with a nauseating oil-slick sheen, and a heat mirage rose from its spine like a ghostly halo.

They fanned out, driving me backward. My heel brushed something brittle—the sand here was thinner, the stone beneath glowing faintly orange through cracks. Something lay under there, and every inch of my body screamed that I *didn't* want to find out what.

The juvenile struck first, springing with a guttural shriek. I ducked, its claws snagging my hair as I rolled. Purple strands fluttered to the sand, instantly singed in the heat. This was not good. The largest lizard charged, maw gaping, and on instinct, I dove between its legs.

Putrid heat engulfed me as I slid beneath its belly, scales scraping my back raw. Its underbelly wasn't armored, just a leathery hide. I drove my elbow upward, aiming for a soft pocket. My bones shook with the impact.

The beast bellowed so loudly it shook stalactites. It bucked, tail slamming down where I'd been half a breath before. I scrambled upright, lungs burning from the sulfur stink.

"Come on, you overgrown gecko," I snarled, voice trembling despite the bravado tearing through my veins.

The oil-slick lizard answered by vomiting a stream of liquid fire.

I hurled myself behind a pillar. Flame splashed against stone, droplets spattering my boot. The synthetic material melted instantly, searing my ankle.

I screamed, and the crowd cheered louder.

"Not fucking today." I edged along the pillar, trying to suck in scorching air without passing out.

The nearest lizard's tail lashed out. I scrambled upward, rock-climbing instincts kicking in as I scaled the unstable column. A claw snagged my boot heel, and I kicked hard, feeling scale crunch under my foot. The lizard recoiled with a shriek, buying me two seconds to scramble up as high as I could.

From this vantage point, the arena spread below me like some demon's playground: cracked stone, churning pockets of lava, spouts of toxic steam. The crowd's jeers shifted pitch. All three lizards circled, acid drool pooling, jaws grinding in anticipation of a meal. One began scaling the pillar, its toes finding purchase in the porous stone. Others prowled below, yellow eyes glinting.

I fumbled for Vyne's vial. The acid sloshed inside, its surface shimmering like liquid rage.

One drop melts steel.

The lizard's head crested the ledge, jaws unhinging. I hurled the vial. It was my only shot, and each heartbeat pounded in my skull as though time itself slowed.

It struck between its eyes.

The explosion of sizzling flesh drowned the crowd's gasps. The lizard tumbled backward, its death throes scattering the pack. I slid down the pillar, boots skidding in gore-streaked sand. My hands shook, the adrenaline a sickening high.

There was no sign of the vial. I could yell at myself for wasting it later. If I survived.

Where the hell was Rath?

A hiss rippled through the arena—sharper, hungrier than the lizards.

I turned slowly, dread pooling in my gut. The ground beneath my boots trembled as a new shadow uncoiled from a deep tunnel, its scales clicking like a death rattle. It was like a living earthquake: pulsing, breathing, lethal.

I backpedaled, ankle screaming where melted boot leather fused to burnt flesh. The creature rising from the pit wasn't lizard—not with those segmented metallic plates rippling along its thirty-foot length, not with the dozen articulated legs tipped in hooked barbs that screeched against stone.

Its head swung toward me on a serpentine neck, faceted eyes reflecting a thousand fractured images of my trembling form. Molten veins pulsed beneath pulsing yellow scales, casting hellish light through the joints in its armor. The stench of rotting sulfur and singed bone clawed at my nostrils as it hissed, spined tail whipping behind it in arcs that carved gouges in the arena floor.

A roar split the air—not the beast's, but familiar.

Mine.

Rath dropped from the ceiling like a comet trailing smoke, wings folding tight against his back as he landed. Twin lava-forged swords blazed in his claws, their edges white-hot as he landed between me and the monstrosity. Sand vaporized where his boots struck, the shockwave knocking me to my knees. His scales glowed with an infernal intensity, veins of orange light flickering in the cracks along his arms and shoulders.

"Stay behind me!" he barked, voice rough, scorching. I'd never been happier to be yelled at.

The wyrm struck.

Rath's swords met its jaws in a shower of sparks. I scrambled backward as acid-green blood rained down, eating pockmarks into the sand. The wyrm's barbed legs scissored wildly, shearing off chunks of Rath's armor. He didn't flinch, driving a blade upward through its palpitating throat. A gush of fluorescent ichor splattered the closest rock face, sizzling on contact.

"Orla! The pillar!"

I turned toward his shout just as a wyrmling—smaller, faster—spewed liquid fire from above. Heat slapped my shoulders, singeing the ends of my hair even worse than before. I dove behind a stalagmite, fists clenched. The stone exploded behind me in a shower of fragments, shrapnel scraping against me.

Rath's wing clipped my side as he soared past, snatching the wyrmling mid-leap. They crashed into the arena wall in a tangle of scales and snapping jaws. I didn't wait—I snatched up a fallen barb the size of my forearm, its edge still dripping wyrm blood that sizzled against my palm.

"Stubborn human!" Rath roared, pinning the wyrmling with a knee to its sparking thorax. His free sword hovered at its shuddering neck. "I said stay—"

The sand between us bulged.

We moved in together—Rath yanking his blade free, me driving my stolen barb downward. The emerging wyrm pup died with a wet gurgle, acidic blood spraying my forearms. I barely felt the new burns, adrenaline numbing everything but the will to keep fighting.

Rath's claw closed around my bicep, hauling me toward a crumbling stone column. He wrapped his arms around me, tail securing me in place, and launched us up. The ground below vanished, swirling steam and predator eyes glaring with ravenous malice.

But there was no hope of escaping the arena. We were

closed in, and I didn't need to be told that the only way out was to win. Whatever winning meant to the Drakarn.

Rath carefully set me down on top of one of the pillars, obsidian shards scraping the soles of my boots. "Stay. Here." His voice thrummed with command.

"Not arguing!" I shouted back, though my pulse hammered in protest.

But there was barely any sanctuary on top of the pillar, just crumbling rock and a panoramic view of certain death. Rath's wings blotted out the arena's hellish glow as he dove back toward the writhing wyrm. I stood alone with the sizzle of my burnt flesh and the acidic reek of dead reptiles filling my lungs, the noise of the crowd rolling in thunderous waves.

Something clicked beneath me.

I looked down. The stone under my boots swam with shadows—no, not shadows. *Scales.* Dozens of them, rippling up the pillar in a shimmering wave. Snakes. Their arrowhead skulls broke the surface first, lidless eyes burning with phosphorescent hate, forked tongues tasting my terror.

I dug in my boot, heart pounding like a war drum, yanking my dagger from my boot just in time.

The first strike came from behind. I pivoted, the snake's fangs grazing my hip as I brought the blade down in a wild arc. Metal bit through scale and bone, severing a skull that rolled hissing into the abyss. Acid blood sprayed my wrist—agony, then a terrifying numbness that spread like wildfire.

They swarmed.

I became a creature of instinct—jabbing, sneering, kicking when teeth closed around my boot. A tail lashed my ribs. Another snake coiled around my thigh, its body searing like a brand. The sound of them—tangled hisses, the scrape of scales on rock—flooded my ears, drowning out the roar of the crowd for a moment.

The world tilted, and the ledge crumbled.

The pillar shuddered beneath me. The snakes' bodies coiled around the column's base, a living noose tightening as they gnawed through rock with fangs dripping corrosive venom.

The crumbling ledge offered less footing than a cliffside ice sheet. Below, a lava pit bubbled hungrily, shooting up flares of liquid rock that made the entire air shiver. Above, Rath's battle cries mingled with the wyrm's shrieks, savage echoes that slammed around the arena in waves of terror and adrenaline.

And the ledge gave way.

I caught a jagged outcrop one-handed, body slamming into the pillar's searing surface. A snake clung to my boot, its weight dragging me toward the lava's orange maw. The heat radiating from below scorched my cheeks. I tasted salt from sweat rolling down my lip.

"Not ... a chance," I snarled, swinging my free leg in a desperate arc.

The snake's skull crunched against the rock. It released me, spiraling into the lava with a hissing pop. I hauled myself onto the outcrop, trembling arms screaming with exertion. Below, the remaining snakes writhed, their acid melting handholds into treacherous sludge, and the stench of dissolving stone added a bitter tang to the suffocating air. The largest snake struck like a piston, fangs glistening with fresh venom. I twisted, driving my dagger upward, praying it would hold.

The blade glanced off its armored snout but lodged in its eye.

It recoiled, shrieking, the dagger protruding from the snake's ruined socket like a gruesome trophy. It thrashed, tail smashing the pillar and shaking the entire structure.

Rock exploded. I fell and caught the snake's spasming body.

We dropped together, its acid blood eating through my sleeve. The lava's heat blistered my cheeks, shriveled my lungs. I wrenched the dagger free as we plummeted, stabbing wildly. The blade struck a chink in its underbelly armor.

Green gore erupted, hissing in midair.

The snake's final throes flung me sideways. I hit a sloping rockface and slid, shredding my palms on volcanic stone. The lava pool yawned inches away, each bubble a promise of burning finality.

Move.

I crab-crawled upward, dagger clenched between my teeth. Rath's roar guided me—a beacon in the inferno. I launched myself the last few feet over a jagged lip of rock, vision spinning with exhaustion. I was still alive.

I crested the slope in time to see him grappling the wyrm, its metallic scales refracting hellish light. One of his swords lay shattered nearby, broken edges still glowing. The wyrm's tail coiled around his torso, squeezing the air from his lungs.

"Hey, glitterlizard!" I hefted my blade, voice raw.

The wyrm's faceted eyes pivoted.

I leaped onto its thrashing tail, driving my knife toward a gap in its plates. The impact jolted my wrist, and my grip slipped. My weapon spun away, clattering somewhere I couldn't see.

"Orla, no!" Rath bellowed, baring fangs as he tried to twist free.

The wyrm shook me off like a gnat. I rolled, snatching a shard of Rath's broken sword—still glowing white-hot. It scorched my fingers, but pain was an afterthought.

The wyrm struck.

I met its jaws with the shard.

Molten steel met crystalline fangs.

The explosion blinded me. A searing flash that devoured all

sound, all light, all sense of direction. When the blaze in my retinas finally subsided, the wyrm lay twitching, its skull split by the shard wedged deep in its neural crest. Rivulets of sickly fluid seeped from the wound, burning channels into the arena floor. Rath stood over it, chest heaving, his remaining sword trembling in his grip.

Raw fury radiated off him in waves.

He stared at me, breath ragged, eyes blazing with the reflection of the crowd's cheers.

I wiped wyrm guts from my cheek. "You're welcome," I rasped, somehow finding the breath to speak.

His tail lashed, stirring up a cloud of dust and ash. "You were supposed to stay on the pillar!"

"And you were supposed to duck." I pointed to the wyrm's barb embedded in his shoulder.

The arena shuddered—a deep, groaning vibration that traveled up through my boots and into my teeth. Rath's hand closed around my wrist an instant before the ground split between us, superheated steam screaming from fresh fissures. The entire stadium pulsed with an ominous quake, as if the volcano beneath us throbbed with a living heart.

"Move!" he roared, yanking me sideways as a geyser erupted where we'd stood, white-hot droplets splattering across the stone.

Three lava-lizards crawled out of an opening near the geyser.

We crashed into the arena wall, my spine slamming against rock still hot from the wyrm's acid blood. Rath's body shielded mine as another vent burst overhead, raining scalding drops that sizzled on his scales. The crowd above howled for blood, their savage chants echoing across the ring.

Three vents formed a tightening triangle. I had an idea. "Drive the lizards into the steam."

Rath's answering snarl held reluctant approval. He lunged left, swords carving arcs that forced the three new lizards toward the nearest fissure. I scrambled up a rubble pile, torn boots slipping on loose shale. My burns screamed with every movement, but I forced my body onward.

The largest lizard wheeled toward me, jaws dripping. It leaped in a swirl of obsidian dust. I ducked and screamed, "Now!"

Rath's blade slammed into the vent's edge, diverting the steam jet directly into the creature's face. The lizard's death throes filled the arena with an earsplitting wail that harmonized with the crowd's frenzied cheers, hunger for violence intensifying their mania.

We fell into rhythm—Rath herding, me hurling chunks of broken rock to trigger the vents. When the final lizard collapsed in a steaming heap, we stood back-to-back, shoulders heaving in sync. Blood—my own, and a nauseating medley of reptilian gore—dripped off me in rivulets.

The wyrm's corpse chose that moment to slide into a lava pit, half-submerged, releasing a final gargle.

The resulting explosion of molten rock sent us diving in unison. Rath's wing curled around me as fiery debris rained down, clanging off his scaled armor. His growl vibrated through my burned cheek, pressed against his chest. "Still alive?"

"Disappointed?" My lips cracked on the word, tasting ash and iron.

His fanged grin flashed in the flickering glow. Despite everything, a flicker of satisfaction sparked in his eyes—a warrior's thrill at survival against impossible odds.

We were alive. We won.

Do you believe in our fucking bond now? I wanted to scream into the stands.

Across the bloodied sand, Zarvash rose from the spectator

stands, his bronze scales polished to a taunting gleam under the shifting torchlight. His presence commanded the crowd's attention, and the cheers fell into an eager hush.

"The Forge remains unimpressed!" he bellowed, ceremonial hammer raised high. A small section of the crowd took up the chant, dozens of claws pounding stone in rhythmic unison.

Unworthy. Unworthy. Unworthy.

The rest of the Drakarn watched in silence, tension coiling in the air like a serpent.

The ground beneath us groaned, fresh steam vents hissing open. Rath shoved me backward as a geyser erupted where I'd stood, the superheated blast singing his scales. Pain flickered across his features, a snarl following in its wake.

"Coward!" Rath roared, twin swords flaring brighter, red lines tracing the steel. "You hide while others bleed!"

Zarvash launched himself out of the stands and glided down, wings spread wide, each leathery membrane etched with golden runes. "Tradition requires *proof*, Flame Heart. Your human barely survived glorified hatchling trials." His copper-tipped tail flicked toward the smoldering wyrm carcass. "The Forge demands a true sacrifice."

I limped forward, ankle screaming like the flesh might peel away. "We just killed your murder pets. What more—"

Zarvash backhanded me with his tail. A blow so swift that I barely caught the glint of bronze scales before it connected. He was fast, impossibly so.

The world whited out. I tasted blood before feeling the split lip, my skull ringing from the impact. Rath moved faster than thought—his sword at Zarvash's throat, heat radiating off him in waves that distorted the air.

"Touch her again," Rath growled, embers dripping from his fangs, "and I'll mount your scales on my wall."

The arena held its breath as the crowd leaned forward in

eager anticipation. Even the lava vents seemed to quiet momentarily, their hissing subdued beneath the tension.

Zarvash laughed—a dry, rustling sound that made my skin crawl. He pressed forward until Rath's blade drew blood. "Strike me down, and the challenge fails. It is not over until the gong chimes." His tongue flicked toward the shadowed alcove where Karyseth's priests lurked next to a massive bronze gong, arms crossed. They made it clear the gong would not chime until one or both of us were dead.

It might have ended there, blood spilled to feed the arena's greed, but Darrokar approached with a thunderous stride, his black wings stirring the dusty air. It took little more than his furious glare for one of the priests to step aside.

Darrokar raised a scaled fist and rang the gong, the brassy note echoing across the volcanic arena like the final toll of judgment.

The challenge was over.

Rath spat at Zarvash's feet, the hiss of saliva evaporating on contact. "You are a coward and the Forge Temple's lackey. Meet me in the ring and repay this insult. *Now*."

THE ARENA'S stench clung to me—sulfur, blood, and the acrid tang of molten rock. My scales still smoldered, the faint glow of heat lines flickering across my arms as I stormed through the training grounds' arched entrance. Orla limped beside me, her human frame trembling with exhaustion, her purple-streaked hair singed and matted with wyrm blood.

She was alive.

That was all that mattered. But the fire in her eyes told me she wasn't done fighting.

"You're insane," she said, her voice hoarse but sharp enough to cut through the haze of my rage. "We just survived that nightmare, and your first thought is to pick another fight?"

I didn't stop walking. This ended today. I would not wait another moment. "Krazath is Zarvash's underling. He wouldn't act without orders. Zarvash orchestrated your kidnapping on behalf of the temple. He put you in that pit. He doesn't get to walk away unscathed."

"And what if you lose?" she shot back, grabbing my arm with a strength that surprised me. Her fingers were small, fragile against my scales, but her grip was iron. "What happens to me then? To *us*?"

I turned, my tail lashing behind me, and met her glare. Her face was streaked with soot and blood, her lower lip split and swollen. But her eyes—those damned human eyes—burned with defiance. She wasn't afraid of me, even now. Even after everything.

Good.

"I won't lose," I growled, the words rumbling deep in my chest. "Not to him. Not ever."

She scoffed, releasing my arm and crossing hers over her chest. "You're not invincible, Rath. You're bleeding, exhausted, and—"

"And I'll tear him apart," I interrupted, my voice rising enough to echo off the cavern walls. The training grounds were empty for now, the usual clatter of weapons and shouts of sparring warriors absent. The crowd would migrate from the challenge grounds soon enough, their need for blood never sated. Even the air felt heavier, charged with anticipation for what was coming. "He threatened you. He put you in danger. That's not something I can let slide."

Orla opened her mouth to argue, but a sharp hiss of pain cut her off. She clutched her side, her face paling as she doubled over. My anger faltered, replaced by a surge of guilt. I'd been so focused on survival and ending this that I hadn't fully registered the extent of her injuries.

"Selene!" I barked, my voice carrying through the cavern to the group trailing us. The human medic appeared almost instantly, her medkit slung over one shoulder and her dark hair pulled into a tight braid. She moved with the efficiency of someone used to chaos, her sharp eyes scanning Orla's wounds.

"Sit," Selene ordered, gesturing to a nearby bench. Orla hesitated, her gaze flicking to me, but Selene wasn't having it. "Now. Unless you want to lose your damned foot."

Orla sat, wincing as Selene began cleaning the burns on her

arms and legs. The medic's hands were steady, her movements precise, but Orla's jaw clenched with every touch. She didn't complain, though.

"I need to do this," I said, my voice softer now but no less adamant. "It won't stop until he feels true consequences."

Orla looked up at me, her eyes narrowing. "Killing him is quite the consequence. Isn't that just going to piss the Forge Temple off more?" She winced as Selene hit a particularly sensitive spot. "I'm not trying to stop you. I'm trying to make sure you don't get yourself killed."

"I'm not going to kill him," I said, tail lashing. "I want to. He kidnapped you. He threw you into that pit. But there are rules to this. If I don't challenge him, he'll think he can get away with it. They all will."

She held my gaze for a long moment, her expression unreadable. Then, slowly, she nodded. "Okay. But I'm not leaving. If you're going to fight him, I'm going to watch."

"You need medical attention," I argued, gesturing to Selene, who was now applying a salve to Orla's burns.

"And I'm getting it," Orla snapped. "But I'm not missing this. Not after what he did."

Selene glanced between us, her lips pressed into a thin line. "She's stubborn," she said, her tone dry. "But she's right. She's stable enough to stay. Watching *only*." Selene jabbed a finger at my mate. Then she turned to me. "You should really have a healer take a look at you before you add to your own injury list."

I growled low in my throat, torn between my need to protect Orla and my desire to make Zarvash pay. In the end, it was the fire in her eyes that decided it. She wasn't just my mate —she was my equal. And if she wanted to stand by me, I wouldn't deny her that.

"You can watch," I said, my voice rough. "But I want you sitting next to Selene."

Orla smiled, though it was strained by pain. "Deal. Now go kick his ass."

Her words sparked something in me—a fierce pride that burned hotter than any flame. I turned toward the training ground's center, where Zarvash was already waiting, his bronze scales gleaming under the faint glow of the heat crystals. His copper-highlighted tail flicked lazily, his expression one of cool amusement.

"Flame Heart," he called, his voice dripping with mockery. "Ready to bleed?"

I bared my fangs. "Ready to end this."

The crowd of Drakarn who had gathered to witness the duel stood in a loose circle, their scales glinting in the light of the heat crystals embedded in the cavern walls and coming through the sky shaft overhead. Their eyes were fixed on me and Zarvash.

I had expected more to make their way from the challenge grounds. Apparently, a simple honor duel was not worth the hike for most.

Pyroth stepped forward, his orange scales catching the light as he moved with the grace of a predator. Crimson swirls in the pattern of his scales seemed to ripple with each step, and his presence commanded the attention of everyone in the room. He was the Blade Dancer, the master of combat artistry.

"Warriors," Pyroth began, his voice deep and resonant, carrying the weight of ancient rituals. "You stand here today bound by the traditions of our people. This is not a fight to the death, but a test of skill, honor, and resolve. Let the flames guide your blades, and may the suns judge your worth."

He raised a clawed hand, and the crowd fell silent.

Zarvash smirked, his tail flicking lazily as he unsheathed his daggers. The blades were sleek and deadly, their edges honed to a razor-sharp finish. He twirled them in his claws with practiced ease, the movement fluid and mocking.

I drew my lava-forged swords, the white-hot edges glowing as I settled into a fighting stance. The weight of the blades was familiar, comforting, even if the sword in my left hand was a backup blade, my favored weapon sacrificed to the Mating Challenge.

This wasn't just about me—it was about Orla, about proving to every Drakarn in Scalvaris that she was mine to protect, and that no one—*no one*—could threaten her without consequences.

Pyroth began to chant, his voice rising and falling in the rhythm of an ancient war song. The words were older than the city itself, and they carried the history of countless battles fought and won. The crowd joined in, their voices blending as they stamped their feet in an ancient beat. The sound stirred something deep within me.

Zarvash's smirk widened. "You will lose," he taunted, his voice dripping with condescension. "You're already bleeding."

I didn't respond. Words were useless here. The only language that mattered was the clash of steel and the roar of flames. I tightened my grip on my swords, the heat from the blades searing my palms, and waited for Pyroth's signal.

The Blade Dancer raised his hand, the chant reaching its peak. The crowd fell silent, tension in the air so thick it was almost suffocating. Then, with a sharp downward motion, Pyroth gave the signal.

The duel began.

Zarvash lunged, moving faster than I expected. He closed in, daggers slashing for my neck. I parried with one sword, the collision sending sparks across the stone. The impact trembled through my arms, but I stayed rooted. I swung my second blade in a counterstrike aimed at his ribs. He twisted clear, a smug grin curling his mouth.

He circled me, wings tense at his back. His footwork was nimble, the daggers an extension of his body. My swords were heavier; I relied on power and reach, but he had speed. He tested me with a quick thrust, then darted away before I could answer. We danced around each other, eyes locked, searching for any opening.

He feinted left. I caught the shift in his stance and recognized the real strike on my right side. Metal screamed as I blocked, but he flicked his tail low, raking a spiked tip across my shin. I hissed through clenched teeth. He was trying to goad me into a rash move.

"Is this all, Flame Heart?" he mocked, voice pitched just loud enough for the crowd to hear. "I expected more from you."

I let the barb pass, keeping my breathing steady. His arrogance was a weapon I could turn against him.

He came at me again, daggers blurring in a flurry of slicing arcs. I managed to block most, but one found a gap and scored a cut along my upper arm. The burn of pain sharpened my focus. I smashed my pommel toward his face, forcing him back. He hopped away, wings flaring to maintain balance, eyes gleaming with the thrill of combat.

We circled each other once more. The watchers pressed in, hungry for blood and a show. I caught the slightest movement near the edge—Orla, standing with Selene, her posture rigid. I reminded myself she was alive, there, trusting me to handle this. That alone fueled me with savage resolve.

Zarvash attacked again, eyes narrowing. He aimed for my torso in a quick combination, then pivoted to strike at my flank. This time, I caught his left dagger with one blade, hooking his right with the other in a crunch of steel against steel. Our locked weapons screeched. I shoved forward, using my weight to push him off-balance. He hissed and skidded back, tail lash-ing, regaining control by flaring his wings.

"Going soft?" he taunted. "Or is it your human mate slowing you down?"

That was it. I would kill the *kervash*.

I lunged, swords blazing in twin arcs. He ducked under the first, but the second sliced a shallow line across his shoulder. He jerked away, blinking surprise. A scowl contorted his features, but he hid it quickly. The crowd rumbled with excite-ment, boots and claws drumming on stone.

His next barrage came in a whirlwind of steel. I locked one sword with his dagger and blocked the second with the flat of my other blade, but he drove his knee into my abdomen. Air whooshed from my lungs, and I staggered. My tail whipped to keep me upright, but he was already repositioning for another strike at my head. Instinct roared through me. I raised a sword in desperation—he deflected it but lost his angle, forcing him to sidestep instead of landing the killing blow.

I reeled back, gritting my teeth. Blood dripped down my side; the earlier cut on my arm stung every time I shifted. But I saw a flicker of irritation in his eyes—he'd wanted me down by now.

He laughed, breathless. "You're persistent, I'll give you that."

I answered by rushing forward. My left blade clashed with his right dagger, and I slammed my shoulder into him, with raw force instead of grace. He stumbled, trying to bring up his second blade, but I spun, driving my tail into his ribs. A wet crack echoed. He coughed in pain and hopped back, favoring his side. My pulse hammered, every muscle shaking with the effort to keep going.

Zarvash tried to mask his grimace with a sneer. His chest rose and fell fast.

I advanced methodically, swords at the ready. He bared his teeth and lunged. Our weapons clashed in a frenzy, metal shrieking. His tail lashed for my legs, and I leaped aside at the last moment, bringing both swords down in a punishing overhead strike. He crossed his daggers to block, but the raw heat from my blades caused him to yelp. The impact forced him to his knees for a moment. He managed to roll clear, panting.

I glanced at Orla again, saw her lips parted, her fists clenched. She might've been bruised and burned, but her spirit flared bright as ever. I inhaled, felt the burn in the air coil in my lungs, and charged Zarvash before he could regain footing.

This time, I anticipated his tail strike and smashed it aside with the flat of one blade. He tried to slash at me with a dagger, but I slammed my other sword against his wrist, twisting it free of the weapon. His blade clattered away. He hissed in pain, eyes wild. He had only one dagger left.

He tried to pivot, but I drove my knee into his wounded shoulder, followed by a vicious elbow to his jaw. He crumpled with a snarl. I pressed the tip of a sword to his throat, chest heaving. The crowd drew closer, hunger on every face. The air smelled of sweat and scorched metal.

"Yield," I snarled.

He glared, blood trickling from his lip. For an instant, I thought he might grab for his lost dagger and keep fighting out of spite. Then a flicker of fear crossed his face. His hands rose, empty. "I yield."

The crowd erupted. I stepped back, my swords still at the ready, but the fight was over. Zarvash had lost, and he knew it. Anything but abject surrender now would mean certain death.

Pyroth stepped in, arms raised to quell any objections. "The duel is finished," he announced, voice echoing along the carved ceiling. "By the old ways, Rath Flame Heart stands victorious."

The small crowd erupted again, their cheers and jeers blending into a deafening riot of noise. I ignored them, my focus shifting to Orla. She stood at the edge of the onlookers, her eyes locked on me, her face pale but determined. Selene was beside her, the medkit still in hand, but Orla's attention was entirely on me. She gave me a small nod, her lips curving into a faint smile, and I felt a surge of pride.

She was alive. She was safe. And she was mine.

Zarvash climbed to his feet, his movements stiff and deliberate. His eyes burned with hatred as he glared at me, but he didn't speak.

Pyroth inclined his head. "Honor the terms of your defeat, Zarvash. You will be bound to Rath's judgement for a year's cycle. If you break the vow, you risk exile—or worse."

Zarvash spat on the stone near my feet but didn't speak. He shoved past the ring of Drakarn, ignoring their jeers, and vanished down a side passage.

Heat pounded in my veins, adrenaline slow to fade. I looked to Orla. She limped forward, leaning on Selene, but her eyes were locked on me. Relief battled with lingering fury on her face.

"You did it," she said, voice tight. "Idiot."

"Is that my mating name?" I slid my swords into their sheaths, fighting the urge to collapse from sheer exhaustion.

Selene cleared her throat, rummaging in her medkit. "Can we tend to you both now, or do you plan on fighting for who keels over first?"

Orla grimaced at that. I gently placed a hand against her shoulder, guiding her toward the bench. "We'll let you do your job," I told Selene.

Orla squeezed my arm. "That was reckless," she muttered, but a hint of pride colored her voice. "I'm glad you won."

I gave her a short nod, not trusting myself to speak. The red haze of my anger still vibrated under my skin. We were alive, together. That had to be enough.

Pyroth approached. "You fought well, Flame Heart," he said, his voice low and respectful. "The Forge has judged you worthy."

I nodded, my chest still heaving from the fight. "And Zarvash?"

Pyroth's lips curled into a faint smile. "He is bound to you now. For a year, he will serve you, as is tradition."

I didn't need Zarvash's service. What I needed was his absence. But I didn't say it. The rules of a traditional duel were complex. Zarvash was not my servant, but he would owe me. It was something I would keep in mind in the coming months.

I had a feeling I would need to.

Pyroth left us, and Orla shuddered. I caught her but stumbled and had to shift my stance to right myself.

"You both need the healing caverns," Selene said. "Now."

This time, neither me nor my mate argued.

I LEANED over the low table, sketching rough lines across my notebook while my tongue caught on the inside of my cheek. My notes were all around me, half-chaotic, held together by a tenuous thread of logic I might lose if I didn't finish this diagram tonight.

Across from me, Rath sprawled lazily on the bed, one wing draped off the side and a faint smirk tugging at his mouth. His brooding had melted away, replaced instead with the kind of loose relaxation that made him dangerous. His focus shifted between his claw—idly balancing one of my pens—and me, his golden eyes glinting with some private amusement.

You would never guess that two weeks ago we'd been limping out the Mating Challenge, skin burned and scales bleeding. My ankle would be scarred forever, but thanks to Selene's mending and some Volcarian healing herbs, we were both almost as good as new.

"You're scowling again," he said, his voice like gravel warming under flame. "I almost pity whatever you're planning to conquer."

I didn't look up from the page, instead using the edge of my graphite to shade another section of the proposed geothermal grid system. "I told you, this isn't for war. It's energy distribution."

"Which is also conquest," he drawled, flipping the pen in a slow arc. It clattered to the floor when his claws misjudged the catch, but he didn't bother retrieving it, his gaze homing in on me now. "Sweeter when your enemy is tradition, no?"

I snorted, finally meeting his eyes. "Tradition as an enemy? I'm sure that would make any Blade Councilor faint just hearing it."

"Not me." His tail flicked once, the spaded end curling around the chaise's base. "But I'm less faint-prone than most. Go on, tell me how this marvel of yours will upend generations."

I leaned back, pushing away the hair that always fell into my face when I was working and leaving a faint, unintentional charcoal streak down my temple. "Right now, Scalvaris relies too heavily on heat crystals and lavaforges. They're inefficient for consistent power. The underground geothermal vents could provide scalable energy storage—enough to keep the city's entire infrastructure running without burning through resources." I jabbed the pencil against the edge of the diagram in emphasis. "It's basic science."

"Basic for you," he corrected, his smile deepening. "Try explaining 'scalable energy storage' to Nyktral from the River's Teeth. I think I saw him lick a rock once just because it was shiny."

Laughing, I tossed my pencil onto the table and stretched my arms, sore from hours of scribbling. "You're not wrong. I doubt they'd listen to anything I said even if I dumbed it down. Humans are still aliens. Outsiders."

His expression flickered, something darker passing over his features before he banished it. "Humans may be new arrivals," he said, voice low, "but ideas are not species-bound."

"It's not the ideas they'll fight—it's me having them." I exhaled, frustration churning my thoughts. "I'm still hearing whispers about whether I 'earned' my place."

Rath shifted forward, leaning his elbows onto his knees until his massive frame made my cramped work area feel even smaller. The hearthlight carved shadows into the planes of his face, highlighting scars I was still learning to trace with my fingertips. "They won't dare call me weak. Not to my face," he said, and though his voice was calm, there was steel hidden beneath the embers. "And they won't call you less than worthy once I've reminded them how valuable you are."

I was getting used to the possessiveness in his tone—it still caught me slightly off guard. Another part of me, the part that had already learned how unwavering he was in his loyalty, found comfort in it. He didn't consider me a weakness; he called me his equal, his strength. And yet ...

"I don't want this to be about you having to defend me. Again," I said, curling my fingers against the edge of the notebook. "I want them to respect me on my own terms."

Rath tilted his head. His amusement returned in a flash. "Foolish mate," he murmured, something softer threading through the words. "You think tearing down centuries of rigid thought happens in a single strike? Lay the foundation for now. I'll keep the others too occupied to sabotage it."

The sudden, delighted laugh that bubbled out of me startled us both. "So your plan is to just distract Scalvaris while I sneakily modernize it?"

"Exactly." He leaned back again. "Swords clash loudly, *shyrarva*, but it's the quiet forge that alters their edges."

I shook my head, fighting a smile as I returned to my diagram. "God, you're impossible," I muttered, but there was no heat in it.

"And you're brilliant." His rumble chased warmth up my

spine, his voice wrapping around my resolve and bolstering it in a way no plan or blueprint could.

His tail coiled and uncoiled lazily as he watched me return to my work. His presence was a strange paradox—calming in its weight, but always charged with the potential for motion, for violence, for some deep and electric possibility. I'd seen him fight, seen the beast in him unleashed, but there, in the privacy of our chambers, he was something entirely different.

When the hiss of his shifting weight broke the quiet, I glanced up to see him rising from the bed with his usual predatory grace. His wings flexed once in a low sweep before folding close to his back, sharp edges catching the firelight. He crossed the room, his broad size shrinking even our spacious quarters, and began rummaging in one of the storage compartments carved into the volcanic rock walls.

"What are you doing?" I asked.

He didn't answer, at least not vocally. His tail flicked in what I'd come to recognize as either amusement or mischief—possibly both—before he pulled something from the compartment and hid it behind his back.

"Rath," I said, skeptical. His eyes caught mine, a slight glint of smugness visible in their depths. "What are you hiding?"

Instead of answering, he crossed back to me, his movements deliberate, and crouched just close enough for his heat to bleed into my space. The sharp planes of his features softened slightly as he tilted his head, studying me, something achingly gentle shimmering just beneath the habitual intensity of his gaze.

"Close your notebook," he murmured.

I blinked, thrown off by the sudden and quietly commanding tone. Then I folded the paper closed, placing it to the side without comment. "Alright," I said slowly. "What's—"

His hand came forward, producing a roll of parchment

with a flourish. The edges were worn—coated with soot and age, its once-dark ink faded to a muted charcoal. He placed it carefully in front of me, sliding it closer before stepping back to observe my reaction.

Curious, I gently unfurled the scroll. My lips parted as the full scope of it came into view: a star chart, impossibly intricate, the precise marks of constellations spiraling outward from a central axis. I wasn't just looking at a map of Volcaryth's night skies—it cataloged movements and highlighted solar alignments with precision that should've been impossible for such an old artifact.

"This," I breathed, running my finger just shy of touching the delicate ink. "This is incredible, Rath. How ... how did you find this?"

"The archives beneath the Blade Keep," he replied, his voice quieter than usual yet brimming with hidden significance. "Forgotten, abandoned in storage with documents no one cares about anymore—old star maps from times long gone."

I swallowed hard, the enormity of it sinking in. "Why now? Why ... why show me this?"

He didn't hesitate. "Because I know your mind, Orla. Your eyes always watch fractured things—the cracks between stone, the marrow in what others throw away. You follow patterns no one else sees." He crouched again, heavy gaze pinning me in place. "You'll see more in this map than anyone else has for centuries. And I wonder what you might uncover."

His words struck something within me, leaving me disarmed. I looked back at the star map, tracing its curves. Part of me wanted to devour it with analysis, to pull its meanings apart and piece them back into a constellation of discovery.

"It's beautiful," I said finally, my voice catching against the lump in my throat. My gaze darted upward. "You're full of surprises."

His lips tugged into a faint smirk, but his tail's restless flick betrayed his satisfaction. "Only for you," he said, his voice dipping into that dangerous warmth that had undone pieces of me before.

I couldn't suppress the smile spreading across my lips as I carefully rolled the star chart back into its delicate form, gripping it tighter than I needed to. It was more than ancient parchment filled with forgotten starlore—it was trust, belief, and an unspoken promise etched in the gesture of giving it to me.

"Rath," I whispered, unable to find words fitting enough for gratitude or depth. Instead, when I lifted my gaze to him again, every unsaid thing burned in the glance we exchanged, a gravity like twin suns aligning.

His hand reached out, the claws soft as they skimmed along my jawline. His wings arched outward slightly, the tension there not from threat but something raw. "I wanted you to have something worthy of your vision," he rumbled, thumb brushing along the hollow of my cheekbone. "And let it remind you, I see in you what others cannot."

My heart was thundering. Not from fear, though the intensity in Rath's gaze could incinerate lesser nerves—but from the overwhelming sense of being known. Of being seen.

I swallowed hard, my tongue darting out to wet my lips. His thumb stilled on my cheek, the motion not lost on him. Of course it wasn't. When I finally managed to speak, my voice emerged softer than I had intended. "You ... you do that a lot, you know."

His head tilted just slightly, his pupils narrowing in curiosity. "Do what?"

"See me." My hand strayed upward, resting lightly on his forearm. "Really see me."

His scrutiny deepened. "Because you are worth seeing,

shyrarva," he said, his voice dropping into something dangerously tender. "Worth everything."

The air between us shifted, like the faint rattle just before a storm unleashes itself. My breath hitched, but there was no holding back the words now scrambling over one another to escape my throat.

"I love you." The admission sounded almost foreign, like it had been sitting just under the surface of my skin, waiting for this precise moment to escape.

Rath froze. Not in shock. It was something quieter, something deeper. A pause as though the very world had stopped to allow his next breath to find its way into his chest. The tension in his jaw eased first, then his wings, which curled protectively inward as he leaned ever so slightly closer.

"Say it again," he growled, low and rough, his tone making the space between my ribs tremble.

A strange, soft laugh bubbled out of me, more exhale than sound. "I love you," I repeated, each word deliberately climbing its way through whatever walls still existed between us. And now that I'd said it, I found I wanted to say it forever.

His broad frame stretched taller, his shoulders loosening like some invisible weight had finally lifted. He sank to his knees in front of me, tilting me forward as his hands—which could shatter steel but touched me like glass—came to rest on either side of my hips.

Rath's gaze burned, the liquid fire of his pupils expanding, engulfing every hesitance in their way. "And I—" His voice faltered, cracked like rock encountering a river, and he paused before adjusting with deliberate clarity, quieter now, but no less powerful for it. "And I love you, *shyrarva*. More than you understand."

There it was. Plain, simple—except none of it was simple. It existed like an avalanche, unstoppable now that it had begun.

My chest felt both weightless and bursting, filled by the thunder of his truth clasping itself to mine.

I smiled. "There's not much I don't understand."

His answering grin was slow. "Good," he murmured, his lips brushing my temple as he rose to tower over me, never letting his hands stray farther than my frame.

His lips lingered at my temple, the warmth of his breath sweeping over my skin. My eyes drifted shut as every sharp-edged worry fell away, replaced by a sense of boundless heat and safety. His hands, one resting on my hip and the other at the curve of my lower back, tightened almost imperceptibly, their claws careful crescents against my body.

"*Shyrarva*," he murmured, pulling back just enough to match my gaze. His voice was a fire-fed growl, but there was no urgency in it this time—just depth and need. "Will you let me show you?"

"Show me what?" The question barely left me, not because I doubted, but because his intensity rendered words almost secondary.

His tail coiled gently around my ankle, claiming the space between us as his claws flexed slightly. "What it means to be mine."

Heat flared in my chest, his unsaid promise an all-consuming weight. I couldn't have defied that pull if I tried—and stars above, I didn't want to try. My fingers lightly traced the ridges along his forearm as I nodded, my pulse loud enough in my ears to drown out everything else.

"Always."

Rath held me carefully, my ribs pressing against the solid weight of his chest as his wings arched slightly. For a creature designed to bring a battlefield to its knees, he carried me like I might shatter if he held on too hard.

He stepped backward until his claws grazed the edge of the

raised sleeping slab in the center of the room, its surface draped in silks.

Rath laid me down, one hand bracing the line of my spine while the other adjusted my shoulders into place until the silks cradled my weight. His wings spread fully for balance before he joined me, the rumble in his chest steady as the earth itself.

"You are ..." His voice hitched, his golden eyes awash with something both worshipful and predatory as his claws curled around one of my thighs. "You are fire itself, *shyrarva*, and you do not know."

"You keep calling me fire," I murmured, my hands sliding up his shoulders until they curled around his neck, fingers grazing the seam where muscle and scale met. "What does that make you?"

"Fuel," he answered, his fangs catching on the word like a vow. "Heat without direction will devour everything it touches. But with purpose?" His tongue flicked along his fangs, his tail brushing over my calf in slow, deliberate arcs. "It sustains, binds, creates."

His mouth captured mine before the quiver in my breath could answer him, his kiss measured and slow at first, then hungrier when I pressed up into him. His claws skimmed just under the hem of my shirt, tracing the faint lines of muscle where the burn scars were beginning to fade.

He broke away just long enough for his fingers to tug delicately at the fabric. "Off," he commanded, his gaze nearly black. His claws rested against the edge of my skin. "Let me see everything."

My clothes joined the folds of silk beneath me, but his lips didn't follow immediately.

Instead, his fingers skimmed over my exposed skin, tracing over burns, scars, and the star tattoos he'd come to know better than I did. His tail looped farther across my legs, pinning me gently in place as his claws caught at the line of my ribs. "They'll know," he murmured, lips finding the hollow just beneath my collarbone. "Every mark etched here is proof of a strength they can never question. Never challenge."

I would have laughed if his thumb hadn't caught on the corner of my hip bone, stopping the sound with a sharp inhale. "You think scars impress them more than schematics?"

"I know," he said simply, his lips skimming lower, tongue brushing just shy of the lines between silk and skin. Every nerve in my body sang under his touch.

"Rath, I—" The words stumbled into the space between us, more reflexive gasp than command as his mouth found the edge of mine again.

Fingertips against my hip flexed, claws hidden away for just the barest press of intention—Rath's reverence was fire made flesh, devouring without destruction. And when his tail dragged higher, the heat at its core left no confusion: He wasn't asking if I understood.

He was showing me.

Claiming me.

Loving me.

I arched into him, the heat from my own need melding with the furnace of his scales as his claws dipped in places that made me shiver. His hips pressed flush with mine as his tail curled tighter—a possessive pressure rather than restraint, his voice lurching into a quiet growl.

Mine.

The word echoed silently as he consumed me, entirely his own.

Shyrarva.

His breath drew short against my ear, claws flexing protectively across my ribs, but his thrusts slowed with effort. His rhythm stuttered before settling—he intended it to, his movements deliberate and languid. No hurry here, not when it was just us.

Just this undeniable pull.

"Rath," I gasped, my hands clawing at him as he brought me to the edge, forcing me to hover there.

He shuddered, his lips at my neck as his pace faltered. "Burn for me, *shyrarva*."

He didn't have to ask. The sensation he wrung from me was already fire itself, but his command set something loose that raged and devoured until there was nothing left.

He joined me in an all-consuming wave, his chest pressed flush to mine, his wings folded tightly over both of us. His breaths came deep and hard, the satisfaction in them unmistakable. When he finally spoke, his voice was a low rumble.

"Never forget who you are," he murmured, his fangs glinting even as his grip softened.

I turned my face against his neck, breathing in the scent of him—charred cedar and embers—as I smiled into his skin. "You can remind them every time I forget."

VYNE

THE MARKET BUZZED—TOO loud, too alive. I hovered at the edge of the chaos, half-draped in shadows. The crystals in the walls seemed to burn, casting fractured light over the crowd. It made their faces sharp, jagged, almost unreal.

Yet her face, among the other humans, stuck out like a spark waiting to catch.

A burst of laughter, human and soft, carried over rattling carts and shouted negotiations. The sound hit me like a foreign blade, unfamiliar and fatally precise. My tongue ached, that strange sensitivity crawling up from the back of my throat and settling deep in my chest.

For days ... longer than days, if I was being honest, I'd tried to ignore it.

I wouldn't be Rath, drawn in like a moth to fire despite knowing how it would scorch. I was sharper than that. My sense of self-preservation still had teeth.

But when she laughed again, my body betrayed me, dragging my gaze toward their group. Four of them together, a tight-knit cluster navigating the crowd with cautious joy. They moved like a flock of sunglow finches, all darting movements and quiet giggles bound by instinctive camaraderie. They were softer than anything else in the market. Their fragility was jarring, delicate within the sharp angles of Scalvaris.

Delicate, but not weak.

Her hair caught my attention first. Light caught the strands as she tilted her head toward another of the women, listening intently to their whispered conversation. A smirk tugged at the corner of her lips. A quiet predator, watching and observing before striking with some dry quip, I wagered.

It wasn't her beauty, though she had enough of it to snap a weaker male's resolve. It wasn't the way she tucked her hands close to her chest when the smallest Drakarn child ran past her clutching sticky scales of stolen candy. And it damn well wasn't the slight upward curve of her jawline showing off the tension in her neck as her smirk relaxed back into something unreadable.

It was her scent—a phantom warmth that lingered on the smoke-filled air. Something sweet, slightly sharp underneath, like phoenix fruit steeped in herb oil. The scent tightened every nerve in my body, something wild yanking at my restraint.

My tongue tingled again, sharper this time, as if some unseen force had lashed it. It made me want to step forward, part the crowd surrounding them, and inhale until my chest finally stopped burning.

I retreated deeper into the shadows, claws twitching uselessly at my sides. What was this, exactly? Was it the same tethering madness that had dragged Rath through the hells for his human? That had made Darrokar act like a fool?

I clenched my jaws, the barbell in my tongue clicking against my teeth. Whatever it was, it needed to stop.

Rath had barely survived the upheaval caused by his bond. He'd fought tooth and claw against Karyseth and the vultures circling Scalvaris's politics.

I didn't have his patience or his recklessness. I'd spent most of my life artfully dancing just under the council's scrutiny, dodging unnecessary risks and skulking out of the spotlight.

Her laughter cut through me again, raw as an open wound. It scraped away the pretense I clung to, the false calm I'd worn like armor for so long.

I was supposed to be good at ignoring stupid ideas. At looking through the fire and thinking about my next move. But suddenly, I was back at the edges of the market without realizing my feet had moved. The women were still there, farther ahead now, lingering near a vendor draped with polished obsidian necklaces. She stood apart from her companions, fingers pressed to a lichen-brushed gemstone, her expression thoughtful.

The ache twisted tighter. My tail jerked in protest, smacking a low crate behind me with a crack, forcing me to snap it, controlled again.

"Fucking idiot," I hissed under my breath.

To her, from a distance, I probably looked no better than some hulking stalker with half a brain.

But she didn't notice me. No one did—not even the vendor, who was preoccupied arguing with another Drakarn over the price of lava-lizard talons decorated in intricate painted patterns. It was easy to slip closer. Close enough to see the faint drag marks in the dust where her boots had scuffed the ground. Close enough to think about reaching out ... for what, I didn't even know.

The scent hit me harder now. Impossible not to notice when it wrapped around me like a second skin, pulling me in like the currents of an underground river. My tongue burned red hot, every sensitive tastebud lighting up with phantom flavor.

It would be so easy to close the distance. To press clawed

fingers lightly to her shoulder so she'd turn. To watch as her wide, unfamiliar human eyes took me in. To speak—just one word, a name, her name. Or to say nothing at all and just let the silence stretch between us, burning this unnatural pull into the fabric of what could become ...

Would become nothing.

I dragged the thought back, sharp as my blades. Nothing. No "could," no "would."

A mate—a *human*—wasn't something I could claim. Not now, not ever. Karyseth's schemes against Rath and Orla proved that truth well enough.

Why would I want to give her another opening? Rath and Orla had already survived enough. I wasn't about to play with lava after their fragile truce.

Something in me hardened as I stepped away again, the ache in my chest twisting into something closer to a wound.

Self-inflicted. Necessary.

I turned, setting my path deliberately away from the market's packed heart. "Be smarter than him, you idiot," I muttered to the emptiness ahead. I repeated it like a mantra, the words as bitter as sand trapped under my tongue.

Be smarter than Rath. Be smarter.

But even as I turned my back on her, I swore I could still taste the way her scent lingered on the grit-flavored air.

And the burn wouldn't subside.

———

SCORCHED BY FATE

SELENE

NOT ALL OF the seven-foot-tall dragon men in Scalvaris were my type, especially not the one picking his nose with a wickedly sharp claw in the stall across the way.

The River Market stretched out ahead of me, loud and screaming with life—sometimes literally from the winged children running and flying wobbly around. Stalls packed with strange, deadly looking objects twisted along the stone paths, each one shouting for attention in ways that only reminded me how far from Earth we were.

Blades gleamed, crystals pulsed, and tangy-smelling smoke curled up from corners where food vendors flipped something that didn't look remotely edible. But this was life on Volcaryth —a mess of fire and survival. You didn't get to be picky.

I'd say we were the opposite of picky. Not a single one of us had *picked* this planet.

"Look at this!" Rachel Voss's voice cut through the noise. She stopped at a little stall draped in faded woven fabric, pointing at a series of pendants strung from a beam. "Am I wrong, or would this one match Kaiya's glasses *perfectly?*"

Kaiya frowned at the pendant and then at Rachel. "They're not a fashion statement. They're prescribed lenses."

Rachel laughed and rolled her eyes. She nudged me lightly with her elbow. "I don't remember anything in med school that prevented matching accessories."

Kaiya adjusted her thick glasses, clearly unimpressed. "What's the point? Now if you wanted to talk about the biodiversity of the materials and their potential similarities to—"

"Nope," Rachel interrupted before I could even open my mouth to weigh in. "There will be no science babble this early into the day. It's against the law."

"I must have missed that one," I said dryly. "And I think we've broken enough laws over the last three months." The dust was still settling from Orla and Rath's rather explosive mating and the sickening show they'd had to put on to prove themselves.

This earned the start of a grin from Rachel and an unimpressed sigh from Kaiya. I wasn't sure if I was proud or not for managing to keep the mood light. It wouldn't last long anyway. Not with Vega here.

She didn't have to say anything for me to know tension was brewing. With Vega, you could *feel* it first, like that second of silence after someone pulls a grenade pin. I clocked her pacing two stalls ahead of us, posture impossibly rigid. Still, I caught up to her. She'd made the effort to come out and be social.

"This is going to blow up in our faces," Vega muttered darkly. She wasn't looking at me as she spoke, but her voice had that razor-edge of judgment wrapped in thinly veiled exhaustion. "Those weird acolytes won't stop staring at us." She used her head to gesture further up the path to where three Drakarn in yellowish robes were not-so-subtly watching us shop.

Kaiya exchanged a glance with Rachel before pushing her glasses up her nose again. "They can watch us all they like. We're not doing anything wrong."

"Last I checked, we don't get to decide what's right or

wrong," Vega said. She glanced warily at the yellow-robed acolytes. One of them—an older male with dark bronze scales—muttered something to his companion, and they both shifted, like they were debating whether to approach us. "They're not just watching. They're waiting."

Rachel scoffed. "Waiting for what?"

Vega scowled. "An excuse."

Rachel rolled her eyes and ignored her. "Say what you want," she said to Kaiya and me, her tone dipping into a teasing smirk, "but Drakarn biology does seem to kind of be working for some of us. Do you think their wingspan—"

"Seriously?" Vega hissed, spinning around to face Rachel like she'd just set fire to her common sense. "I'm over here worrying about execution orders, and you're busy ogling their damn wings?"

Unflustered, Rachel crossed her arms and tilted her head, smirking lazily. "I hear it's not just their wings."

"You're unbelievable," Vega grumbled, rubbing at her temple and clearly weighing whether or not she could strangle Rachel before any Drakarn noticed. If they would even care.

"Enough." This had to stop before they could land any more barbs. "We're not fighting in public." There were only ten humans in all of Scalvaris, on all of Volcaryth as far as we knew. We had to be a united front, or they'd tear us to shreds.

Rachel smirked again but didn't push it further. Vega, on the other hand, scowled harder before turning and stomping out of the market, her steps brisk and just shy of furious.

Kaiya fell in step beside me as we continued deeper into the rows of alien wares. Her fingers twitched, as if itching to grab a sketchpad or start dissecting every new sight. "For the record," she said, her voice carefully neutral, "I'd still like to understand the biological implications."

I laughed under my breath. "I'm sure you can add it to your growing list of scientific obsessions."

Kaiya ducked her head, a hint of a blush creeping up her cheek. "I am a xenobiologist. I've spent my life studying alien life. This ... well, I never expected so much hands-on experience."

"Hands-on experience?" Rachel asked, a mischievous sparkle in her eye. "If you want hands-on with one of Scalvaris's finest, I'm sure I can arrange an introduction. I bet that guy over there has a tail for days. Very aerodynamic, I imagine."

"Why do I even try to have a serious conversation around any of you?" Kaiya muttered, her blush deepening as she adjusted her glasses for the third time. If she pressed them any harder against her nose, they'd probably fuse to her face.

I snorted, letting the banter run its course. Admittedly, it was nice to hear something other than discussions of survival plans and escape routes, even if the levity was probably doomed to be short-lived. Somewhere in the pit of my stomach, I could already feel the weight of Vega's earlier words.

She wasn't wrong. Execution orders or not, Scalvaris was a pressure cooker—and humans were just one more volatile ingredient thrown into the pot.

Before I could spiral too far, Rachel jerked her chin toward one of the stalls off to our left. "Check it out; that blade looks like some wizard shit."

The weapon on display was stunning. Long and curved ever-so-slightly, its edge gleamed with a sharpness that whispered deadly promises. Intricate heat crystals glowed along the hilt, the golden light flickering like trapped embers. The craftsmanship was undeniable.

It wasn't just a weapon; it was a masterpiece.

And it did look a little like something that could start

shooting magic fireballs with the right words. But in my experience, aliens were real, magic? Not so much.

I stepped closer, letting my fingers hover just shy of the blade's surface. I wasn't stupid enough to touch it outright—some Drakarn got real tetchy about their goods being handled by strangers.

The vendor—an older Drakarn with scales the color of ash—leaned forward, his piercing orange gaze taking me in. "Admiring the fine work, human?" His voice rumbled low, carrying an edge of pride. Not threatening, which was refreshing for a change. Still, I straightened unconsciously, keeping my expression carefully neutral.

"It's ..." I faltered, searching for the right words. What could you even say about something this impressive? "It's beautiful. Did you ..."

The vendor's narrow pupils flicked from me to the weapon, a satisfied smile pulling at his lips. "It is the work of Vyne," he said, like that name alone should mean something to me. When I tilted my head, he chuckled. "One of our finest forge masters. His precision is unparalleled."

Vyne. I rolled the name around in my head, my brain immediately conjuring up the image of a certain Drakarn warrior I'd crossed paths with a few times—once in the healing caverns when I'd been learning from Mysha and again when he'd silently stepped in to help unload supplies without a word.

Dark green scales, broad shoulders, a face that could stop a woman in her tracks ... and hands as skilled as they were lethal.

Rachel's elbow nudged me lightly. "Oh no. I know that look."

I shot her a dry glance, shoving aside the very real mental image of Vyne, flickering forge light catching the sharp planes of his face. "I wasn't thinking about anything," I lied, struggling —and mostly failing—to sound convincing.

Rachel only smiled knowingly.

"Well, if you're interested," the vendor offered slyly, his scaled fingers drumming on the edge of his stall. "It's not often I have his blades to sell. He normally works on commission."

Words fizzled in my brain, refusing to form, which only fueled Rachel's growing amusement. She was going to hold this over my head for weeks.

Kaiya, probably sensing my rising discomfort, leaned forward to ask the vendor something about the heat crystals—her tone dripping with scientific curiosity. I was grateful for the diversion, but my mind had already run off on its own tangent, fixating on the absurdity of it all.

Strong hands. Precise craftsmanship. Quiet strength.

Damn it, Selene. Snap out of it.

If Vyne could pour that much focus and care into something like a blade, what else might he be capable of? What *would* it feel like to have those claws not carving metal but pressed gently to my skin, not as a weapon but—

Nope. Not going there.

I needed to get fucking laid. I'd joked about having a Drakarn of my very own to Orla not long ago, but jokes were one thing. Inviting one of the dragon-men to my bed? I wasn't so sure.

I tore my gaze from the weapon and cleared my throat, forcing my attention back to my surroundings. The noise of the market seemed sharper now, every sound a little too loud as I tried to wrest control of my spiraling thoughts.

"It's getting late," I said briskly, cutting through Kaiya's excited chatter about living crystals. Rachel raised an eyebrow at me, clearly biting back another comment, but thankfully, she let it go.

The back of my neck itched like someone was watching me.

I glanced backwards, looking for ... well, green scales if I was being honest. But if someone was watching me, they were doing it from the shadows.

Maybe this planet was getting to me after all.

THE MARKET BUZZED—TOO loud, too alive. I hovered at the edge of the chaos, half-draped in shadows. The crystals in the walls seemed to burn, casting fractured light over the crowd. It made their faces sharp, jagged, almost unreal.

Yet her face, among the other humans, stuck out like a spark waiting to catch.

A burst of laughter, human and soft, carried over rattling carts and shouted negotiations. The sound hit me like a blade, unfamiliar and fatally precise. My tongue ached, that strange sensitivity crawling up from the back of my throat and settling deep in my chest.

Selene.

For days ... longer than days if I was being honest, I'd been aware of her. Not actively—but in the way you notice the flare of forge-light in the dark, or the lingering echo of a hammer-strike after the sound fades. Today, she wasn't just another foreign presence in Scalvaris.

Today, something felt different.

I wouldn't be Rath, drawn in like a moth to fire despite knowing how it would scorch. I was sharper than that. My sense of self-preservation still had teeth.

But when she laughed again, my body betrayed me, dragging my gaze toward their group. Four of them together, a tight-knit cluster navigating the crowd with cautious joy. They moved like a flock of sunglow finches, all darting movements and quiet giggles bound by instinctive camaraderie. They were softer than anything else in the market. Their fragility was jarring, delicate within the sharp angles of Scalvaris.

Delicate, but not weak.

Her hair caught my attention first. Light caught the strands as she tilted her head toward another of the women, listening intently to their conversation. A smirk tugged at the corner of her lips. A quiet predator, watching and observing before striking with some dry quip, I wagered.

It wasn't her beauty, though she had enough of it to snap a weaker male's resolve. It wasn't the way she tucked her hands close to her chest when a small Drakarn child ran past her clutching sticky scales of stolen candy. And it damn well wasn't the slight upward curve of her jawline showing off the tension in her neck as her smirk relaxed back into something unreadable.

It was her scent—a phantom warmth that lingered on the smoke-filled air. Something sweet, slightly sharp underneath, like phoenix fruit steeped in herb oil. The scent tightened every nerve in my body, wild yanking at my restraint.

My tongue tingled again, sharper this time, as if some unseen force had lashed it. It made me want to step forward, part the crowd surrounding them, and inhale until my chest finally stopped burning.

I retreated deeper into the shadows, claws twitching uselessly at my sides. What was this, exactly? Was it the same tethering madness that had dragged Rath through the hells for his human? That had made Darrokar act like a fool?

I clenched my jaw, the barbell in my tongue clicking against my teeth. Whatever it was, it needed to stop.

Rath had barely survived the upheaval caused by his bond. He'd fought tooth and claw against Karyseth and the vultures circling Scalvaris's politics.

I didn't have his patience or his recklessness. I'd spent most of my life artfully dancing just under the council's scrutiny, dodging unnecessary risks and skulking out of the spotlight.

Her laughter cut through me again, raw as an open wound. It scraped away the pretense I clung to, the false calm I'd worn like armor for so long.

I was supposed to be good at ignoring stupid ideas. At looking through the fire and thinking about my next move. But suddenly, I was back at the edge of the market without realizing my feet had moved. The women were still there, farther ahead now, lingering near a vendor draped with polished obsidian necklaces. She stood apart from her companions, fingers pressed to a lichen-brushed gemstone, her expression thoughtful.

The ache twisted tighter. My tail jerked in protest, smacking a low crate behind me with a crack, forcing me to snap it controlled again.

"Fucking idiot," I hissed under my breath.

To her, from a distance, I probably looked no better than some skulking stalker with half a brain.

But she didn't notice me. No one did—not even the vendor, who was preoccupied arguing with another Drakarn over the price of lava-lizard talons decorated in intricate painted patterns. It was easy to slip closer. Close enough to see the drag marks in the dust where her boots had scuffed the ground. Close enough to think about reaching out ... for what, I didn't even know.

The scent hit me harder then. Impossible not to notice

when it wrapped around me like a second skin, pulling me in like the currents of an underground river. My tongue burned red hot, every sensitive tastebud lighting up with phantom flavor.

It would be so easy to close the distance. To press clawed fingers lightly to her shoulder so she'd turn. To watch as her wide, unfamiliar human eyes took me in. To speak—just one word, a name, her name. Or to say nothing at all and just let the silence stretch between us, burning this unnatural pull into the fabric of what could become ...

Would become nothing.

I dragged the thought back, sharp as my blades. Nothing. No "could," no "would."

A mate—a *human*—wasn't something I could claim. Not now, not ever. Karyseth's schemes against Rath and Orla proved that truth well enough.

Why would I want to give her another opening? Rath and Orla had already survived enough. I wasn't about to play with lava after their fragile truce.

Something in me hardened as I stepped away again, the ache in my chest twisting into something closer to a wound.

Self-inflicted. Necessary.

I turned, setting my path deliberately away from the market's packed heart. "Be smarter than him, you idiot," I muttered to the emptiness ahead. I repeated it like a mantra, the words as bitter as sand trapped under my tongue.

Be smarter than Rath. Be smarter.

But even as I turned my back on her, I swore I could still taste the way her scent lingered on the grit-flavored air.

And the burn wouldn't subside.

3

SELENE

THE FORGE WAS A BEAST.

Heat slammed into me the second I stepped inside, thick and heavy enough to drown in. It burrowed under my skin, snagged in my lungs, a dare to even try and breathe. The noise was a physical assault—hammer on metal, the shriek of steam.

Mercy for sensitive ears or headaches? Forget about it.

Definitely not my happy place.

Sweat already slicked the back of my neck as I crossed the threshold. Mysha's list was crumpled tight in my hand, a knot of worry cinching tight in my chest. The elder healer's fainting spell from earlier wouldn't leave me alone, even if she'd snapped at me and waved me off like it was normal. I wasn't buying it. Not after that glimpse of her hands—bruises under the scales, faint and mottled.

Something was wrong, and it wasn't just her temper.

The noise clanged louder, deeper, as I moved farther into the cavern. Tables overflowed with tools, metal scraps, and surprisingly delicate sketches of blades pinned to the rough rock walls. Chaos, but organized chaos. Everything had its place, even if it looked like a disaster to anyone else. I got the symmetry of it, even as I edged around things that looked sharp enough to slice me open by accident.

Then I saw him.

Dead center in the forge's heart. Heat and firelight framed him like he'd clawed his way out of the flames themselves. Broad shoulders, green scales catching shadows of black, wings folded back but still massive. He moved like he was born to this, hammer rising and falling on a glowing blade, muscles flexing under his scales with each strike. His focus was a laser, locked on the metal as if daring it to disobey.

I stopped at the edge of his space, shifting my weight. Underneath the worry for Mysha, I was suddenly too aware of being an outsider. Even more than usual. The forge was *his* territory. I was just ... human and wrapped up in human problems he probably couldn't care less about.

I cleared my throat, voice quiet against the forge's roar. "Vyne."

He didn't falter, hammer still in its rhythm, but his eyes flicked up. Sharp, slit pupils narrowed as they found me. His chest rose in a controlled breath, a flicker of irritation crossing his face before it smoothed out. Neutral. Not friendly, not warm. Just ... less annoyed.

"You're early," he said, voice rough as rocks grinding together. The hammer came down one last time, then he plunged the blade into a shallow pool of liquid. Steam hissed up, like an angry spirit escaping.

I arched a brow, holding up Mysha's wrinkled list. "I didn't realize there was a schedule."

A ghost of a smirk touched the corner of his mouth. It didn't quite make it all the way. He tossed the hammer onto the workbench, the clang echoing and making me wince.

"Let me see it." Hand out, palm up, claws twitching. I hesitated for a beat. But he didn't owe me a kind tone. I stepped closer and held out the crumpled list.

His fingers brushed mine as he took it, and one word slammed into my brain before I could block it—warm. Too warm. Hot actually. Like fire licking skin, but without the burn, just that unsettling, sharp pleasure that faded too fast. Vyne's touch was ... something else.

Something dangerous.

I snatched my hand back, tucked it behind me like it had suddenly betrayed me. He didn't seem to notice. Or care. His attention was glued to the list, eyes narrowed at the scribbled handwriting.

"Is Mysha trying to kill me with this?" he muttered after a second, tilting the paper like that would magically decode it.

I bit back a laugh. "I'm pretty sure her penmanship is worse than her bedside manner." I was still struggling to learn to read the Drakarn language. My translator made speaking easy. Reading Mysha's handwriting was like trying to decipher hieroglyphics.

That got a low huff of amusement.

"Half of this is gibberish," he grumbled, squinting harder at the messy script. "You sure she didn't spatter ink on the paper and call it good?"

"I wouldn't rule it out." I folded my arms, shifted my weight. The forge was roasting, but the back-and-forth made it almost pleasant. "But she wouldn't ask for anything we didn't need."

"Since when is it a we?"

I bristled. "I've been training with Mysha since we got here." No need to specify when. To say that me and my fellow humans had made a splash in Scalvaris was an understatement.

Vyne's head tilted, and I caught a flicker of something almost ... soft ... in his expression. Wry. Maybe even amused.

Then it was gone, locked back behind the hard lines of his face.

"It'll take time," he finally said, rolling the list into a loose tube and setting it on his bench. "Some of this is ... finicky. The apprentices can handle most of it, but I'll have to tackle this," he pointed to one indecipherable line, "myself."

"And here I was, thinking you'd have it all ready by yesterday," I deadpanned, arching a brow.

That ghost-smirk again. Not quite softening, but there. "I'll have an apprentice get started on what's available. The rest might take a few days."

His gaze flicked to me again, sharp and assessing, and heat crept up my neck. Maybe it was just the forge finally getting to me. Yeah, probably that.

"Thank you," I said, ignoring the tightness in my throat. "Mysha's not exactly patient. But I'll pass it on. If she's not happy, she can fly down here and complain herself."

That earned a snort—a real one this time. His wings shifted, rustling in the heated air. "I'd like to see her try," he muttered, then inclined his head toward the doorway. "You should get moving before the heat does more than just flush you pink."

I jolted and damn it if my cheeks didn't get even pinker.

When I looked up, there was something in his gaze—not exactly indecent, but *knowing*. Too knowing. Like he'd noticed more than just the heat getting to me. My flushed skin, the way I couldn't seem to stop glancing at his hands.

Damn those hands.

The last thing I needed was to start imagining what they might feel like against my skin. And the rest of him?

Damn it again.

I cleared my throat, nodded, and turned, getting out of there before I could embarrass myself further. But even walking away, I could feel his stare. His eyes tracked me across the forge, a pressure on my back I didn't want to think too hard about. I bit the inside of my cheek, focusing on putting one foot in front of the other until I was past the threshold, back in the blessedly cooler tunnels.

I blew out a breath, dragging a hand over my damp forehead. My heart was still hammering, too fast, like I'd just escaped a fight. Except it wasn't fear driving my pulse. It was something sharper. I didn't want to name it, but I wasn't stupid.

A male like Vyne, he pulled you in, even if you fought to stay *out*.

I didn't need this. Not now.

I forced my thoughts back on track. Mysha. The list. The illness that had her leaning against the wall earlier like standing upright was too much effort.

By the time I reached the healing caverns, the tension in my chest had eased a little. Whatever had been fighting for my attention in the forge had no place here.

Something had been wrong for days. A tension in the air, a sluggishness in the way some of the healers moved. Mysha had been snapping at apprentices more than usual, rubbing her temples like even the dim cavern light was too much.

The orderly calm I associated with the Drakarn healers, their smooth efficiency, their collected focus, was fractured. Whispers, low and urgent, volleyed over prone bodies. Fabric rustled; muffled gasps and groans filled the air.

I froze just inside the entrance as the picture snapped into focus, sharp and ugly.

Mysha wasn't the only one sick.

Two other healers lay nearby, sprawled like they'd collapsed mid-step. The strange bruises weren't faint marks now—they spread dark and web-like across their calves and arms. A few other Drakarn moved through the room, jerky and clumsy, eyes glazed, clawed hands fumbling with supplies they couldn't seem to manage.

Rachel was crouched over one of the healers, brow furrowed in concentration. Kaiya moved between makeshift tables with frantic energy, her tension leaking out in sharp, tight movements.

"Selene!" Rachel's head snapped up as soon as I moved farther inside. Her voice was loud, sharp, but controlled enough to cut through the chaos. "Get over here. The shit hit the fan."

"What the hell happened?" I asked, crouching next to the closest Drakarn, not touching yet, just observing. Their chest barely lifted, shallow breaths that didn't seem to suck in enough air. The bruising was darker, spreading out from their torso. Veins under the scales were raised and angry. Beside them, bandages soaked in a green residue lay useless in a bowl of water that had somehow turned murky.

Rachel shook her head, standing, wiping her hands on her pants as she came closer. "Mysha collapsed just after you left. Then Sharyth and Nyzarin. It's spreading too fast to track. Symptoms are all over the place—muscle spasms in one, vascular issues in another. And I have no idea what's causing it. Kaiya's been consulting her notes, but we don't know *anything*."

"So the universe is being a bastard again." It came out harsher than I meant, but I wasn't there for soft words and handholding.

Kaiya spoke before Rachel could, appearing at my side, strung tight with tension. "We need samples. Data, patient histories," she said, voice clipped but precise. "Maybe they were exposed to something ... specific. Or maybe this is a known disease. I was trying to compare what I know about—"

"Kaiya," I interrupted, fixing her with my no-nonsense look, the one for when things were going sideways and we were out of time for theories. "Focus. What's workable now?"

To her credit, she didn't flinch, though her fingers twitched, betraying the battle to hold back the flood of ideas in her head. "Rachel's doing triage, trying to stabilize vitals. I tried a microdose of Earth antibiotics, just to rule out—"

"Good," I cut her off again, not unkindly. Focus was Kaiya's lifeline and reeling her back when she got lost in her own thoughts was part of the deal. "Stick to what's working. Rachel—"

I turned to her as she packed another vial into her med kit, sharp eyes already scanning the room like she could fix it with sheer will. "Did Mysha give us any hints?"

Rachel's lips tightened. "No. She's unconscious now, same as the others. Her symptoms are getting worse." Her gaze flicked to the makeshift triage area, the cot where Mysha lay still, face pinched even in sleep.

It took effort to keep panic out of my voice. "Do we need contamination protocols? Any signs it's jumping species?"

Rachel paused, weighing her answer. "Nothing yet. We're exposed, obviously, but we seem ... unaffected. So far."

"Not exactly comforting," I muttered, already pulling gloves from the kit and snapping them on. My hands moved on autopilot, finding the pulse at the neck of the nearest healer.

Weak, thready. Fuck.

I glanced around again, the harsh light bouncing off hollow cheeks and ragged breaths. The air felt thicker, pressing on my lungs like the forge, but this was worse. The forge was simple heat. This was ... hell.

"Alright," I barked, pulling my voice sharp, the tone they responded to because it sounded like I had a plan. I didn't. Not yet. But I'd fake it until I did. "Rachel, keep triage going. Airway stabilization first, and—"

"God damn it." Rachel's voice was dry, almost flat. I followed her gaze across the room to a younger healer clawing at the wall, movements twitchy and frantic, like he was trying to rip something invisible out of his own body. Then, like his strings were cut, he crumpled, face-first on the floor.

"Shit," I hissed, already moving, but Rachel's hand shot out, hard on my shoulder. "Bad idea," she said, firm.

"No choice," I snapped. "We have to contain this."

"You touch him, we risk exposure."

That stopped me. For about a second.

"We're already fucking exposed," I said, fierce, crossing my arms despite the growing weight in my chest. "Not touching him doesn't magically make us safe, Rachel," I continued, voice dropping harder, colder than I usually let it get. "We control what we can, or we watch everyone in this room die."

4

SELENE

ONE WEEK *Later*

It smelled like sickness. Like death.

My boots scuffed against the stone floor as I darted from one makeshift quarantine area to the next, eyes scanning for any signs of change in the afflicted healers.

Drakarn who had once stood tall and composed now sagged against stone benches, their scaled bodies limp and marked with angry, festering sores. Most barely moved. Some didn't move at all. The only sound they made was a wheeze, too weak to cough or cry out.

A creeping ache settled low in my gut at the sight, but I pushed it down. I'd been learning Drakarn healing ways for weeks, and now ...

Focus.

The murmurs and steady rhythm of the healing caverns were gone. Instead, rushed footsteps, clipped voices, and the scraping of trays across stone replaced normalcy. My throat tightened from the acrid sting in the air, something chemical and *wrong* that we couldn't identify. The healers were dropping like stones, and nothing seemed to be stopping it.

"Kaiya, double-check the gear for all the humans. Vega, I

need this entire section cordoned off—no one without protection gets near it. Rachel, go through the patient notes again. We must've missed something."

I wasn't a doctor, and I'd never felt it more than now. But as a combat medic, I understood triage.

And some of the Drakarn definitely wouldn't make it.

Kaiya's anxious nod and Vega's sharp grunt of acknowledgment were quick—exactly what I needed. They moved, figures cutting through the flickering light of the caverns. Rachel hunched over Mysha, her hand hovering over the elder's still form before quickly moving to assess her vitals.

The head healer hadn't stirred in hours.

I crouched beside a young Drakarn who had collapsed earlier, inspecting the inflamed sores spreading along his throat. My gloved fingers pressed near the edge of one on his neck. The swollen lump gave slightly beneath the pressure, and a thin trail of yellowish fluid leaked out. It was wrong.

It didn't behave like anything I'd seen before, but it also reminded me of far too many things. This was an alien disease on an alien planet. I wished for a computer, a research book, *anything* that might give me a clue to what we were dealing with.

"We need to keep them hydrated," I said quietly, the words more for myself than anyone else. I turned to Rachel. "This isn't just lethargy. None of them have shown a real thirst response, even now."

"We're handling fluids," Rachel replied steadily, but the tightness around her mouth betrayed her apprehension.

In another area of the hall, Orla was trying to rig brighter lighting using salvaged human tech. Her muttered curses reached me even from here. Every single human on Scalvaris, all ten of us, as if that was anything, was involved in trying to keep the healers alive. I didn't want this disease spreading to the Drakarn in the city. So far, us humans seemed immune.

Movement from the perimeter caught my attention. Vega pushed back a Drakarn warrior who had ventured too close, her hand planted firmly against his chest. I stood just as her voice rose, clear and firm.

"Stay back," she snapped, her posture rigid. "We don't know what's causing this yet or how it spreads. Do you want to risk carrying it through the city?"

The warrior growled something low, his tail flicking in agitation, but he didn't argue when Vega jabbed a gloved finger toward a nearby guard post. He backed away with a sharp lash of annoyance.

"Good," I called out tersely. "Keep it that way."

Vega glanced at me over her shoulder, and I could see the tension in her. She trusted exactly no one right now, and I couldn't say I blamed her. But aggression wouldn't help, either. I walked toward her as I pulled off my gloves to swap them for a fresh pair from the kit at my belt.

"Don't be too hard on them," I muttered as I passed her. "We'll get better cooperation if you're not threatening to shank anyone who breathes near us."

She crossed her arms. "Cooperation isn't going to help if this spreads."

I paused but only for a moment. "Noted."

Kaiya was carrying a tray of cleaned medical tools repurposed from both Drakarn and human supplies. The hybrid assortment made my stomach twist. Most of these were improvised; none of them were right for what we needed there. I examined the tray, my movements brisk, but the frustration gnawed at me.

Too clunky. Too wide. Scalpel edges dulled. Forceps too large for precise work. The designs of their tools weren't suited for the nuanced procedures we needed to treat a condition like this. They were weapons repurposed for healing, without the finesse required for something this delicate. My hands hovered over the instruments, imagining the strain of trying to use these on something like infected glands or necrotic tissue. I forced down a sharp exhale.

What we had wasn't enough, and what we needed ... Damn it.

"I'll be back," I told Kaiya before stalking towards the decontamination station and out of the caverns.

The forge wasn't far. Its heat seeped into the tunnels leading there, wrapping around me with the oppressive weight of the magma that flowed through the heart of Volcaryth. I was practically running, Drakarn dodging out of my way as I took corners too fast and nearly flung myself into a wall in my haste.

We needed better tools to stand a chance against whatever this thing was.

A disease? Poison? Parasite?

When I stepped into the forge's main chamber, the world tilted. The air was thicker there, throbbing with the energy of molten metal and the clanging of hammer on steel. Forge masters worked in silence, their movements fluid. But it wasn't them that drew my focus.

It was him.

Vyne stood at the far end of the forge, his back to me. Broad shoulders framed by wings flexed as he adjusted the angle of his anvil.

He worked with a focused intensity, his clawed hands guiding a thin blade under the precise heat of a Drakarn forge light. Shadows flickered across the lines of his emerald scales, giving them a deeper shine that caught coppery hues buried beneath the green. I didn't have time to notice, but my body didn't care what my brain was trying to do.

His scent hit me like a caress—subtle, warm, and irritatingly familiar even though we barely knew each other. But now, in the thick heat of the forge, it surrounded him like a second skin.

My tongue tingled, and I swallowed hard, pushing the feeling away, even as my body burned from more than the heat of the forge. My fingers ached to reach out for him. Clearly, exhaustion and stress were getting to me.

This wasn't the time or place.

"Vyne," I called out, keeping my voice steady as I stepped into the sweltering forge chamber.

His back was to me, broad and unyielding, but his movements faltered for the briefest moment. The metallic ring of his hammer paused mid-strike before picking up again, slower this time, as if he were deliberating something. He didn't turn.

"What are you doing here, human?" he said, his voice gruff, like gravel scraping against steel. "I had an apprentice deliver everything you asked for."

I crossed the stone floor, ignoring the heat clawing at my skin and the prickle of awareness under it. The Drakarn had a way of making you feel like you didn't belong, but I wasn't about to let him push me out. Not when lives were at stake.

"The healers are collapsing," I said bluntly, cutting past any pleasantries. "Mysha's sick. Whatever's hitting them is spreading fast, and we have nothing precise enough to work with. I need tools that aren't clumsy, that fit human hands. I need you."

His hammer froze mid-strike, the unfinished blade glowing beneath his claws.

Slowly, he turned, towering over me even across the modest distance between us. The flickering glow of molten fires caught the ridges of his scaled face, sharpening every detail—the scar cutting through his left brow, the flick of his tail that betrayed his thoughts more than his stoic expression did.

His yellow eyes locked onto mine, and it felt like the air in the forge shifted. Heavy. Different.

"You need *me?*" he repeated slowly, with just enough skepticism to make me grit my teeth.

"I need your tools," I corrected, stressing the word. This wasn't time for games. "You're the best forge master in the city, aren't you? I've seen your work. You're ... precise. Fast. And that's what I need right now."

If my words flattered him, his face didn't show it. That cold, assessing gaze stayed fixed on me, searching, like he was looking for the real reason I had walked into *his* forge and demanded his skills. The silence stretched a little too long, the heat of the room pressing down on me harder by the second.

"I don't know what's causing it," I continued, softening slightly, "but I know we can't treat it with what we have. I need finer instruments."

His jaw tightened, and for a second, I thought he'd sneer and shrug me off. But then his gaze shifted, lingering on me just a beat too long before he finally exhaled through his nose.

"What exactly do you need?" he asked curtly, moving toward a nearby workbench without waiting for me to answer.

The tension in my chest loosened, and I stepped closer, the air between us feeling too charged and strangely fragile.

"Fine-tipped forceps, micro-serrated scalpels, tools precise enough to work between scale and muscle without damage," I said quickly, listing off items as I pictured the mess in the healing halls. "Retractors shaped for Drakarn anatomy, articulated probes—"

The faintest quirk of his brow stopped me mid-word. His eyes glinted with something unreadable—sharp, calculating, and maybe a little irritated.

"You speak like someone who's spent too much time thinking about my blades," he muttered, grabbing a chunk of heat-resistant alloy and turning it over in his hand.

For a moment, my tongue tied. The way he said it, quiet and under his breath, made something in my stomach twist.

"I've spent a lot of time thinking about saving lives," I corrected, shaking off whatever weird feeling tried to crawl up my spine. I clenched my hands into fists at my sides. "You can forge these, can't you?"

He snorted, almost amused, as he dropped the alloy onto the workbench and reached for another. "I can forge anything. Question is whether your humans know how to use what I make ... or if you're just wasting my time."

I bristled, taking another step forward. "It's wasting time to talk like this when people are dying. You want to sit here and mock humans while the sickness spreads through *your* kind?"

The flare of defiance in my own voice caught me off guard, but I didn't step back.

Finally, Vyne's gaze softened—barely. Just enough for his brow to furrow instead of sneer as his claws dragged across the table's surface with a sharp rasp.

"You'll have them by dawn," he said, finally. Then he turned back to the forge, dismissing me entirely.

Even as relief coursed through me, I didn't move right away. I couldn't, not with the crackling heat of the room lingering in my lungs and his scent digging into senses I didn't know could react so strongly.

I exhaled sharply, ripping my attention back to the reason I'd come here in the first place.

The healers. Focus on the healers.

"Good," I said stiffly, already angling back toward the exit. "Don't make me chase you down for them."

HAMMER STRUCK METAL. The sound echoed all around the forge, ringing in my ears. I forced rhythm into the chaos, controlling each movement. The forge's heat clawed at my scales—hot even for a Drakarn—but I didn't let myself pause. Each strike burned more energy into the tools taking shape beneath my claws.

Forceps. Scalpel. Something articulated, precise.

These weren't weapons. But the urgency was the same.

Sweat gathered along the edges of my scales as the tools inched closer to completion. The alloy's glow dimmed under the shaping, its heat yielding to my control, but not without resistance. Each adjustment demanded focus, every shift a test of my patience. My claws twitched against the metal.

The ache of tension rippled through my chest again, sharp as the scent that had refused to leave my senses since she was there. It lingered in my head, maddening and intrusive. I clenched my jaw hard enough to make the barbell in my tongue press into the roof of my mouth.

My hammer didn't slow. Letting it stop would mean letting those thoughts in.

Her voice had settled into the forge, too. Not its tone—no,

that was already fading from memory. What clung to me was its edge. A command without invitation. A sharpness that didn't back down, born of necessity, not arrogance.

I growled low, pressing the blade of my hammer against the edge of the forming scalpel to narrow its contour. Self-preservation urged me to scrub every trace of her from my mind. But self-preservation was never good at winning when instinct screamed its demands. Not with her scent still burning through the air.

This was ridiculous.

The forge cracked around me, molten currents bubbling beneath reinforced grates. Time blurred as I moved from one tool to the next. The hiss of metal bending was the only sound louder than my rhythm. The edges of tools sharpened, taking clearer shapes like whispers pulled into focus.

I thought of her hands as I crafted. Smaller than a Drakarn's; the adjustments for human size needed precision finer than I liked. It had been hard enough to balance efficiency with my usual sense of perfection. Now it was harder with her face flashing through my memory in brief, cutting fractures.

Focused. Strong.

Her face wasn't supposed to linger. But it did.

Selene.

The tips of my claws scratched against cooled metal as I set the last tool down on my anvil. My breathing steadied slowly, and I stood there a moment longer than I needed to.

The ache took root again, curling beneath my ribs like it had always been there, and I fought the urge to smash the nearest unfinished blade to pieces just for the brief release it might bring.

It had been this way for weeks now. Ever since Rath's situation had nearly killed him and his mate, I'd kept my distance. Seeing how it had nearly drowned him—and brought chaos to all of Scalvaris besides—should've quenched any flame before it started.

But no matter how many walls I built in my mind, Selene's scent hit them like a battering ram.

I looked at the finished tools on the anvil. The glow of their tempered steel mirrored the heat crawling through my chest. This wasn't about her.

This was about the work.

About the healers, and whatever sickness clawed them down like prey picked apart by stealthy predators.

I gathered the tools into a sturdy leather wrap, folding it with care. My movements were efficient, detached. Anything to keep my thoughts chained to the task, not to *her*. The ache still gnawed in my chest.

The path to the healing caverns was quiet. News of the sickness was spreading, and healthy Drakarn were keeping their distance. Only the occasional flicker of heat crystals lit my path, their light fractured and uneven. My grip tightened on the bundle of tools.

When I entered the cavern, the stench of sickness assaulted my senses, burning against the cool edge of healing salves and sterilized metal. The space buzzed with tension, low murmurs from humans and the occasional rasp of a dying breath filtering through the stillness.

Selene was at the center of it all, moving with quick precision. Her black hair was tied back, stray strands sticking to her damp skin as she worked. She was bent over a table, inspecting a makeshift chart pinned to the surface, her hand stilling against the edge of it as she processed something. Her expression was stone—you'd think she wasn't panicking. But her hand tensed, small but unmistakable, and I saw the edge of fatigue carving its place into her jawline.

She needed to rest. I wanted to rush in and demand she

return to her chambers, or, better yet, mine, and sleep until the darkness faded from under her eyes.

I had no right.

A Drakarn guard jostled past me, his tail narrowly avoiding my own. I didn't move.

She hadn't noticed me yet.

Part of me wanted to leave. To set the tools down and vanish before she turned, before her eyes met mine and triggered that ache that refused to burn out. But my feet ignored me, carrying me farther into the cavern until my shadow stretched across her table.

Her head snapped up at the movement, dark eyes flicking toward me. For a second, relief flickered across her face, subdued but unmistakable. "That was fast."

"Done ahead of schedule." The words came out sharper than I meant, their edge sinking into the air between us. My claws flexed against the tool wrap. "Are the healers still alive?"

She gave me that tight, no-nonsense look, the one that made it annoyingly difficult to shake her off. "Barely," she said, her tone clipped but calm. Her hands reached out as I lowered the bundle onto the table.

She unwrapped the tools with care, fingers running over each one like she was memorizing their shapes. The forceps, the scalpel, the retractors. Her focus stayed on the metal, her lips pressed into a line of concentration.

"These are ..." Her voice trailed off before she glanced up at me again. "This is ... good."

I didn't reply. The gratitude in her tone should've been satisfying. It wasn't.

I wanted more.

Her fingers lingered over the scalpel, testing its balance, its weight. She set it down carefully, her eyes finally lifting to mine.

"You didn't have to deliver these yourself," she said, and there was no accusation in her voice. Only curiosity.

"I needed to stretch my legs," I muttered, crossing my arms. My own excuse felt weak, even to my ears.

Her gaze narrowed, assessing me in a way that turned the air between us heavier than the forge's heat. She nodded, an arch of her brow betraying amusement. "Thank you, really. But you need to leave now."

I snorted. "So soon?"

Her expression was grave. "Whatever this is, it spreads fast."

That brief flicker of relief was gone. Now it was all focus again, all energy coiled into tension she wouldn't let herself release. Watching her was like watching an arrow pulled back too tightly against its bowstring.

I should've turned and left. I didn't.

Instead, I stepped closer, forcing her to look up again. My claws tapped once—twice—on the edge of the table. "If you're short on hands, I'll help."

Her eyes widened, only for a moment before she tilted her head back to that same assessing stare. "We have this under control for now."

I was close enough now to pick out the scent clinging to her again. Krysfruit soap. Smoke laced within it. Something sharper, too, adrenaline-laced, lingering just above her skin. The ache I'd melted into the tools roared back, uncontained.

I wanted to argue. I had no business here, nothing but rudimentary knowledge of how to treat wounds in the field. But I spotted at least half of the humans in Scalvaris tending to Drakarn, and exhaustion was dragging at each and every one of them.

If they didn't find a way to treat this illness soon, they'd be the ones in need of help.

"Let me know if you need more tools," I said. As if that was sufficient.

Selene nodded, and I was dismissed.

When I stepped back into the tunnels, the air shifted again. Colder. Stale. Yet I still swore I could taste her on every inhale, as if leaving the caverns hadn't been enough to escape the burn.

The council was restless. And scared.

Never a good combination.

Mektar stood near the central table, wings tucked tight against his back, his shadow sharp. Zarvash lingered at the far end, hunched over one of his maps as always, his claws tapping idly against the surface. Khorlar's broad frame towered over the others, his stone-gray scales making him an even grimmer fixture against the firelit backdrop. Darrokar and Rath spoke to one another in hushed tones.

I didn't like the stiffness in the room. It promised nothing good.

Mektar didn't waste time.

"The humans," he snarled, voice low and biting. His midnight-blue scales caught silver streaks from the heat crystals as his tail jerked behind him, one curved claw tapping in measured strokes against the stone. "Their presence. Their interference. And now, their poison."

I stiffened. My claws curled at my sides, but I forced restraint into my voice. "Poison?"

Mektar's expression darkened further. He turned slightly, angling his body toward the central table as if expecting allies to rise from the shadows of the chamber. "Do you think it's coincidence this sickness began now? That Mysha herself—an elder—has fallen? We are not blind, Vyne. The Forge Temple—"

Rath groaned. "The Forge Temple sees enemies in every shadow."

My jaw twitched. Mektar's voice grated on every nerve I had grown tired of sanding down. "The humans have no more idea what caused this than we do," I said, my tone flat and edged in mirthless humor. "But yes, brilliant theory. Let's assume they crashed landed on our planet, waited several months, attempted to integrate into our society, and then whipped up an illness targeting our people, all while volunteering themselves to die along the way. Master strategists, clearly."

Sarcasm coated the words like molten slag, and I didn't bother softening it. Mektar shot me a glare. His claws scraped louder against the table as his tail flicked erratically. "Their weakness invites sickness! Their blood carries it! They are frail creatures, and whatever infects them spreads faster than wildfire. Shall we wait until it has taken root in each of us before acting?"

"Is that an actual question?" I asked lightly, leaning back on one foot. "Because while we're slinging paranoid accusations, perhaps you should consider someone more credible. Anyone from the Temple make an unannounced visit lately? Say, to the healing caverns? To stir things up a bit, as they tend to enjoy doing?"

Zarvash's brow quirked at that—subtle, but there—and Mektar's expression darkened. For all his bristling and righteous indignation, the accusation landed just close enough to the truth to irritate him. His wings flared before snapping back against his spine.

"You think the Forge Temple would harm our healers?" Mektar sneered, brushing the words aside like ashes in the wind. He was trying too hard. "The Forge Temple stands to protect our people's traditions, not poison them."

"Of course," I said dryly, crossing my arms. "I'm sure that's precisely what they're thinking when half their low-ranked acolytes hound Rath, screaming about divine judgment because he claimed a mate. Very hospitable. Truly guardians of reason and decency."

Rath let out a short bark of laughter from the other end of the room, and even Zarvash couldn't stop the twitch of his lips that threatened to resemble approval. Mektar's irritation boiled over, his claws leaving visible divots in the table now.

"Enough foolishness!" Mektar growled, glaring across the room like he was daring anyone to challenge him outright. "The Blade Council should stand united in protecting Scalvaris—not indulging in childish deflections. The Forge Temple—whether you agree with their methods or not—speaks to the heart of this matter. We should listen."

Rath rolled his eyes so hard I thought his head might snap backward. "Oh, absolutely. We should let the priests guide our survival. Maybe throw a few humans into the lava while we're at it, just to cleanse their 'weak blood.' Who shall we start with? Darrokar's mate? Mine?"

Darrokar growled.

Mektar snarled in response, but before he could launch into whatever drivel passed for a counterargument, Zarvash clapped his hands once, the sound sharp even in the fire-lit chamber.

"Enough," Zarvash said coolly, his tone slicing through the tension with a dangerous calm that carried no room for argument. He tilted his head, keen gaze sweeping across Mektar before settling briefly on me. "Mektar, do not be foolish. The humans did not spread this disease. And you, Vyne, know the Temple would do no such thing. We've wasted enough time chasing our tails. Here is what we know: The humans' quarantine methods are working—for now. Their intervention has stopped any spread into the city. The humans seem to be immune to whatever is causing this."

His words had just enough venom to make Mektar twitch again, but Zarvash didn't stop. "If we exile the humans now, what exactly do we gain? Crippling fear? Spreading this sickness? I don't want them here any more than you do, but it would be foolish to punish them now for helping."

Zarvash, the voice of reason. Since when?

From this angle, I could see Mektar's claws tap against the stone, too forceful to be casual. "Maybe we should form a committee," I offered, my voice perfectly bland. "One to vote on who gets to deal with the crisis first: the humans with brains and solutions, or the Temple with prayers and sacrifice. I'd love to see how those results come back."

Mektar hissed under his breath, his glare cutting toward me more murderous than it had been all night. "You tread too close to heresy, Vyne."

I exhaled through my nose, unbothered. "If heresy means valuing practicality over fanaticism, allow me to fetch the shackles myself."

Zarvash made a sound halfway between a sigh and a laugh, low and exasperated but not without amused acknowledgment. He straightened, fixing his gaze once more on the room's larger audience, deliberately dragging the focus away from me and Mektar before the latter self-combusted.

"If we intend to approach this situation *logically*," Zarvash said once more, with renewed emphasis, "then I suggest no more delays. Order additional supplies drawn from the lower stores. Work with the humans—not against them—to analyze the sickness's source and treatment. Above all, ensure cooperation, or risk this disease spreading throughout the city."

The silence that followed wasn't quite agreement, but it wasn't argument, either. It hung there, brittle and unresolved, but quieter than anything Mektar would risk answering with.

Finally, Khorlar grunted from his corner. His stoic expression hadn't changed, but his agreement—or at least his refusal to dissent—carried weight. For now, Zarvash's logic would hold.

Mektar bristled visibly but didn't speak. I didn't bother hiding my satisfaction, letting the faint flicker of a smirk cross my face as I rose to full height. Mektar caught the expression well enough; his sneer returned swiftly.

I left without waiting for his next fumbled insult.

The council chamber's heated tension clung to me as I strode away. Mektar might splutter or rise against Zarvash's surprisingly even logic later, but not tonight. For now, I'd won. Or rather, Zarvash had—his careful threading of caution and reason had defused the worst of it or delayed the inevitable explosion. Mektar's paranoia wasn't extinguished; it was merely smoldering, banked embers waiting for any excuse to blaze.

The path back to the forge was empty. Quiet. A reprieve from the council's festering fear. The tunnels curved ahead, the usual dim lighting casting an even glow across the uneven stone. It should've been a relief to return to solitude.

It wasn't.

The quiet only amplified my thoughts. They tripped over themselves, restless and sharp-edged, leaving trails of unease. The weight of Mektar's accusations mingled with the ache stirred by Selene's presence in the cavern. The momentary distraction of council politics wasn't enough to silence the pull she ignited—not nearly.

Her scent lingered as if she were standing beside me now, that subtle sharp tang of adrenaline threading beneath it. It burned clearly enough in the caverns that it chased me through the tunnels.

I shook my head sharply as I entered the forge, the heat's familiar, oppressive weight closing in fast. It swallowed errant thoughts more effectively than I could. Routine would reset the balance, suppress whatever inconvenient chaos simmered below the surface.

Let it burn out there. Let the heat melt these edges back to something sharp and manageable.

I grabbed a chunk of heat crystal from a supply chest, its grain rough beneath my claws. The chamber was sweltering, hotter than before, but I welcomed it. Anything to sweat out this ridiculous storm in my mind.

It wasn't enough.

The ache that had spread deep within my chest didn't seem to care about logic. It pushed like a simmering pulse against my ribs now, low and insistent. The hammer in my claw was supposed to relieve it. Instead, it dug in further.

I didn't notice I'd started shaping something new until the clang of metal echoed differently, the sound resonating sharper, crisper than my usual molds. A half-formed blade—a simple design, nothing ornate—formed something rough in my claws.

Selene didn't need weapons. She needed solutions.

But I had none to give.

6

SELENE

THE CAVERN WAS QUIETER NOW. The murmur of the sick had stilled, replaced by the hushed voices of Rachel and Kaiya. They were bent low over the wooden table, barely large enough to hold the fragments of gear Orla had pieced together for them. Soft light glinted off Rachel's sweat-streaked hair as she adjusted her makeshift lens, her hands steady as steel. Kaiya hovered beside her, fingers twitching with nervous energy, curiosity radiating like heat from embers.

My gaze flicked between them and the motionless figures of the healers on the other side of the cavern. The air hung thick, metallic with the scent of spilled blood and old herbs.

"Focus the light here," Rachel said, her voice calm despite the tension buried beneath it. She leaned closer to the sample spread thin across a shard of glass. "We need to confirm the structure. If this doesn't match ..."

She let the words trail off. They didn't need finishing. If the medical researcher and xenobiologist couldn't crack this puzzle, it wasn't getting solved.

Kaiya adjusted the light source, her curly hair sticking to her damp forehead. "Got it. There—look. The edges. It's forming those patterns you mentioned." Her voice pitched upward, eager, like she'd forgotten the dead-weight anxiety pressing down on the room.

I stepped closer. "What does that mean?" My voice came out rougher than I meant, but they didn't flinch.

Rachel straightened. Her finger traced the edge of the sample through the lens. "The biochemical structure is consistent with what Mysha described before she passed out. If this plant extract works the way she implied, it should bolster their immune systems and support recovery."

"You're talking about a cure?"

Rachel screwed her face up. "Not exactly. We don't know what's causing the illness. I've been reading Mysha's notes. Or trying to. My Drakarn is still—" She cut herself off. "If anything is going to help, it's this."

"What is it?" They had a vial of dust on their workstation, and there was some kind of paste in a mortar and pestle.

"It's called vyrathis."

Kaiya was wide-eyed. "We've got enough for one dose."

An ache twisted somewhere deep in my chest. I kept my expression steady. "Then we dose Mysha." I stared at the fragment of fluid and crushed leaf spread thin on the glass. The pungent scent of the plant pricked at my nose, sharp and earthy.

It didn't look like salvation. But it felt heavier than anything else in the room.

"How long will it take to see results?" I asked, shifting my weight as I glanced toward the elder's still form, half-buried under blankets.

Rachel exhaled low. "No idea." Her voice stayed calm, but her eyes narrowed in focus as she carefully lifted the sample away and moved toward the small vial beside her. "Are we doing this?"

I let my gaze drag across the cavern again. The sick

Drakarn were barely breathing, their scaled chests barely rising. Mysha's form looked small in the wide space. Fragile. It wasn't a word I'd ever associated with the Drakarn before arriving here.

I shoved the thought deep.

"Do it."

Rachel's motions were exact, her hands moving with care honed from years of research in the lab. Kaiya hovered beside her, chewing her lip as she held the light steady.

Mysha was impossibly pale beneath the glow of the heat crystals. Her breathing rasped faintly, like it was dragged from the depths of her chest against her will.

Rachel knelt beside her. "Lift her head, slowly."

I obeyed, gently sliding my hands beneath Mysha's scaled shoulders and cradling her head as Rachel leaned forward with the tube and Kaiya clamped her fingers on either side of Mysha's mouth to make her lips pucker open.

It seemed to sit in her mouth for several seconds before Kaiya stroked her hand down Mysha's throat until she swallowed.

We had to wait.

Mysha's breathing remained shallow, each rasp a reminder of how close she was to slipping away. I let my hands linger beneath her head for a moment longer than necessary, as if holding her steady might anchor her to this world.

No one spoke. Every sound—the shifting of fabric, the bubbling echo of the underground river beyond the far cavern wall, the shallow breaths of the sick—felt amplified in the absence of movement.

Mysha's chest rose and fell weakly.

"Now what?" Kaiya's voice broke the stillness, soft and unsure for a change.

"Now we wait." Rachel straightened from where she

crouched. Her hands were shaking slightly, the only crack in her otherwise eerie composure.

Rachel and Kaiya returned to their bench, poring over notes and calculations. I stayed. My eyes were glued to Mysha's face. Her breathing stayed steady now—not stronger, but no worse.

It wasn't much, but it was something, and in the absence of worse news, I'd cling to even the smallest sliver of hope.

The minutes oozed by. Even in my combat days, time had never felt this slow. My muscles were like coiled springs, tension wrung into every inch of me as the acidic thought twisted in my mind—what if this didn't work? What if it was already too late, and we'd held onto hope as only another cruel delusion?

Almost worse, what if it did but we couldn't find more vyrathis to go around?

Mysha shifted, just a bit. Her jaw slackened, lips parting as if her body was remembering it was supposed to breathe. My own breath caught as her claws twitched under my hand.

I scanned her closely. Her chest rose and fell again—but deeper this time. The rasp clinging to her breath seemed to let go, if only by a fraction.

"Mysha," I whispered, leaning closer like the shift in weight really mattered.

Her head tilted into my touch, and for the first time in days, I swore I saw her scales take on a hint of healthy glow on the edges, faint but unmistakable. Hope kicked in my chest, sharp and sudden.

"She's waking up," I called, voice low but urgent.

Rachel and Kaiya dropped what they were working on and hurried to my side. I hadn't moved, hadn't dared to, as they crouched on either side of Mysha. Rachel's fingers hovered just over Mysha's forehead.

Rachel pressed against the healer's neck. "Heart rate is still weak, but it's not erratic anymore. That's ... good. Very good."

I didn't let go, even as the others hovered, like keeping my hands where they were might hold Mysha together just a little longer. A groan left her throat, soft and strained, and her scaled lips twitched fractionally apart.

"Mysha," I said again, firmer this time, leaning in close enough to catch any change in her breathing, her expression, her still-closed eyes.

Her eyelids fluttered open, just barely, enough for the glow of the nearby crystals to reflect off her slit-pupil irises. Her gaze darted sluggishly before landing on me. Recognition flickered there, weak but clear.

"Hum ... human," she rasped. Her voice was wrecked, sandpaper and gravel grinding through the single word. But it was hers, and it filled the space like a signal flare in the dark.

"Yeah, it's me," I told her, fighting to keep my voice steady. "You're safe. Rest. Don't try to talk."

She didn't listen, of course. Drakarn never did—not when sheer force of will was basically embedded in their DNA. Her lips worked again, another groan scraping its way out.

Kaiya's hand fluttered toward her own mouth, nerves flooding her expression, but Rachel placed a steadying arm on her shoulder. "Let her speak."

It took several agonizing seconds for Mysha to string something together. Her chest hitched with the effort, muscles jumping beneath her sheer determination. "Rare," she ground out finally, her voice breaking on the single syllable.

I frowned, leaning closer. "What's rare? The illness?"

Her head shifted, a shake side-to-side, and her claws twitched uselessly against the blanket. "Vyrathis ..." The word came slower, harder, like dragging stone uphill, but its weight dropped between us all the same. "H-har ... Harrovan."

Her strength gave out just as she forced the word through clenched teeth. Her eyes fluttered closed again, but her body had eased in my grip, her breathing leveling out into something quieter—steady, almost peaceful.

Rachel blew out a long breath, tension visibly bleeding from her shoulders. Kaiya leaned back on her heels, clutching her knees, her energy deflating into something closer to numb relief.

"Vyrathis," Rachel repeated. "I'd say that's confirmation we're on the right track."

Kaiya straightened, almost too quickly, her hands shaking with nervous energy again. "But what the hell is Harrovan?"

"That's the next thing we figure out."

I stood, letting my body shift into motion. The ache I'd felt these past days didn't loosen, not fully, but it shifted into something else.

Purpose, maybe.

"You should head back to your quarters and sleep," Kaiya said. "I think Kira said she was going to try and make some bread for us. Rest. You've earned it."

I looked at each of the fifteen unconscious healers and shook my head. "Did either of you sleep last night? At all?"

The doctors shared a guilty look.

"Go sleep. Vega and Terra will be coming in for their shifts soon. There's nothing more you can do right now."

Rachel's eyes were practically black with exhaustion. Kaiya's skin had gone a bit sallow. It didn't take much insisting for them to leave me to it. And, as promised, Vega and Terra showed up.

But I still slept on a little slab in the back of the healing caverns, unwilling to leave my patients.

———

I adjusted the blanket over Mysha's still form, smoothing it against the cool scales of her chest. Her steady breathing wasn't loud enough to break the silence, but it carved through the oppressive fear clinging to the room. It was quieter in my head now—a small victory.

Mysha was alive, and there was a trail to follow.

The hope sparked by her words hung in the air, tantalizing but incomplete. Harrovan. The word was a puzzle piece in a language I barely understood. And the weight of what would come next made my fingers twitch with restless energy.

I didn't leave her side. Couldn't bring myself to.

The subtle scrape of claws on stone made my ears prick, and my head turned toward the entrance. Vyne's imposing frame filled the cavern doorway before he ducked to enter fully, his wings folding tighter as he navigated the narrow space. He carried a bundle across his arms, wrapped in thick cloth.

The sight of him sent a strange pulse through my chest, as sharp and sudden as it was unwelcome. My focus snapped back to Mysha, tamping the feeling down as fast as it rose. I didn't have time for *feelings* of any kind.

Vyne's steps were careful, but the air between us shifted as he neared the slab where Mysha rested. His scent again—smoke and something distinctly him—curled into my senses like it belonged there.

"You're back."

"You sound surprised." His voice carried its usual edge of dry disinterest, though it softened slightly. "It's late. Shouldn't you be sleeping?"

"I could ask the same of you." My response was automatic, my eyes still on Mysha's weakly glowing scales. "What's in the bundle?"

He shifted, and the fabric rustled as he set it on the table beside the elder. "More supplies. Forge tools. Salves. Whatever I could gather that might help."

I glanced at the bundle, barely resisting the urge to pick through it. "Good. Thanks."

He huffed once, a sound too soft to be a laugh but still close enough to catch my focus. It made me finally meet his eyes. The dim glow from the crystals caught on the emerald green of his scales, the black diamond-like patterns down his arms and chest marking him like armor.

His gaze didn't waver, though there was something sharper in it. "What happened?"

"Kaiya and Rachel found something that helped Mysha wake up for a bit." The words felt heavier than they should, and for a second I let them hang there, waiting for his reaction. "She gave us a word. Harrovan. She passed out again before we could get anything else."

Vyne's head tilted, his eyes narrowing—not in irritation, but thought. "Harrovan. The mountains."

I blinked. "Mountains?"

"It's a range far east of Scalvaris. The tallest peaks on Volcaryth." His claws tapped once against the stone of the table, the motion measured. "Days away by wing."

Days away. I pressed my lips together, the realization settling uncomfortably. I wasn't sure we had days.

"Someone's going to need to go there," I said after a long breath.

Not me. I couldn't leave. Though my mind flashed briefly to what it might be like to spend a days, a week even, with only Vyne. Heat jolted through me. Even with all the stress of the sickness, a small part of me *wanted* that.

"There's a plant. Vyrathis." The words felt heavy, weighted not just by the distance but what it implied. Logistics, risks, expectations. It wasn't fear—not exactly—but the weight of responsibility wouldn't loosen its grip.

Vyne's eyes stayed on me. They held that same sharpness I'd noticed before, unreadable but somehow too focused, like he could sense the thoughts twisting through my head. "I know it. It's rare."

"And I'm guessing it only grows in the Harrovan mountains?"

His expression didn't shift—no dramatic scoff or flinch, only the tiniest upward quirk of his brow. "Or so I've heard."

"Damn it."

Vyne's wings twitched, a flicker of movement that drew my eyes before I could stop them. He didn't respond, just waited, watching me with that maddeningly calm stare. His presence felt too steady in a moment where everything else frayed at the seams.

"I'll speak with the council," he said. "If you need vyrathis, you'll have it."

7

VYNE

THE COUNCIL CHAMBER SMOLDERED. Not with fire but with something sharper and far less controlled. Anger. Fear. Weakness masquerading as strength.

Darrokar loomed in the center of the room, the weight of Scalvaris balanced on his shoulders like it was carved there the day he rose to the role of Warrior Lord. His voice bit through the thick tension with the precision of a freshly honed blade.

"It has to be you, Vyne."

I almost laughed, but the flick of my tail was the only visible reaction I allowed. Restraint took effort. "You can't be serious," I said sharply, my voice low but steady. "Send a scouting team. Trained wings accustomed to Harrovan. Not—"

"You." Darrokar's voice cut through every word I hadn't yet said, leaving no cracks for debate. He stepped forward, his wings stretching in a silent warning. "I need someone I can trust. Mektar's causing trouble, and I don't know what in the hells Zarvash is up to. If they put their soldiers on this ..."

My claws curled, dull against the curve of my palms as shadows danced across the blackened stone walls. "Send someone else," I said evenly, though beneath the surface, tension coiled hotter than the nearby forge tunnels. "A group.

Resources. You're asking one to accomplish what you need a team to do."

"Two," he corrected.

The room seemed to gather more heat, though perhaps it was just me. A hiss escaped my teeth before I could bury it. "You can't mean one of the humans."

"Yes," Darrokar said simply, his gaze meeting mine without a flicker of doubt or hesitation. It almost made me hate him. "Selene."

Heat crawled beneath my scales. The mere mention of her name made the ache I'd kept chained in the shadows push harder against my ribs. Her scent threaded its way through memory, brighter than the fires in the forge.

I dug my claws into the stone of the table hard enough to leave divots. "She'll die out there."

Darrokar sighed. "She won't. She's resilient. She was a soldier, just like my Terra. And a medic. She is uniquely suited to this mission."

"Resilient is not immortal," I snapped. "Do you want to give this city another reason to distrust her kind if we fail?"

"She is necessary." Darrokar's words were calm but heavy, clearly chosen with care. "She's been working with the healers for weeks. She knows their ways, their methods. She's already proven her value tenfold. If anyone can identify and handle the vyrathis when it's found, it's her. And I'm sending you with her so you *don't* fail."

"And when the predators out there smell her blood?" My wings shifted, pulling tighter against my back as I spoke.

Darrokar stepped closer, his gaze locking onto mine with that unreadable steel he kept sheathed until moments like this. "Do you doubt me so much, Vyne?"

The air thickened between us. My tail flicked, carving a

line through the heated silence. "I don't doubt you," I said finally. "I doubt the wisdom of this."

Darrokar tilted his head, the movement as deliberate as every measured step he'd taken until now. "Do you?"

I hated how clearly he could see through me. Beneath my objections, my resistance, the truth pulsed too close to the surface: It wasn't just the danger of the Harrovan mountains that made my chest tighten with every second of this discussion. It was her. Selene. The thought of spending days—and nights—alone with her, her scent driving every instinct to places I couldn't afford to go. I doubted myself more than I did the world beyond Scalvaris.

But some truths wouldn't be spoken here. Darrokar didn't press further, though his gaze stayed sharp.

"I trust you," he said instead, his tone deceptively simple. "So will you trust me?"

"Trust doesn't make mountains less deadly."

"And doubt weakens resolve," he countered, his arms crossing over his broad chest. "Which will you carry into this mission?"

I closed my fist against the stone table, letting the heat seep deep into the muscles of my arm before I finally forced the words from my throat. "Fine."

Darrokar gave a single nod, one that somehow carried more weight than the anvil in my forge.

"Good," he said simply. "You leave at dawn. Report to Selene tonight and ensure she has what she needs. I'm trusting you with this."

I didn't respond beyond the sharp lash of my tail against the stone as I turned toward the chamber's exit.

As I stalked into the tunnels, the heat of the council chamber faded behind me. But the ache in my chest—sharp, heavy, and distinctly hers—burned hotter still.

———

The air outside the healing caverns clung to me like ash settling over scorched earth. This small alcove, cut into the outer wall of the tunnels, was a place meant for reprieve—a moment of peace amid chaos. The world here didn't burn; it breathed. Quiet. Cool. Patient.

And yet, the tension in my chest pulled taut as I took in the figure sitting against the ledge.

Selene.

She was curled in on herself in the way someone does when fighting sleep too long, her legs drawn up, arms hooked loosely around her knees. Her dark hair, usually pulled back tight like she was braced for battle, hung limp in loose waves over her shoulders.

The lines of her posture screamed weariness, but her eyes, locked on some unseen point in the dim haze beyond, glinted with a determination I doubted even her own body could quench. Shadowed though they were above the pale hollows of her cheeks, they burned, defying everything around her, even herself.

Her head tilted, her shoulders stiffening an infinitesimal amount. It wasn't defiance, just awareness. Preemptive defense, perhaps. This woman was carved of sharp edges and blunt truths.

"What are you doing here?" she murmured. Her voice was low, roughened at the edges, yet calm. Steady. Like someone who wasn't surprised anymore by disappointment circling back for another hit. "Come to give more bad news?"

The bitter edge under her tone cracked something in my chest I hadn't realized was fragile in the first place.

"I come with orders," I said, stepping fully into the meager light.

Her lip quirked, the shadow of that sharp humor pressing through exhaustion. "Figures."

Her head peeked to the side, sparing me a glance cut from steel and smoothed by something too soft for either of us to name. Whatever she was bracing for—criticism, dismissal, more endless pressure—it sat coiled behind that glance, an invisible wall built brick by goddamn stubborn brick.

I lowered myself to the stone beside her without asking. My tail curled once, instinctively tucking to the side so it wouldn't crowd her space. Selene shifted, not away but inward, crossing her arms like she had to build another barrier between herself and whatever weight she'd been forced to carry all day.

I waited. She would speak when she wanted to and not a moment before.

It didn't take long.

"One of them died." Voice flat. Heavy. Not cracked or broken, but brittle, like glass about to shatter under its own strain.

Every muscle in my body stiffened. "Who?"

"A young one. Yaris." She exhaled hard, fingers dragging briefly through her hair before falling limply at her sides again. "He wasn't ... he wasn't doing well by the time we got to him, but I thought—I thought maybe ..." Her voice trailed off, unfinished, swallowed by the vast emptiness carried in her too-quiet breath.

She shook her head sharply, but not to erase what she'd said. Just to shove it somewhere else, some dark corner she wasn't going to look at long enough to let it sink fully in.

"Barely old enough to be here," she muttered, quieter now but no less sharp. "He had this laugh. Quick and stupid and bright—damn near drove Kaiya insane this past week." Her lips twisted, as if memory could still find humor in agony. "Then he just ... stopped."

Guilt flashed across her eyes. The kind that left scars deeper than any blade could carve. I knew the weight well; it lived in my own chest some nights with wounds I'd long since buried.

"You did what you could."

She barked a laugh—not cruel, not humorless, but something sharp and self-deprecating. Her head tilted down briefly. "I couldn't do shit."

The air tightened around us—not choking, but charged. I wanted to reach out, to tug that weight from her shoulders and crush it under my claws before it swallowed her whole. But my hands stayed where they were, clenched against my knees. Her scent was sharp in the stillness, krysfruit wrapping around the ember-smoke of grief laced in her skin. Everything about her pulled against the ache in my chest I'd tried—and failed—to quench since the first time I'd met her.

I should have left. Should've delivered my orders and gone to deal with the rest of the mission's logistics. But the thought of walking away while Yaris's shadow still lingered in her expression made my claws curl hard enough to bite into my own palms.

"He wasn't on you," I said finally, my voice low enough it barely carried across the space between us. "None of this is."

She didn't look at me. But her lips pressed into a tight line as her hands curled at her sides, nails dragging against the fabric of her pants.

"Harrovan." My voice shifted deliberately, the single name slicing into the quiet between us, though the tension in it made my stomach twist.

That made her finally look at me. "What?"

"That's where we're going." The words left me heavy as the stone beneath us. "Darrokar ordered it. You and I leave at dawn."

Her reaction wasn't what I expected. Not anger or frustration. Not even the exhaustion driving everything else. It was just stillness. Like she hadn't registered the words yet. Like her mind was playing catch-up with her defenses.

Her lips parted once, then snapped shut. She shook her head, faint and definite. "No."

I blinked. "No?"

"I mean no. As in, not happening. As in, my place is here," she said, steel sparking through the weariness clogging her voice. "You can't just ... Hell no. I'm not leaving the healers now. They need me."

"They need you to retrieve the cure."

Her frame stiffened, her arms raising to cross tightly over her chest as though bracing against me—or perhaps herself. "They need me now."

"They'll need you more if they're still alive when we return."

The response silenced her, but her eyes cut dangerously toward mine, a flicker of heat beneath both her defiance and grief. "You're so sure we can even find it?"

"Yes." I meant it, even though the rough trek through Harrovan clawed over my mind like a poorly woven net. Her mortality against its dangers would haunt me every step beyond the city's barriers, but here, now, watching her try to climb a wall made of her own stubborn will and bruised instincts—I wouldn't let her crumble only to chain herself to failure's corpse.

Selene's jaw twitched, tension tracing her frame as she exhaled sharply through her nose. "You've been up there, then? Harrovan?"

"No." My tone stayed steady; it softened only where her shoulders stiffened further. "But I'll make sure you're not left to face it alone."

Her lips almost curled into a smile before her eyes dropped again, low and far away from the dim blue glow of the river.

The silence pressed down again, heavy but not the same weight as before. It shifted too much, too soon. Too clear. Above the grief thick in the air, something else edged closer, closer to the space we'd left untouched since the moment we first crossed paths.

I crossed it before I could think better of it.

My hand moved first—not grabbing, not holding, but hovering above her shoulder as my wings shifted open, slow, deliberate. The tip of my left one curled toward her back, brushing her upper spine like a shield offering itself where words would always fail. "Let me give you strength," I murmured, my voice low and rough-edged against the quiet.

She didn't jerk away. Didn't move at all, in fact, as my claws hovered against her, hesitant to thunder through whatever fragile thread she was clinging to here in this little alcove. After too many suspended heartbeats, her body softened, muscles easing toward the contact.

Her voice barely breached the quiet, but when it did, it refused to waver. "Just for a little while."

Something in me cracked wide open. It wasn't a break, not really, but a fracture deeper than I cared to name. As her weight shifted just slightly against my wing, I felt her warmth leeching through the fragile space we'd allowed between us.

I let it happen.

The world around us drew quiet, as if Volcaryth itself had decided to hold its breath. Her exhaustion had a gravity of its own, pulling everything close into its orbit, me included.

Her hair brushed against the curve of my wing, barely a whisper, but even that little touch sent my instincts reeling. Every sinew of restraint I held threatened to fray as her scent wrapped around me—smoke, krysfruit, and something sharper, tinged with sadness.

I exhaled through my nose, steady and slow, while my claws curled against the stone beneath us. "We will make it back," I said, breaking the stillness between us. My voice was rougher than I intended, lower, but steady. "To the healers. To this place. I won't fail you."

Her head tilted, her cheek brushing the edge of my wing, whether consciously or not I couldn't tell. She let out a soft, humorless laugh, the kind that didn't belong to someone who fully believed what they'd just heard. "And what if we do?"

Her question wasn't meant to challenge. It wasn't defiant. It was quiet and jagged around the edges like a blade that hadn't been polished properly.

"You and I don't fail." I said it again, slower this time, stronger, hoping she could pull the weight of those words into her chest and carry them with the same intensity I felt.

Selene raised her head just enough to glance at me. The shadows of her exhaustion and stubbornness waged war in her eyes, dark and cutting but too human for her to conceal entirely. For a moment, I could see the soldier in her fighting the medic. The part of her that wanted to move forward, to push and charge and fix, battling the part that had known loss and carried it far longer than anyone deserved.

"That easy, huh?" she said, the faintest flicker of dry humor threading her voice. "Why don't you package that up for the rest of us mortals?"

I snorted softly—the sound rough and unpolished even to my own ears. "Mortals?" I echoed, the word rolling over my tongue like there'd been a joke buried in it once. "Hard to believe you think of yourself that way."

Her brow quirked, a spark of something sharper flashing in her tired gaze. "Oh, don't worry. You Drakarn don't let us humans forget where we fall on the food chain." The corners of her mouth twitched upward, though not quite into the shape of a smile.

That humor was enough to kindle something warmer, brighter than the ache underneath. It was enough to anchor me against the instinct clawing beneath my scales.

"Harrovan isn't the food chain you need to worry about," I said, though my tone stayed lighter than the words themselves. "But if it helps, I'll make sure any predators out there know exactly where they fall."

Her lips tugged upward a little more, though the weariness in her expression still weighed her features down. "Big talk."

I leaned back, letting the tilt of my wings shift just so, not enough to pull away but enough to cut the sharp edges of what still lingered between us. "Big claws."

That earned a small laugh—real but wry, edged with disbelief but unharmed by it. She shook her head but leaned forward again, her breath soft and even as she stared past me.

For a while, neither of us said anything.

Her scent lingered in the alcove, threading through the cool air like a constant reminder of things I had no right to think about. The warmth of her shoulder, so close to brushing mine—and the quiver of her resolve beneath it—snared my focus in a way I hated but couldn't seem to shake.

No predator worth its fangs ignored what was right in front of them, but this was something else entirely.

I shifted against the stone. The scrape of my claws filled the silence, breaking it just enough without fracturing the fragile calm that had settled. "We leave at dawn," I reminded her, my tone softer, less edged now. "Get some rest."

Selene turned her head a little, her dark eyes cutting upward to meet mine. There was no sharpness in her stare this time—no challenge, no defiance. Just tired steel. And beneath it, something that flickered too faintly to trust the shape of. "Easy for you to say," she murmured, her lips curling in a sardonic edge. "Pretty sure you Drakarn can fall asleep standing upright."

I huffed, a sound small and guttural in the back of my throat. "We can. But you're not Drakarn."

"No kidding," she said wryly, pressing her palms into her knees as if preparing to rise. Her glance dropped, and the shadows along her face deepened under the quiet glow of the river's light. "But seriously—look at me. You think I'm just going to flip myself 'off' after this?"

I tilted my head, my wings giving the slightest flick of acknowledgment. "You need to try." My voice lowered further, rough and honest. "Exhaustion gets you killed. Especially where we're going."

Her lips parted, argument at the ready. But her words caught somewhere between her mind and her mouth, and what finally escaped wasn't anger or sarcasm, just a long, quiet exhale. She leaned forward, bracing her elbows on her knees, and dragged a tired hand through her hair. "You think I haven't been trying?"

I made no reply. None was required. The rawness in her voice—quiet as it was—said more than anything I could offer.

The silence stretched between us, softer this time. Not heavy, just steady. Long minutes passed, or maybe only seconds. I didn't count. I just stayed still, watching her from the corner of my eye while the ache buried beneath my ribs pressed harder with each passing breath.

Finally, Selene rose to her feet, the motion practiced but stiff. The fatigue etched in her posture caught the glow of the distant light, shadow and glow playing against her every step. She turned just enough to glance over her shoulder, one hand resting on her hip as her other reached up to tuck a stray strand of hair behind her ear.

"So," she drawled lightly, the humor barely masking the honesty beneath it, "dawn, huh?"

I smirked—a flicker of warmth that betrayed more than I cared to admit. "At dawn."

Her brows quirked in response, her lips tilting upward in a humorless smile. She held my gaze just a moment longer before looking away, her jaw tightening as she shifted her weight on her heels.

"Don't be late." Her words were almost teasing, as though speaking them aloud lightened the atmosphere just enough to make it tolerable again.

"I'll be waiting."

8

VYNE

PRE-DAWN WAS QUIET IN SCALVARIS. Time blurred under the rock, the suns just a hint through the skyshafts that pierced the ceiling of our city.

The air was heavy. Tense. And in that quiet stillness, I could feel the city bracing for the threat creeping ever closer to its borders. It was more than the sickness festering in the healers' caverns. It was something larger—something clawing at the edges of Scalvaris, unseen and unspoken.

The weight pressing against my chest wasn't the city's fear. It was something sharper.

Selene.

Krysfruit. Smoke.

It tickled my nose before I heard her footsteps.

She emerged from the edge of the quarter, her figure cutting a sharp line against the glow spilling over the stones. Her hair was tied back, though already some loose strands curled and stuck against her skin. The strength of her frame—the set of her shoulders, the weight in her step—didn't waver, but something else clung to her.

Weariness. Hesitation. Quiet grief behind a mask of sharp focus.

My tongue—traitorous, damnable thing—tingled at the edges, a phantom sensation I couldn't banish no matter how tightly I locked my jaw.

When our eyes finally locked, it hit harder than I anticipated. She stiffened for just a moment, a flicker of something unguarded before those dark eyes leveled me.

"Not too many early risers in Scalvaris?" Her voice was even, carefully controlled, though the faint humor threaded in it betrayed her efforts.

I forced a wry smirk, though the weight in my chest didn't loosen. "You're late."

"Am I?" I could see the ghost of a smile tugging the corner of her lips as she stepped closer. "You could have left without me."

"You must be lucky."

Her expression sobered, the humor retreating back into the quiet defenses she always carried. "Lucky's not exactly what I've been lately."

The words weren't sharp enough to cut, but they landed heavier than a mere observation. They sat awkwardly in the space between us, refusing to be smoothed over or walked around.

I tuned my senses back to the mission, letting practicality sand down the edges of everything else. "We'll make our way through the tunnels first, then out to the peaks." My wings shifted, the scrape of my claws mimicking the restless twitch in my shoulders. "We'll stop where we can find shelter come midday."

Her chin dipped, a small, fractional motion that said enough. Her fingers fiddled with the straps of her pack as she adjusted its position with combat trained precision.

Her motions were steady and calm as I studied her. She'd been a soldier once, and it showed. I shouldn't have cared beyond how it would help the mission. I shouldn't have noticed. But every inch of her stole my focus anyway.

Her scent. The set of her jaw. The stubborn line of determination cutting through exhaustion in her eyes.

Gods above, she was— No. Stop.

I forced myself to glance away, my gaze sweeping over the morning glow of the river instead. "Ready?"

Selene huffed softly and adjusted her pack again. "Lead the way."

Her voice might have been steady. Her steps resolute. But as we moved toward the tunnels carved into the cavern wall, that same weight coiled tighter with every step. It clung to the silence between us, unspoken but impossible to ignore, no matter how far we went.

I could hear her breathe. Too clear in the tunnels. Too close. The soft rhythm of it was steady, to her credit—controlled despite the strain of exhaustion I knew ate at her body and mind. Her pack jostled against her back, the sound blending with the quiet scrape of her boot against stone.

She brushed against me, her arm, her shoulder, maybe both, catching against the tough curve of my own as the path narrowed to little more than a cramped corridor. The contact was light, but the spark it sent through my nerves lingered. Heat prickled along the ridge of my spine. I forced my wings tighter along my back, trying to reclaim the space between us, but there wasn't any.

Selene stepped back to compensate, muttering, "Bit tight in here, huh?"

Her voice was low in the winding echoes of the tunnel. But the way it cut through the silence between us was sharp enough to draw my attention.

"Only for those who aren't paying attention." My voice was as dry as I could make it. A reflex. A defense.

She gave me a narrow look, though the faintest twist of amusement tugged her lips upward. "Of course. Because your wings don't seem to be taking up half the path."

"They're efficient. Unlike your stride."

She let out a sharp breath just this side of laughter. Her pace didn't falter, and when her shoulder brushed mine again, this time she didn't pull back so quickly. I didn't think it was on purpose, but the contact lingered.

My claws flexed against the rock for balance, the scrape unnervingly loud in the too-close air. Her scent was even stronger now, distinct and maddening. My tongue tingled again, that same cursed sensitivity pulling my focus where it didn't belong.

We crossed a sudden dip in the floor—a pocket of uneven stone that split the path where magma had once scorched through centuries prior. It forced her step to falter, her footing catching awkwardly, though she masked it quickly and pressed forward. I caught her movement before my mind registered what I was doing, my wing shifting instinctively to steady her balance.

Her hand shot out, reflexive. It wasn't enough to grab me— she didn't—and instead her fingers caught the edge of the wall beside her.

"Careful," I muttered before I could stop myself.

Her head tilted, sharp and questioning, though her pace didn't falter again. "I've got it."

Her dark eyes cut toward me as much as the tunnel allowed, the shadows obscuring the finer details of her expression but not enough to dim the glint of teasing steel in her gaze.

"Is there a reason we're not flying? Or are those wings of yours just for show?"

I bristled, wings flaring, sharp taloned tips scraping against the narrow cave wall. "The path to the Harrovan Mountains would take us too close to a field of noxious gas given off by one of the volcanoes. If we leave by the entrance at the end of this path, we'll avoid it. And keep breathing."

"Breathing is the preferable option."

The tunnel opened after a sharp bend, giving us a bit more room to breathe. Selene exhaled low, like she'd been carrying the weight deep inside her and could finally draw a full breath.

I glanced over at her. A scar ran along her temple, thin but sharp enough to suggest violence, caught the light as she turned and something dangerously close to *need* clenched in my chest.

"That scar. Is it from fighting for them?" I asked quietly, the words slipping before I could rationalize the cost of asking.

Selene paused, her brow tightening in confusion. "Them?"

"The humans. Whatever you call them. Your warriors."

She didn't speak immediately. Her fingers brushed against her temple, tracing the old wound. Finally, she rolled one shoulder in a small shrug, though the motion looked heavier than it should have. "No, my scar didn't come from battle. A piece of glass hit me when I was fourteen. From a broken bottle. Wrong place, wrong time sort of thing. I joined the army for the usual reason: college."

My jaw tensed, muscles pulling tight in my throat though I wasn't sure why. "I don't understand." What was *college*? She spoke Drakarn now, thanks to some little piece of Earth technology, but the word didn't translate.

"School," she said, and this time I knew the word. "I was supposed to serve out my contract and then they'd pay for my education. Then my superiors offered another option. I could leave early if I volunteered to go on the generation ship. They needed more medical professionals. I'm not a doctor or anything, but I was promised more education. More room for advancement. And it wasn't like there was a life I was missing out on at home. I'm not like Kira; I'm not missing a sister or anything like that. I thought this would be the opportunity of a lifetime."

"And instead you ended up here."

"This was definitely not what I was promised." She cast a sidelong glance my way. "But it's not all bad."

Her scent burned sharper against the compact air, and I swore the space had grown smaller again, closer. Too close.

When I spoke, my voice came quieter, rougher at the edges. "Good."

"What about you?" she tossed the words out casually, probing but not prying. "How did you become a forge master?"

"I forged my first blade when I was eight," I said. "It wasn't sharp, but I liked the shape. My father liked the ambition. That was enough."

Her expression flickered—soft, if only slightly. "Eight. Damn."

Selene's steps faltered briefly, her boot snagging over an irregular break in the rock, and for a moment, her weight pitched forward. My arm shot out before my brain caught up, steadying her without finesse until she was flattened against my chest.

I let her go quickly, but it was useless. The tunnel narrowed again, forcing her step closer to mine. As her arm brushed mine for the second time, any rational thought left unraveled, fraying at the edges faster than I could hide it.

Her scent burned sharper now. It wrapped around me in the confines of the tunnel, teasing the fragile chain of control I'd forced around my instincts since the moment I'd first tasted the air near her.

For the forge's sake.

My gaze dropped briefly, catching the subtle shift of her shoulders—the sharp cut of bone against her skin, her frame wound just tightly enough that I could feel her bracing for something invisible but inescapable. She wore her strength like armor, too heavy in some places, but almost too worn near others. And it only made the ache inside me twist deeper.

Damn it all.

I fixed my stare forward again, unwilling to crumble under the instinct clawing against sense. There wasn't space here— not now, not in this tunnel, not anywhere between us for what my body sought so painfully.

The tunnel's oppressive grip finally began to loosen as light from the end—faint and pale, but unmistakable—glimmered ahead. My steps slowed.

Selene caught my hesitation, her own movements faltering briefly before she drew up alongside me. Her breathing was quieter now, steadier, though her stance remained sharp-edged, like she was bracing for whatever lay just beyond our line of sight.

She stepped forward, her boot scratching against the stone as she moved closer to the growing glow. The dim warmth of the rising suns had started to bleed into the cool blue hue of the crystals, casting flickering shadows that danced along the rough walls. The air felt lighter here, cooler, though brimming with a strange tension that hummed beneath the surface like unseen currents.

I moved up beside her, wings rustling as they adjusted to the wider space. I took a moment to savor the more open space, but only for a moment. I didn't want her to think I was hesitating.

Selene looked out over the distant horizon. Quiet tension radiated off her. "It's beautiful," she said softly, almost as though the words weren't meant for me to hear.

"It's beautiful, but it burns," I responded. Even with my scales, the surface of Volcaryth was unkind.

She didn't look at me. "I figured as much."

The steep drop from the tunnel mouth to the terrain below yawned open just steps away. The winds swirled through the air, teasing the edges of my wings.

"You're not afraid of heights," I said, more statement than question. Her steady stance told me as much.

"No." Her response was clipped, matter-of-fact. But she still glanced at the distance below with a narrowed gaze. "But that doesn't mean I'm not cautious. It's not like I have wings."

"That's why you have me."

She blinked, finally turning toward me. Her lips curved, though the humor in her smile didn't quite reach her eyes. "Are you always this reassuring?"

"Only when it's warranted."

"Lucky me." Her tone softened, faint amusement lacing her exhaustion.

I stepped closer. The rock beneath my feet shifted, but I ignored it, wings flaring as I gestured toward the open sky beyond the ledge.

"Get closer," I said, my voice cool, though something in my chest twisted as her gaze flicked toward me with an oddly suspicious arch of her brow.

Her jaw tensed, but she didn't argue. Instead, she inhaled sharply through her nose, muttering something under her breath that sounded like either a curse or a prayer. Then she stepped closer to the edge of the tunnel. Her frame was still as strong as ever, but I caught the flicker of hesitation in her stance as she glanced one last time at the drop awaiting her.

I opened my wings fully, the stretch of them casting shifting shadows that sliced across the rock at our feet. The motion forced her step closer, keeping her within reach. I extended an arm, my claws flexing briefly before curling tightly against the leather guard at my wrist.

"Don't flinch."

Her eyes narrowed. "What—?"

Before she could finish, my arm circled firmly around her waist. It wasn't rough—precisely measured, controlled, but undeniably close. I pulled her against me as my other arm moved to steady her back, claws grazing just briefly against the strap of her pack. My wings closed, angling around her frame without fully enveloping her. Not yet. I wrapped my tail around her legs to keep her as close as possible.

Selene stiffened, her breath catching at the contact. Her hands instinctively shot to the front of my armor, gripping the edges of the leather as her stance fought against faltering completely.

"This is practical," I offered, though my voice was rougher than intended. She didn't need to know how much it cost me to keep my control. "For both our sakes."

She didn't respond immediately. Her gaze flicked toward the open sky behind me, her hands still gripping the edge of my worn leathers like she was weighing every possible escape plan.

"Right," she said finally, though the edge of her voice gave away her own internal battle. "Practical."

Stars help me.

That close, every sense I had was on fire—her breath warm against my throat, the heat of her skin radiating through the armor and scales separating us. My claws itched for purchase they couldn't take, my wings shifting instinctively to tighten around her, shielding her fully within their span as the wind curled tighter around us.

"Ready?" I asked, my voice softened by a restraint that grated against everything primal inside me.

She nodded once, her grip tightening. "Don't drop me."

The faintest twitch curled at the corner of my lips—a bitter, aching smile rising to fight the storm raging beneath the rest of me. "Not a chance."

9

SELENE

THE WIND HAMMERED at my face, sending a wild snarl through my hair and a hot spike of terror through my stomach. My arms tightened around Vyne's neck—not because I didn't trust him, but because trust wasn't about to overrule every screaming survival instinct raging in my chest.

The ground plummeted away beneath us like it hated me personally, and for one long, dizzying second, I swallowed the sharp, indignant protest of a species that had never been meant to leave the ground.

Vyne's hold didn't falter. One arm braced across my back, the other curved beneath my thighs, anchoring me against the unshakeable heat and strength of him as his wings unfolded and snapped open with merciless precision. The sheer size of them—dark, rippling planes of muscle and membrane stretching impossibly wide—made the clipped edge of awe lurking beneath my anxiety harder to shove down than I liked.

I was trying not to think about the tail wrapped around my legs. Judging from the blushes I'd seen from both Terra and Orla, Drakarn could be wickedly precise with their tails.

Volcaryth unfurled beneath us, a hellscape alive with fire and stone and smoke. Crimson sands twisted into blackened cliffs, their jagged spines punctuated by menacing veins of rivers that glowed molten-bright against the scorched ground. Steam hissed from unseen rifts below, curling up into the shimmering waves of heat that distorted everything into a feverish haze. The air cut sharp and sour in my throat, tinged with sulfur so thick it clung to the back of my tongue no matter how carefully I breathed.

It was hell. And somehow ... it was beautiful.

I glanced down, curiosity overriding my better judgement for half a second. Mistake. My stomach flipped violently as I registered how far we already were from the tunnels of Scalvaris. The cliffs were tiny teeth now, sharp and impossibly far away. I squeezed my eyes shut before the lurch in my stomach could claw its way up to my throat.

"You sure you've got me?" The words escaped before I could think about stopping them. I tried to make the question sound teasing, but it came out tighter than I liked.

Vyne's voice cut through the chaotic wind, rough around the edges but maddeningly calm. His tone held no sense of strain despite the sheer size and weight of me that he carried as easily as breathing. "Do you think I'd bring you this far just to drop you?"

It was the dry precision in his words—not teasing, but not quite cutting—that had me snorting despite myself. "No."

His wings adjusted, catching a rising thermal draft with an expert, calculated shift that had the cruel audacity to make me feel momentarily weightless.

Without meaning to, I was noticing things about him again. Details I didn't want to focus on, like the ripple of his muscles beneath my legs and the press of heat through the smooth hardness of his scaled skin where it touched mine. Even his scent beneath the sulfuric sting of Volcaryth was distractingly, infuriatingly distinct—something rich and scorched and impossible to name.

It was too much. Too close.

My jaw clenched against the strange coil of unease threading low in me, and I resettled my grip on him like that would do something. His heat washed over me, unrelenting even against the hot currents of air buffeting us higher.

"You can relax," he said. His voice dipped into something low and firm. "You're safer in my arms than you would be on the ground."

"Tell that to gravity," I retorted, though not even sarcasm could steady my voice.

His wings snapped outward in a subtle tilt that sent us gliding on a slower descent now, the currents catching waves to lift us against the searing sky. "Humans need to adapt if they want to survive here," he replied, the blunt, matter-of-fact cadence of his words landing heavier than they needed to.

I aimed a sharp glance upward at him, my lips twitching despite myself. "Wow. Thanks for that astute insight."

He didn't respond. But there was something almost deliberate in the flicker of his wings again as he settled further into the air current, arms shifting at my waist like the motion was every bit as natural to him as breathing.

By the time his wings cut into a sharper angle upward again, I could feel the strength in his frame flexing with every shift of the flight. It was natural, fluid in a way that couldn't quite be called effort. His focus was sharp and unnerving, but there was never hesitation. Not in the way he moved. Not in the way he latched his hand tighter at the closest pull of hot wind, his claws brushing just barely against my skin.

The world blurred below, marked by endless fractured spines of rock glowing faint with the veins of lava that scoured the surface. The heat pushed harder and harder against my body with every fucking mile. And I hated it—hated the way I could feel the rhythm of his wings aligning quietly with the pounding pulse in my ears, hated the strange steadiness it offered when my instincts wanted chaos.

I sighed. "Is it always this goddamn hot?"

"It can freeze at night," Vyne responded, his clipped reply carrying just enough authority to kill any expectation of sugar-coating.

"Hell of a tourism ad."

One wing shifted just slightly, setting the wind curling close enough to rattle the strands of hair clinging to sweat at the side of my face. "We don't get many tourists."

A hot wind slammed against us, fierce with its timing. His grip tightened briefly, just enough to keep me steady as he adjusted in a single motion. That seamless control—sharp and effortless, even as the gust clawed at us—set something coiling low in my stomach. I ignored it. Tried to. But it lingered, sparking against frayed nerves and tuning me too closely to the heat of his body pressed to mine.

We flew on like that, stretched tight between the hovering nowheres of earth and sky. The weight of his closeness grated against my already shredded composure, impossible to shake. By the time the broken peaks of volcanic cliffs rose beneath us, cracks against the sky, my muscles felt stitched together with something fragile and thin.

"Hold on," Vyne said, his voice cutting through the thick air.

Instinct tightened my arms around him. Before I had the chance to second-guess, his wings folded in, angling us into a dive so sharp it seemed to pull the breath right from my chest. The wind churned around us, violent and hot, testing his control, but his hold didn't falter—not once. Just before we hit the outcrop where rock jutted out from the cliffs, his wings snapped open. The force of it caught us, slowing us just enough for what should've been a smooth landing.

For him, at least.

My knees immediately tried to quit on me the moment my boots hit the ground. Adrenaline licked through me in waves, raw and unsteady, but his hand stayed firm on my arm, keeping me upright until I finally found my balance. Blood pounded in my ears, tangled up with the burn in my chest and the heat soaking into my skin. When he let go, slowly, it was almost too careful. Like he wasn't sure if I'd crumple or not.

I didn't. Not physically, at least.

A breath rattled through me, but it scraped too harsh, nearly sticking to the thick heat swallowing the plateau like a second atmosphere. My hands drifted to my knees as I leaned just far enough to keep the vertigo at bay.

"That," I said between gulps of air, my voice cracking at the edges, "was objectively terrifying."

A low sound escaped him—not quite a laugh, but close enough to knock my focus off-center. "You held up better than I expected."

"You're lucky I didn't ..." I trailed off. No way I was about to admit I'd been five seconds away from losing my lunch all over his armor. "Forget it."

Vyne's gaze lingered, heavy enough that I didn't need to look up to feel it. It was the silence that got me more than anything—the weight of what wasn't being said. Loud and crushing, louder than any words ever could've been. I straightened, swallowing hard against the dryness clawing at my throat.

A shadow flickered in my periphery, and I turned to see him holding out a small canteen. Its surface gleamed against the distorted light—dented and scuffed, as though it had survived more miles of this harsh terrain than I had any hope of matching.

I hesitated, just briefly.

Then I reached for it.

Our fingers brushed.

The contact was so small, barely enough to count, but it sparked through the noise of everything else. The heat of his hand—too warm, somehow even hotter than the blasted air around us—touched the clammy bite of mine, and something inside me jolted. My spine stiffened, my lungs turned traitor, choking my breath into a brief, stuttering hitch before letting go again.

He flinched first.

Just barely, but it was there. The canteen passed into my hand, but his fingers pulled back like he'd touched live flames. A sharp, gruff sound slipped from him, as if he'd meant to smother the reaction but hadn't quite managed to rein it in. His wings twitched, a tension barely breaking through before snapping back under tight control.

I looked down, pretending I hadn't noticed. Pretending my hands were busy with something as ordinary as unscrewing the cap of the canteen and not still trembling.

"Thanks," I said, my voice scraping against the dryness in my throat as I uncapped the canteen. I focused wholly on the cool stream of water sliding past the harsh burn of the sulfur-thick air. For a moment, it was the only relief in the oppressive heat pressing on every part of me, carving its way through the metallic taste left there by Volcaryth's unrelenting assault.

Capping the canteen, I tossed it in his direction—not out of recklessness, exactly, but out of some base-level frustration that had hitched itself to my nerves and refused to let go. Vyne caught it so cleanly he might as well have anticipated my motion, his claws folding around the dented metal without a word.

"Rest." The command was impassive, his focus barely

darting toward me before it turned to survey the ridge surrounding us. "We'll camp here for the night."

"You don't have to tell me twice," I said, retreating to a wide, flat rock hugged tight to the plateau's central ridge. The surface burned against my skin when I perched on it, but I sank into the contact anyway, resisting the urge to lean back fully for fear my shirt might melt into the stone.

Vyne moved with sharp efficiency, every step precise. His tail snaked behind him, shifting grains of stony grit as he crossed the edge of the plateau to comb its perimeter. His body remained taut with focus, though nothing about it telegraphed alarm. It was a rhythm of constant readiness, practiced and almost predatorially smooth—the kind of presence that demanded awareness even when it didn't actively threaten.

I hated that he drew my focus the way he did. His movement, the way the dark gleam of his scaled form swallowed every trickle of heat shimmering between the molten landscape below and the rock pressing beneath me. With each measured turn, his arms adjusted their balance against his armor, claws flexing—not in unease but in idle control, as if each sharpened edge had been designed down to its smallest detail for lethal purpose.

He wasn't handsome, not really. That word was for softer things. Safer things.

What Vyne was ... it didn't fit into anything soft or safe.

And that dip in my stomach as my gaze moved along his line another fraction farther?

Definitely the heat.

———

Darkness descended on Volcaryth in a slow, simmering fade, turning the molten glow of the landscape into something ember lit. Even the heat withdrew, leaving a sharp breeze behind. I huddled against a wedge of stone, arms wrapped around my knees, trying to ignore the clammy cling of my sweat-drenched clothes.

Vyne settled across from me, rummaging through the pack by his side. Weariness seeped into my bones after the day's flight, but it was the gnawing anxiety over the healers that kept me restless. I watched him produce a few strips of dried meat, and my stomach knotted. When he offered one, I accepted, chewing carefully.

His tail drifted in a lazy arc behind him, but there was nothing lazy about his vigilance as he scanned the sky every so often for threats. Even so, he placed a canteen of water beside me with a gentle motion. For a moment I resented that kindness, how it stirred a raw, unfamiliar ache.

"You're worried," Vyne said at last.

No shit. I swallowed the dry hunk of meat, trying to gather my thoughts. "The healers—the sickness." My throat tightened, forcing me to reach for the water. "I keep picturing them, waiting ... running out of time."

His eyes searched mine. "We'll find this blasted plant," he said. "They'll hold on until then."

"You can't know that," I whispered. Fear and guilt twisted in my chest.

Vyne exhaled, his tail brushing once against the stone before it fell still. "What use is it to fear otherwise? Now eat." He handed me another strip of meat.

I forced it down.

Later, Vyne beckoned me toward a slab of rock that formed a partial windbreak. I glanced at the sky's bruised purple glow, night swallowing the last thread of daylight.

"You should get some sleep."

The dropping temperature made me shiver even harder,

and I wrapped a cloak around my shoulders and settled in, my knees pulled tight against my chest as the wind hissed over the ridge. My mind felt too loud for sleep, every half-formed worry fixating on Scalvaris and its ailing patients.

Time slipped.

It could have been minutes or hours of half-dream, half-wake, when the rustle of wings startled me. Vyne knelt close, his face caught in shifting shadows, the draconic lines seeming even more alien in the faint light.

"You're trembling," he said. "Are you cold?"

"I'm okay," I muttered, but I couldn't hide the way my teeth were practically chattering.

"Suffering will do neither of us any good." He hesitated, then extended one wing around my side. The great, leathery span shut out the wind and was almost shockingly warm.

A ripple of heat spread through me. I breathed in, trying to collect my wits as the sudden contrast—bitter cold on one side, radiant heat on the other—made my awareness spike. Who was I kidding? Awareness and Vyne went hand in hand. Every time he was near, it was like my entire being was attuned to him.

Still, I shifted closer, letting my shoulder rest against him.

He lowered himself so that we lay side by side, not quite touching beyond the drape of his wing. His wing formed a canopy, deflecting the punishing wind, and gradually, my shivers calmed. I hovered in that strange half-sleep again, the day's exhaustion pulling me under with awkward, uneven surges of rest.

At some point, I must have drifted into sleep. If I dreamed, I couldn't say of what, only that the shadow of a Drakarn warrior stood over it all.

When dawn finally came, it snuck in on a faint, pewter glow. My eyes blinked open to discover the cloak had been pushed aside in favor of something warmer—Vyne. My cheek tucked against his shoulder; one of his arms curved around my waist, claws splayed over the hem of my shirt. His other arm was beneath my head, his fingers near my ear in a loose, almost protective grip. Even more startling, his tail coiled possessively around my calf.

My pulse thudded in my ears. This was too close, too comforting. His body heat soaked into me, each breath measured and slow. I knew I should recoil, should disengage from the intimacy that threatened to tip over the line if I so much as breathed too hard.

But I didn't. Not right away. I relaxed a fraction, letting the lingering chill recede a bit further. There was no time to waste, but for just one moment, I let myself steal the comfort.

COMFORT DIDN'T LAST LONG. After a breakfast of more dried rations and the sips of water we could spare, Vyne was on his feet and holding something out to me.

"Here."

I stiffened just slightly at his tone. Cool. Professional. Not at all the sound of a man—alien—who'd wrapped me in his arms overnight like I was precious.

Get a grip, Selene.

He was holding out a blade now, its blackened edges flat against the light that flared over the ridge. The knife gleamed, a sickly edge of reflected heat glinting off its curving, jagged design.

"A souvenir?" I asked, taking refuge in dry humor like an escape route as I took the knife. It was heavier than I expected and rough-textured, carved with distinct grooves that made it feel impossibly deadly.

Vyne cast me a glance, just flat enough to make its point. "A precaution," he said evenly. "These mountains are rife with scavengers. Both of the Drakarn variety, and vicious beasts."

Something flickered uncomfortably in my chest, and I gripped the knife harder. "Got it," I said, a low puff of words meant less as agreement and more as a line drawn under every conversation we weren't about to excavate.

Vyne was scanning the horizon again, his sharp lines settled against the violent sprawl of the ridge behind him. He didn't glance back when his wings gave a flick, catching enough sunlit distortion to create a sudden burst of heavy air between us. He simply turned, every part of him a calculation, threw his next look pointedly at the crevice hugging the edge of nearby crags, and then eased his hand into the curl against one side of his belt.

"I'm going to scout out the area before we leave to make sure we don't encounter any company on our flight. Stay alert," he said. "If something finds you before I'm back ..." He trailed only half a beat too long before finishing, "Scream."

Right. Just what I needed to hear.

"Not sure dramatic death screams are really my style." I angled the blade properly at my side as I stood, though exhaustion made even that feel heavier than it was.

"Scream loud enough, *Zhyvarin*, and you won't die."

He burst into the air before I could ask him what the hell *zhyvarin* meant.

No use lingering on it. I leaned back just enough to close my eyes for a breath or two, the knife resting across my lap like a shield, and tried not to give in to the gnawing sense that, clever blade or not, I didn't belong here.

The suffocating quiet of the plateau stretched around me, leaving me to stew in my own thoughts while the heat bore down on me. I would give almost anything for some shade.

Some small, logical part of my brain told me to conserve energy, to ease my muscles and let the restless ache fade from my joints before I had to move again. But that part of my brain always forgot who it was dealing with—it was the soldier in me that braced, kept the flex of my hands curling and uncurling around Vyne's blade, and sent every nerve into overdrive at the sound of even the faintest crackle of rock sliding somewhere beyond the ridge.

The sound wasn't new. Not really. The mountains were alive in their own way—rocks falling, distant steam geysers erupting with gut-punch force every now and then. But tension didn't leave much room for distinguishing natural from unnatural—not when survival depended on treating every noise as a threat.

And survival was always the game, wasn't it?

I lifted the blade once more, testing its weight in my palm, its smooth handle fitting snugly into the curve of my fingers. There was a grim comfort in the way it fit with every subtle change in my grip—it felt like Vyne knew, somehow, what size and heft I'd need, like this thing had been crafted with some maddeningly intimate knowledge of what fit my hand better than, say, the hand of an average Drakarn.

A sound came again. Louder now.

I sat up straighter, fingers tightening on the hilt as sound rolled over me like a boulder I hadn't been quick enough to dodge. My throat worked past the flat dryness of the air, my pulse climbing its way up to my ears as my senses flared to life.

There was nothing natural about the scrape of claws against stone.

The quickest way to die in unfamiliar territory was to assume you had the upper hand. One misstep, and your throat might end up torn out. I'd seen it before—trainees who wanted to play hero, underestimated an opponent or a situation until it ate them alive.

Literally, in some cases.

The mountain air thickened in my lungs, hemmed in by the heat swirling like smothering mist around the plateau.

There—a flash of movement below the ridge, quick and

sharp. My stomach twisted. It wasn't Vyne—too large for him, and it moved wrong. Too slick, too feral.

I dropped into a low stance before my brain fully caught up, bracing one foot instinctively on the uneven rock. Adrenaline hit fast and sharp, slicing through the oppressive heat stretching tight across my ribs.

Assess, position, anticipate.

The first rule of combat. It had been drilled into me in training until it mapped itself into my muscles—not always neat, not always perfect, but ready despite the brutal terrain now pressing in around me.

There was another flicker of motion. Closer this time, clearer in its sharp, bounding trajectory over the blackened rock below.

I swallowed hard and adjusted my grip. My thumb brushed the hilt of the blade, the hilt pressing familiarly against my skin.

The scrape of claws on stone echoed sharply.

The first figure crested the ridge, his hulking frame outlined against the heated shimmer of the air behind it. The light carved shadows over his scaled body, revealing dark, gleaming patches of multicolored scales that reflected the searing sunlight in fractured patterns. His face split wide with a sharp, guttural hiss, exposing rows of curved, serrated fangs that looked built for shredding through anything unfortunate enough to land in their path.

And that tail—thick and scaled like a living whip—lashed with restless precision, the tip twitching as though eager to sink into flesh. It wasn't just a movement of balance but an anticipatory one, alive with violence.

Another followed close behind, snarling low as he scrambled across the uneven ridge, his talons clicking loudly against the stone. His scales were duller than the first, mottled with scars and darkened staining that looked somehow wrong, like old blood that had been absorbed into the flesh. The same unnervingly long tongue flicked out with a sharp twist of his head, tasting the sulfur-heavy air like it could already smell me —like he had singled me out as prey.

More followed behind him.

They were Drakarn.

Too much like Vyne to be mistaken for anything else but filled with so much hate and vicious intent they almost seemed like another species.

They didn't just look like they wanted to kill. They looked like they would enjoy it.

They were circling.

The largest of the group—a massive brute with scales that shimmered like bruised firelight—stepped forward, lowering his head. Heat waves rippled up from the ridge behind him, distorting the violent sprawl of its body to something almost monstrous. Every step brought him closer to me, like he had already decided the next move was mine, but I wouldn't survive to make it. Its wings flared, the membranes semi-translucent against the molten brightness of the landscape.

Some awful instinct within me screamed when his snake-like tongue hissed out again, moving viscously against his fangs before he drew it back into its mouth. A sound escaped it then —a sharp, snarling hiss that vibrated low and guttural through the air before it rose in pitch, slicing like a knife through the oppressive quiet. It was nothing like the commanding tones of Vyne. This was wild, all hunger and rage and malice stripped back to its rawest form.

Think, Selene. Move.

The massive Drakarn lunged without warning, and pure instinct yanked me sideways before his talons could rake across my midsection. I tumbled low, crouching to regain balance as his strike crashed rock where I'd just stood, the impact sending shards of stone skittering across the plateau. My grip on the knife tightened, nerves sparking with electricity.

Before I could adjust fully, another one came barreling toward me from the right—faster, smaller, but no less dangerous. I spun to meet him, feeling every ounce of strain tearing through my ribs as I slashed upward with the knife against his advance. The blade connected cleanly with his lower arm, biting into the gap where softer sinew met rigid plating. The Drakarn staggered briefly, his injured limb snapping backward with a shuddering cry, but the movement didn't slow him for long.

Momentum. Don't lose it.

I dropped to one knee as another lunge—this one viciously fast—sent talons ripping just above my head. My free hand gripped the slick ground as I braced upward and slashed again, the knife biting deep into the sinewy stretch of his leg this time. Dark blood sprayed, hot and metallic smelling, across the rock inches from my face.

The injured Drakarn reeled with a voracious hiss, wings snapping wide and throwing a violent gust of air against me as I rolled away painfully, barely catching myself on the uneven ground.

More were closing in, their distorted shadows flickering across the plateau. A shuddering frustration climbed in my chest alongside pure, searing exhaustion. I hadn't been ready for this. Not for all of them—not for the speed or the raw physicality that turned every motion into a gamble between cautious calculation and blind desperation.

Then the largest one—the brute—moved again.

I stumbled, crashing hard against the craggy rock, though sheer stubborn force kept the knife gripped tight in my hand.

The pack's movements shifted then, slowing but somehow more dangerous.

They had me cornered now. Trapped at the edge of the plateau where the drop below opened like a yawning death sentence.

The brute took another step forward, his claws clicking ominously as he tilted his head. Those slit-pupiled eyes glimmered against the reflected light of the molten rivers below. There was something almost ... amused in its gaze.

If he was going to kill me, he wanted me to feel it first.

Fuck that.

I straightened shakily, muscles burning, but kept the knife angled upward between us as a defiant snarl tried to pull itself up past my throat. My pulse pounded loud in my ears, stubbornness clawing sharp and vivid through the fear choking my lungs.

If this hellscape wanted a fight, I'd give it one.

The brute surged forward, wings flaring wide. I knew I wasn't fast enough to avoid this one properly—but at the last second, as I sucked in a sharp, desperate breath, a flicker of movement pulled my gaze upward.

And then the air changed.

No—the air cracked.

A massive shadow collided full force with the brute, sending him spiraling sideways into the jagged rock as a shockingly loud snarl burst through the suffocating quiet. It wasn't until the edges of the shadow sharpened—unfolding fast, precise, and rippling wings caked in black heat—that I realized what I was looking at.

Vyne.

He moved so fast it barely registered—the sleek motion of his wings slicing through the stifling air as his tail swung in a sharp arc, knocking one of the smaller Drakarn clean off the plateau.

THE SCENT HIT ME FIRST.

Hers.

Something darker hung in the air with it; blood, bile, the feral stink of fury unchained. Of Drakarn rage.

My muscles coiled tight, instinct sharpening into something closer to weaponry than thought. Something was wrong.

The ridge came into view faster than I should've managed—faster than the ache clawing at my wings could complain. My descent sliced clean through the air, every violent beat of my wings driving me closer. The landscape blurred, streaks of crimson and volcanic black giving way to brutal clarity as the plateau rushed toward me.

Selene.

If they'd— If she—

No. Don't think. Act.

I saw her as the details burned into place—a momentary impression, devastating for how quickly it tunneled into me. Cornered.

Her back pressed against the ridge's precarious edge, knife raised in a desperate line of defense. Defiance painted every exhausted line of her battered frame, her small human form trembling on the verge of collapse but refusing to yield.

They circled her. Rogues.

Drakarn who'd traded honor for savagery, their movements small, calculated, cruel. Their tongues flicked, claws raking across stone as they prowled closer, vicious intent hanging heavy in the heat.

Not just death. They wanted worse.

The sky all but shattered when I hit them.

The gust from my landing sent two of them sprawling, their bodies slamming against the ridge's unforgiving surface with sickening force. Stone buckled underfoot, splintering as shards cracked outward from where my talons anchored deep.

The third rogue—the largest of the pack—spun toward me, hissing out a sound that was equal parts rage and surprise. His movements were sluggish compared to my strike, his slick, too-bright scales catching nothing but failure as my claws drove deep into the heavily muscled curve of his chest.

The sound he made—a wet, gurgling screech—satisfied something cold inside me.

"You touched her. You die."

My voice grated low, unrestrained. It didn't simply echo across the ridge; it commanded. Final. Absolute. A promise etched into the rock beneath me.

None of them moved fast enough.

The smallest rogue lunged at the edge of my wing—but before he could strike, my tail lashed out, slamming into him with a crash that made him collapse. He dropped first to his knees, then fully forward into the dust, lifeless.

The brute recovered quickly, roaring as he lunged forward with a ferocity born of desperation. Massive claws swiped wide, aiming for my midsection—an attack too clumsy to merit caution. I didn't pull back. Not back. Never.

Pivoting sharply, I darted to the side, the swing of his strike skimming the air I left behind. My wings hammered back fiercely, propelling me straight toward him as I slammed my claws into the side of its maw.

Something crunched. Fangs caught briefly on my gauntleted hand before I tore myself free with a force that sent gore splattering across the rock behind him.

He staggered, stepping back with a mangled snarl, his blood dripping thickly in rough streaks that sizzled against the heat of the ground.

I advanced. My arm shot forward, carving into the column of his throat with exacting force. My weight collided with his bulk, each motion deliberate, powered by bloodlust honed into something sharper than instinct.

The brute swayed, refusing to fall. His massive frame reeked of defiance, but it didn't hold when my tail speared into the connective joint of his wing.

The scream he let out tore through the thick air, primal and broken.

My wings flared wide, anchoring me against his failed resistance as I drove him down. He buckled hard. Collapsing under the crushing combination of clawed strikes and raw, unrelenting weight. As his chest hit the ridge beneath us, he squirmed one last time—half resistance, half instinct pushing him toward survival.

The brute fell silent.

Behind me, the remaining rogue scrambled back, his panic-laced hissing scraping over molten air as he turned to flee.

Two steps.

That's all he got.

My tail hooked sharply into his back leg and dragged it over the splintered ridge. His snarls turned desperate, sharp claws carving scratches into the agonized rock as he fought.

Futile.

"You don't get mercy," I said. My voice was quiet, almost thoughtful, but the edge of it could've cleaved the ridge itself.

My claws sank neatly into his throat. Twist. Tear.

Silence.

I stood over the remains of them, breath dragging through my lungs, the remnants of the fight settling low in my limbs. Scented with blood. With violence.

And underneath it all—her.

Selene.

The heat simmered around me, pulsing sharp and fevered as I straightened. Every inhale dragged currents of heated air into my chest, its weight clinging as though trying to anchor me in the aftermath. Her scent threaded through it all, sharper now, intertwined with the adrenaline and ash-slicked air pressing hot onto the ridge.

She was barely standing.

Her back was rigid, though exhaustion nearly buckled her frame. One hand gripped the hilt of the knife I'd given her, her knuckles white where her resolve tried to bleed into the steel. The way she held it—not raised in threat but trembling with raw defiance—was a testament to her. She wasn't fearless; no, she was far too human for that.

But she was breathtaking all the same.

My knife. *My* woman.

The truth of it didn't matter, not now with my blood running hot and battle riding high.

Even bruised with blood streaking the soft edges of her brown skin, she stood like a creature made of fire and spite, still ready—still fighting—even with nothing left to wield but that knife and whatever shards of stubbornness she could cling to.

Her dark eyes darted to me briefly, then away. She wasn't shaking anymore, but her stance betrayed the truth—heels edging into bad footing, muscles braced too tight, her body locked somewhere between ready-collapse and survival instinct.

"You're not hurt."

Not a question. A demand.

Her gaze snapped upward, locking onto mine with a sharpness that would've made a weaker creature falter. Her lips trembled, but only long enough for her to bite down and press them tight against the emotion straining there. Her chest rose unevenly, breath catching before she answered with a force that nearly cracked under the weight of its own stubbornness.

"I'm fine." Her voice was strained. Fractured at the edges.

I didn't believe it for a single burning second.

"You're shaking." The words came out harder than I intended, sharp enough to strike the tension between us, and her response cut back with a biting force that tried masking the cracks beneath it.

"Adrenaline," she said, her chin tipping upward, pride lacing every inch of the stubborn line she drew between us. "That's how it works."

It might've worked—on anyone else. But the brittle flame in her eyes, flickering right alongside every sharp inhale, told me otherwise.

I moved forward again, closing the space with steady steps. She didn't step back. Not fully. But she stiffened, the knife angling between us, more barrier than threat.

I stopped just short of swinging range. Not that I was braced for a fight—no. I'd die before I raised a claw against her, but there was something about the way she planted herself there, stubborn and almost trembling, that made me tread carefully.

Softer. Not weaker, just quieter.

"You don't smell like adrenaline." The observation left my

throat rough, my voice barely above a growl, and the way her skin flinched at the sound cut something low through me. "Your fear is soaked into the air. So is the blood."

Her sarcastic laugh cut sharp across the heat, bitter and jagged. "I hadn't noticed."

But her bravado did nothing to mask the tremor trailing through her fingers. The trembling tip of her knife faltered again, though her knuckles stayed white from gripping too tightly.

My gaze swept downward, dragging over her weakening stance, the wobble of her knees where exhaustion rippled through her frame. I searched for blood, for anything hidden in the curve of her arm or the desperate rise of her breath that she might be trying to shield.

Because if she was bleeding unnoticed— If she couldn't even tell ...

"Stop." Her voice cracked against me, breaking harder than the knife she still held like it meant anything. Her free hand rose suddenly, palm lifted toward me like she could push me back with a single word. "Don't look at me like I'm about to fall apart."

Her stubbornness might as well have been a current drawn straight from the molten vein of Volcaryth itself, snapping bright and furious against something more fractured underneath.

I blinked slowly, jaw clenching against the instinct to bare my teeth in a snarl. My next step was sharp, harder than I meant it to be, but precise enough to close the final stretch of space that separated us.

"Let me see," I said, quieter now but still sharp. The low press of my voice coiled like heat breaking under pressure, and my claws flexed where they hung just within reach of touching her.

"I told you—" she tried, but I silenced her.

"Let me *see*." The growl came unbidden, rough and low, carrying the force of a command she didn't have room to argue with anymore.

I wanted to say it was instinct. Or desperation. But it was neither.

It was something harsher, sharper, thrumming dangerously low in the pulse of my blood.

Her jaw tightened again, her lips pressing together as if she was fighting to anchor herself against more resistance. Her chest rose briefly, enough for her chin to tilt higher, but her defiance cracked under some unspoken, mutual weight that neither of us knew how to place.

She shifted. A step. Small.

Enough.

I moved closer, closing what little distance still lingered. My claws reached carefully—angling for the curve where her shoulder met the sleeve of her shirt even as my senses flared sharper beneath her scent.

Selene stiffened immediately, her muscles tightening, but she didn't pull away. My grip steadied gently—not restraint, not fully, but angled enough to guide her. My gaze swept her shoulders, tracing over the flush of her skin, over the streaked minerals and ash scattered across her arm.

No punctures. No claw marks.

No blood. At least none of hers.

The coil in my chest—tight, suffocating—began to ease around the edges. Even as heat simmered dangerously low beneath each rasping breath.

"You're reckless." My claws uncurled, releasing the tiny sensation of contact they'd kept where her arm burned beneath them. I didn't move far. Didn't withdraw.

My hand remained there a moment longer than it

should've, hovering just near the edge of where her steady defiance began softening into frayed exhaustion. "Reckless," I muttered again, quieter this time. Something between relief and accusation wedged itself thick into my throat as every nerve threatened to fray. "*And stubborn.* I told you to yell for help."

Her strength—astonishing in its raw, stubborn humanity during the ambush—was fading. Here, under the suffocating quiet that followed the fight and the crushing heat of Volcaryth's ridge, she was cracking.

My claws ached with the need to steady her.

"I—" she began, her voice uneven and splintered, barely piecing itself together. Her weight shifted, grounding slightly against the ridge beneath her feet—but just barely. "I didn't have time to think. Those things ..." Her words faltered, lost somewhere in the raw scrape of memory and the overwhelming chaos still clawing at her veins. "I didn't—"

"Stop."

My voice came sharper than I intended, biting through the fragile space she'd carved for her protest. The flicker of softness lurking in her defiance startled into something wide-eyed.

"If you think I need an excuse, save it," I growled, every syllable taut with restrained weight. "You're alive. You fought back. That's the only thing keeping this entire ridge from being painted with scavenger blood."

Her lips twitched—the hint of a frown brushing against her brow before she leaned into a sharp, uneven laugh. Bitter, almost broken. "Then what's all that?" she nodded to the splatter left by one of the beasts before I cast him off the plateau.

The quip fell flat, though, trailing off somewhere beneath the heat stretching between our bodies like a fault line ready to rip wide open. Her gaze twitched downward briefly—not submission; no, not her—but something tangled and cautious. Maybe even strained. Her grip on the knife slackened before dropping entirely.

The blade clattered against the stone.

"You're trembling," I said again. Not accusing her this time, just noticing, just reading her the same way I read every shift in battle, except this war was entirely different. Entirely maddening. "And it's not nothing."

"I didn't come out of that unscathed," she replied, cryptic but unconvincing. The false strength wavering over the brittle layers of her voice only sharpened my awareness further. "I'll be fine. I just need—"

Her hand rose briefly, brushing across her face as though she could physically press the lingering panic aside. "I need—" She stopped again. Her line of thought broke with a sharp breath before looking back up at me.

Her expression was fiercer than I'd anticipated. Fiercer, too, than I was prepared for.

"I'll deal with it," she said, quieter now, but with every ounce of strength her emotions had left to offer. "My fear. My shaking. All of it. It's mine."

"No."

The word came without thought—without restraint. Low but deliberate, sharper than the hiss of hot air pouring from the distant geysers below us. Every sharp instinct, every fraying edge of my mind burned in protest against her words, against the thin walls she attempted to build between us.

Her gaze snapped sharply upward, dark and unyielding as disbelief flickered there. "What?"

"Give it to me," I murmured, claws twitching where they hovered near my sides. "Your pain, your exhaustion—it's what I'm here for."

12

VYNE

I STOPPED MYSELF.

The edge of my tongue scraped against my fangs, heat surging up my throat as something inside me howled at the thin, slipping leash I'd kept anchored around the truth.

Her expression hardened again—a flare of defiance. "I'm not something to be—"

"Gods." My hand shot forward—not sharply, not in anger, but steeped in the raw frustration she pushed into every space between us. My claws brushed against her shoulder, featherlight, then froze when I felt her flinch beneath the soft but unyielding pressure.

Every ounce of me recoiled, a surge of self-control wrenching through my chest. But before I could pull back fully, her own movement stopped me. She leaned, imperceptibly but undeniably, just barely toward me. When my grip stilled—steady but quiet along the curve of her arm—she didn't step away.

I couldn't stop looking at her. At the fragile tremor carved into her jawline, at the roughness blooming over her cracked lips, at her lashes dusted with the ever-present ash streaking the rest of her face.

Her scent—fates above, her scent—threw every part of me into restless chaos. I burned brighter than the veins twisting deep through Volcaryth's blackened heart.

Krysfruit. Smoked salt. Her. Always her.

"Selene," I murmured, without meaning to. Her name cracked through my throat, more growl than word. "You don't get to carry it alone."

She stiffened a little beneath my touch, her gaze flickering over my expression like she was trying to read something there. "I do. I have to. I—"

"You don't," I ground out, cutting her protest short. My head dipped lower, the motion instinctual, undeniable. The words I needed wouldn't come—couldn't. Nothing could bridge the aching space threatening to splinter everything. "Not from me."

Her lips parted as if to argue or push me back into whatever tactical distance she thought she needed for logic to breathe between us. But nothing came.

And the sound of that silence was shattering. Deafening. Ripping whatever restraint I had left into useless fragments.

Her scent sharpened against me in unbearable waves.

I lowered my head without thinking. Closer. Dangerous. Every part of me screamed at once—not just desire, not just instinct, but something brighter, terrible in its force.

Her knees dipped, shifting her weight forward, closer to mine. And her breath—ragged and too quick—hitched just enough to shatter the careful tension strangling the ridge.

"Selene," I growled again, hoarse and rough, a surrender wrapped in her name.

Control was gone. Fully. Terrifyingly.

I kissed her.

It wasn't careful. It wasn't soft. The moment was too raw for any of that. My lips crushed against hers before I could think myself around it; before I had time to stop and consider what it might cost.

Her warmth bled into me; her taste hit the back of my fangs—salt and heat and something maddeningly sweet beneath it all—and everything unraveled.

She gasped against me, surprise giving way to something low and startled, but she didn't pull back. She moved toward me instead. Her lips, soft but cracked, parted beneath mine, not yielding, but answering.

Her hands—uncertain and shaking from adrenaline—caught the edge of my armor, trembling before curling tighter. The heat of them—small, human, too fragile—seared through even the thick, fire-forged metal, cutting into me sharper than any clawed strike ever had.

My claws flexed briefly. Just enough to linger near her sleeve and then tighten ever so slightly, careful but protective, just shy of helpless.

Her taste.

It built heat behind my ribs and poured tension into every inch of me I couldn't anchor. My tongue flicked against her bottom lip—primal, entirely unbidden, entirely maddening in its sensitivity—and that was it. The last thread of restraint frayed itself to ash.

I angled my head, deepening the kiss until her breath hitched sharply against mine, a trembling gasp escaping her throat as her hands tightened against my scales. Not resistance. Not anymore. Her grip wasn't something born of fear or hesitation; it was something closer to instinct, to need, raw and unfiltered in its desperate hold on me.

Her lips moved tentatively beneath mine, uncertain at first, but growing bolder. Her body tipped infinitesimally closer, shoulders rising with every fractured breath racing between us. The brush of her fingers clinging to the scaled edges of my neck made something deep in my chest curl tight, heat sparking low and dangerous where her nails raked against flesh.

Gods below, she wasn't pulling away.

Sensations poured into me in waves. The tremor in her frame as it eased closer. The scent of her, impossibly rich and sharper now with her sweat. The sound she made, a soft, involuntary noise escaping her throat, when my claws shifted, just barely, to ghost along the curve of her neck.

My restraint wasn't just fraying—it was disintegrating.

What was left of the logical side of me screamed to pull back, to stop giving in to the raw instinct and rein in control before everything tipped past the point of no return. But the connection between us was already burning too bright, too consuming. Her scent invaded every inch of my senses. Her taste lingered on every edge of my tongue, more potent than any flame Volcaryth had ever birthed into existence.

I couldn't think.

Only feel.

My claws, still trembling from restraint, flexed where they cupped the slope of her shoulder. It wasn't enough. Couldn't be. The undercurrent pouring heat straight into my blood demanded more.

I slid one hand lower until my claws hovered delicately at the edge of her waist, the thin fabric of her shirt a useless barrier against the blistering heat growing between us. Her breath stuttered as soon as she felt the shift, her chest rising sharply against mine before melting into the pull of my weight anchoring her closer.

Her lips parted farther, and the brush of her tongue sent electricity sparking up my spine, setting fire to every thread of self-control I still had.

I growled—low, deep, possessive—a sound I barely recognized as mine.

Her response? She trembled, yes, but not from fear. Instead, her body leaned forward, tipping against me as though drawn into the same unbearable pull threatening to unmake me. Her nails dug against the curve where my neck met my shoulder, testing the edge of my scales, and the subtle scratch of it sent another shudder rippling through me.

Something feral clawed its way to the surface. Buried for too long, ignored for longer. The sheer rightness of her against me—of her taste, her touch, her breath threading into mine— forced every sharp edge of my instincts into blinding want.

She fit against me too perfectly.

I broke the kiss, though it felt more like wrenching myself out past the event horizon of something unstoppable. My lips dragged away slowly, reluctantly, while every inch of my body fought the loss. I stopped when only the smallest space separated us, our shared breaths still mixing in shallow, uneven rhythm.

My wings trembled, the strain of holding them tight against my back just as agonizing as the distance I now forced between us. Her scent—gods, her scent swarmed my airways, still heavy, still drowning me in her.

Her lips—kiss-swollen and perfect—parted as though she wanted to say something. But the words didn't come. Only her breath emerged, soft and battered, her chest rising too fast and too unevenly as her heartbeat thumped loudly enough for my heightened senses to catch all of it.

Her eyes burned into mine, wide and searching, her expression wide with an emotion I was too afraid to name. Confusion. Need. Awe. Fear. All of it swirled beneath the ash-dusted surface of her gaze.

"*Zhyvarin,*" I rasped.

It wasn't just a word. It was the name I'd dreamed up for her in the nights when I couldn't ignore what she truly was to me, when the dreams wouldn't let me go. It was lightning, scoring its way through my chest—a sound shaped by fate, dragged from the deepest corner of whatever I was becoming beneath her touch.

She blinked. Once. Twice. Then something sharp sparked in her expression again—less confusion now, but caution. Her brow furrowed as realization caught up to the shock threatening to carve its way through every sharp edge between us. Slowly, her hands loosened from their grip on my scales, her fingers trembling as they hovered, uncertain, in the burning air between us.

"What—" Her voice broke, soft at first, then sharper, biting out against the searing quiet surrounding us.

A thousand answers burned on the tip of my tongue.

None dared leave my mouth.

Instead, I reached for her wrist, careful to catch it lightly, my claws brushing just barely over the fragile edge of her pulse. One step closer. Just one. Just enough for my gaze to find hers again, unflinching.

"*Zhyvarin.*"

The word slipped out again, unbidden but undeniable, soft and soaked in reverence.

Her brow furrowed again, the bite of defiance curling over her lips. "What?"

I couldn't explain. Couldn't risk it. Not now. Not with every nerve in me still locked between the ache to hold her and the fear of breaking something irreparable.

"Never mind," I muttered, though the weight in my voice betrayed the words as a lie.

It did matter. More than anything. And the way her gaze lingered then flickered back to my lips, her own still trembling, told me she knew it, even if she couldn't say it.

The silence between us coiled tighter, broken only by the

distant hiss of geysers erupting against the ridge. My claws loosened reluctantly against her wrist, slipping back into the void that lingered between warmth and absence.

She didn't move right away. She stayed there, shoulders caught between tension and uncertainty, her frame too frayed to dare finishing whatever storm of thought hung in her expression.

13

SELENE

VYNE WALKED BESIDE ME, his gait steady and sure, like the uneven rock beneath us posed no challenge at all. There wasn't so much as a hitch in his pace.

I tried not to let my gaze linger on his tightly folded wings or glinting scales. Not when there were enough reasons already to keep my attention fixed squarely on the crumbling path ahead. The terrain wasn't the only thing I had to watch for.

Two days.

That was how long it'd been since the kiss.

Two days since he'd breached every armored wall I'd thought I'd built, and I'd been stupid enough to kiss him back like breaking apart beneath him was inevitable.

Now, there was nothing between us except the grind of rock underfoot, the heavy press of the air, and the occasional sound of tremors rumbling under the surface.

Maybe I should have been grateful for the silence. But it only made the memory harder to ignore.

I yanked my focus forward, sparing no more than a second to tighten the scarf clinging against my face to help block out the rancid air. Each step dragged a little harder than the last, exhaustion pressing in sharper than the heat clinging to the air.

Vyne didn't even look winded. His focus stayed locked onto the path ahead, scanning every jagged cut in the mountainous landscape.

I cleared my throat. "Do we even know where this stuff grows?"

"Unstable ground," he replied, his voice as even and unshaken as his movements. "Anywhere the earth has split wide or the heat vents through cracks. Vyrathis will stand out from the surrounding rock."

That was frustratingly non-specific. Just vague terrain descriptions paired with every possible hazard the Harrovan Mountains had to offer.

Perfect.

"Helpful," I said, dry as the air threatening to crack my lips. My sarcasm felt like the only weapon I had left.

It earned nothing more than the faintest glance from him, his brow lifting in unbothered acknowledgment. "Would you like me to conjure the plant from thin air instead?"

"If you could do that, you should have tried three days ago," I shot back.

The corner of his mouth twitched—so faint that it might've been melted into the ambient heat of this place, except I recognized it for what it was. Not quite a smile, not quite not. And damn it, I hated how it sent some small sizzle through me.

This awareness of Vyne was going to be the death of me.

Dragging my attention back to the ridge ahead, I kept my pace steady. The ground was shifting more there, the blackened rock glittering with oppressive heat. Treacherous footing at best. But that's when I saw it—a shimmer caught in the light, something alive amid this endless stretch of dead stone.

"Wait," I said, sharper than I meant to. My hand twitched vaguely toward the glint of color as I slowed. "Is that ...?"

There was no hesitation in how Vyne moved. Before I

could say anything else, he stepped ahead of me, his wings shifting as he assessed the terrain. His claws flexed against the rock, finding safe purchase where I'd struggle.

I followed him anyway. Sitting still had never been my thing, and I wasn't going to let him handle this alone.

There it was—low and barely there against a black fissure: vyrathis.

Its thin leaves shone with a metallic sheen, curling outward like it had grown in defiance of the oppressive heat swallowing the landscape. The glow of the plant was a small pocket of alien color against the harsh black of the mountainside.

"Shit, that's it," I breathed, tension easing just long enough for relief to rush in sharply.

"Careful." Vyne's voice came low, guarded. He crouched near the plant, his claws hovering just above the ground. "There's a gas pocket nearby," he said, his voice quieter now, his wings pressing outward in readiness. "The ground's unstable underneath."

"Great," I muttered, irritation vibrating louder than fear in my voice. "The one thing we actually need, and the whole mountain's ready to swallow us for it."

I crouched down beside him, the vyrathis close enough that I could feel the heat emanating from its fragile leaves. My hand moved toward my pack, fingers brushing against the stiff edge of the container Rachel had given me before we left.

I crouched at the plant's edge, my fingers gripping the container with care, keeping it angled just right. My free hand moved toward a small tool strapped to my thigh—a sturdy but lightweight blade meant for shearing samples cleanly. I worked quickly, each motion precise as I trimmed the silvery leaves away from the delicate stems.

The air was thinner there, sharper somehow, though I couldn't tell if it was my mind playing tricks on me or the gas

Vyne had warned about seeping up from somewhere deeper in the mountain below. My pulse jumped, but I forced it down. Focus. I didn't need to think about imaginary disasters when the real ones were waiting just underfoot.

"Selene."

His voice cut through the thin air. A warning. I froze, my hand hovering mid-motion with the blade angled near one of the stems.

"What?" I asked.

He didn't respond immediately. Instead, his eyes locked onto the fissure directly beside where I crouched. His wings twitched as the sound of shifting rock rumbled low beneath us.

"Don't move," he snapped, firm enough that it left no room for argument.

I froze.

My grip tightened on the container in my hand, and my pulse hammered against the silence stretching between us. Vyne's claws flexed as he stepped closer. The scrape of rock shifted under his weight, audible even over the heat-warped air squeezing the mountainside.

Vyne was all precision, anchoring into the nearer edge of stone while his tail wrapped around a thicker outcrop behind us for extra support. It was painfully clear just how much stronger his body was than mine—as if the terrain itself bent beneath his touch, unwilling to argue against the force he carried in every movement.

He applied pressure to the fissure nearest the plant, testing it. His wings shifted again, catching currents of air rising from somewhere deeper in the rock. I didn't realize I'd been holding my breath until he finally straightened and nodded at me.

"Go on," he said, the protective angle of his wings shielding me from whatever unseen threat still lurked.

I resumed my work, my focus tightening as I clipped the

last of the vyrathis stems and sealed them carefully in the container. The silvery surface of the leaves glinted, catching patterns of light that seemed almost too delicate for a place like this.

"We need more," I said, rising carefully from my crouch.

Vyne's green eyes flicked toward the container in my hands, and for a moment, there was something like relief written in the sharp lines of his expression. Not warmth, not exactly—but close enough to knock me off-center.

My eyes darted down to his lips, and I squeezed them shut before any thoughts about what those lips could do rose up.

Too late.

Shoving the container back into the secured pocket of my pack, I straightened, wincing at the ache settling into my shoulders.

Without a word, Vyne moved closer, his claws brushing against the ledge for balance as his hand extended toward me. His large frame cast long shadows over the tiny ridge, and his gaze fixed on me with that same irritating intensity he always carried.

I hesitated, just for a moment. Then, gripping his offered hand, I caught his wrist with mine and allowed him to guide me away from the edge.

The vyrathis was easier to spot the second time. And the third. I lost track of time, but the ache in my legs and the burn in my lungs told me it had been hours. My bag was full to bursting with vyrathis, container stuffed full.

It had to be enough.

The healers would live. If we got it home to them in time.

Vyne put down a marker at the biggest bed of the plant, a stake in the ground with a brightly covered piece of cloth tied to the end that could be spotted from the air so Drakarn from

Scalvaris would know where to look if we had to send them back for even more.

We'd done it.

For now, at least, it had to be enough.

The ground was growing more unstable by the minute, and we couldn't linger. I stepped into Vyne's arms and let him launch me into the air as we began our flight home.

The place we stopped at wasn't much of a campsite, but it was flat, and that was good enough for me. It was carved out of a small space in the mountainside, shielded by a curve of sharp black rock that jutted outward like broken teeth.

Heat shimmered across every surface, but now the air softened just a little compared to the suffocating press from earlier. I wouldn't call it breathable, but I wasn't choking on every inhale now either.

Small mercies.

Our packs were slumped against the outcrop, their rough fabric streaked with ash and dirt from the endless journey. I collapsed against the rock wall, letting out a long, unsteady breath as I tugged the scarf from my face now that the rock was blocking some of the worst gusts of sulfurous winds. The deceptively light vyrathis container rested in my lap.

The trip wasn't over—not even close—but for the first time since setting out, the sense of triumph outweighed the exhaustion clinging to every single muscle I had.

Vyne moved a few feet away, crouching and holding onto the stone like it was nothing. He didn't look worn out—hell, he didn't even look inconvenienced. His movements lacked any sluggishness as he pulled a water flask free, uncapping it with the same ease he carried in every action.

"Could you at least pretend you're as exhausted as I am?" I muttered, craning my neck to glance over at him. The consequences of the flight and search pressed against my ribs, but irritation felt like a better distraction than lingering on how much energy I'd burned.

Vyne paused, mid-motion, then glanced at me with a lift of his brow. "Would it help?"

"Yeah," I shot back, quick enough to feel the pull of amusement creep into my voice. "Solidarity and all that."

He tilted his head, expression calm but a bit edged. For just a moment, I thought I caught the bare flicker of something like humor somewhere beneath all the unreadable layers he wore like a shield.

"Noted."

I huffed out a shallow breath, leaning my head back and letting my gaze wander past him to the horizon beyond our fragile little camp. The Harrovan peaks stretched endlessly, their silhouettes rising against waves of twisting heat and sulfuric haze. Everything about this place was wrong—hostile.

Beautiful, sure, but ready to remind you just how easily it could kill you.

I slid the vyrathis container into one of the pouches in my pack, protecting it from the harsh environment. I made myself linger on the process—adjusting, tying the straps—anything to keep my hands busy. But when I stood, shaking the tension out of my legs, I swore my movements pulled his attention again, heavy, steady, and impossible to ignore.

"You should rest."

His voice broke through my thoughts more firmly this time, less suggestion and more instruction. When I glanced back toward him, he'd finally shifted out of that perfect crouch, standing in a smooth motion that sent his wings flexing. His stance was too steady, his gaze too focused, and I hated that the sharp edge of it made my pulse falter.

"What does it look like I'm doing?" I snapped.

His narrowed gaze didn't budge. The huff that followed

was subtle, barely audible, but it cut all the same. Without saying anything, Vyne stepped closer—his tall frame shadowing me.

"Selene." The sound of my name wasn't harsh. He said it with just enough force to dig under every fragile excuse I wanted to give. "You've done enough."

I swallowed hard, the air clinging between us too heavy. This close, Vyne wasn't just sharp edges and brutal efficiency anymore—there was something else to him. Something softer, buried beneath the skin of his alien presence like a broken ember glow, threatening to burn brighter the longer I looked.

The moment pressed down like everything else in this place—the heat, the sulfur, the rocks underfoot. But this—this was heavier in a way you couldn't run from. I felt the sharp edges of it cutting through every breath, twisting tightly as Vyne's gaze stayed locked on me.

"You've done too much," he repeated. His voice dipped lower this time, rough but steady, like he could force the air itself to yield. "Rest. Now."

Something flared in me—not defiance, exactly. Not quite. Just the reflexive need to push back against whatever told me I couldn't keep going.

Pride was a hell of a thing. I wasn't about to let it go.

"I told you, I'm fine." The words came out sharp, but not sharp enough to cut through the tension clinging stubbornly between us. "We rest here for a few hours and then head out."

Vyne didn't step back. Of course he didn't. I hated how steady he was; hated the way that same steadiness made something underneath my walls crack.

He tilted his head, his expression shadowed but calm, like he was holding back more than I could ever read. The sharp line of his jaw twitched, dragging every inch of my focus straight to him.

"You're lying," he said simply. Blunt. No malice. Just a cutting sort of truth that landed harder because of how quietly he wielded it.

Something snapped. Exhaustion, maybe, or frustration from how tightly he'd held me under that unreadable gaze. Either way, I exhaled sharply, letting the angry, restless part of me rise to the surface.

"Yeah? Well, we can't all be untouchable super-warriors." My voice cracked just slightly at the edges, but I twisted the words into a dry sneer, hoping they'd be sharp enough to hold their own weight. "Let a girl have some damned pride."

"I'm not untouchable," he said, his voice quieter this time. But something in the way he said it—sharp-edged in a way it didn't need to be—made the hair along the back of my neck lift.

His claws shifted at his sides, the restraint in the motion all the more noticeable because it was too controlled. Like something far deeper simmered just beneath his composed surface. Something real.

He took another step forward, closing the already narrow space between us, and my first instinct was to stiffen. Not out of fear, but because the weight of his presence—sharp and focused, frayed but unyielding—felt like it might crush me if I let it.

"You're not weak," he said firmly, the words catching me off guard enough to throw me silent. His green eyes pinned me in place, their intensity like a wrecking ball through every wall I'd carefully built. "But even the strongest need their rest. We wait out the night. Push now and we might break."

My throat worked against the dryness pressing in, the heat running rough fingers against every inhale. His words clung tighter than the sulfur to the back of my mouth, and for half a second, I didn't have the energy to fight them off.

"That some lesson they teach you in Drakarn warrior

school?" My tone slipped somewhere between sarcasm and bitterness. But the edge of my voice cracked, betraying me when I least wanted it to.

"No," he said without hesitation. His gaze stayed soft—not in its strength, but in the way it didn't waver, didn't narrow the way it might if his patience was thin. "It's something I learned because I didn't. Not soon enough."

That admission hit differently—quieter, smaller, but sharp all the same. He didn't elaborate, and I couldn't bring myself to ask. The space between us hung too heavy for words to do anything but pull everything tighter.

I shifted on my feet, trying not to let the air clawing its way between my ribs sound too uneven.

But Vyne didn't let me drag myself away too far. He moved again—not a full step this time, just enough that the edge of his hand brushed against my arm.

Not forceful. Not demanding. Just *there*. Subtle.

And stupidly, infuriatingly steady.

I didn't pull away. I wanted to. Wanted to shove the strange weight of his presence out of my space until I could think clearly again. But the pull it created kept me frozen where I stood.

That same steadiness in him left me undone.

Before I could second-guess the sharp, restless twist building in me, I moved.

The decision hit like an earthquake. Sudden. Destructive. My arms lifted, looping around his neck without ceremony, hugging him close. My pulse hammered against the hollow space carved between us—far from calm but no longer lost to hesitation.

Vyne froze.

For a fraction of a second, it felt like I'd crossed some unspoken fault line between us, and my stomach twisted with uncertainty. But then his hand shifted—his claws ghosting lightly against my side before they curved, careful and caring, to rest just against the small of my back. Not pushing. Not needing to.

Just keeping me steady.

His body, all too solid, didn't lean all the way into me, but his wings curved inward, their outline enough to block out the fading glow of the barren landscape around us. The motion felt unintentional—like he hadn't even noticed himself doing it—but it was enough to set something fragile alight inside me.

His heat should've burned hotter than the magma tearing through Volcaryth beneath us. But it didn't. It didn't hurt at all.

It felt like relief. Like safety.

When I finally let my head tilt upward, the sharp edge of his carved features came into focus—closer than they'd ever been. His breath brushed against my skin, scattering along the small spaces too narrow for heat to settle in fully.

And then he kissed me.

HIS MOUTH tasted like promises and burnt honey.

Not the saccharine stuff people baked into pastries; this was darker. Charcoal bitter and still a bit sweet. I gasped into the kiss, fingers clawing the scales of his neck, their edges biting into my palms. His claws shredded the rock wall behind me, shards raining down around us. Heat radiated from his chest in waves, almost too much to bear.

His heat was a shield, pushing back the icy dread I carried for the healers back in Scalvaris. Just for a moment, I could forget the sickness, the uncertainty, and embrace what it felt like to feel safe.

To feel *alive*.

I didn't know which was louder—the geysers vomiting steam below or the jackhammer of my pulse. My spine ground against the stone as his wings snapped open, blotting out the hellscape's fading glare.

His tongue—long, relentless, perfect—flicked against the seam of my lips. I opened on a broken noise, letting him devour me like I'd been starved for this exact flavor of ruin. The growl vibrating against my mouth wasn't human. Wasn't gentle. His hips pinned me hard.

I wanted more.

Fear coiled low in my belly, a sharp reminder that I was playing with fire—a fire I wasn't sure I could control. But it was a beautiful fire, and my better judgement could take a backseat for once.

The rumble in his chest deepened. One clawed hand let go of the wall to grip my hip, talons careful but the pressure bruising. His tail lashed, gouging fresh ruts into the mountainside.

His pupils were narrow slits, dark shards splitting golden irises. Nostrils flared, drinking my scent like I was the first clean air he'd tasted in forever. My hands shook where they clung to him, torn between shoving him back and dragging him closer until our bodies fused.

"Vyne," I rasped, voice stripped raw.

His thumb brushed my jaw, calloused pad rasping over split skin. "You're shaking."

"Adrenaline crash." I bared my teeth in something too wild to be a smile. "Human thing. We don't usually tongue-fuck walking furnaces when we're hanging off mountains."

A muscle twitched along his jaw. His gaze dropped to my mouth, and I realized my lip had split. I didn't know if it was from the harsh air or his fangs. His growl returned, lower now, as he closed the distance. I braced.

He licked the wound.

The flat of his tongue dragged from my chin up to almost my nose. My breath hitched, nails carving trenches between his shoulder scales. He groaned, the vibration rattling my ribs, and did it again.

"Salt," he murmured against flesh. "Sweet."

It wasn't just lust now. It was possession, a claim. A shiver wracked me, not entirely unpleasant.

"Infection risk," I choked, clinging to medic-mode like a lifeline. "Your mouth's dirtier than a field medic's—fuck!"

Blunt fangs grazed my earlobe. The hand on my hip slid around to grip my ass, hauling me flush against him. Every scaled inch scorched. The thick ridge of his cock pressed through our clothes, that unnatural fleshy tip writhing against me.

"Still scared, *Zhyvarin?*"

The alien word rolled against my neck. I didn't know it. Didn't care. The ledge tilted or maybe my brain short-circuited as his tail coiled around my calf, tip stroking a path above my ankle.

"Terrified," I lied, raking nails down the groove of his spine. "Can't wait to see how you devour me."

God, I *was* terrified.

I was barreling headlong toward a disaster I wasn't sure I could avoid. But I couldn't show it. Couldn't give him that power. So I told him the truth in the voice of a lie, pushing him to the edge, hoping he'd pull me back. Or maybe that he'd push me over.

He laughed and reclaimed my mouth, and it felt like breathing after being held underwater. For once, I didn't care about anything other than him and me; that was what terrified me. The kiss was surrender and conquest, all teeth and dominance. I bit down hard and felt the metal of the barbell in his tongue.

He snarled, wings battering the cliff face as he spun us, pinning me against the heated stone his body had shielded.

Ash clung to the sweat-slick planes of his chest, collecting around shining nipple rings. My shirt hung in ribbons.

"Mine." The declaration seared my throat.

The mountain quaked beneath us. I didn't answer.

Didn't need to.

His claws froze holding the shredded remains of my bra, the curved tip trembling millimeters from the clasp. The tremor in his hand would've been invisible if my chest weren't flush against his, feeling the live-wire tension corded through his muscles. My smile felt like a blade—sharp, defensive, honed on decades of triage bravado.

"Need help?"

I dragged my nails down the ridged valleys between his back scales, savoring the full-body shudder it ripped from him. His green scales glistened under Volcaryth's fevered glow.

Vyne's growl quaked through my sternum. "Cease testing me."

"Funny," I breathed, rolling my hips to grind against the throbbing ridge of his cock still trapped under his pants. "I thought warriors lived for challenges."

His gaze dropped to my exposed chest, pupils swallowing the last slivers of yellow. Sweat pooled in the hollow of his throat. My tongue darted out, traitorous, and his restraint shattered.

Blunt fangs scraped my collarbone—not a bite, a brand. Claws cinched my hips, lifting me until my legs locked around his waist. Sharp stone gnawed my shoulders, the bite dull compared to the furnace of his scaled torso.

"Don't," he rasped against my sternum, tongue lapping salt from my cleavage. The tip seared a path down my breast.

My laugh broke into a gasp as I felt his tail climb up my thigh. The ridged underside ground against my inner knee while the tip pricked a warning trail up my calf.

I fisted the dark hair at his nape, wrenching his head back. "Then quit treating me like I'll shatter."

Feral light ignited his gaze. A claw split the band on my chest, shredding the bra's last threads. The material fluttered downward. His palms—scaled, searing—claimed my breasts, testing their give against his callouses.

"Yes," he grated, reverence roughened by lust. A claw-tip

circled my nipple, catching just enough to sting. I arched into the burn, and he groaned, canines gleaming. "Say it."

I nipped at his neck, trying for anything I could reach. His hips pressed me harder against the cliff wall, tail teasing my legs wider. "Make me."

His claws took care of my pants, exposing every part of me. Bitter air kissed my thighs as he shredded fabric.

Breath scorched my ear. "*Zhyvarin*."

That word. It sent a spike of heat through me.

His tail was a fucking menace. And I loved it. The ridged underside ground slow circles over my sex, each stroke making me shudder.

"More," I begged.

Vyne's snarl vibrated through me as he fell to his knees, and his tongue—fuck, that endless, wanton tongue and the metal nub within it—speared against me. He inhaled sharply, wings flaring, nose buried in the slick heat between my legs.

"Hot," he growled, the word mangled by fangs. Claws pricked my waist, blunt tips threatening bruises. "You burn."

I couldn't think beyond the feelings. His tongue flattened against me in one all-consuming swipe.

Lightning.

My spine arched, a shattered scream tearing free. He growled—possessive, feral—and continued the motion. Again. Again. The wet slap of muscle on flesh echoed off stone, rhythm syncopated by my ragged gasps.

"Fuck—Vyne—!"

He jerked, a sound like splitting stone erupting from his chest. The tail and tongue at my core stroked harder, ridges snagging swollen flesh. I came apart with a choked wail, thighs squeezing against him as reality splintered into shards.

He didn't relent.

The coil snapped again before I could breathe, his tongue

now devoting obscene focus to my nerves. My nails found the membranous gap between his wing joints, gripping delicate tissue.

"Again." The command left his throat raw.

I broke—body bowed, vision going white. The orgasm ripped through me, wringing a sob from my chest. Vyne finally withdrew, chin glistening, eyes void-black pits.

The fleshy hood of his cock twitched, weeping indecent pre-cum.

Where had his pants gone? I didn't care.

I stared at the scaled monster, vein-like ridges pulsing under strained flesh. Before fear could take root, I took hold of the base.

This was new. Something both alien and ... intimate. Not just his touch, but seeing him so completely unleashed, so vulnerable. With the fear came a heady rush of power and ownership.

He froze.

The strange tip curled toward my grip, the alien appendage brushing my knuckles. Velvet-soft. Alive. Madness overrode survival instinct. He'd tasted me. Turnabout was only fair.

Vyne recoiled. "No." The denial strangled itself. He tried pulling back, but I tightened my hold, thumb smearing slick across the slit. His tail spasmed around my thigh. "Can't be ... gentle," he rasped, jaw clenched hard enough to fracture. "Need you."

"Then fucking take me."

He hissed, claws raking across rock above my skull. Then he grabbed only my hips and hooked one of my legs around him.

The first thrust shattered me.

He buried himself to the hilt, the alien girth of him stretching in ways no human anatomy allowed. I gasped out his name, nails tracing the scales between his wings. His cock pulsed—a living thing, veined shaft throbbing in me.

"Fuck—!"

He didn't withdraw. Didn't move. Just hovered, trembling, tail coiled around my thigh like a steel cable.

"*Zhyvarin.*" That word, that special name for me, sounded like a prayer in his throat. Damnation. Worship.

I answered by driving my heel into the back of his knee. "Please."

He growled and dragged out slowly. Agonizing. The scaled base of his shaft stroked against my sex, each ridge striking sparks. His cock's swollen lip peeled away with a lewd pop, leaving the sensitized flesh throbbing.

"Need ... you ..." His claws cratered the ledge above my head.

"Try." I locked my ankles at the small of his back, yanking him home.

He sheathed himself with a snarl, the snap of his hips rocking my spine against basalt. The fleshy hood fluttered against me, alive, as if it had its own rabid pulse. Pleasure scorched up my nerves, white-hot and vicious. I bit his shoulder, flesh and scales flooding my mouth, and he groaned, the vibration shredding my last tether to sanity.

"Look." He wrenched my chin down.

His scaled hips pistoned. The tip of his cock arched upward with each withdrawal, glistening head questing for my clit like a starved beast. Alive. Ravenous. His claws nearly drew blood at my hips, the sting dissolving under the ache pooling in my gut.

"Vyne—I can't—"

"Can." Fangs scraped my jaw. "Take it. Take me."

The ledge quaked beneath us.

"Shit—!"

His wings thundered open, hauling us backward as stone crumbled. We slammed into the opposing wall, his forearm cushioning my skull. The impact drove him even deeper.

A supernova burst behind my eyelids. My spine arched off the rock as the orgasm tore through me, convulsive and raw. He roared, hips stuttering, release scalding my insides.

"*Zhyvarin.*" His forehead pressed to mine, the word a fractured oath. "Mine."

His tail coiled tighter, underside grinding that spot as he wrung my orgasm dry. I thrashed, oversensitive and broken apart, but his claws pricked my hips, forcing me to take every drop.

When reality staggered back, we were a knot of limbs and heaving breath. Vyne's forehead pressed to mine, his purr vibrating through my marrow. His tail flicked against me, flexing lazily.

"Mine," he rasped again, quieter. Surrender. Demand.

I laughed, the sound stripped to bone. My tongue was tied in too many knots to say anything in response.

15

VYNE

SELENE LAY TANGLED AGAINST ME, her breathing uneven but slowing into something calm. Sweat slicked her skin, the salty tang of it lingering where her pulse beat faintly at her neck. Her warmth pressed into mine, every soft edge of her fitting against the sharp, unyielding lines of me. My hand rested low on her hip, claws carefully curved back because I didn't trust them—not with her like this. Fragile. Human.

Mine.

The thought struck, sharp as any blade. It rooted itself too deeply, twisting through me with brutal certainty.

Mine.

And fates take me, nothing had ever burned quite like the satisfaction wrapped up in that word.

Her dark hair clung in damp, chaotic waves to her skin, streaked with ash and grit stolen from this unforgiving landscape. And still, nothing—not Volcaryth's heat, not the volcanic terrain threatening to destroy us both—could dull how fierce she looked in the bare afterglow. Fierce but soft, utterly untouchable despite the undeniable way she melted in my arms.

My wings gave a flick. The motion curled the edges inward, shrouding her body where she rested against me, offering her a quiet shelter she didn't even know was there. Her weight grounded me, warm and too close, leaving nothing—not battle, not rage, not reason—to distract me. It was just her. Her scent in the thick air, the tension still crawling sharp under my skin, and the knowledge of what had just passed between us.

Stars above, I was already failing.

My instincts snarled, wild and unrelenting, demanding more of her. Touch her again. Taste her again. Claim her utterly.

I stilled, forcing a sharp inhale into lungs still aching from exertion. The sulfur-tinged air clung to my ribs, its bitterness scratching at my throat. But it wasn't what filled me now. No, all I could taste was her—the maddening sweetness beneath the salt tang of her sweat, the wild scent of something citrus. It clung to my tongue, lingering like a punishable indulgence, and some reckless, bone-deep urge wanted to taste it again. To remind her of this bond in ways she couldn't ignore.

Not yet. That leash was tighter than want, though the edges frayed enough that my claws twitched at their cage. I couldn't give in, not while her body still hummed with exhaustion pressed into my chest.

Selene shifted against me. The small motion—so subtle yet intimate—tore across every frayed nerve. My grip tightened on her hip, my palm warm and calloused against the thin fabric of the shirt I'd scavenged from her pack. Her fingers stirred against my ribs, a soft twitch that shouldn't have tugged at something deep inside me. And yet ... I memorized her, almost unconsciously, with a sharpened focus I couldn't explain even to myself.

I wished she was lying naked against me, but no amount of

lust could overcome the reality of our location, and we'd hastily pulled on clothes before collapsing beside one another.

Her exhaustion softened her edges, and for half a moment, her guard gave way to something gentler. Her brown lashes rested softly against her cheeks. Her chest rose in steady rhythm beneath my hand. I dragged my gaze over the shape of her.

Sanity should've returned by now, except it hadn't. I'd crossed every boundary I had no right to touch ... and still, it wasn't enough. The heat pulling tight through me hadn't dulled; it didn't burn out the way it should have. If anything ... it burned sharper now. Hungrier.

Mine.

Mate.

It wasn't something quiet anymore. The word crawled red-hot through every breath, every nerve, an ache gnawing sharp at the center of my chest. I hadn't said it aloud. I didn't need to. Every time my fingers skimmed delicate bones beneath too-fragile skin, I came closer to losing the leash entirely.

She wasn't just mine. She was *her*—stubborn, maddeningly human, and so gorgeously unbreaking she made all of Volcaryth look brittle by comparison. No molten river could claim her, no volcanic ridge could match her stubborn, radiance. And she still didn't know, did she?

Selene tilted her head, a soft brush of her temple against the dip of my collarbone. Heat sparked, unbidden and familiar where her pulse beat. My throat locked around the need coiled there, wrapping tight through sinew and muscle. Every part of me wanted to take more—to feel *more*—but instead, my fingers eased into that moment.

I forced myself still. Anything less threatened whatever frayed balance I'd clawed back. The whisper of her name burned against my tongue, bitter smoke tight at the edges. If I'd let it slip now, if I'd told her—

Forge save me, I wanted to tell her.

If she saw everything unraveling in me now, she'd never believe it. The truth. That no ridge, no fault line, no uncharted piece of this godless terrain could break me half as easily as she could.

And if I wasn't careful ... she *would*.

"I can *feel* you thinking," Selene muttered, her voice soft and frayed at the edges, though laced with a bit of humor. Her hand nudged weakly at my chest—not a push, not even close, but strong enough to pull my focus back to her because of course she'd notice.

Of course *she* would find space to tease even now.

I blinked down at her, the corners of my mouth twitching despite myself. "You should be sleeping."

"So should you."

I tilted my head. "Are you fussing at me?"

My claws shifted against her hip, the motion careful, restrained. She didn't pull away. Didn't stiffen. But she did look up at me, eyes catching reflections of distant light. The glow carved firelight into her expression, pulling tight against every stubborn edge of her.

"You're impossible," she muttered. The softness beneath the words caught somewhere deeper—fragile, not from weakness, but from something she wouldn't offer easily.

"And you're still here," I replied.

Selene snorted, though the sound lacked edge. Fragile. Tirelessly human. The tension between us dulled—not into emptiness, but into something quieter. Something heavier. It settled there, like this volatile mountain ridge couldn't shift it.

Her head tilted, gaze slipping past me toward the expanse

of Volcaryth unfolding just beyond the crumbled plateau. The landscape was vicious in its beauty, a sprawling labyrinth of broken black rock and shimmering heat. The rivers of lava threading veins deep into the mountains glowed, casting distorted shadows across her sharp features.

"What is this place to you?" she asked quietly, her voice tinged with something sincere enough to unbalance me.

I stilled.

My focus cut away from her face, following the long spires of dark peaks breaking against the stifling haze. Her tone was soft but unflinching, brushing against the edges of something I hadn't intended to acknowledge.

"It's a proving ground," I said finally. "There was a time when young Drakarn warriors who thought they'd finished their training came here. The Harrovan Mountains are cruel, but surviving them ..." My claws flexed against her side. "The ones who came back weren't just warriors anymore."

"It's different now," I continued. The weight tightened in my chest before I could stop it, rougher than the air clawing its way through the rocky expanse under us. "The terrain is too unstable. Fewer came back. And Ignarath has expanded their territory; we're not far from the border." My thumb moved along the curve of her waist. "They would not take kindly to this mission."

Her lips parted, not in argument, but with questions lining the space between us. She didn't ask them.

Her head shifted, brushing against my chin. I should have held her still, anchored her completely into this moment before her restless thoughts took her another direction. But I couldn't bring myself to do it—not when it was Selene, not when her fire kept breaking apart things I thought I'd buried long ago.

She settled back against me, and her soft, shallow breaths melted into an even sleep.

I sat there for awhile before finally, my own eyelids drooped, and I joined her in the peace of slumber.

Then it shattered.

A scream split the still air, and I jerked upright, looking for its source.

VYNE'S GROWL vibrated through the stone beneath me just as a scream ripped through the air like shattering glass.

My mind scrambled to catch up as I jerked awake, muddled by the haze of sleep, but that scream—the shrill, fractured sound of it—dug hooks into my ribs and wrenched me into full awareness.

Burnt air clawed my throat, a rush of sulfur and steam making my lungs sting with each breath. Vyne was already moving, a shadow of coiled muscle and tension at my side.

I sat up too fast, nearly tangling myself in his wings as they flared wide. They blotted out what little morning light there was, stretching like shields over me while his claws flexed against the ground, nearly carving into the stone with the force of his restrained fury.

Another scream echoed, high and desperate. My stomach twisted.

That voice was human.

"Stay," Vyne growled, not looking at me. Just one word, clipped and commanding.

"Wait—" My arm shot out, but too late. He moved faster than I could keep up, his entire frame lifting into the air with a single beat of his wings. Wind whipped over me as his shadow disappeared into the sulfur mist hanging above.

My pulse thundered in my ears.

Stay? Seriously?

Not in this fucking lifetime.

The scream echoed again, and instincts I couldn't argue with shoved me upright.

The grip of fear clawed its way up my spine, but it was overrun by something heavier, louder. *Move.* My body, my muscles, every ounce of my awareness latched onto that need.

The ridges leading upward were unforgiving. Shards of volcanic rock scraped at my palms as I climbed, the grit slipping underneath my boots and threatening to spill me onto the unstable terrain below.

By the time I crested the ridge, I could barely think through the heat and the choking pressure in my chest. But my focus narrowed fast when I spotted the source of the chaos.

First, the woman. Ragged and trembling, trying to hold her ground even as her feet scraped against loose rubble edging toward a fissure. Her clothes were tattered, her bare arms streaked with grime, hair clinging to her sweat-soaked skin in uneven clumps.

She was human. There wasn't any mistaking that.

Then her pursuer. He was Drakarn. His scales shimmered red, shot through with golden undertones. I didn't recognize him or the armor he was wearing. Was he one of the Drakarn from Ignarath that Vyne had mentioned?

He moved with almost lazy slowness, stalking toward her like the whole mountain belonged to him. And her? She was nothing to him but something breakable.

My heart, already pounding hard, lurched.

Far above them, the clash of wings and roaring snarls shattered the silence. Vyne. Locked midair with someone equally massive. Their bodies tangled into an overwhelming storm of claws and fangs that blurred beyond my ability to follow.

But it was the woman's scream—the sharp, splintered crack of it—that dragged all my attention back. Her legs wavered beneath her, inching across the ridge. And that red-scaled bastard? He took another step forward, his pupils fixed on her with something too cruel and calculated to ignore.

I moved before I could think.

The knife Vyne had given me felt too small, too light in my hand as I gripped it tight enough to turn my knuckles white. What I wouldn't give for a gun right now.

Fear buzzed under my skin, clashing against the instinctive pull roaring through me to *do something*. My pulse hammered loud in my ears, drowning out everything but the scrape of my boots over the rock.

I descended the ridge, staying low, moving fast against the unstable ground. Shifting grit slipped underfoot, rock scraping against my palms and knees every time I braced myself against a drop too steep for balance.

Ahead of me, the red Drakarn shifted his weight forward, wings twitching just enough to draw attention to the brutal size of his frame. He stalked toward the human. It wasn't a question *if* he was going to act, only *when*.

Another half-sob, half-choking sound wrenched its way out of the woman. She stumbled another inch backward, and her heel skidded dangerously close to the wide fissure cutting through the ridge.

Hot air hissed from steam vents near the cracks in the earth, the sound sharp and uneven enough to claw through my focus. My legs burned from the scramble, my breath coming too fast, flooding my lungs with sulfur-tainted air.

But there wasn't time for pain, for doubt.

When I dropped the last few feet from the ridge and

shoved myself between them, the red-scaled Drakarn finally noticed me. His head shifted, eyes locking onto me with a predatory calm.

I raised the blade to level with his chest.

"Get back," I said, though the quaver in my voice betrayed something thinner than confidence.

The woman went still. Her breathing was still too loud, too ragged. I'd worry about that later.

The Drakarn drew in a breath through wide flared nostrils, his lips quirking upward enough to reveal serrated fangs.

"You're either brave," he drawled, voice dark and unnervingly smooth, "or stupid."

"Try me."

It wasn't my cleverest line, but my grip tightened around the knife all the same. The edge of its hilt dug sharp into my palm as I shifted closer, as steady as I could force myself to be.

The red-scaled bastard chuckled, low and sharp as breaking rock. It wasn't loud, but it hit heavy, curling out with enough force to vibrate through the ever-thinning space between us.

"Stand aside, human." He tilted his head slowly, his tail flicking behind him with a few unhurried snaps. "This one is mine."

"Not anymore." I took one step back. Far enough that he'd have to do more than swing lazily to reach me. For every inch I moved, though, it felt like I was sinking deeper into boiling water.

Behind me, I could feel her trembling. Her panic, her desperation, was a raw heat spilling into the space like the sulfuric air hissing dangerously from the nearest vents. She had to keep it together. If she made a break for it, there wasn't anything I could do.

The Drakarn's gaze burned, yellow and sharp, catching at the thin line of my knife like nothing more than child's play.

For a moment, I thought maybe—maybe—he'd say something else. Some drawn-out breath of mockery to give me the chance to step back, shut him down before this could escalate even further.

But no.

His whole body shifted instead, his weight rolling forward into one swift strike.

It came fast—too fast. The whip of his tail lashed through the air a half breath before his claws could follow, spiking against the loose rubble ahead of him as I barely threw myself back far enough to evade.

Heat stole the air from my lungs, pulling a searing gasp out of me as my boots scraped against stone, and the knife twisted forward on instinct alone.

The strike didn't land. He was faster, and his twisted grin made sure I knew it.

"Sloppy," the Drakarn taunted.

I couldn't waste time trading jibes with this beast, but it was everything standing between the woman and the narrowing sliver of rocky ridge left beneath us. I stepped forward again, blade steady, pulse anything but.

Come on, Vyne.

It was almost enough to keep him in place. Almost.

Then the sound hit.

The thump of a limp and heavy body crashing against unforgiving stone.

Then the roar.

Louder, more raw, deeper than my knife or his claw could have cut past.

It carried sharp across the ridge, rough and furious, breaking control of every sound or thought I'd tried to hold onto in the moment.

When Vyne came down from the air, it *wasn't* calculated,

smooth, or finely executed as I'd come to expect from him. This wasn't control.

This was rage, and it hit with force enough to split the ridge wide beneath both Drakarn.

The red Drakarn bucked under Vyne's impact, claws scrabbling against crumbling rock as he reeled forward. His wings flared for balance, but Vyne didn't let him recover. Talons locked deep into his opponent's shoulders, ripping downward in a vicious arc that sent blood splattering across the ridge.

The clash was deafening—snarls and bone-rattling roars that echoed around us. Vyne's movements were sharp, relentless. Calculated violence gave way to unpredictability, and I caught the glint of his fangs as he lunged for the red-scaled warrior's throat.

Air rushed past me in dizzying bursts that stole my breath. The fight was too fast, too brutal—green and red scales blurred in and out of the sulfur haze rising from the heat vents.

This wasn't the Vyne I knew. His precision was still there, but it was wrapped in something unrestrained. Something that didn't stop for control or reason.

My chest tightened painfully as I forced myself closer to the woman. Her ragged breathing was practically a wheeze now, audible even above the hiss of steam and the crashing of claws on stone.

"I'm here," I managed, my voice sharp and strained as I crouched low. My knees pressed into the unstable rock, hands tightening around the knife until the metal cut cold into my palm. She flinched at the sound of my voice, her eyes cutting toward me in recognition before another tremor in the ground wrenched her focus away.

Above us, the battle whirled in unpredictable surges. Vyne struck fast—aiming for weak points with brutal efficiency—but the red-scaled warrior lashed out harder, the weight of his strikes threatening to overpower Vyne's speed.

A snap of wings. A hiss of claws. The silence of held breath before a tail cracked the air.

Vyne twisted mid-dodge, his wings beating downward in a ruthless push that drove his enemy farther back toward the ledge. His claws sliced clean along a vulnerable patch of scales near the other Drakarn's chest, and the snarl that erupted in response sent a spark of panic rocketing through me.

I couldn't look away. Couldn't even blink.

The red-scaled warrior lunged, his claws reaching wide with a force that could crush bone—and barely missed. He stumbled under his own weight as Vyne rolled out of the way, dragging a second strike along the length of his enemy's exposed side.

Blood splattered the ridge in dark streaks.

It was violent. Brutal. Terrifying.

The woman whimpered again behind me, tearing my attention away just long enough to see how badly she was shaking. Her hands clutched at her sides, fingers pale and trembling, her chest rising and falling too fast as she gasped for air she couldn't seem to find.

"It's going to be okay," I said to her firmly, keeping my voice low and steady despite the nauseating churn of dread in my stomach. "Just stay behind me. I've got you."

Her head jerked in what might have been a nod—hesitant, broken—but her weight shifted forward like she meant to try. She didn't say anything, her cracked lips trembling as her eyes darted between me and the fight above.

A hiss snapped my attention back to Vyne just in time to see the red-scaled warrior's body twisting unnaturally at the ridge's edge. A final swing—a desperate last strike—broke through Vyne's attempts to pin him fully down, and the larger Drakarn's wings flared wide as he slashed upward.

The blow grazed Vyne's wing, ripping through the delicate membrane as he snarled and pressed in harder.

Together, their weight sent a tremor crashing through the ridge as the unstable ground beneath them buckled again.

"Vyne!" I shouted, my voice sharp enough to cut over the volcanic hiss.

He didn't hear me—or if he did, his focus stayed locked entirely on his opponent.

His claws drove forward, ripping through the edges of armor-like scales and drawing a guttural, labored roar from the other Drakarn. Even through the blood, the snarling, and the unrelenting violence of the moment, Vyne's purpose rang clear.

He wasn't just fighting. He was finishing this.

The ridge groaned under their combined force, crumbling farther as the red-scaled warrior's claws lost their grip.

But as the fight tipped all its weight into the battle above, it left the ground beneath *me* wobbling too close to breaking.

Another fissure split through the stone just inches behind my heels, and I grabbed the woman's arm fast to pull us both back before the broken edge of the ridge could give way entirely.

Her hands clung tightly to my arm now, fingernails digging into my skin like she didn't trust her own legs to hold her upright anymore.

I caught her eyes again.

"Please," she begged softly, her voice cracking under the force of what should have been louder words. "Please, help me. Save me from these monsters."

17

SELENE

I TIGHTENED my grip on the woman's arm as her knees faltered, pulling her upright as the unstable ground shifted beneath us. Tiny cracks webbed across the ridge, sulfuric steam hissing erratically through stone. One wrong step and we wouldn't just fall—we'd vanish into volcanic hell.

Her fingers clung to me like a lifeline, trembling so violently I thought she might hurt herself. She wasn't just scared—she was unraveling. Her breath came shallow and unsteady, each gasp sharp enough to punch holes in her control. But I didn't let go.

"Hey!" I snapped, keeping my voice low but firm. "Eyes on me. You're okay—I'm not going to let anything happen to you, alright? We're getting out of this."

A low, guttural roar erupted from higher up the ridge, rattling the heat-laden air around us. The sound froze her, her whole body tensing as she flinched hard into my side. I didn't have to look to know where the fight was coming from. I trusted Vyne. I knew he wouldn't let the bastard get anywhere near us —but she didn't.

"It's okay," I murmured, shifting my grip so I could keep

her closer, steadier. "I need you to breathe. Deep and slow. Focus on my voice."

Her whimper broke my momentum. It was a quiet, splintered sound full of something I recognized far too well—panic that didn't just come from this one moment. This wasn't fear of an immediate threat. This was someone who'd been living on edge for far too long, stripped bare by circumstance.

How was she here? There weren't supposed to be any humans on Volcaryth outside of my people back in Scalvaris. I wanted to ask, but she wasn't in any place to answer. Not yet.

"Come on. One step at a time. Don't look back." I spoke with layers of calm I didn't feel, keeping it steady as the adrenaline clawed at my chest.

She stumbled, legs folding mid-step. My arm shot out, snapping around her waist to keep her upright. She gasped, her breath hitting like broken glass, but she didn't try to resist when I steadied her again.

"Deep breaths," I said, a little softer now. "You're doing fine. Just keep your feet—steady now."

Her knuckles were bloodied, her fingers curling against me so tightly it felt like she'd carved grooves into my side. Too strong for her to be completely powerless, but too desperate for it to matter. She wasn't thinking anymore; she was surviving on raw instinct, and I had to be enough for both of us.

Every inch we covered rattled underfoot. Tiny fragments of volcanic stone scattered with each shifting step. The ground hissed beneath us, not quite stable but stable enough. I kept us moving, slow and steady, even when my muscles barked protest. There wasn't another choice—not if we wanted to live.

I let out a slow breath as the ridge sloped downward into smoother terrain. "Okay," I murmured, more to myself than her, though she clung tighter in response. "We're getting there. Just a little farther."

Her head shook, her response staggered and broken. "I ... didn't think anyone ..."

Her voice cracked into silence. Her whole body jolted against me when another echoing roar rippled through the air, closer this time.

Her trembling grew fiercer, her voice trembling loose again in barely audible fragments. "... anyone would come."

The words, slurred and barely there, hit somewhere I couldn't place. My jaw tightened. But this wasn't the moment —not to process, not to dig deeper. Her survival—*our* survival— had to come first.

"You're not alone now," I told her plainly, adjusting my grip as the incline leveled out into an uneven path along the ridge's edge. My boots skidded, but I dug in to steady us both. "Keep moving. We're almost there."

I could see the edge of the campsite past an outcropping, and for the first time since we'd started moving, relief crept into my chest.

Just a little farther. We could make it.

The ground leveled out beneath us just as her knees gave way completely. She collapsed where she stood, crumpling back against the blackened rock. Her thin shoulders heaved with each gulp of air, trembling as though even breathing was a battle she wasn't sure she could win.

I crouched in front of her, keeping a firm hand on her shoulder to hold her steady, grounded. "You're safe," I told her, my own breath pushing hard through my lungs. "Do you hear me? We're safe for now. Breathe." A pause. "In through your nose—slow. I need you to slow it down."

Her bloodshot eyes, wide and panicked, snapped to mine. They searched me wildly as if looking for any crack in my composure that might justify her spiraling fear. I didn't give her one. I stayed rock-solid in front of her, forcing calm into my voice where my muscles only screamed for rest.

She nodded shakily and dragged an uneven breath through her nose. It hitched but didn't spiral right away. Promising. The next breath was a bit steadier, though still a far cry from ideal.

"Good," I said, my voice lowering into something soothing, steady. "Keep it up. You're okay—we're okay."

Even as I reassured her, I couldn't stop my clinical instincts from taking inventory. Up close, she was worse off than I'd realized. Deep bruises shadowed her skin, swelling and discoloration scattered unevenly between deep gashes and ugly scrapes. Her clothes were burnt and torn, as if she'd crawled out of the steam vents themselves.

Too thin. Ribs showing beneath her battered skin, her limbs trembling from both dehydration and exhaustion. She was a human-shaped survival instinct at this point, hurt and collapsed within herself, and still somehow breathing.

"What's your name?" I asked as I reached for my supply pack.

Her lips trembled, just shy of a reply. Then the quietest whisper slipped through her cracked mouth. "Reika," she rasped, the word catching like shards in her throat.

"Reika," I repeated gently, giving her shoulder a reassuring squeeze. "Alright, Reika. I'm Selene. Nice to meet you." I unclipped the tiny water pouch from my kit, ignoring how worryingly little remained inside. "Here. Drink—but slow, alright? Don't push it too fast."

Her trembling hands reached out, faltering before brushing the pouch. For a split second, I thought it might drop between us, wasted completely. But she managed, gripping the edge with shaking fingers and raising it hesitantly to her lips. Her gaze stayed pinned on me the entire time, like she was waiting for me to snatch it back or slap it from her hands.

Small, steady sips left little trickles at her mouth's edge, but she didn't choke, didn't splutter.

"Good," I said. Her breaths came easier now—rough, yes, but better. "Alright, let's take a closer look at those cuts."

She didn't protest when I reached for her forearm. An ugly gash ran deep enough to graze muscle beneath her sunburned skin. I grabbed what supplies I could from the remains of my med kit, working quickly to clean it out.

"This one's going to sting," I warned her quietly. "Tell me if it hurts, and we can stop."

"Why ... why are you helping me?"

I paused and really looked at her. It wasn't suspicion I saw there. It wasn't anger or even gratitude. Just ... confusion. Unfiltered confusion that radiated like a wound of its own.

"Because you need it." The simplicity of my tone didn't waver as I resumed cleaning the wound. "I'm a medic. That's how this works."

Her silence spoke louder than anything else after that.

I finished wrapping her forearm, then moved lower to inspect the uneven swelling along one ankle. There were blisters there, crackling like ruptured masses across swollen flesh. The burns from running this volcanic hellscape were clear—painful and likely pricking at every nerve with hot rods of agony. She clenched her jaw tight as I lifted the ankle, saying nothing but letting out a sharp, unsteady exhale as I worked.

"Alright, I've got you," I murmured when her trembling turned harsher at one particularly deep press. "Stay with me. You'll be good as new in no time."

A weak scoff croaked out despite her pain—brief, edged with disbelief but still there. That was something. I gave her a short glance, arching my brow in mock challenge.

"Too soon for jokes," she rasped.

I shrugged, the corner of my mouth twitching into a hint of a smirk. "It beats screaming."

She blinked like she didn't know how to respond to that, and I turned my focus back to her injury. The bandages pulled tight against the weakened joint, stabilizing it enough. I couldn't promise miracles, but she'd survive. That was enough for now.

The beat of wings blew hot rock dust toward us. My pulse jumped, though not out of fear this time. I straightened, glancing behind me just as Vyne picked his landing spot across the wide edge of our makeshift perch.

The impressive slam of his claws against the charred rock sent tremors skittering along the stone. His bloodied scales caught the dim light, and there were brutal shadows around him. His scent made the air sharper, though it wasn't rage he carried back with him.

Reika stiffened to stone beside me.

"Shit," I cursed. Her head snapped toward Vyne, and her eyes exploded with panic. Every trace of calm dissolved before I could react further.

She screamed. Loud, wrenching, full of wretched terror that ripped the fragile silence apart. Before I could think to restrain her, she scrambled blindly against the rough slope, dragging herself backward on bloodied palms and shaking arms.

"Reika!" My voice was sharp, a cutting force meant to ground her. "Stop! He's not going to hurt you."

Her panic swelled even more, animalistic and frantic, fueled by something deep and unrelenting. Her lips trembled, chest heaving violently. "M-monster!" she stuttered, though it fractured midway between a sob and a hiccup of air. "He's one of them! He's—he's—"

"Enough," Vyne's command thundered ahead of him,

barbed and hard enough to shake the air itself. It hit like steel clashing against metal, his low growl carrying authority designed to break panic rather than stir it.

Reika froze completely. Her body locked, trembling harder now, on the perilous edge of total collapse.

I shifted between her and Vyne, one hand lightly pressed to her shoulder again as I murmured quiet reassurances. "You're safe. He's with me. He won't hurt you."

Vyne's glinting, yellow gaze burned sharp through the remnants of smoke between us—controlled, restrained. After a long beat, he stepped back, his wings folding tight.

"You're hurt," he rumbled at me. His voice was low, tension radiating from every fiber of his frame.

"I'm fine. Bruised, maybe," I said quickly, brushing dust from my scratched forearms. I was too focused on Reika to think about my own pain.

When the silence stretched too long, I sighed, folding my arms across my chest to mask my wobbling exhaustion. "Seriously, Vyne. It's nothing."

"You've seen better days," he growled softly, moving closer with talon-scraping steps over the rock. His chin tipped down, eyes locking onto mine.

Reika hissed in a sharp breath and started to judder with fear. Her breaths came in fast. She was hyperventilating now.

If I couldn't calm her down, I had no idea what to do. We couldn't just leave her there.

"He's different from them. Trust me. I wouldn't bring a threat near you."

Her lips quivered, every line in her face clinging to disbelief like it was the only thing between her and oblivion. "You don't know," she whispered, broken and terrified. "You don't understand."

"Maybe not," I said softly, still holding her gaze. "Look at me, Reika. I know enough to bet my life on him. I need you to trust me, just for now. Believe me when I say you're safe with us."

Her breathing continued to hitch, but the trembling slowed a little, her muscles inching closer to unfrozen. She shuddered —not entirely convinced, but no longer drowning in pure terror.

"We need to leave," Vyne said. His eyes swept over both of us, lingering on Reika just a beat longer before cutting back to me. "More are coming. They'll smell their fallen before long, and when they do, they won't come alone."

I looked at Reika, her fragile state etched in the tight cords of her trembling frame. She'd stopped trying to crawl away, but her fear still radiated like heat, coiling tense and unrelenting. She wouldn't make it far on her own, and carrying her across the ridges would slow all three of us to a death sentence.

I didn't allow my focus to linger long before shifting it to Vyne. His massive wings, even folded tightly against his back, couldn't hide the damage stretching from the nasty tear along the edge. Blood seeped out with each twitch of his movements, though he held himself upright, impassive. His strength was undeniable—but strength had its limits, and his were closer than he let on.

He was hurting. She was barely holding on. And all I could do was try to hold the weight of that in both hands without anyone slipping through.

"We need speed," Vyne said, bracing one shoulder against the rock as though the admission itself irritated him. "I can fly her ahead. There's a second ridge farther west—secluded enough to lose the Ignarath if we move quickly. She'll be safer there."

"No," Reika rasped, cutting him off violently before I could answer. Her voice cracked on the word, panic rising sharp as claws, latching onto any semblance of control she thought she could salvage. "No. You can't—you can't let him take me."

Her breath grew rough again, and she pressed herself harder into the rock, trembling visible anew. "He's just like them. I can't— I won't—" Her words stuttered, and she started shaking again.

"Reika," I interrupted, kneeling down and catching her frantic gaze before the spiral could fully consume her again. "Reika, listen to me. He's not like them. I need you to hear me."

She shook her head so hard I feared she might hurt her neck, her wide-eyed panic driving her further into denial. "You don't understand!"

"Then help me understand." My voice stayed firm—unshaking, despite exhaustion pressing cracks into my resolve. "Tell me what happened."

Her body jolted at the words, her gasp rough and staccato, but she stopped moving. Her trembling didn't vanish, but she stared at me now, not through me. Something in her wild gaze softened—or at least tolerated the possibility that my words weren't a trap.

I exhaled, gesturing between the three of us. "We don't have options right now. We can't win if more come. So, here's the question: are you willing to get out of here alive, or do you want to face the Ignarath again?"

She didn't answer. Her lips pressed thin and pale, punctuated with blood pricking at the cracks. Her eyes tipped downward—not toward rocky escape paths, not back toward Vyne.

After what felt like minutes compressed into seconds, she nodded—the smallest, reluctant tilt of her head. "No flying," she insisted.

I swallowed hard against the surge of frustration. Turning, I met Vyne's gaze. "We have to walk," I said, my tone final. "You need to rest your wing."

"You're too stubborn for your own good," he muttered, more to himself than me. But he didn't argue. That told me how much his wing had to be hurting.

He took a careful step back, giving Reika space to breathe even as his presence still filled the ridge's confined air. And with that same controlled precision, he angled closer to me, his body a fortress of heat and vigilance.

"She won't keep pace long," he warned, though his tone had softened by now. "If her strength fails—"

"It won't," I said, cutting him off. The conviction in my voice tasted stubborn even to myself. "We'll figure it out."

I turned back toward Reika and extended a hand once more. She hesitated just a fraction before gripping it shakily and standing.

I hitched my pack over my shoulder and tried not to think of the vyrathis inside as Vyne led the way down a narrow path.

18

VYNE

I SCANNED THE PATH AHEAD, blinking only when the sting of sulfur forced it. Wind shifted around us in thin, sharp currents—too erratic for comfort, too quiet for complete safety. We had to keep moving.

Behind me, Selene murmured softly, voice calm and almost stern. "Just breathe through it, Reika. A few more steps. We'll rest soon."

Selene moved with no hint of hesitation, her focus so tightly woven into tending to the fallen woman it was as though the volcanic landscape didn't even exist.

And, stars above, it wrecked me.

Selene should've been the one resting. Her temples glistened with sweat, smudged with streaks of soot she either hadn't noticed or hadn't cared to wipe away. Scratches scored her exposed skin in uneven patterns.

She deserved better than this journey. Better than this ridge.

Better than me.

She slowed, giving Reika another of those delicate touches —her fingers ghosting over the woman's trembling wrist in a silent reassurance only she could make believable. I exhaled and turned my focus forward again.

It was safer to study the path. Safer not to let myself get dragged under whatever storm she stirred in me: longing, hunger, something deeper I couldn't name without risking it breaking loose.

Selene's tone turned teasing despite her heavy burden. "Eyes up. The rocks are more afraid of you than you are of them."

Reika's clipped response was little more than a broken grunt. Progress, of sorts—she wasn't screaming or cowering anymore. I'd lost count of how many times the woman had locked up mid-stride, her terror bracing through even the smallest glance in my direction.

Her gaze hadn't met mine for longer than a heartbeat since Selene had convinced her to move. But she *was* moving, and that was what mattered.

But more than that ... Selene wouldn't let her break further. Her boundless, maddening kindness wouldn't let her. And something in me knew better than to pretend I didn't admire that.

Maddening. Beautiful. *Mine.*

Control coiled its leash tight through my ribs again, its strain aching. I rolled my shoulders briefly, peeling the tension out in careful movements as my claws flexed against my sides.

"We need to stop." Selene's attention lifted toward me. "I need to clean her cuts before they get worse."

I fought to keep my voice steady. "Stopping too long is a risk. If the Ignarath come back over this—"

"Don't start with me." Her tone cut sharply, then dipped lower when I turned. "We need fifteen minutes."

I swallowed back a sharp retort, releasing a low growl

instead. My wings snapped out for a brief stretch, and I winced at the ache. "We can spare five."

Her jaw twitched, but she nodded.

The moment I stopped moving, the pain caught up like a rival who'd been waiting for their chance to strike. My wing burned in gnawing pulses I could feel down to the bone. It was the kind of pain you could bargain with—if you didn't mind bleeding through every demand.

The tear wasn't deep, but every shift turned the injury into a throbbing reminder of my limits. I flexed my shoulder experimentally, keeping my wings tight against my frame. No use letting Selene catch the tremble as my body betrayed me. Not that she'd miss it for long.

Behind me, her voice was soft and low, pulling some semblance of calm from Reika's frantic breaths. Watching Selene ease the woman out of panic was almost worse than the pain—each word weaving that impossible warmth into this barren land, each steady hand doing what my claws never could.

I clenched my jaw and turned my focus forward, scanning past the darkening shadows of the ridges cutting against the hazy horizon. Volcaryth was unforgiving in its silence, but no fresh tremors rattled beneath us. No sulfur-drenched breeze tipped me off to Ignarath warriors cutting through the paths we'd left behind.

We'd crossed the edge of their claimed territory and were safe.

For now. But we had to keep moving.

Rest time was over.

We walked for over an hour before Selene's voice drifted over. "Vyne." One word, carrying the weight of so many unsaid.

I glanced over at her. There she was, crouched beside Reika, her hands steady.

Her tone turned firm, leaving no room for refusal. "She can't go much farther. We need to make camp."

My claws flexed in resignation. "Soon." The word came out clipped, more at myself than her. Her lips twitched in fleeting triumph, though her gaze stayed heavy.

"Good."

I dropped to a crouch. The sharp pulse of pain still pounded steadily when I tucked them tighter, but nothing quieted the deeper pressure buzzing beneath it.

The outcropping up ahead wasn't much, but it was enough. Stone walls jutted between us and the open ridgeline, creating a half-shelter tucked against the mountain's angry edges. No overhead cover to hide us from any Ignarath scouting aerial paths, but it kept the worst of the sulfurous winds at bay.

It would have to do.

Selene already had Reika settled near the base of one wall, propping her up with a pile of shredded fabric pushed under her head like a pillow. Her improvised med kit lay scattered across the ground.

Reika's breaths came shallow and uneven, and her eyes fluttered closed against the world. Exhaustion had overtaken her panic for now. That alone did more for our chances of survival than any words I might have offered.

Selene's head turned toward me, sharp and direct—an acknowledgment, not an invitation. Her hands stayed carefully busy, adjusting the thin strips of bandage around Reika's bruised wrists. The movements were methodical, practiced.

"Selene." Her name tasted unfamiliar on my tongue, drawing something gentler out of me. "Enough. She's fine."

For once, she didn't argue. She breathed out, shoulders sinking. I wasn't sure if it was exhaustion or agreement, but it didn't matter.

Instead, she shifted subtly toward me, propping her back

against the same slope of rough stone wall. Her hair fell loose over one shoulder. Without the distraction of motion, sharp exhaustion shadowed every inch of her.

"Let me see your wing." Her tone was low but pointed.

I stilled, my own exhaustion heavy enough to blur the words before they sank in. "It's nothing," I countered too quickly. Vainly.

Her hand nudged toward my arm, not with force but with enough weight to slice through my half-hearted response. Her touch was light, but the slow trace of her fingertips across my wing struck deeper than her sharpest arguments ever had.

"I told you—" The words dissolved when her fingers pressed gently against the torn edge of skin along the membrane. My thoughts scattered in an instant, as though her lightest touch had broken them on purpose.

Her fingers withdrew in one swift, careful motion. "You'll live."

My own hand lingered just beside hers without thought—brushing lightly against the edge of her wrist.

It wasn't enough.

It wasn't ever going to be enough.

I settled against the rock, muscles tight despite the attempt to rest. Selene leaned into my side without hesitation.

Her breathing was steady now, slower than before but still weighed down by exhaustion. The tension in her frame hinted at an ache she refused to let show. Even now, when her body craved rest, her thoughts cut through the thick silence between us. I didn't need to read her mind to know she was thinking of a dozen questions she wouldn't voice, not yet.

She broke the haze of heat and silence with a pointed question. "How long will it take us to reach Scalvaris on foot?"

I turned my head. Her hair was still mussed, half sticking to her temple in damp streaks, but her eyes never wavered. Stubborn, focused, and entirely unyielding.

"A week." The subtle twitch in my wing flared as if protesting. "Maybe more, depending on how far west we must go to avoid Ignarath patrols."

Her lips parted to argue—or worse, suggest something reckless—so I cut her off. "Don't even think about it." My words came out in a low growl. "If you're about to suggest I fly ahead to deliver the vyrathis, forget it. I'm not leaving you out here alone, in enemy territory, for days."

Her brows furrowed, annoyance flickering bright for a heartbeat before she sighed. "I wasn't going to say that." Her tone remained low. "I figured out three hours ago that you'd say no."

I huffed a quiet laugh, shifting my weight to adjust the angle of my aching wing. "You're learning, *Zhyvarin*."

That earned me a weak glare, but she let it drop. Instead, her eyes flicked briefly toward Reika, who lay asleep—or unconscious—on the uneven ground not far from us. The soft rise and fall of her chest barely betrayed she was still with us.

"I know the healers need the vyrathis, but we can't abandon Reika. Not like this. What do you think they did to her?"

"I don't know." My attention flicked to the fragile human shape crumpled against the stone. "Ignarath aren't kind to outsiders."

The weight behind her silence was heavy. I didn't look at her; I didn't need to. Her emotions were loud, even when she buried them behind reason. "And Scalvaris is so friendly?" The bitter humor in her voice was muted but still sharp enough to hit.

I laughed. "Compared to the Ignarath? Yes."

She blinked, as if genuinely startled by that response, and

for a fleeting moment, her eyes shifted toward the landscape beyond the narrow ridge.

Her voice lowered. "Do you think she was on our ship? Is it possible there are more humans on Volcaryth? That they survived?"

She would know better than me. There were ancient stories of people from far away planets woven through our history, but I had never given them much thought until Selene and her fellow humans had crashed into the burning sands outside the city.

"You'll have to ask her."

Selene didn't respond. I watched her in stillness, torn between wanting to do something—anything—to ease the weight she carried and the impossibility of action. Despite the razor edge of the situation, she still glowed. Stubborn as ever.

Mine, whether she knew it or not.

We were close now, both of us leaning against the walls that formed our makeshift camp. Her shoulder brushed mine— barely, but enough for my mind to fixate on it. Exhaustion should have dulled my senses, but no. The awareness of her warmth so near, the scent that clung to her as though even Volcaryth's heat couldn't burn it away.

I looked at her again, unable to help myself. Her profile was drawn in dimming light and shadow, and none of it was diminished by the grime and exhaustion streaked across her features. No, this was Selene at her rawest: worn but unbreaking.

And gods help me, I wanted her. Every stubborn, infuriating, breathtaking part of her.

I reached up and brushed a strand of her dark hair back, freeing it from where it clung to her temple. My knuckles grazed her skin—warm, impossibly soft against the sharp edges of this volcanic hellscape.

Her breathing hitched, just a bit, as her gaze darted to mine. She didn't pull away.

"*Zhyvarin.*" Her mating name settled rough and reverent on my tongue.

Slowly, carefully, I tilted her face toward mine, my clawed thumb brushing her jawline with cautious precision. Her skin was fire beneath my touch—fragile and fierce all at once.

I leaned down, the world narrowing to the maddening slice of space between us. When my lips brushed hers, it wasn't with urgency. No battle raged in that moment, no ferocity vying for control. The kiss was slow, soft but consuming, a quiet clash of heat and restraint. Her lips trembled against mine before she leaned in, her entire frame pressing closer with painstaking grace.

I could have drowned in that.

Her hands found their way to my chest, resting lightly against the scales just above my heart. I felt her hesitation—not because she didn't want this, but because she did. Just as much as I did, perhaps more. The truth lingered between us, fragile and undeniable: there was no turning back from this.

And gods, for a moment, I didn't want to.

But then she pulled away, her forehead resting lightly against mine as her breaths came shallow and quick. The space between us lingered, crackling with unspoken intensity neither of us dared to tip farther toward.

"We can't." Her whisper broke the hush, voice heavy but steady.

My claws curled into my palms to keep my composure. "I know." The admission tasted like ash. "You should rest. I'll take first watch."

It was going to be a long night.

REIKA TRUDGED BESIDE ME. Her trembling had eased enough to keep her upright, though exhaustion clung to her shoulders like dead weight. Every step she took was driven by sheer will.

The strap of my pack cut into my shoulder, the clinking of the vyrathis container a reminder of what this delay could cost.

"How did you end up on Volcaryth?" I asked, keeping my voice low. If I'd been any less exhausted, I might have spent the night tossing and turning, desperate for the answer. Instead, I'd slept only a foot away from Vyne and wished I was brave enough to lie down in his arms.

This thing between us ... I wasn't sure I understood it. I could practically still taste him, the memory of his tongue a brand on me.

And I couldn't think about it. Not now, not when I had to keep Reika alive and get the vyrathis back to Scalvaris before it was too late.

Reika didn't respond. Not surprising—she still flinched whenever I said her name. Her gaze flicked toward Vyne's shadow ahead of us before her jaw clenched and she refocused on her uneven footing.

I tried again. "Were you on a generation ship from Earth? Maybe your pod got ejected somehow?" As best we could tell, that was what had happened to me and my fellow humans.

Her voice cracked when she finally spoke. "Does it matter?"

"It might," I said. "If there are others out there, they might need help."

She stopped. For a moment, I thought she'd stay silent, but then her lips curled into a sneer, her voice sharp and bitter. "If anyone else made it, you won't find them alive. You'd be lucky to find their bones."

The edge of her bitterness grated, but I swallowed my irritation. Pushing her wouldn't help, not while she was still bruised and battered. What the hell had she survived to leave her this cut open and closed off?

"What about you?" I pressed. "How long have you been out here?"

She didn't flinch this time. "Long enough."

She wore her silence like armor. And whatever survival instinct had dragged her through this volcanic deathtrap still burned under her exhaustion, just enough to keep her moving.

The terrain didn't help. The deeper we pushed into this wasteland, the more Volcaryth's suffocating hostility seeped into my bones. This world wasn't just a planet—it was a predator. Every shadow, every sulfur-choked breath in the air felt like it was waiting for one moment of weakness to strike.

Vyne moved steadily ahead. He knew the terrain better than either of us, but even he couldn't fully hide the tension. He saw something there—felt it.

He's worried.

That thought stuck to me harder than the heat. If Volcaryth had Vyne watching the shadows, we were already treading over the edge of disaster.

Reika kept moving, her steps growing steadier. Her breathing, still labored, was getting stronger. Whatever strength had dragged her through hell planet still burned inside her, faint but alive.

Then the first warning hit—a shift in the air, enough to make every nerve in my body tighten.

"Move." Vyne's voice cut like a knife.

Instinct took over before my mind could catch up. I shifted fast, dragging Reika toward me as I adjusted the pack against my back. My gaze darted upward to the surrounding ridges, searching desperately for whatever had Vyne's wings flaring.

Nothing. At least, nothing I could see.

"Eyes up," Vyne growled, his gaze locked on the rocks above. He stopped short, his imposing frame coiled and ready.

Then I saw them—shadows slipping over the peaks, moving too quickly and too precisely to be anything but a threat.

Shit.

"Reika." I kept my voice sharp and low, stepping closer to shield her as I reached for my knife. Vyne's knife. Whichever. All that mattered was it was sharp. "Stay close. Keep moving. Understand?"

She nodded stiffly, her breaths shaky but steady enough to keep her upright. Good. That was good. I could work with that.

The air thickened, tension coiling around us. It prickled behind my neck, each heartbeat louder and harder against my chest.

Then they appeared.

The first Drakarn, they had to be from Ignarath, burst from the haze, red and gold scales glinting. He slammed into the ground, his claws scraping deep gouges into the ridge just meters from Vyne. His wings flared sharply as he straightened.

A second leapt forward from the ridge to our left, blue-scaled and bristling with dark armor so polished it seemed to drink in the shadows. Above us, a third circled.

"Stay behind me," Vyne growled. His body coiled, every muscle taut and ready.

I didn't argue. There wasn't time. Instead, I eased my stance, gripping the knife tighter in one hand while keeping my pack secured against my back with the other.

The first Ignarath launched himself at Vyne, claws outstretched. Vyne met him head-on, his strike brutal and precise, claws tearing at scales with surgical precision. Their impact echoed off the rocks, shaking the ground beneath me.

But as I tracked their fight, movement from the second Ignarath snapped my focus back. His eyes locked onto me. My stomach tightened. Big. Fast. Dangerous.

He lunged.

I dove low, heart hammering as his claws swiped just over my head. My blade sliced upward as I turned, grazing his flank. He let out a sharp snarl, twisting quickly to face me again. He was angry now—his tail snapping violently behind him, his gaze predatory and locked.

He swiped again, claws fast. I twisted, throwing awkward steps backward, barely keeping ahead of his momentum. Each move scratched away at whatever sandpaper-thin margin of survival I had left.

Focus. Keep moving.

His claws slashed wide, too fast for me to dodge. I threw myself sideways, the motion wrenching at my shoulders and sending me skidding on loose volcanic rock. Pain flared sharp along my ribs as I found my footing.

The bastard in front of me lunged again, claws slashing. I ducked, my knees scraping rock as I drove my blade upward. The edge of his wing caught my knife, tearing webbing and sending him reeling back with a guttural snarl.

The Ignarath growled. He was gauging me now—he hadn't expected resistance. His arrogance was personal. If I could exploit it, even for a moment ...

Footsteps.

No—pounding claws. Heavy, fast, closing in.

I turned sharply to see the second Ignarath, the blue-scaled brute, barreling toward Reika. Her scream sliced the air just as he reached her, his fangs bared and gaze alight with cruel intention.

Damn it.

"Reika!" I yelled, my heart slamming into my ribs. My body reacted, moving before my thoughts could catch up, muscles burning as I sprinted toward her. She was defenseless, frozen. I—

No. She wasn't.

She gripped a wickedly sharp piece of volcanic rock, her hands trembling. Her wide, panic-stricken gaze locked on the blue-scaled Ignarath, but there was a shift in the air. A thread of something wild sparked in her movements, shaky but there. Her terror turned sharp, desperate—but not paralyzed.

As his claws reached for her, Reika lashed out with the shard, the wide swing catching him clean across his forearm. Dark blood sprayed hot and fast against the stone, and the Ignarath's snarl turned to a roar of pain.

"Reika, get down!" I barked. She stumbled backward, the shard still clutched in white-knuckled hands.

The Ignarath recoiled, his fury radiating off him in near-tangible waves. He swiped again, and I barely had time to react, my body twisting sharply as he crashed into the ridge beside us.

My hands tightened around my knife as I maneuvered between Reika and the advancing Ignarath.

Fight. Survive. Protect.

That was all I could focus on now.

The Ignarath stalked closer, slow and steady now. He knew I was trapped. I could see it in the sharp curl of his lips, the evil grin that split his scaled face. His claws flexed, mocking, as if savoring the kill before he delivered it.

We were losing ground fast. I glanced past the Ignarath, trying to track Vyne, but I couldn't see him. The Ignarath snarled, his hand snapping out. A claw skimmed over my shoulder—not enough to tear flesh, but close enough to send me stumbling. Pain shot down my arm.

The bastard wasn't letting up. His massive wings folded to gain tighter control as his claws flexed and struck again. This time, I couldn't dodge fast enough. His hand clipped the side of my pack, dragging the weight of it hard against my ribs and knocking the air from my lungs.

The ridge around us felt alive—unstable rock shifting and groaning beneath the pressure of his sheer brutal force. My footing wavered as I stumbled farther back, the fissures widening behind me. He followed every step with relentless precision, cutting off any paths of escape with calculated strikes. This close, his size was overwhelming, his shadow swallowing the light as he pressed forward.

I just needed an opening. Anything.

A sharper sound cut through the air above us—a sudden rush of air displaced by powerful wings. My pulse kicked hard as I shifted my focus upward to the hulking shadow descending fast from above.

The third Ignarath hit the ground behind the first with a force that felt like an earthquake.

This one was broader, darker, his scales nearly black. His massive frame loomed, unnatural in its size and weight. His eyes burned, piercing gold—locking instantly on me, his wings still tucked tight against his back, claws flexing as he moved closer.

No hesitation. No slow circling this time. They weren't waiting anymore.

The weight of everything hit like a punch. My breath felt heavy and raw as my hand trembled harder around the knife hilt.

Vyne's roar broke through. I whipped my head toward him just as the emerald flash of his scales collided brutally with the first Ignarath. His claws tore into his opponent, forcing him toward the edge of the ridge. The fight was blood-slick and loud.

He didn't pause—didn't falter. Even with his wings frayed and blood streaking his sides, Vyne dominated the fight. But there were too many of them, and for every advantage he gained, it only pushed me harder into the realization:

He wasn't going to hold for long.

They weren't there to test our limits. They were there to tear them apart.

20

SELENE

MY KNIFE WAS TOO small against the sheer size of the Ignarath warrior in front of me. No time to second-guess; no time to think. Just react.

He circled closer, a predator toying with its prey. Claws sliced the hot, sulfurous air. Behind me, Reika's breaths were panicked gasps that clawed at my focus. I couldn't afford to look back, not even for a second. One wrong move, one glance away, and this bastard would gut me.

The Ignarath tilted his massive head, his slitted eyes narrowing in what I could only interpret as cruel amusement. "I will suck the marrow from your bones."

Great. He was going to enjoy this. Mockery on top of the very real threat of murder. The crimson streaks across his wings shimmered in the light, like hell's own tapestry come to life and intent on killing me.

This was bad. Beyond bad. Vyne was battling two of them now, his snarls and the sickening clash of talons echoing off the rocks. I tasted the metallic tang of fear on my tongue. How much longer could I keep this up?

Reika choked out a gasp, a fragmented attempt at a warning. I was too slow to process it, her voice splintered and lost in the fight, and that was all it took.

His claws lashed out, catching the strap of my pack and yanking me violently off-balance. I stumbled, one knee cracking hard against the hard stone. Pain exploded through my leg, white-hot and blinding. I swore and barely managed to throw my knife up in a useless defense as he bore down on me.

He came in again, faster this time, claws aimed with deadly precision straight at my chest. I braced uselessly, knowing this was it.

A wave of regret washed over me. Thinking of what could have been, all the things I wanted, this was the last thing I should be doing. But for a second, all I could think of was the taste of Vyne's lips against my own, of the way his body melded with mine. Of the creeping suspicion that there was something more, something *bigger* between us.

Or there would have been. If we had a chance at a future.

I'm sorry, Vyne.

But the blow never came.

The world shifted in a heartbeat. A thunderous slam echoed off the rocky walls as another massive figure collided with the Ignarath like a living firestorm of muscle and fury. The force of it sent shockwaves through the ground, knocking the crimson-scaled bastard back on his heels, his claws skidding uselessly against the stone as he scrambled to regain his footing.

Granite-gray scales gleamed as he straightened, his massive frame a nightmare—for my enemy, at least. For me? Relief flooded in, a surge of desperate strength.

I recognized this warrior.

Khorlar.

He didn't spare me so much as a glance. His narrow eyes burned only for the Ignarath in front of him, his jaw set, a terrifying stillness about him. It was clear: his next move was already decided, and it wouldn't end well for whoever stood in his path.

The Ignarath snarled, his wings flaring as he prepared to strike again. But Khorlar was faster, a blur of motion. He lunged forward with brutal efficiency, his claws burying themselves with a sickening, wet crunch into the Ignarath's shoulder.

The bastard roared, a guttural, enraged sound that was abruptly cut off when Khorlar's other hand slammed hard into his ribs with the force of a battering ram. The blow sent the Ignarath crashing against the blackened rock wall, fissures spiderwebbing out from the point of impact.

It was over before I could fully react. Precise, devastating strikes. He wasn't just fighting—he was dismantling his opponent, piece by piece. There was a terrifying economy to his movements, a cold, calculated brutality that left no room for doubt.

Above us, the shadow of the third Ignarath loomed closer, circling lower with clipped strokes of his massive wings. I swore under my breath. There was no way even Khorlar, as powerful as he was, could hold both of them off.

Vyne's opponent was backing off, shredded scales a testament to Vyne's vicious efficiency—but he was bleeding too, favoring one side. Exhaustion was clear in every movement.

Another growl, closer this time, pulled my attention back down to Khorlar. He had already turned his focus on the second Ignarath. I started to move forward, ready to throw myself into the fray—stupid or not, I couldn't just stand there— but the granite wall of a warrior didn't need my help.

Khorlar stepped into the attack. He ducked low under a sloppy, rage-fueled swipe, then drove his fist upward with explosive force into the Ignarath's exposed underbelly. The sound that followed was visceral, sickening—the crunch of scaled flesh and bone against the impact of volcanic strength. I winced, despite myself.

The blue Ignarath stumbled back, a mangled roar tearing from his throat, his wings twitching spasmodically as he jerked upward in a desperate attempt to retreat. Blood marred his once-pristine scales, leaving crimson streaks dripping in his wake, the volcanic air carrying the acrid scent of his pain and labored breathing before it all faded into the relative silence.

The ridge stilled.

I stayed frozen where I stood, my knife still clutched tightly in one hand, every nerve screaming for me to act, to react, to *do* something. But there was nothing left to do. The Ignarath were gone—either dead or retreating—and we were, miraculously, still alive.

Vyne landed behind me with a heavy thud, the turbulence of his wings stirring up a cloud of ash and dust around our feet. His breathing was steady, if strained, but I could see the tightness in his jaw, the almost imperceptible stiffness in the set of his shoulders. He was injured, no question, though he didn't give me a moment to ask, to assess.

"Hurt?" His voice was sharp, his concern settling on me. His gaze swept me from head to toe, his eyes narrowing when they caught on the shallow cut along my arm and the way my chest still heaved with exertion, each breath a ragged reminder of how close we'd come.

"I'm fine," I said quickly, waving off his concern with a dismissive flick of my wrist as I swiped the back of my hand across my dirt-streaked brow. "Nothing a shower wouldn't fix. What about you?" I needed to know, needed to see for myself. I wanted to throw myself at him, wrap my arms around him and never let go.

This thing between us was more than just lust. If I had

more than a second to think about it, I might even call it ... No. There was no time. Not now.

Fuck it. I reached out and brushed my fingers against his arms, that little contact all I could allow, one little point of contact all there was to assure me he was still there, still alive.

It wasn't enough.

I wasn't sure if I imagined him leaning into my touch for just a second.

"Not relevant." He shifted his focus, his gaze moving to Reika, who had pressed herself as far back into the nearest rock wall as she could get, her bruised and battered frame trembling in the aftermath. Her wide eyes flicked frantically between me, Vyne, and Khorlar, as though she couldn't decide which of us was the bigger threat.

"Reika." My voice softened, my knife slipping back into its sheath with a practiced flick. I crouched down near her, careful to keep my movements slow and non-threatening. "Hey. You okay? It's over. We're alright." *For now.* I kept the last bit to myself.

She didn't respond at first, her gaze locked on Khorlar with an intensity that spoke volumes. He still stood silently amidst the wreckage, a stoic, unmoving sentinel, radiating an aura of contained power.

Slowly, her trembling fingers loosened their death grip on the shard of volcanic glass she still clutched. Her breathing hitched, then steadied, her arms dropping heavily into her lap as if the weight of them had suddenly become too much to bear.

I exhaled heavily, a slow release of tension that had been mounting up throughout the fight—hell, ever since we'd left Scalvaris. Progress, even if she wasn't going to accept it yet.

Khorlar's raspy voice, devoid of any emotion, finally broke

the heavy silence that had settled over us. "There'll be more. We need to move."

He was right, of course. If their scouts didn't report back, reinforcements would follow. And they would be even more determined, more cruel.

Vyne was a steadying force despite the lingering adrenaline still crackling through my system. "We can't keep going like we have," he said, his gaze flicking between Reika and me, calculating. "We need to fly."

Reika stiffened immediately, her head snapping up to meet my gaze, a flicker of renewed panic in her eyes. "No," she croaked, the sound small and broken, filled with a deep-seated terror. "He'll ... he'll drop me. He'll hurt me. He'll—"

I was about to give her reassurances that I had no way of backing up when Khorlar came up to kneel in front of her. He held out a clawed hand. "I swear on my life you will be safe." His voice was rumbly. "I have never once dropped someone. I will not today."

I thought she might scream, might cower. She looked at Khorlar like he might grow a second head. She blinked rapidly, her chest heaving with shallow, unsteady breaths. For a long, agonizing moment, I thought her fear would win. But then, her lips parted, and a soft, wavering, "Okay," escaped.

Thank you, universe, for small favors.

It took longer than I'd have liked to coax her away from the relative safety of the wall, but eventually, she moved closer, her steps stiff and reluctant, carrying her toward Khorlar.

He growled softly, a low rumble, his wings tilting as he crouched down to better position Reika against his broad, scaled frame. Her trembling hands clutched at his arms, her knuckles white as she adjusted to the unfamiliar sensation of being supported, of trusting a Drakarn.

With a powerful thrust of his legs, Khorlar launched himself into the air.

I stepped into Vyne's arms, and he did the same.

21

VYNE

HIGH CANYON WALLS concealed our resting place from above, but the narrow space would trap us if anyone tracked us on foot. The air was too still, too oppressive. A warning.

Khorlar settled Reika against a concave fold near the canyon's edge, the shadows of burnt stone forming an uncertain cradle around her. She slept fitfully, the day's strain having gutted what little strength remained. Khorlar sat sentinel beside her, his massive frame an immovable barrier.

It was a good position—secure enough to rest, with clear visibility for watching the canyon's labyrinthine offshoots. The kind of place that would have let me relax, once—before all of this.

Before her.

Selene moved ahead, careful and sure on the uneven ground. The strap of her pack dug into her shoulder, and her jaw ticked with tension. She wouldn't complain. Not aloud. But I saw.

She set the bag down but stared at it for a long moment, like she was worried it might disappear. After how far we'd come to get it, I could understand.

I approached her, my hands itching to touch, but I could

feel Khorlar's watchful eye. We needed privacy, needed a moment alone. "The canyon's clear for now. Let's find a place to bed down. Khorlar has the girl and first watch."

Selene eyed me, more intuitive than I was prepared for. She studied me like she was calculating angles, risks, vulnerabilities—not from our enemies. Mine.

"Is something wrong with right here?" she asked.

I took the opening. "My side is bothering me." The admission was clunky, but her focus snapped immediately to me.

Healer's instincts—merciful and maddening.

"Why didn't you say something sooner?"

I blew out a breath and gestured toward a side passage just ahead. The fissure was painted in an uneven glow by some mysterious reflection of the suns. "It's nothing serious."

Selene didn't respond. Words weren't necessary; her expression had already shifted to a mask of calm authority.

She followed me down the offshoot, small enough to force us to flatten against the warm stone to fit through. She didn't complain, her lips a tight line as the space opened ahead of us— a shallow alcove carved into the volcanic rock, hidden well beneath the canyon's natural shadows. Safe enough. For now.

And private.

I had to hide my grin.

"Alright," she said, dropping her pack with a muffled clink as tension cracked loose from her shoulders. She turned toward me. "Sit."

I arched a brow.

She bristled. "I mean it, Vyne. Let me see."

Shaking my head, I lowered myself onto a curved outcropping of stone and let my wings flare for balance. The warmth of the rock pressed into me, soothing muscles I wouldn't admit were aching. Her eyes flicked toward the way I held my arm against my ribs, how my wing shifted stiffly.

"Where does it hurt?" she demanded.

I flexed my arm, tilting to expose the stretch near my armpit —the shallow line of torn scales where the edge of an Ignarath talon had glanced me. The graze wasn't deep, barely more than a persistent sting and a sticky patch of dried blood. A minor wound. Negligible.

For Selene? It may as well have been catastrophic.

She sucked in a harsh breath. "Why didn't you tell me?"

"Because it wasn't relevant," I murmured, watching her.

"You're bleeding," she said flatly, daring me to argue.

"Not badly."

She huffed, pulling a small pouch from her belt. "Not the point."

The unexpected sting of her fingers brushing near the wound rattled something in me, and not from pain. She was so careful it hurt—like she assumed I'd break apart under her touch.

"It's not bad," I said at the growing line of panic in her frown. "Stop worrying."

Her lips thinned into a line as she continued, a damp cloth already pulling the stickiness of blood away from the torn scales. "Worrying's part of the job," she shot back, voice tight. "Especially when wounded warriors decide they're too tough to tell anyone about their injuries."

I almost laughed. Survival instincts choked it back.

When she finally pulled a roll of bandages from her kit, I caught her wrist lightly, fingers grazing the soft edges of her pulse. She froze, her gaze snapping to me.

"Selene." My voice dropped low, her name heavier this time. "It's nothing."

Her eyes held mine longer than they should have. The air thinned. For a brief flicker of time, the weight of the rock around us didn't press quite so hard. There was only her—brilliant, stubborn, impossible.

And, gods help me, mine.

But I let go, forcing the tips of my claws to unhook one by one. She kept watching me for a moment longer before dropping her gaze, her hands moving mechanically now as she wrapped the bandage. The heat of her fingers barely touched me. It wasn't enough.

"Done," she said, brushing residual dust from her palms and stepping back. "You should have told me sooner. What if you'd weakened during—"

"What? The flight?" I interrupted. "I would never drop you."

"You don't know that." Her tone was frustrated, her teeth worrying at her lower lip. This wasn't only a medic's training resonating beneath her skin. It was more.

I couldn't resist pushing. Couldn't resist tugging at the unspoken.

"Why does it bother you, *Zhyvarin*?" I asked.

Her breath hitched. But she didn't answer.

For all her control, all her intellect, she faltered. And the warmth it lit through me melted the last of my restraint.

My hands slid to her hips, easing her backward until her back met the rock wall. The pale glow of light painted shadows across her cheek, catching the edges of her features. For a moment, she still radiated tension—that stubborn refusal to surrender.

So I didn't give her the chance.

My mouth captured hers, and there was nothing gentle about it. This was possession, pure and unfiltered. A claiming I'd held back from for too long, and now, with her warm and alive in my arms, I could hold back no more. Her lips parted on a startled gasp, her hands gripping my shoulders, but she wasn't pushing me away.

I let the growl rumble deep in my chest, my wings flaring against the narrow confines before folding tightly back. Her heart beat against my ribs, insistent and wild, as I tilted my head to deepen the kiss, my tongue flicking past her lips.

Her taste wasn't just sweetness. No, it was spice and fire—a challenge that dared my control as much as it unraveled it. My claws flexed against her hips, careful not to pierce but tracing every soft curve beneath her clothes like map lines.

The kiss turned hungrier. My tail coiled around her ankle, the underside brushing bare flesh as it slid upward. She moaned into my mouth, low and throaty, sending lightning ripping through my control.

Restraint? Never heard of it.

Her fingers clutched the raised grooves of my scales. When her nails caught against the sensitive edges of my neck, I groaned. She wasn't shy. Not here. Not with me.

This was a firestorm.

"Selene," I said. My forehead rested against hers, sweat and heat mingling. My claws framed her shoulders, bracketing her wrists lightly against the wall. Gods, I didn't want her steady.

Her bottom lip caught between her teeth, swollen and glistening, and I had the urge to reclaim it, to lick and nip and taste until she dissolved entirely.

"Fuck," her voice was raw, eyes shining with something fiery and unreadable. "This is insane. We can't."

I let the smallest smile tug the edges of my mouth. "Then tell me to stop."

A laugh—breathless, intense—tumbled from her lips, and I pressed closer, our bodies aligning. Skin heated through fabric until there was no separation, and the delicious friction of her body against mine sent sparks rolling through every nerve.

"Say it," I demanded.

"Don't stop."

Her head tilted back against the stone, exposing her throat, the curve of it begging for a bite I wasn't sure she was ready for. My mouth found her jaw instead, tongue tracing the subtle line down to the hollow between her collarbones. Her breath hitched, the pulse beneath my lips pounding like drums.

"Vyne ... I—" Her words broke off into a whimper as my tail tightened, flexing with precision against the skin of her calf. The sound hit like fuel on an open flame. There was no going back now.

"Tell me to stop," I murmured against her skin, my voice ragged. "And I will."

Her response came in the form of her hands gripping the edges of my jaw and pulling me back to her lips with a fervent intensity. I devoured her, backing her tighter against the warm, uneven wall as my hands slid up, tracing along the curves of her waist and slipping under fabric until her skin sang against mine.

My talons carefully pulled at the offending layers of clothing, easing the fabric off. Her hands gripped my shoulders tighter, pulling herself closer as the last remnants of cloth fluttered to the ground.

"Selene," her name was a plea and worship as my mouth dropped to the exposed skin at her collarbone and down to the swell of her breast. My hands explored the softness of her curves, every ridge and hollow memorized.

I didn't give her time to retreat, to think, to argue. I didn't want her doubts. I wanted her surrender. Her trust. Her everything.

Falling to my knees was an act of reverence. And I wasn't done. Not even close.

As I kissed down her stomach, her response echoed louder in the alcove.

And gods, I wanted to hear more.

The moment my lips brushed the soft heat between her thighs, her fingers twisted into my hair. Not a protest—a demand. A claiming. Her hips arched off the wall, subtle at first, then a desperate, unashamed offering, every choked-back sound vibrating through the marrow of my bones, a siren's call I couldn't resist.

Her scent was heady and salt-edged, the familiar tang of her arousal undercut by something darker, something deep that made my fangs ache. My tongue lashed upward in one long, slow, punishing swipe.

"Fuck—Vyne!" Her thighs trembled against the sides of my head, the smooth human skin in contrast with my rough scales, as I pinned her tighter to the stone. The wet slap of my tongue plunging into her, delving deep, echoed off the canyon walls, her taste, her unique essence, bursting across my senses—burnt caramel and reckless, unyielding humanity, a combination so intoxicating it threatened to shatter my control.

She tasted like war, like survival, like Volcaryth itself—fire and resilience intertwined.

Her nails scored the sensitive ridges between my shoulder blades, a painful pleasure, drawing a sound that was more beast than Drakarn. My tail, acting on its own instinct, moved up her calf with slow, sure pressure until the tip teased the soaked, sensitive apex of her thighs.

She shattered instantly.

A silent scream ripped through her, a tremor that shook her entire frame, every muscle locking as her thighs vise-gripped my skull, holding me captive. I drank her down greedily, lapping, sucking, savoring every shudder, every drop of her essence. Her scent, intensified by her release, filled the air.

"Again," I said against her quivering, exquisitely sensitive flesh, the word a rough demand, a promise, a prayer.

My tongue speared deeper, seeking out every sensitive fold, every hidden pleasure point, until she responded, a broken, beautiful sound. Her second climax came faster, harder, severe —a wounded animal sound breaking past her clenched teeth, a testament to the raw power of her pleasure.

When her knees buckled, threatening to send her collapsing, I rose in one fluid motion, pushing down my pants without ceremony. I would have ripped them to shreds with my talons if I had another pair to spare on this journey.

The scaled base of my cock glistened under the glow of the canyon, thick, dark veins pulsing with urgent need beneath the stretched, sensitive skin as the tapered tip flexed hungrily. That traitorous, wonderfully sensitive fleshy rim peeled back, revealing the flushed, engorged slit beneath—already oozing the thick, musky fluid that would brand her; a silent, invisible claim.

Her eyes darkened, pupils swallowing irises whole, leaving only pools of desire. A deep hunger mirrored my own.

"I need you," she breathed, the words a ragged plea, a challenge, an invitation.

The last thread of restraint snapped.

I hauled her legs around my hips, her soft human skin sliding against my scaled thighs, the contrast a delicious torment, my tip nudging her entrance with possessive, sure pressure. She was still spasming from her last peak, her body clenching around nothing—needy, desperate, exquisitely sensitive. The sight, the feel of her pulsing heat, nearly undid me, threatening to send me spiraling over the edge before I'd even fully claimed her.

"Watch," I commanded, my voice a low rumble, my thumb

hooking her chin, forcing her gaze downward. "Watch what I do to you, *Zhyvarin.*"

Her wrecked sound vibrated through every scale, every nerve ending. That flared, sensitive rim of my cock stretched her obscenely, the overstimulated nerves making her scramble for purchase against my shoulders, her fingers digging in. Inch by brutal, agonizing inch, I seated myself, pushing, stretching, filling her, until the scaled base of my shaft kissed her swollen flesh.

Her eyelids fluttered, a soft sound escaping her lips. "So ... fucking ... big—"

"You take it. All of it. You're mine, *Zhyvarin.* Made for this. Made for me."

Her answering grin was pure rebellion, a flash of the fierce, resilient spirit that had drawn me to her. She rolled her hips, taking me deeper, accepting me fully.

The world went red with untamed need.

I pistoned into her without mercy, each powerful snap of my hips slamming her into the volcanic rock. That serpentine ridge along my cock's underside stroked against her internal walls with every slow, sure withdrawal.

"*Zhyvarin,*" I said, my breath hot against her sweat-slick throat, the word a prayer. "Mine. Mine. Always mine."

Her teeth sank into my shoulder as her climax took her. And I responded, a deep sound of release, slamming home one final, earth-shattering time. My release surged into her, claiming her from the inside out.

We hung there, suspended—her trembling legs locked around my waist, my hands embedded in the stone above her head, holding her, claiming her, possessing her. The musky, potent scent of our joining, of our mingled scents, clung to the air.

Somewhere beyond our ragged, uneven breaths, I heard

Khorlar make a sound—a warning, a reminder of the world outside, of the dangers that still lurked.

Reality crashed back, unwelcome, intrusive.

But for now, none of it mattered.

My forehead pressed to hers. Selene's grip on my shoulders loosened, her fingers tracing lazy, aimless patterns across my scales, each touch a spark against my cooling skin.

I shifted, easing my weight, but not breaking the connection. Not yet. My tail unwound from her, the tip lingering to brush a slow, sure path down her spine, a silent promise. Her answering shiver was involuntary.

"You ..." she began, her voice hoarse, uneven, the word trailing off as her eyes fluttered closed.

Exhaustion finally claimed her, a heavy weight settling over her features, softening the hard edges of her spirit. Watching her sleep, vulnerable and utterly spent in my arms, something shifted. The possessive fire still burned, but it was tempered, edged with a tenderness I hadn't known I was capable of.

"You're my mate, *Zhyvarin*," I whispered.

My confession was lost to the stillness, unheard by the one person who needed to hear it. She was oblivious to the weight of the truth I'd finally acknowledged.

The irony stung. I'd spent weeks, months even, fighting this connection, fearing the consequences, the chaos it could unleash. And now, when I'd finally surrendered, when I'd finally embraced the undeniable truth ... she couldn't even hear me.

It didn't matter. We'd be home in Scalvaris soon. She'd be safe in my quarters, in my bed, soon enough. It took almost no effort for me to imagine her on my sleeping slab, hair spread out around her, the space somehow bending to her will.

Carefully, I eased us down, settling her against the curved outcropping of volcanic rock where I'd sat earlier. Her head lolled against my shoulder, her dark hair spilling across my chest. She murmured something unintelligible, a soft, sleepy sound that tugged at something deep within.

I wrapped my arms around her in a protective embrace, my wings shielding her from any threat. I would protect her. I would fight for her. I would do whatever it took to keep her safe, to keep her by my side.

She was my mate.

And I wasn't letting her go.

22

SELENE

EVERYTHING ON VOLCARYTH was designed to kill. Knowing that didn't make breathing any easier.

Worse was the rhythm around me. Vyne's wingbeats. Steady. Unyielding. With every stroke, the pressure of his body shifted. I was cradled against his chest, his scaled arms locked around me. My brain told me I was safe. My stupid human, survival-instinct brain disagreed.

And I was trying—desperately—to survive my own mind.

His warmth clung to me. I swore I could still smell him on me. And my body ached in all the places that reminded me just what we'd done together. Vyne was life and danger wrapped in one unbearable pull, and after last night ...

Fuck.

The memory of his lips, his touch—of the way we'd fit together—made my heart kick against my ribs. Sparks of what we'd shared still crackled where the tips of his claws brushed my side. I wanted nothing more than to lie back down with him and stay lost in the pleasure.

But then the weight returned: what I *should* have been doing. The vyrathis. The healers. The hollow-eyed, rasping bodies in the healing caverns. I'd lost hours with Vyne. Hours we could have been flying back. And now, with the precious container of vyrathis tucked in my pack, every second screamed at me. Time we didn't have.

It didn't matter that both Vyne and Khorlar had made it clear we couldn't fly at night, that they needed to rest their wings.

We could rest when the healers weren't dying.

The thought made my chest tighten, and I shifted. His arms locked firmer, claws coiling protectively under the curve of my back. "Don't wriggle," he growled, voice low against the wind. "Unless you want to test how good I am at catching humans mid-fall."

I kept my tone dry. "I wasn't planning on taking any dives. How much farther?"

Vyne's eyes narrowed. "Not long," he said. "We'll be able to enter through one of the sky shafts from this approach. No need to climb through the tunnels."

Ahead, Khorlar flew steadily, massive gray wings militaristic in their precision. They didn't falter, even with the human shape clinging weakly to his broad chest.

Reika.

From my position, she looked impossibly small, a curled shadow cradled against Khorlar's scaled arms. The pale streak of her skin was faint against the muted gray of his leathers. But even from a distance, I could see the shaking. Her wrists trembled, and her head slumped awkwardly. Exhaustion had her in a chokehold, and the rough lines of fever were unmistakable.

I should have done something for it before we left. The red streaks webbed around the cuts on her arms and shoulders— delicate but dangerous threads that coiled inward. Infection. Her breathing, too shallow, too labored, told me enough.

It wasn't the sickness plaguing the healers. This was

simpler, caused by exhaustion and dirt. But it could be just as deadly.

One crisis at a time, Selene. Deal with the healers first.

A shift in the air cut through my thoughts. The wind grew sharper, warmer, as we descended through the narrow sky shaft that would take us into Scalvaris.

Vyne angled his wings, leaning into the wind as he adjusted our trajectory. My stomach flipped as the updrafts pushed against us. Every muscle in Vyne's body tensed as we veered closer.

"It's safe?" The edge in my voice was unavoidable.

Vyne's lips twitched. "I'd hardly take you down here if it wasn't."

I hated that I liked the quiet authority in his voice.

Khorlar shifted positions, descending faster, his broad gray wings slicing through the heat. He landed heavily just ahead of us, raised claws creating a protective barrier as Reika shifted weakly.

A sick, horrible sound rasped from her throat.

The second I was on solid ground, I rushed to Khorlar.

"Get her straight to the healing caverns," I snapped. Duty cleared my mind. "She's burning up."

Khorlar's gaze was steady. He said nothing, simply turning toward the nearest corridor and carrying her away.

Vyne touched my arm. "Selene, I—"

"No," I couldn't do this now, whatever it was. "The vyrathis first." Vyne and I ... there was something there. Something real. I wanted it so bad it hurt. But I could deal with the delay. Delaying our mission meant death for the healers.

Emotions had to come later.

The passageways narrowed, the unbroken stone brushing against my arms as I ducked low into the heat of the city. But my pace didn't falter, even as the familiar glow of heat crystals guided me. My mind stayed locked on the bodies waiting below.

Waiting. Fighting. Clinging to the edge of existence.

I couldn't fail them.

When we reached the healing caverns, it felt like death. The thick, acrid scent of sickness pooled, mingling with the tang of sweaty bodies and burnt herbs. It was worse than I remembered.

Rachel and Kaiya were in the center, heads bent over one of the makeshift tables overflowing with vials and crushed plant matter. Smudged lines of exhaustion painted Rachel's features, dark shadows pooling beneath her eyes.

Kaiya's hands flew between a mortar and pestle, crushing something with frantic energy, her curls plastered damp and flat against her temples. They were both close to collapsing— two women, stretched far beyond their limits, but still fighting.

A choked cough from a nearby bed drew my focus. One of the healers—a broad-shouldered Drakarn male—shook violently, his once-brilliant red scales dull and marred with dark, web-like veins. His breathing was shallow, punctuated by strained, wet gasps.

I looked to the other beds. The sight sent a sharp twist deep into my chest. The healers were crumbling. The same spread of bruises marred every weak body. Wings hung limp. Mysha's bed was at the far end, her breathing low and weak, but, thank god, steady. She still had a chance.

"Selene!" Rachel's voice cut through the haze. Her relief was visible. "Tell me you have it."

I swung the pack off my back, setting it on the table with a thud that made Kaiya jump, though her hands kept working. "Yes. Here."

Rachel's hands were on it instantly, pulling the container

free with care, her fingers quick. For all her exhaustion, she moved with practiced precision.

"How much did you find?" Rachel asked. Her words were coated in cautious hope.

"I hope it's enough."

Rachel nodded in sharp agreement, already moving to prepare the medicine. Another cough dragged my attention to the far side of the cavern, where a younger healer thrashed weakly.

My gut clenched.

Behind me, Vyne cleared his throat. Of course, always watching, always steady, always too near and too far. His presence loomed, an anchor I couldn't let drag me down. Not now.

"You need rest, *Zhyvarin*," Vyne said quietly. "Let's go to our quarters."

Our quarters?

What?

His words landed, and my brain stuttered. I snapped my gaze to him. "Our quarters?" My voice came out ragged. "What are you talking about?"

We'd slept together twice. Since when did that mean living together? Or was I jumping to conclusions? A week on the surface of Volcaryth had nearly knocked me out, and relief now was mixed with exhaustion. Whatever Vyne was saying, I was probably misunderstanding. We were just ... hell, I didn't know.

You know it's more than that.

I shoved the thought away.

His wings shifted. He spoke low but steady, each syllable careful. "You need rest. You've done enough. More than enough. Come home with me."

A bitter laugh clawed up my throat. "Enough? You honestly think this is enough?" My hands jerked up, motioning toward the rows of beds. Drakarn lay on them, motionless or writhing, their breaths rasping. "In case you haven't noticed, they're still dying, Vyne. Until that stops, nothing is enough."

The truth scraped my throat, but I didn't care.

Tension rippled through him, though his voice remained calm. Too calm. "I'm not telling you to stop," he replied slowly. Measured. "But even you know you can't pour from an empty vessel. You need rest. You need time to—"

"To what?" Anger flared, hot and sharp. "Rest? Recuperate? Learn to live with failure while I sit back and watch them die?" The words tumbled out, and I couldn't pull them back.

His gaze dropped, briefly, to my hands. The tremble betrayed me. I curled my fingers into fists.

"You're my mate," he said, softer now, but the word shook me to my core. "I won't let you burn yourself out."

Mate. Mate. Mate. It seemed to echo off the walls around us.

"Stop." The word came fast, sharp, exploding from somewhere deep in me. My voice cracked. I didn't mean it to come out that way—cold and rough—but it was the only thing I had. A shield. "Just stop. Please."

The tension between us shifted. He stilled, expression hardening, his wings pulling close to his body. His eyes—so sharp, so unrelenting—found mine again. He didn't falter.

"You're mine." It was a declaration.

Those words—those two damn words—crushed me.

Shock surged up, tangling with everything else I'd shoved down—fear, exhaustion, anger, grief. How could he say that? How could he just ... drop this on me *now*, here, surrounded by dying healers? How could he say *mine* as though it wasn't going to rip me open?

"I—"

There was too much. Too much to feel, too much to think,

and no space for anything in the middle of this crisis. My chest tightened, and I tore my gaze from his, desperate to focus on anything else.

This didn't make sense.

But my body knew otherwise. Even as fear and doubt trembled through my limbs, I felt a steady beating in my chest. Something undeniable. And I hated it. I hated how it pulled.

"I can't do this," I bit out. My hands clenched, nails digging crescents into my palms. "Not now. I can't—"

Vyne stepped closer, his movements careful, as if I was something fragile. "You're overwhelmed," he said low, a hint of a growl threading his voice. "But I'm not wrong. I know you feel it."

I shook my head, hard. I needed to stop this, stop him. "Don't call me that—your mate. I can't—"

"You *are*." His tone unraveled me further. "You've been mine from the moment I first saw you. This," he gestured between us, "is too strong to ignore. I've tried."

Every muscle tensed. Fight or flight screamed in tandem, and yet, I couldn't do either.

Because he wasn't backing down. He wasn't walking away. And that terrified me more than anything.

But there was no room for this. Not now. Not here. Not when my responsibilities threatened to crush me.

Someone cleared their throat. Kaiya was standing a few paces behind us. Her face was pale, her shoulders tight. "Sorry to interrupt," she said tightly, her eyes briefly flicking between me and Vyne. "Selene, I need your help. Rachel needs a second set of hands preparing the vyrathis extract so we can start administering it ASAP."

She didn't have to say more.

"Of course," I replied, stepping toward her. My priorities

were crystal clear. I shot Vyne a glance over my shoulder. "Go," I told him. "I ... We'll ..."

I had no idea what I was supposed to say.

Vyne tensed, but he didn't argue. And with one last lingering look that burned, he turned and left.

Kaiya seemed to shrink in on herself. "Thank god you're here," she muttered, already rushing back toward the central table.

I threw myself into the work. It was that or think of Vyne. And if I did that, I might actually go crazy.

23

VYNE

NIGHT HAD SETTLED over the makeshift infirmary, but no rest came with it—only a thick, stifling heaviness that pressed in, as though the stone around us devoured every flicker of hope. That same oppressive feeling slithered beneath my scales and knotted in my chest.

I carefully removed a half-formed metal clamp from the forge, its heated grip making my claws tingle. This was the fifth clamp I'd made in the last hour. They were simple and a little crude, but maybe they'd save lives.

Usually I'd craft weapons there—blades to fight things with teeth and claws. Now, I was shaping medical tools that Selene and the healers needed to survive.

Once the clamp had cooled in a bucket of water, I slung it with a few others in the crook of my arm and set off down the corridor. Darkness pressed close in these tunnels, broken only by the sullen glow of heat crystals embedded in the rock. My steps fell into a determined rhythm, matching the tension in my thoughts.

I'd already cursed myself a hundred times for how I'd handled our arrival back to Scalvaris. This wasn't much, but I would give her what help I could, show her that I knew just how important she was. To the city.

And to me.

When I entered the infirmary, it was the usual sight of cramped beds and tired faces, human and Drakarn alike. The air felt thicker than the forge's blaze—clogged with infection, antiseptics, exhaustion. A few Drakarn, sporting half-mended scales, dozed or stared off in silence. Human healers bustled quietly, measuring powders, boiling water, checking pulses.

Selene stood across the room, tending to a bronze-scaled Drakarn who looked dangerously fragile. She leaned in, gently pressing a cloth to a reopened wound at his neck. There was a careful tenderness in her movements, but I saw how stiffly she held herself.

I ached to cross the room, to help. To pick her up and *make* her rest. But I held back. She glanced up, looked at me, and then away as if I wasn't there at all.

Kaiya beckoned me over to a table crowded with half-empty bowls, jars, and fresh bandages. The pungent smell of herbs stung my nostrils. She clutched a mortar and pestle, her eyes dark with fatigue. When I placed the clamps on the table, she gave me a weary smile.

"How many more can you make?" she asked.

"As many as you need."

She nodded. "We'll need plenty. Anything you've got, really."

I only nodded. My gaze slid to where Selene was gathering supplies near a cracked crate. Her hair was falling out of the string she'd used to tie it back. Even from there, I saw fresh shadows under her eyes. She rose and walked toward us with purpose, looking at me once, so briefly I might have imagined it.

"Are those the new clamps?" she asked Kaiya. I might as well have not existed.

Kaiya gestured at the metal pieces. "Yes—Vyne just brought them."

Selene lifted one of the clamps, working the hinge with her fingers. For a second, I thought I saw approval in her eyes. Then her expression went flat. "They'll do." She set the clamp back onto the table and marched off. My chest tightened at the dismissal.

This was worse than I thought.

A fit of coughing erupted nearby, sharp and grating. One of the sick—an older male I recognized but couldn't name—lurched in his bed.

Selene was already moving. "Kaiya, get me a clamp—and more bandages, quickly!" She rushed over, fear barely masked behind focus.

I was right on her heels, crossing the space in a single stride. "I've got him," I said, bracing the convulsing Drakarn's upper body. His tail flailed dangerously near Selene, and I tightened my grip, trying to keep her out of harm's way. My own tail shot out, wrapping with his and wrangling it down like we were wrestling.

The smell of blood tainted the air; the Drakarn's wound spurted a fresh stream of foul fluid. Selene pressed her hand to his cheek. "Easy," she soothed, though I could see the fear in her eyes. "You're tearing your wound wider. Let us help you."

He roared again, but his voice cracked, the delirium looking painfully close to panic. Claws raked the air, nearly catching my arm. I shifted, tucking one arm under his and gripping tight so Selene could work.

Kaiya dashed back with bandages. Selene snatched them, her face set in fierce concentration. She juggled disinfectant and the clamp, pressing the wound's edges together while the Drakarn bucked. My arms trembled with the force of holding him.

"Stay still," I growled into his ear. He gave another ragged bellow, head snapping back against my shoulder.

Selene finally fitted the clamp into place, securing the torn flesh. The male let out a guttural groan, his body dropping from fevered tension to exhausted stillness. "Almost done," she whispered, grabbing a suture kit and stitching around the clamp's edges. Her touch was deft, every movement swift but precise. When she finished, she exhaled, pressing one hand over his wound to keep the clamp from slipping.

I let out a long breath, easing my hold. The Drakarn sagged onto the cot with a weak moan. Blood matted my forearm—mine or his, I didn't know. My shoulder stung from the line of fresh cuts, but I barely noticed it. I was too busy watching Selene.

Her eyes lifted to meet mine. For an instant, we were the only two people in the room. "Thank you," she said.

A ripple of something like longing passed between us. The moment cracked, and she pulled away, dabbing blood from her hands as she spoke to Kaiya. Without another word, she slipped into the corridor to wash. My entire body hummed with tension. I wanted to follow her, demand she let me hold her, comfort her, take her away from this place. But the braced line of her shoulders was a warning: not now.

Kaiya gave me a quick nod before turning back to the patient. The healing caverns settled down as the crisis ebbed, leaving me with nothing to do but stare at the space where Selene had disappeared.

Anger churned in me that I couldn't fix this, that I couldn't protect her from any more pain. She needed room to breathe. All I wanted was to shield her from the world so she could.

The glow of crystals lit my path back to the small, stuffy forge. A half-finished anvil sat waiting, flickers of heat dancing over the coals. I moved toward it, hammer in hand. Work was the one thing I could do without question, the one way I could still stand beside Selene—indirectly if not literally.

Drawing a deep breath, I plunged a fresh bar of steel into the embers, coaxing the orange glow until the metal softened. I withdrew it with a pair of tongs and laid it on the anvil. Sparks flew at my first strike, bright motes that collapsed before hitting the ground. My muscles ached from overuse, sweat already slicking my scales. But I kept swinging, forging a tool this time —a delicate, curved retractor that Selene and Kaiya might use to hold tissue in place for sutures. If I could improve even one procedure, maybe Selene would suffer fewer nightmares of watching her patients bleed out.

Each blow of the hammer became a vow: I would do everything in my power to prove I was more than trouble and hunger. I'd stand beside her, bolster her when she wavered. If the best I could do was to twist steel into useful shapes, then I'd do it until my arms failed. In this hush, I made a promise to her, to us, even if she didn't hear it right now.

If she needed space, I'd give it. If she needed time, I'd wait. But I would not vanish.

I placed another steel bar into the coals. I wasn't stopping until dawn. That was the one thing that felt certain: keep forging, keep giving, keep proving. No matter how many blows it took.

24

SELENE

I PACED through the makeshift infirmary, boots scraping softly across uneven stone. Somewhere in my mind, Vyne's voice kept replaying like an echo stuck on repeat.

"You're mine."

I tried to pretend I had everything under control, but that declaration rattled inside me, refusing to fade.

The Drakarn's ragged breathing pulled my attention back to the present. Their condition was improving, but each breath still sounded like it fought through a layer of sickness that didn't fully want to let go. The vyrathis extract had helped stabilize them— enough that their labored wheezing wasn't quite so ominous—but it wasn't a miracle. We had to wait for healing to happen naturally.

I hated leaning on hope that felt so fragile.

I stopped by Mysha's cot, checking her temperature with the back of my hand. The soft glimmer of her scales was reassuring. She felt hot, but not feverish. Her chest rose and fell in a steadier rhythm than yesterday, but there was still a long way to go.

I exhaled slowly, letting my hand drop back to my side. The memory of Vyne heated my thoughts. His gaze, his strong grip.

I was trying to push those feelings aside, but each time I remembered the slow burn in his eyes, my stomach fluttered traitorously.

Now was *not* the time for that. These people needed me focused. I shook my head, forcing my mind to return to the scene in front of me.

Then there was Reika

She looked so small in a space intended for towering Drakarn warriors. Her breathing was shallow but steady, and her forehead glistened with fresh sweat. At least the fever was no longer raging like it had been. She didn't stir when I approached.

But I wasn't her only visitor.

Khorlar watched her with a stillness that made my skin prickle. I swallowed, unsure if I should say anything. The hush in the cavern was almost loud in a strange way, and I didn't want to disturb it.

Khorlar rose in one swift motion, ignoring me outright, and marched away, tall frame melting into the shadows near the exit.

What was he even doing there in the first place?

I kneaded my temple with my thumb before lowering myself at Reika's side. Gingerly, I brushed a damp lock of hair off her forehead. Her breathing hitched under my touch, though she didn't wake. Dull purple bruises mottled her arms. I hated to think of what had been done to her.

The hush abruptly broke as distant footsteps raced toward us. The way they thudded—a rapid, uneven cadence—made the fine hairs on my neck rise. Kira lurched into the healing cavern, looking winded and wild-eyed.

I stood and took a step toward her, worry punching through my own exhaustion. "Is everything okay?"

Her gaze darted from bed to bed. She didn't respond to me; I'm not even sure she saw me.

"Where is she?" Kira's voice rang through the cavern, cutting through the moan of the sick and stirring an uneasy flutter among the Drakarn who weren't fully unconscious. "Where's Larissa?"

Her eyes were frantic. "Kira," I edged closer, "who are you looking for?" But I had a sick feeling in my stomach. I already knew.

Kira's chest heaved, words tumbling out almost incoherently. "My sister. They said there was another human. That you found someone. Where—"

Then she spotted Reika. The color drained from Kira's face as she hurried over, dropping to her knees with a raw cry. My pulse stuttered. I'd never seen someone's heart break right in front of me before.

"No," she gasped, voice dissolving in a half-sob, half-denial. "No, no, no—"

She gripped Reika's arms, as though if she held on tightly enough, Reika might become the sister she was so desperately wishing for. Her one wrenching sob tore at my gut. I stepped in behind Kira and crouched down.

"I'm sorry." It felt so hollow.

Tears rolled unchecked down her face. "I thought if I just kept hoping ..." Her voice broke, and she bowed her head until her forehead touched the edge of the cot. "She's dead, isn't she? They're all dead."

My own heart twisted. "We can't know that," I said, as gentle as I could manage. "But maybe Reika can tell us what she knows. When she wakes up."

There was no telling if Reika had been on the same ship we'd been on. It made sense. How many ways were there for humans to end up on Volcaryth? But jumping to conclusion could give Kira false hope. And she was already on the edge of falling apart.

She sniffed, nodding in a jerky motion, tears still brimming in her eyes. Slowly, she loosened her hold on Reika. Just as she was getting herself steady, a new presence disrupted the quiet.

Vega entered in her usual brash fashion, scanning the rows of beds with a quick, sweeping look. "So we found another human. The guys in charge are going to *love* that."

I was already bracing myself. "Not now, Vega."

She raised an eyebrow, glancing at me and then at Kira's hunched form. "Don't get your hackles up. Am I the only one that remembers that we're here on sufferance? Or did you forget how they almost killed Orla for a bit of accidental trespassing? As far as they're concerned, more humans equal more trouble. I'm trying to keep us alive here."

Kira rose unsteadily, turning on Vega. "If you're so eager for doom and gloom, go preach it somewhere else," she snapped. "We don't need you making everyone feel worse."

Vega's eyes flicked over her. She looked as though she might lob a retort but then seemed to think better of it. An uneasy shrug took over her stance. "Fine. But this place is a powder keg waiting for a spark."

I pinched the bridge of my nose, a headache nudging its way behind my eyes. "Let's just not," I said, keeping my tone level through sheer force of will. "We can't afford it." I hesitated, then exhaled. "Why are you even here, Vega?"

"I'm a helper, didn't you know? I've been in here every day, cleaning up unspeakable messes and trying to keep the dragon-monsters alive." Her face wrinkled in distaste.

"Let's not call our patients monsters." I dreaded to consider her bedside manner.

Vega shrugged and walked off to get started with her shift. I didn't try to stop her. She had an attitude, but we needed the hands.

The silence she left behind felt loaded, all the more claustrophobic in the dim light. Kira gave me a look so full of exhaustion that I felt another wave of guilt rising.

Kira brushed her knuckles across her damp cheeks. Anger and sorrow mingled in her eyes. "Let me know if she says anything about Larissa."

I nodded. "I promise."

Without another word, she spun on her heel and headed for the exit. My heart ached for her—and for all of us, really. We were trapped beneath this mountain, clinging to uncertain alliances and half-fixes.

I looked at Reika. She was still, aside from the movement of her breathing. Then my own doubts started circling—and inevitably, my thoughts landed on Vyne. I told myself I was just tired, but even the mention of his name in my head made something hot twist in my gut.

I stood there, fists clenched, letting the memory of *"You're mine"* pound against the inside of my skull.

He had the shittiest timing on Earth. Or, well, Volcaryth.

What would happen if I gave in? If I let myself believe? My stomach knotted, torn between wanting him in some undeniable way and knowing I shouldn't risk it—not now, with so much chaos.

I owed Orla an apology. Looking back, my advice to her about her situation with her own Drakarn warrior felt glib. I'd even joked about wanting one of my own.

I had no idea what that meant.

"Are we going to talk about it?" I nearly jumped out of my seat when Kaiya's question lashed me like a whip.

"The healers are doing better. We can figure out Reika's

situation once she's up." There was so much to do and not enough hands, but we were making do. "Is Rachel sleeping?"

"I hope so, but come on, Selene." She sat down on a stool beside me and gave me a *look*. "You slept here last night. Are you hiding from Mr. Tall, Green, and Obsessed with you?"

Yes.

No.

I didn't know.

I groaned. "Can we not? Please."

"Are you one of those people who solves everyone else's problems while letting your own fester?" she asked, diagnosing me faster than any therapist back on Earth.

"I'm one of those people who doesn't let others die because I have issues in my personal life." It felt like a weak retort, but I didn't have anything else.

Kaiya stared at me, waiting for me to break.

I wouldn't. I was stronger than that. I didn't need to vent. I could handle this on my own.

Who was I kidding?

"We barely know each other. The mission was all stress and excitement and ... fuck if I know. And now he's telling me I'm his mate, as if I have time to deal with that while all of *this* is happening." I spread my hand out, gesturing towards the healing Drakarn. "What was he thinking?"

"Oh, no, you're totally right on that part. His timing sucks. But I saw the way he looked at you. He wasn't lying."

"I know that!" I clamped my mouth shut, like that might call back the words.

If I knew all that, why was I stressing?

I groaned. "Do you have any advice, or are you just going to ask pointed questions?"

"You don't need advice, just a little kick in the ass. Our lives are completely messed up. It's not like any of this was planned. So maybe embrace the good stuff?"

Before I could say more, she patted me on the shoulder and walked away to tend to one of the moaning healers.

I didn't want to obsess over Vyne. I didn't want to think about what it meant if I was his mate.

The problem was, I couldn't stop.

With a grunt, I got up and walked away from Reika and resumed checking the other beds. Mysha stirred under my hand, blinking in brief confusion before drifting back into sleep. I listened for any trace of that deep, hacking rasp that had haunted them all before, but it seemed to be fading. Hope flickered inside me, fragile but alive.

After finishing my rounds, I tipped my head from side to side, stretching until my spine popped. The oppressive space pressed in. It smelled like damp stone and stale air, and the walls felt closer than they had hours ago. I needed to leave this ward, if only for a few minutes.

But as I leaned against the wall, the rasping coughs of the healers echoed in my ears, and under that were Vyne's unforgettable words.

You're mine.

25

VYNE

THE FORGE ROARED AND GLOWED. Familiar heat pressed against my lungs, each breath thick and laced with iron tang. The hammer in my hand rose and fell in a vicious rhythm, a metallic heartbeat echoing through the stone. Each strike against the battered blade on the anvil should have eased the discord growing inside me.

It didn't.

My arms burned from fatigue, sweat coursing over my scales, but I couldn't stop. Every swing was a question I couldn't answer, a frustration I couldn't name. If I kept hammering, maybe I could outrun the regret that gnawed at the corners of my mind:

Selene.

She was everything I'd never asked for—fury, a spark, and a fragile softness all tangled in one. The memory of her lived in every breath, every flare of muscle. A storm I couldn't calm and didn't want to. But that storm had pulled away, and the fear of losing her forever lodged deep in me, more suffocating than the forge's heat.

It was all my own damned fault. Some need had possessed me to claim her then and there, as if exhaustion hadn't weighed heavy on us, as if Selene hadn't spent the last several days, all edges frayed with worry for the healers.

I drove the hammer down harder, as though I could pound answers from the metal. Sparks ricocheted in orange bursts, scattering into the air. The steel warped beneath each blow, but no matter how many times I struck, the chaos in me only grew.

A heavy presence filled the doorway behind me before he spoke. I knew who it was by the slow scrape of his talons against stone, by the weight in the air that always announced him. Khorlar.

"You'll ruin the blade," he observed, his deep voice steady. "Or yourself."

I scowled, not taking my eyes off the battered metal. "I can fix it."

"Can you?"

Clenching my jaw, I lifted the hammer again. The strike was so forceful it jarred my shoulder. A rough growl tore from my chest. "Why are you here?"

Khorlar folded his massive arms across his dark-gray scales. "Because I'd rather not see you destroy good steel."

I barked a short laugh. "Close your eyes, then."

Silence thickened, punctuated only by the clang of metal. My wings twitched, restless, but I forced myself to keep going. I couldn't stop, or I'd feel too much.

"Is this about the human?" Khorlar asked, finally.

My grip tightened around the hammer, claws scraping against the worn handle. "She has a name."

He inclined his head, unruffled by my sharp tone. "Selene," he corrected. "Another human mate?"

I slammed the hammer down, and the blade cracked under the impact. I tossed the hammer and the ruined blade aside.

"You don't know a damned thing about it."

He let out a low snort. "I haven't suggested that I do."

Fury flared, but I caught myself. This wasn't just anger—it was fear, an old enemy wearing a new face. "She made her desires, or lack thereof, very clear."

"Do you think that sound doesn't carry in a canyon? Because what I heard wasn't a lack of desire."

He was lucky I'd dropped the hammer. Rage flared hot and fast. He had *no right* to hear what sounds my mate made when I gave her pleasure, no right to intrude or say a word about it.

My heart thumped in a ragged rhythm, answering a call deeper than logic. Selene was mine—even if she doubted it.

"Leave me." I didn't need his prying or his opinion. Khorlar had no love for the humans, and if he spoke one sour word about my mate, I'd be forced to test the ruined blade sitting in the discard pile.

He hesitated for a moment before doing as I asked.

I closed my eyes and swallowed hard. I was hitting the wrong target. No amount of metal would shape itself into glass. Thunder rumbled in me, a pulse of longing that tasted like desperation.

Sweat dripped from my brow, the forge's heat melding with the searing temperature of my own blood. My temples pounded, but this time, I let the ache in, forced myself to feel it. If I was going to fight for Selene, I needed every ounce of pain, every shred of need. This bond was stupid, maddening, and the only thing that felt real.

My heart lurched as her scent tickled my nose. I thought it was a phantom at first, but she stood in the doorway, haloed by the forge's angry glow.

She looked exhausted—hair tousled, worry lines carved into her brow—but her gaze was steady on mine. She smelled like the healing caverns: herbs, sweat, and under it all was just *her*. Something I wanted to drown in.

Selene and I stood there, the forge sputtering sparks that

died in the hush between us. When she finally spoke, her voice had the rough scrape of resolve and heartbreak. "I think we should talk."

I forced a breath, setting my shoulders. "All right," I managed.

Everything in me wanted to yank her close and demand she believe that she was mine, that I'd keep her safe. But I held back. I had to.

It was hell.

Her arms were wrapped around herself like a shield. The light highlighted the tired circles beneath her eyes. I hated knowing I was part of why they were there.

"Yesterday ...," she said softly, "Vyne, I—" she huffed out a breath. "We've known each other for a week, and you tried to take over my life like you owned it."

My immediate instinct was to argue. I dug my fangs into my tongue until I tasted copper. I wouldn't mess this up again. Not now. Not with her.

She swallowed hard. "My entire life flipped on its head the second I ended up here. And every time I think I'm adjusting, something else breaks under my feet. Everyone freaked the fuck out with Orla and Rath. And don't think I haven't heard what people whisper about Darrokar and Terra. You and I, it's ..."

"It's real." I wasn't going to push, but I couldn't let this go. "I told myself to stay away. I tried. Gods below, I tried." I took half a step forward and forced myself to stop. "Do you think I want to bring trouble to you?"

I could almost taste the fear behind her anger, the vulnerability she tried so hard to hide. My claws twitched, itching to grab her and prove how real it was. But I'd come too close before, only to see her shut down from the weight of it.

I stepped forward until only a breath separated us. Softly, I cupped her chin, forcing her gaze up to mine. "I'm your mate, *Zhyvarin*," I said, letting every thread of truth coil in my voice. "It means someone in this gods-forsaken world will fight for you, bleed for you ... die for you, if that's what it takes."

Her lip quivered, and for a moment, I was sure she'd bolt. But she stayed.

"The others need me," she whispered, as if it were an apology. "I can't allow myself to be distracted, not when people are dying, when—"

"Selene," her name was a vow. "I don't want to strip you of your responsibilities. I just want to stand beside you while you fulfill them. Let me."

Emotions flickered over her face: anger, hope ... terror. One by one, they warred for dominance. Finally, she dropped her head, breath shuddering. "I'm not sure how," she murmured. "And now, you're telling me to open up ... That you want me as what, exactly?"

"Everything," I breathed. "I want everything."

Before I could stop myself, I dropped to my knees, the motion swift and sure, every last shred of control leaving me as I knelt in front of her. My hands moved to frame her hips, steady but reverent, claws curling under against the soft fabric of her clothes without piercing—without risking breaking her.

She deserved better than my fire. But I couldn't stop offering it to her.

"What will it take to make you mine?"

Her eyes widened. But she didn't run. With a single exhale, it seemed like she let go of something heavy. "I think ..." Her words came quietly, voice hitching. "I think I've been yours for a while now, whether I liked it or not."

The heat in my chest flared brighter, roaring hot and unrelenting as though she'd poured molten steel into my ribs. Her confession settled deep in the raw places I'd been trying desperately to keep from fracturing further. It wasn't an admission; it was a collision—a force slamming into me with the weight of all the words she hadn't said before.

For the first time in weeks, the fire inside me didn't feel like it was trying to hollow me out. It felt like fuel.

"Then stay," I said softly, my voice hoarse but unwavering. The words cut low from the depths of my chest, layers of feeling I'd long buried spilling freely now. "Stay with me."

Her lips trembled, a breathless exhale escaping before she dropped to her knees, her hands finally reaching for me. And gods help me, the way she touched me—light but certain, like she was still deciding if she should've claimed me sooner—ignited the only answer I had left.

Mine.

Always mine.

The forge roared hotter around us, and I embraced the burn.

26

SELENE

IT WAS hard to tell if the room itself was hot or if Vyne was the one heating it. Probably both.

His room was buried deep in Scalvaris—some hybrid of a forge, a bedroom, and an artist's den. Not far from where I stood, a broad stone slab topped with silks served as a bed. If I looked too long at it, my heart started hammering.

But Vyne was the main attraction.

He was standing near the center of the room, wings half-furled, glancing my way with this tension that made me think of coiled springs. His scales caught the light, shimmering in that dark-green shade that reminded me of polished emeralds. Though he wasn't moving, he was brimming with energy—a wildfire held behind a flimsy barrier.

He didn't say a word. Didn't have to. I knew exactly what he was waiting for, and I realized I'd been waiting just as desperately. My feet closed the distance between us, while inside me, everything seemed to stutter and surge at once.

He met me halfway, wings curving around in a slow sweep that made my breath catch. It was intimate—those tough, scaled membranes forming a secluded world for just the two of us.

One of his hands rose, thumb brushing my jaw. A quick spark lit my nerve endings, and my focus tunneled in on him alone.

I wanted to say something—anything—but my mind was too tangled by the intensity in his gaze. His breath fanned across my cheek, warm as the forge's embers, and my lips parted in anticipation before he moved. Then he was there, leaning in, claiming my mouth in a single, searing kiss that stole the last of my composure.

That first contact struck like lightning—pure, charged need. My eyes fluttered shut as tingles raced from the press of his lips to the tips of my fingers. I clung to his shoulders, half afraid my legs might give out from the sheer heat of him. Each slide of his mouth over mine stoked that inner flame, making my pulse pound so loudly that nothing else existed. The worries, the obligations ... they dissolved into the background noise of the world.

His tongue teased the seam of my lips, a coaxing pressure that sent a small gasp tumbling out. He seized the sound, deepening the kiss even more. When his fangs grazed my lower lip, drawing a startled, breathless hitch from my chest, a surge of hunger jolted through me. His taste was salt and fire, a sensation that set every nerve alight.

I melted into him, fingers digging into the hard muscle of his back as though anchoring myself to reality. But reality shifted—narrowing down to the rough planes of his body beneath my hands and the muted growl resonating behind our joined mouths. Instinct took over, guiding me to open for him farther. His kiss grew more urgent and confident, each slow, thorough stroke enough to make me forget breathing.

The world tilted as he guided me backward, the edges of my vision hazy with want. My spine met the platform behind me in a less than gentle thump, jolting us just enough to break our lips apart. A ragged breath left me, matching his own uneven exhale. Our eyes met in that heartbeat of distance, and then he tugged me close again, our mouths catching in another all-consuming kiss that left no air between us.

I didn't give him time to ask if I was sure—my answer was obvious. I grabbed a handful of his top, tugging him closer. He made a low, rough sound. Next thing I knew, he was slicing my shirt off with the edge of a claw, neat as a seam ripper. A startled laugh escaped me, cut short when his lips covered mine again.

He tasted urgent, like we'd put this off for far too long, even if it had only been a day. His wings shifted, brushing my bare shoulders. Everything felt fevered. When his tongue slid down my throat, I couldn't stop the shudder, or the way my fingers fisted in his hair, searching for something to hold onto.

He had me up on the stone bed before I realized it, his body wedging between my knees. My thighs squeezed around him, and for a wild second, I remembered how strong he was—this Drakarn warrior who could bend steel and slice rock. Somehow, all that power was cradling me with a careful sweetness.

And he was all mine.

His kisses skimmed my collarbone, teeth grazing in a way that made me arch into him. Electricity fizzed along my nerves. I reached for the fastenings of his leathers, fumbling them loose, while he slid his hand down my side, claws pricking gently in warning. That tiny sting had my pulse kicking even faster.

Once his chest straps dropped away, I paused to stare. The crystals in the room cast him in half-shadows, revealing lines of muscle and scale, plus faint silver scars from old battles. I'd never get used to how gorgeous he was in his brutal, inhuman way.

Now I had all the time in the world to stare. No Ignarath

warriors were chasing us down. The healers had the vyrathis they needed to heal.

And Vyne was my mate.

I was still getting used to that.

Vyne shifted closer, pressing me into the welcoming softness of the silks. He trailed kisses over my stomach, hungry but unhurried. I gasped when he finally moved between my thighs. His breath sent tingles through my hypersensitive skin.

Then that tongue of his, longer and rougher than any human's, flicked against me. He traced the length of my slit, flicking and teasing in a way that sent electric jolts through me. Each pass of that rough tongue felt shockingly vivid, as if he had tapped directly into my nerve endings. He lapped at me like he was savoring the finest honey, slow and sensuous.

I trembled beneath him, skin flushed and hypersensitive. When he found my clit and zeroed in on it, I nearly screamed. He circled the sensitive nub with the tip of his tongue, just barely grazing it, until I was shuddering and writhing helplessly against the slab. His wings enveloped us like a cocoon of heat and anticipation.

Just as he had my climax coiled tight, ready to spring, he abruptly withdrew. I made a strangled noise of protest, hips bucking uselessly. Vyne chuckled low and sultry, the sound reverberating through me.

"You want more, *Zhyvarin?*" he purred, eyes glinting wickedly in the firelight.

I could only moan in response, utterly at his mercy. The knowledge only seemed to fuel his desire.

I tried to stifle a cry. No chance. It tore out anyway, echoing off the stone walls. He made a satisfied sound deep in his chest, the vibration nearly pushing me over the edge. My fingers clamped around his shoulders, nails scraping at his scales. Each pass of that wicked tongue felt shockingly vivid, until I was right at the point of toppling into oblivion.

But he pulled back before I finished. My outraged whimper must've amused him, because he had a half-smile on his lips when he crawled back up my body. That look disappeared into another kiss, scorching and immediate. I could feel the press of his cock—heavy and alien, with that odd, flared lip at the tip—stretching me in ways that made my vision haze.

He hesitated, just for a heartbeat, long enough for me to see the question in his eyes. I answered by rocking my hips, urging him. A growl rumbled through his chest. That single sound turned every nerve in my body to liquid fire.

Then he drove into me, slow at first, letting me adjust. My head fell back, a ragged moan bursting from somewhere deep in my chest. He felt impossibly big, stretching me wide, filling me completely. A strange tension unwound inside me as his thick length slid into my wet heat. It was like part of me had been waiting forever to slot into place with him, a perfect fit.

He buried himself fully with a trembling groan, chest heaving and muscles rippling beneath my fingers. "Selene," he grated out, voice raw with need and emotion.

"Vyne." My fingers found the wiry ridges at his nape, hooking there as I lifted my hips in response. He bit back a curse, pinning me down with strong hands, his grip both possessive and worshipful. My body shivered, and tingles spread along my skin from his touch.

That was all the warning I got before he started moving, a heated rhythm that built and built inside me. His hips rocked and bucked, driving into my core with firm, purposeful strokes. The slick sounds of our joining and our mingled pants and groans filled the air.

With each pass of his hard length, the tension inside me

gathered and pulled taut, a coiling spring of building pleasure. I could feel myself growing hotter and wetter around him, my slick walls clenching and fluttering. My sex throbbed, a tight, focused ache that demanded to be filled and scratched.

He pounded into me, each powerful thrust jostling my body, rocking me with his force. That full, stretched feeling of his cock stroking deep grew sharper, more insistent. The drag of him across my senses was deliciously, exquisitely overwhelming. I wanted to be consumed and digested by the consuming pleasure until nothing remained but the infinite, inescapable finish of him.

I fisted a handful of silk, crying out. My climax rolled through me in dizzying waves. I barely came down before he pounded forward one last time, letting out a ragged cry that shook my bones. His wings flared wide, tail lashing against the stone. The sudden burst of warmth deep inside me made my body clamp around him all over again, a final spasm of shared passion.

It took awhile, but we unfurled from that state of frantic bliss, panting like we'd run a marathon. The heat of the room folded in around us, but for once, it didn't feel stifling. Our bodies stuck together with sweat, but I was in no rush to pull away.

His weight pressed into me for a minute, heavy and protective. Then, carefully, he slipped free, leaving my limbs quivering. My face felt hot, but my heart felt strangely light.

He settled at my side, half propped up on an elbow. I laughed under my breath. "I can't feel my legs," I murmured.

"Good," he was all male satisfaction. He reached down, dragging the silks over us, and the subtle thoughtfulness made my chest tighten in a whole different way. A girl could get used to this.

For a while, we lay there, listening to each other breathe. His tail drifted over my leg in a lazy caress.

My gaze landed on Vyne's face. He was watching me with this intensity that could have been intimidating if I didn't know him so well. I traced a faint scar along his collarbone. "I love you, you know," I blurted.

He stilled. For a split second, I wondered if I'd gone too far. Shit. This whole mating thing was too new, too unexpected. Emotions were running high. Endorphins were screwing with my head. I could make a dozen excuses, and none of them would be true.

Then his eyes softened. "I ... I love you too, *Zhyvarin*," he said, so quiet I barely heard it, a secret encapsulated by the rock walls around us.

My throat squeezed. It felt like I'd spent years stumbling through chaos, only to finally land there, wrapped in this Drakarn's arms. My earlier guilt poked at me—there were still so many people outside this room who needed help. But I couldn't argue that this moment was essential, too.

I couldn't do this without Vyne. Without my mate.

When I curled in closer, he tucked me under his chin, a fierce tenderness in the gesture. The last remnants of the tension I was carrying started to bleed away.

"We should rest," he said. "Tomorrow will be ... complicated."

I huffed a wry sound, already imagining the avalanche of tasks waiting. "It's always complicated. But at least I'll have you to help me through it."

My voice was heavy with lingering exhaustion, so the last few words came out tender, almost shy. That was new and startling, but he didn't seem to mind. He pulled the silks tighter around us, sealing in the comforting weight of this private forge filled only with our mingled breath.

I pressed a final kiss to his scaled neck, letting my eyelids sink shut. Somehow, even amid all the chaos forever swirling in this world, I felt ... safe. It was a luxury I barely felt like I deserved.

Sleep claimed me gently as Vyne's breathing evened out, and my last thought was simple:

Finally, I'd found something worth letting myself fall for.

27

SELENE

I MADE my way through rows of stone beds I knew by heart now, each step a reminder of how hard we'd fought to keep the Drakarn here alive. I heard few raspy breaths and more gentle sighs, and my own pulse eased in response. My fingers automatically brushed table edges to check supplies. But something was different this morning. I felt lighter, steadier.

I could see progress.

The Drakarn who'd been near death two days ago were no longer caught in that frantic half-consciousness. Their scales still lacked their full luster, but there was a definite shimmer there—life returning to their bodies. It was enough to flood my chest with cautious hope.

Mysha was sitting, her back propped up by pillows and her hands cupping a steaming mug. She glared at me as I approached, and I couldn't stop the smile that spread across my face. If she was feeling well enough to glare, she might actually pull through.

"What mess have you made of my healing caverns, human?" Mysha demanded, setting her mug on her bedside table.

"I think that's a question I should be asking you." I sat at the end of her bed, careful to avoid her legs and tail. "We used vyrathis to aid in healing, but I have no idea why you or the other healers got sick. The illness only affected the healers, as best we can tell." I paused for a moment, but she would want to know. "Three died."

Mysha sneered and hissed. "Damnation. How long have I been ill?"

"About two weeks."

She thought for several moments, reaching for her mug and sipping again before setting it back down. "Healer's Fatigue."

"What?" My fingers itched for a notebook, but I wasn't going to leave when Mysha was giving me answers.

"It's an old illness, and rare. I haven't seen it in my lifetime, but my mentor told me about a spell of it that nearly wiped out Scalvaris a century ago. Remnants of illness lurk in all of us, and in healers, it can mount until it reaches a saturation point and transform into something deadly. It first spreads through the healers, then to anyone who helps, then the rest of the city. Vyrathis is the only known treatment. It gives our bodies a chance to fight the illness. I must have told you before I succumbed." She nodded, satisfied with her deduction.

It wasn't exactly right, but close enough that I saw no reason to contradict her. "Will you tell Rachel and Kaiya about this? If you're up for it?"

She tried to swing her legs off the bed. "I'll be up and tending to the sick. They can find me after."

I placed my hand on her leg. "Maybe tomorrow, elder. Your body needs a bit more healing."

She hissed again, but didn't try to stand. She must have been truly fatigued. I left her to her rest.

I spent the next several minutes making check after check. Supplies? Holding out. Pulses? Steady. Fevers? Seemed to be back under control.

I spotted a large silhouette hovering near the beds in the

back. Khorlar. His imposing figure blended into the rock—broad shoulders, dark gray scales, wings folded so tightly against his back he almost vanished into the cavern wall. He might have gone unnoticed if I didn't catch the glint of light reflecting off his scales.

He didn't look to me as I approached. Still, I knew he was aware of me; I'd seen his battle instincts firsthand. His wings stayed clamped to his spine, and he stared at a point on the wall like he was trying to memorize every chiseled contour.

"Khorlar?" I kept my voice quiet, not wanting to disturb anyone else who might be sleeping.

He finally glanced my way. His eyes narrowed slightly in acknowledgement. He was silent for an uncomfortable stretch before he answered, "Checking."

I tilted my head. "Things are improving," I said, my tone gentler than I'd expected. "Thank you. We wouldn't have made it back if not for your help." I didn't want to imagine what the Ingarath would have done to us. They hadn't gotten the chance.

He didn't nod, just flicked his tail once against the stone. "I honor my duty," he said. It was so formal, carefully worded. I wondered what he was really doing there. But I doubted he'd welcome more questions.

After a moment, he turned on his heel and prowled to the passageway. He didn't look back.

I didn't have time to waste on mysterious Drakarn.

Reika was right where I'd left her—still frail but getting stronger. Her hollow cheeks and bruises looked less brutal this morning, and her breathing was relaxed, if shallow. She appeared to be healing in slow, steady increments. I knelt beside her, studying the lines of tension that still marred her brow. Even in rest, Reika seemed poised on an invisible edge.

"You're safe here," I whispered. I wasn't sure if I said it for her benefit or mine, but it felt like a necessary vow.

When her fingers twitched against the sheet, my heart gave a tiny leap. I didn't know if there were more humans out there, more Reikas who needed saving. If there were, we would find them. We had to.

I pushed to my feet, rubbing my sweaty palms on my thighs. "Rest easy," I mumbled.

A shuffle near the entrance made me turn. My stiff shoulders loosened when I spotted Vyne, and my cheeks strained with a smile. This thing between us had me looking like a fool.

I didn't care.

"Long shift?" he asked. His voice, that low rumble, always made me feel safer.

"You could say that." My body ached. "But there's progress. Mysha woke up for a bit and was able to explain what happened."

He glanced at the cots the same way I had, that fierce intelligence of his taking in details. "Good. They need you."

Heat prickled across my face, and I was thankful for the murky lighting that might hide how flustered I felt. "I'm just doing what I can." Then, I gestured toward the exit. "I think I've earned a break. Walk me home?"

Vyne offered a smile, the kind that made my heart stutter. He closed the distance, holding out his large, claw-tipped hand. I didn't hesitate, sliding my smaller one into his, and everything inside me clicked into place.

We left, the air outside the cavern cooler, though the city itself never truly cooled. We walked in silence for a while, letting the labyrinthine corridors of Scalvaris swallow us.

"Vega wants to go searching for more humans. She isn't wrong—it's important. I'm guessing the council isn't going to like that." They hadn't when Vega escaped the city to come rescue me and the civilians I was hiding with in a cave not far from our initial crash site. I had no idea how that might have turned out if Terra wasn't snuggled up with their leader.

Being snuggled up to a Drakarn of my own, now I saw the appeal.

His fingers tightened around mine. "They won't," he said. "The Ignarath will demand retribution for the scouts we killed. Sending a human like Vega out anywhere near their territory could court war if she manages to survive."

I cursed. "I don't know if anything can stop Vega, short of throwing her into a cell. And even that didn't work for long."

He released my hand and turned, his broad shoulders blocking some of the corridor's pale glow. "That is not a problem for today, *Zhyvarin*."

I might have argued, but I was tired from my shift and right next to my mate. I didn't want to waste time worrying about Vega and her future.

We walked again and made it to Vyne's—*our*—room. The heavy door slid shut with a stony thump, locking out the noise of the city.

Vyne let go of my hand to undo the leather straps across his chest, removing one layer of armor. His wings came free, then settled behind him. I stared a fraction too long, every inch of him reminding me just how good he looked, and how much he was mine.

"Sit," he ordered gently, gesturing to a cushioned ledge along the wall. I did as asked, too tired to protest. My legs throbbed in relief when I sank into the seat.

He knelt in front of me, massive and graceful. The heat of his scales radiated through my clothes. "You're pushing yourself hard," he said, blunt as ever, though his tone was oddly gentle. One clawed hand lifted, brushing hair away from my face. "You do so much, Selene. For them. For us. Don't lose yourself."

I tried to reply, but I didn't manage more than a shaky exhale. The exhaustion I'd been pushing aside the entire day suddenly crashed down, and I realized I was trembling. Vyne's hands came up to frame my face, holding me steady in a way that seemed to say, I've got you.

"You don't have to say anything," he murmured, pressing his brow to mine. His breath, hot and steady, ghosted over my lips, and his wings flared forward to cocoon us. It was so private, so comforting, that something in my chest cracked open.

When I found my voice, it wobbled. "Thank you," I managed. It felt woefully inadequate, but it was all I had.

Vyne's thumbs rubbed small circles along my jaw. Then he tugged me toward him, arms wrapping around my waist. I fell into his chest, catching the deep, resonant thump of his heart, the scales shifting across his broad shoulders. Every inch of me seemed to unravel in that slow, careful warmth.

"You're mine, *Zhyvarin*," he whispered. "No matter what wars or storms come."

My heart lurched. I pulled back just enough to see his face, sliding my fingers over the rise of scales on his shoulder. He shivered beneath my touch, eyes slipping half-closed as he leaned into my hand. The trust in his expression nearly undid me.

He guided his mouth to mine, sealing the moment in a slow, tender kiss. No urgency this time, no desperate clash. Just a soft, lingering exchange that tasted of devotion and everything we would build.

I wrapped my arms around him and surrendered.

I STOOD PERCHED on a rocky outcropping, arms crossed. Below, trainees sparred with varying degrees of competence, most displaying defensive formations as porous as the atmosphere above Volcaryth. A flicker of impatience ignited in my chest—an instinctive urge to snarl corrections or bark orders. I suppressed it. Not yet. Let them taste failure, scrape their hides raw. They'd learn more from bruises than lectures.

My gaze moved restlessly between sparring pairs, weighing their intent against clumsy execution. Bad habits, unchecked now, would bleed them dry later. A head thrown too far back during a strike, a tail dragging where it should provide balance ... my patience frayed, but remained, for the moment, intact.

Then my gaze drifted, pulled across the cavern to the far side: the humans.

They weren't sparring Drakarn today. Their exercise centered on scaling the treacherous rock faces, navigating the uneven terrain with a painstaking focus. Boots scraped against sharp edges and loose rubble, their small, strange hands finding purchase along jagged holds. Where my kind relied on tails for balance and powerful wings for controlled descents, the humans compensated with an unnerving precision, gripping tighter, crouching lower. It wasn't natural—it couldn't be, for them—but they were relentless.

One caught my attention.

Hair pulled back under a utilitarian leather band, a face that radiated composure despite the exertion evident in every controlled movement. It wasn't unusual for me to observe the humans as they moved through the caverns; curiosity was simply practicality draped in the guise of observation.

But this one ... she was singularly focused. Intent.

She studied the rock face before her as though it were a puzzle to be solved, not merely an obstacle to overcome. A sharpness edged her gaze, darting and aware, registering movement and depth in ways I hadn't noticed in the others.

Without conscious intent, I edged closer to the platform's edge, my breath measured as I watched her ascend. She was precision incarnate ... until she wasn't. One of those leather boots dislodged something loose, a hairline crack spider-webbing across the rock face in an instant.

Then everything happened almost too fast for reaction.

The crack widened, a series of sharp pops and snaps that broadcast disaster as physics caught up. Her hand shot upward, grasping for a higher hold. She didn't scream, didn't freeze, but some instinct drove her to try and stabilize as the rock beneath her gave way.

First, loose stones slammed against the cliff face, falling in an uncontrolled cascade. Then, her body followed, moving too fast. She twisted mid-air, clawing desperately for purchase, but collided hard against another outcropping several feet below. Another slip, a mere inch more, and she'd have plunged off the ledge into oblivion.

The rockfall wasn't stopping. Dust clouded the dim light, obscuring her small, curled form.

"Damn it." The words were a low growl ripped from my throat.

Instinct surged, burning white-hot, obliterating every other thought. My claws scraped against the rock as I launched myself forward. Survival demanded timing, precise calculation—not reckless action—and yet there I was, abandoning calculation entirely.

My kind did not make mistakes on terrain like this. My hands gripped the heated rock, tighter than iron, carving a path downward with an unforgiving mix of force and control. The stones that had crumbled toward her still rained around us.

Her scent hit then. Even amidst the acrid chaos of dust and falling debris, it struck me like a whip. I refused to acknowledge the sensory jolt, the sudden hypersensitivity that flared on my tongue.

Everything sharpened, refocused, as though a lightning bolt had struck me.

Her scent was closer now: crisp and alien, deceptively light, yet sharp enough to draw blood. Beneath the atmospheric noise of the cavern, I could almost hear the frantic beat of her pulse—faint but rapid, defying her outward composure.

The last few feet were the most treacherous. Sharp stones forced an awkward perch, wings momentarily extending for balance as dirt and gravel shifted. Any lesser warrior would pause, regroup, resist the urge to charge blindly.

No time for that.

Seconds mattered. Less than that.

Then she was there—fingers white-knuckling a warped, unstable ledge that offered no real security. A smear of blood at her knuckles. A precarious overhang threatened to collapse near her left leg. I landed close, but not close enough, not yet at her side.

This place offered no kindness, no quarter.

"Don't move!" My voice thundered, an imperative, not a request.

Everything else dissolved as I extended my clawed hand to her. Any sweetness lingering beneath her scent was ruthlessly ignored, my focus narrowing to necessary efficiency as I sought a more secure foothold. The chaos subsided, leaving lingering instability in its wake.

I pulled her away from the ledge.

The world narrowed to the visceral—the grit of her bloodied hands slipping against my claws, the searing heat of the broken rock, her weight against my grip. Every sense screamed for focus, demanding I lock down instinct and channel it into precision.

The tension ratcheted tighter, some unseen thread pulling at a place I hadn't had time to name—something wild and ancient, testing the limits of my control as her scent flooded the space between us, closer this time. My tongue burned as if branded, the acrid metallic tang of danger mingling with her phantom sweetness.

This was not the moment for distraction—damned if my own body didn't agree—but the sensation was suffocating, scalding. It deepened as I wrapped my other clawed hand around her waist, sharp focus overriding any resistance. No matter how fast I worked, the heat radiating off her lingered, clinging to me.

"You weigh less than an ash cat," I grunted, hauling her upward. "Stop fighting me."

"I'm not fighting!" she hissed, her voice sharper than expected. She kicked her legs toward the collapsing rubble below, struggling for a foothold. I swore and pulled harder, drawing her body flush against mine.

"Then stop squirming!" I snapped.

The moment her weight fully shifted into my grasp, the

tension snapped—not just in the rock, but somewhere deeper. My tail flicked against the ledge as I propelled us upward, clearing the worst of the debris. My wings flared briefly, catching the air to stabilize us, and finally—finally—we landed on solid footing.

Her breath hitched, the first unguarded sound of emotion slipping past her carefully constructed exterior. For a moment, we were utterly still. Dust settled in the faint light, coating her bruised and dirt-streaked skin like motes of gold.

Her scent lingered. Unforgivingly.

"Are you injured?" My voice was gruff, harsher than intended.

Her chest rose and fell rapidly. She tilted her head, those sharp, assessing eyes locking onto mine as though calculating some equation that couldn't be spoken aloud.

"Nothing broken," she rasped, exhaustion evident in her tone. "Thanks."

There it was—a flicker, a crack barely noticeable, as if she'd loosened her grip on the vigilance she wore like armor. When her fingers brushed briefly against the clawed hand still gripping her waist, I felt her relax.

That wouldn't do. Not here. Not now.

Not with *her*.

"Be more careful next time," I ground out, my voice cracking like a whip. Without ceremony, I released her, the distance I needed achieved as she staggered to her feet. She didn't fall, though; her legs steadied quickly, and she held herself like a queen.

Her expression shifted imperceptibly, mouth settling into its former sharp line. The momentary vulnerability I'd glimpsed dissolved as quickly as it had appeared.

Good. Better this way.

She took a breath, her jaw working as if considering something to say before closing her mouth again. Straightening her spine, she moved stiffly past, her scent trailing after her like smoke.

I stood rooted, my chest tightening under the weight of it all —her scent, the phantom warmth of her body pressed against mine, the impossible ache that clawed through me like something ancient trying to awaken.

It couldn't awaken. It wouldn't.

The burn on my tongue refused to fade.

———

Read *Fated to the Drakarn Warrior Lord* to find out who Khorlar rescued and how he claims his mate!

———

Thank you so much for reading *Bound by the Drakarn: Drakarn Mates Volume One*!
Your support means the world to me. If you enjoyed the story, it would mean even more if you could take a moment to share your thoughts in a review or leave a rating.
Hearing from readers like you makes all the difference!

Drakarn warrior, deadly enforcer, feared mentor, and shield to the weak in a world of molten rock and razor-sharp wings, this is what I am. I never waver...until she crashes into my fortress and demolishes every ironclad rule I've ever held.

Hawk is human: smaller than my kind, yet braver than any warrior I've ever known. From the instant her scent sears my senses, I know two truths: she is mine, and I will break worlds to protect her.

But forging a bond with an alien female inflames ancient grudges and council politics—each side eager to shred our alliance before it blooms. And when enemy forces appear demanding human blood, there are those in Scalvaris eager to give her up.

They call me ruthless for locking her in my private quarters, for guarding her every step, but she's too precious to lose.

Rival clans plot war, temple priests preach doom, and eagle-eyed enemies circle for the kill. I'll face them all—wings flared, claws bared—to keep her safe.

A Drakarn's mate isn't a choice. She's fate. And a Drakarn warrior never surrenders what belongs to him.

Drakarn Mates
Possessive, primal, and unstoppable.
On the fiery world of Volcaryth, Drakarn warriors claim their human mates. They'll defy rules and battle enemies to protect the women fate has bound to them.

Claimed by the Drakarn Warrior Lord
Echoes of Fire
Scorched by Fate
Fated to the Drakarn Commander
Chained to the Champion

Dragon Brides
Dragon Princes. Fierce Women. Love.
Fated mates, fierce women, and dragon princes are ready to find their mates.
Crux
Ranger
Saber
Cipher
Storm

Drake
Asher
Knox
Flint
Pine

———

Guarded by the Shifter

Werewolf. Bodyguard. Mate.
The origins of these shifters are shrouded in mystery, but they're determined to protect their mates from any harm that comes their way.
Also available in audio!
Hunting Season
On the Prowl
Stalking Magic
Hungry for the Wolf
Wolf Cursed (novella)
Wolf's Temptation

———

Stealing the Alpha

The thief takes what she wants, but the alpha keeps what's his...
Join shifter thief Mel as she clashes with lion alpha Luke in an explosive trilogy of two opposites who can't keep away from one another.
Also available in audio!
The Alpha Heist

Entangled with the Thief
In the Alpha's Bed

———

Alien Mates: Planet Exile

Guerran is no place for pretty human women. But these alien heroes will protect their mates!
Also available in audio!

Exile's Hunter
Exile's Adored

———

Zulir Warrior Mates

Kidnapped humans. Alien Warriors. Electric wings.
The Zulir Warrior Mates series brings you human heroines and heroes abducted from Earth who find love – and wings! – with the alien warriors who rescue them.
Also available in audio!
Synnr's Saint
Synnr's Hope
Synnr's Spark
Synnr's Kiss
Synnr's Ride

———

Mated to the Alien

Fated Mate Alien Romance
Detyens are doomed to die young if they don't find their fated mates.
Follow along as these mated pairs fight off aliens, corrupt dictators, prejudiced humans, pirates, and more! The books can be read or listened to in any order, though some characters show up in multiple stories.
Select books available in audio.
Pick a book and jump into the action today!

Ruwen
Tyral
Stoan
Cyborg
Krayter
Kayleb
Shayn
Braxtyn
Doryan
Dekon

———

Detyen Warriors

Detya was destroyed a hundred years ago. These doomed warriors are out to find justice... and their mates.
The Detyen Warriors series brings you kick butt heroines, alpha alien heroes, fated mates, and relationships strong enough to span the galaxy!
The entire series is also available in audio!
Soulless
Ruthless

Heartless
Faultless
Endless

———

Detyen Warrior Outcasts
Fated Mate Alien Romance

These doomed warriors were abandoned by their people and live on the edge. Their mates hold the key to their salvation. Pick a book and jump into the action today!

Dangerous Bond
Intrepid Bond
Wayward Bond

———

Alien Holiday Romance

Christmas... in space????
These alien holiday romances look beyond Earth's winter holidays and ring in the season across the galaxy!
Select titles available in audio.
Snowed in with the Alien Beast
The Alien's Winter Gift
The Alien Reindeer's Wild Ride
Trapped with her Alien Mate

———

Alien Outlaws

Outlaws, schemes, and love... it's all there in the Alien Outlaws series...

Andie Munster is sick of life on Ixilta, the planet she got dumped on after being abducted from Earth six years ago. And when the mysterious and dangerous Xandr shows up looking for a way off the planet, she's half-prisoner, half-co-conspirator in a wild rush to escape.

Rogue Alien's Escape
Rogue Alien's Woman
Rogue Alien's Secret
Rogue Alien's Legacy

———

Find more by Kate Rudolph at www.katerudolph.net

ABOUT KATE RUDOLPH

KATE RUDOLPH IS a paranormal and sci-fi romance writer who lives in Indiana. She loves writing about kick butt heroines and the steamy heroes who love them. She's been devouring romance novels since she was too young to be reading them and had to hide her books so no one would take them away. She couldn't imagine a better job in this world than writing romances and sharing them with her fellow readers.

If you enjoyed this story, please consider leaving a review.

www.ingramcontent.com/pod-product-compliance
Lightning Source LLC
Chambersburg PA
CBHW061532190726
48289CB00004B/1016